the
FANTASIST'S
ASSISTANT
Gill Jackman

For WM
Builder of sheds, maker of tea, mender of hearts.

Prologue

From the very first, the idea of making a balloon navigable was worrying the inventors. Suggestions ranged from the sensible idea of propellers, through oars and sails, to the picturesque solution of bird-traction. This last has, of course, a noble history throughout myth and legend.
Ballooning by C.H.Gibbs-Smith

The long day in the Healing Field had not healed everyone. People still streamed through the hazel archway, amazed by the tissue-paper flowers above their heads. Five days of sex, drugs and rock and roll, and even in the early years of a new millennium, Sunday reached out to them like a day of rest and hope.

One hundred thousand party-goers who have drunk and smoked and whizzed and tripped their way through a week can't be wrong. Men and women threw themselves on the grass and lay like star-fish in the makeshift gardens of our still-green Arcadia where the air was free of burger fat and the ground free of mud. I watched them from the canvas porch of my frame-tent. Cider-slugging youths casting shifty looks at us hippies from the safety of their peer group. Single women passing hopefully by the crescent of notice boards promising tantric massage or karmic untangling. One paused at my Tarot sign, ambivalent about catching my eye.

I pretended not to see. Midsummer magnifies everything, and savaging illusions is not an art to pursue once you're tired.

Midsummer can be a dangerous time.

I shut up shop, slipped into some crocs and strolled past the Medical Herbalists to the dusty drag. A second later, I saw Tom's bald head bobbing above the river of people. And then his face was in front of mine, skin as soft as a baby's and plump as a home-made pie, but I wasn't fooled. I knew him and he knew it because we'd spent every spare moment over the course of a year arguing and agreeing, fighting and fucking. So when, with both of us exhausted, he'd finally pleaded, "Take me for granted," I had. Typical of him to floor me with the unexpected.

Instead of turning left and heading down to the music as planned, we turned right and headed up. The massive discrepancy in our height had no impact on our pace. We climbed the hill, adapting our strides to one another, disrupting no one. The people in our path must have passed round us, or maybe we passed through them.

When we saw the top of a yellow hot-air balloon billowing above the furthest hedge, we turned to take it all in. Glastonbury. City of our birth. Field upon field of canvas and hardboard shops, dissected by paths and rolled-out metal roads. Two fields down, a tree-lined disused railway track separated the green sector from a triumph of pylons and big-tops and helter-skelters and the punks. Far to the right the thinnest haze could still be seen from the ball of flame that exploded every twenty minutes and beyond that, the flat roofs of police Portacabins. Above them and out on all sides, hills were covered with nylon tents packed close enough to be a refugee camp. Then, up to the very tops, the outer circle; acres and acres of sparkling cars, banished to the suburbs. Across it all, sun spots glinted off metal stages. A trapeze swung from a crane. At midsummer, the stars came to earth.

You'd think the music would be lost at such a distance, but something in the acoustics of that late afternoon in this giant amphitheatre combined to make those hills a whispering gallery. Sound blasted and faded in the breeze as Radiohead blew suddenly into Toots and the Maytals, Shirley Bassey and back to the stomping Maytals. Enough talent and success on a hundred stages spread over half a square mile to make me feel special for just being there. So when 'Hey Jude' came on, we both knew this was the real thing. Partly because that fully inflated, thirty foot high balloon peeping above the tallest hedge on the hill behind us had the words *Paul McCartney* blazing across it.

Tom took my hand and we climbed the last field until we reached a five bar gate. PASSES ONLY. But the men in yellow t-shirts only smiled as they swayed in one mind to the blessed Paul, and we slipped through. Tom could have that effect on people. One man approached us as we sauntered up a track of flattened grass to the balloon, but Tom smiled at him. Gave him a flash of those uneven teeth and then tried to hide them behind those large soppy lips. That smile always made shorter men feel churlish. Anyway, the security guard slowed his pace and, too distant for him to see properly, we twirled the passes for our own fields and he waved us on.

So on we went, Tom's billiard-ball head nodding like the Queen's from an open carriage, and he actually waved a final wave with his elegant hand.

I grappled with one of the figures-of-eight that tethered the balloon to the ground, then clambered over the lip of that oversized picnic basket as Tom loosed the others. I never gave a thought to what we were about to do. Too busy concentrating on pulling Tom safely in as we lifted off. Even as he shouted to be heard over the bump, bump, bump on the drift back down the red carpet, I only laughed, excited just to be with him, because I wasn't really listening.

Once we'd left the ground we hardly moved at all, but Tom pressed the button to ignite the gas and we roared slowly up until the last plumes of bonfire smoke became curls on the head and chin of a great Green Man, his eye a stripe of big-top, his smile the showers and plunge-pool that curved across the Greenpeace field.

We hung, suspended in the sky. Tom's arm snaked around my shoulder, big hand tangling my hair as he held my head steady. He gazed at me, sober as a hangman. "The strength you have... I know I can do anything as long as I've got you, and I have got you, haven't I?" And he kissed his conviction into me. "I love you as a man loves a woman. I promise, my soul is in your keeping. You are my future."

Up there, surrounded by stillness, we seemed fused into one. "I talk slowly," he said, "because I try to measure my words; to weigh them; to check their veracity. I... love... you." And my hearing seemed none other than the vibration of his voice or his body (I don't know which or if they are different). My cheek was his cheek; the smell of warm air only a dream of his breath drawing me in and out of life. And taste? "I promise, happily... " he put his hand on his heart, "that it's my responsibility, to look after you. I'm yours, always." And he covered my own heart with this same hand. And on we kissed, if kiss you can call it. More accurately, we drank, and he was as pure as oxygen, as tasteless as air becomes when you have been breathing it involuntarily all your days.

I turned to lean over the edge of the basket. *All You Need Is Love* was radiating from the stage and yellow balloons drifted up the sides of the surrounding hills, tickling the Green Man who shook his hair and beard and laughed them upward. One of the balloons passed so close by that Tom leaned out and waved it towards me. I swear I saw a minim float from it and pop into his mouth.

Copying him, I scooped my own arm through the air. Paul was no longer onstage and the crowd had taken up the anthem in a hum of love so potent that it sliced a path to let him leave. I knew then, watching the great man reach to touch the hands of those lining his route, that there was no difference. Tom *was* Paul McCartney and through Tom, I caught glimpses of how I, too, was so deeply embedded in this flow of light and land and laughter that all notion of being outside it made me giggle. And relax. And finally, weep.

Tom begged me then. "Promise me, promise me you'll remember my promises," and a single tear rolled down the crease of his cheek and into my mouth. "Please. Please. I can only go on, knowing I'm yours."

He pressed the button again and we shot up until the air thinned. He grabbed my hand and I clung to it, giddiness intensifying both into a single prayer. As he pulled me, I felt the lip of the basket crash against my ribs, the air expelled from my lungs and the roughness of the wicker graze my stomach. Then he lifted me by the back of my jeans until I leaned right over the edge. "You know I love you?" he said, sliding the heel of his hand hard up my spine to the back of my head until I stared down. The festival site was almost lost, a tiny buzz of colour among the cool green slopes of a Picasso Goddess, all thighs and breasts and cheeks. "Oh, yes," I gasped, but as he turned my head in his palm and his face drew close to mine, his big lips curled in an expression of amusement and triumph. "We have to jump. We have to jump together. You know that, don't you?"

As briefly as a star shoots through the sky, I saw his brow, usually so high and unassuming, loom thug-like towards me and his soft cheeks freeze into spots of ice. I barely had time to push the thought that Tom could be other than I believed from my mind and smile, nodding into the eyes of my eternal soulmate, before he launched himself headfirst out of the basket, yanking me with him.

For a moment we were weightless, surfing through a bed of water pearls so tiny they passed through every pore and cell. I remember reaching out from some notion of us flying entwined when my forearm struck a solid object and everything below my elbow seemed to shatter. The force threw me onto my back, and into a rushing wind. The skies flashed like stretched sheets before I, or maybe they, began to scream. Torrential rain sounded in my ears but when I opened my eyes I saw blue sky and an angel above me in the shape of a huge dove, wings outstretched to frame its body in a halo of white. Then the wind turned me. Hands, warm as God's, silky as silt threw me over and over until I was as breathless as a child pleading, 'Enough.' The ground, I knew, was coming up to meet me and I couldn't imagine how the great bird in the sky would make it down in time to catch me, but I remembered my promise. To remember his.

Words. Curves to slide down. Circles to hide in. Pillars to cling to.

Chapter One

The M25/M11 route from Stoke Mandeville Hospital to Cambridge was one Beatrice usually avoided. Major roads mesmerised her and she had feared they might contribute to her brain deteriorating. Either way, the less you used it, or a smaller road, the more likely it was to become extinct. But today none of that seemed to matter. She cruised onto the M25 with the idea that a road was just a road and a motorway had fewer speed cameras on it.

The return to work, even for a 'staged return' assessment, had been far more tiring than she'd anticipated. Now her Audi purred along at eighty, driven by the need to get back to her semi-detached Victorian Villa, where Ralph seemed more present these last six weeks than he had when he was alive. Within an hour she was turning off at the Cambridge junction. A record, even for her. Bumping over a road at the edge of town that seemed to have had its tarmac gouged up by a giant fork, Beatrice spotted a speed camera just in time. *Contra-flow*. On either side, warehouse-sized shops seemed to flip past on a loop. *CurrysNextB&Q. MatalanTescoHome.* A cartoon landscape and herself running, running. She tightened her grip on the steering wheel, tried to cut across the east side of town, but found herself swerving instead onto a housing estate that she was certain hadn't been there before. An empty road led to two cul-de-sacs. She caught the flicker of a wall-sized plasma television through a window. No room for books.

A not unpleasant strength filled her chest as her heart went arrhythmic, but she soon felt panic banging on her throat, demanding she get home. What was a speeding fine compared to being stuck here? She drove back and along the main road as fast as the traffic would allow, turning after twenty minutes into a wide avenue lined with mature sycamores.

The giant laurel that brushed the front wing of the Audi on the way up the drive needed cutting back. The thought reassured her. Doing anything to the bush had no more of a place in her intentions now than when she'd said the same thing every week to Ralph on their return from the supermarket. She smiled, familiar thought following familiar thought. When she got a new car, she'd *have* to cut the bush back to stop the scratching. She'd *have* to have expensive insurance, too. Really, modern life was just one long 'for want of a nail the kingdom was lost', only in reverse. *For want of a car, insurance was needed, for want of insurance, a job was needed*, Ralph sang, in her head. *And all because of an eco-car.* The train of ideas ended, as always, with the decision to keep her battered, diesel-consuming wreck in the hope that she would fall apart first.

The wooden porch was rotting. No one had replaced it in PVC or spilt paint on the tiles. Happily, Beatrice opened the front door, threw all the post, apart from the letter marked Cambridge University Library, into the green plastic recycling bin outside, and retreated to the rear living room. Gently, she placed the letter on top of the grand piano. Common wisdom would have her dreading the isolation, weeping as she wandered through the empty house, but the truth was that at sixty-four she felt more settled with the dead than with the living. Her earlier meeting with Occupational Health had disturbed her – a checklist ticked off by an apparently human appendage of artificial intelligence. It smiled. It spoke. It asked the questions on the screen. It was concerned that 'the Trust might not be meeting the requirements of its duty of care.' Her skin was too thin, she knew, to complete her secondment as Senior Consultant for Psychiatry, but they hadn't asked about that, so back in a fortnight it was. Something to do. A place to return from.

Here, company was simply a matter of switching on the standard lamp that had once belonged to her mother. Or pruning the roses with her father's own secateurs, rusting, even when he'd taken the cutting from his own prize bush. Ralph himself seemed now to be permanently in his Parker-Knoll armchair, reading the paper and sharing the occasional funny misprint. She smiled at him, as if she were already curled up on the sofa. He'd never complained about the amount of papers she kept in piles or spread over the carpet, despite her having a designated study in the attic. He'd never really complained about anything that mattered.

The French windows squeaked on their metal hinges as she pushed them wide and stepped onto the crazy-paving. A wood pigeon cooed once and was quiet, hidden in the bower of the overgrown garden. She turned back into the high-ceilinged room and lifted the lid of the piano. Sitting on the stool, she eased down the soft pedal as gently as if it was her hand on Ralph's back at first light.

Eyes closed, little finger stretched to G, middle finger raised to B, her left hand found the shape of sadness. Down she pushed, hand, foot, heart quietly speaking of loss and longing, the first beat of each bar vibrating into the empty room, house, world like a shout that hadn't meant to be so loud, but couldn't help itself. Halfway through the fourth bar her left hand slipped down the keyboard, from major to minor and down to the next major and down to the next minor as if the bottom could never be reached. Beginning the phrase again, she brought her right hand to bear, each singular, plaintive note a statement of its separation from the roiling harmony below. Alone, its attempt to express pain would mean nothing, would be as one-sided as words without a context, as trust without agreement.

As it was, with both hands playing together, the melody sounded as if it were trying to escape. Beatrice hit top D with her little finger, increasing the pace, before returning to where the music had begun, the downbeats on the left hand insistent, dragging the right to face the loss, moving down the keyboard more quickly than it had the first time round. This time, the right, more familiar with its options, doubled, tripled in speed, reached higher; the left, patiently witnessing this hopeless struggle until the right quieted, like a hysterical child that had run out of breath. Until time was up. Until it really was case of putting the inevitable foot down. Beatrice crashed along the keyboard, acknowledging one last bid for freedom with a brief foray of her right hand before the lowest major chord swallowed up all dissent.

Long after she closed the lid, Chopin's Prelude no.4 in E minor vibrated on through the low shafts of sun in the kitchen, the silent hall, the egg she boiled for herself, and the wide, empty bed.

*   *   *

Blue and yellow blur into purple. Huge weights crush each limb.

A spade digs into my chest. Everything is scoured. Fingers, toes, arms, legs. Skinned.

A steel band is crushing my head. I hear rasping. Claws rip open my stomach and I light up in a bright scream of lightning. Bones spike at right-angles from a forearm, jut from a shoulder. I am a fixed pattern.

Sound bubbles. "Hospital are in you."

Antiseptic, thick as tar, sticks me together but my jelly-joints hang loose and boulders nestle in my eye-sockets.

"You are in hospital."

I try to smile, feel my face twitch, hold it steady, imagining the twitch will disgorge the mess of liver and kidneys that peer out from between my intestines. But perhaps they are pinned in place by the bones?

I must be mostly pelvis then, sitting in the bed. I feel relieved. Intact. A bowl of clean lines after all that scrambling of parts. I know the pelvis is important, worth saving, but every time I breathe, a little of my heart muscle is shaved by the steel grater in my chest so I concentrate on keeping my sips of air shallow.

"Try not to move."

If I'm in my bedroom, it seems I have shifted the furniture around so that my mother has to lean over me to place my tea on the bedside table. This time I will not move and she will not spill it on the bed and then shout at me.

"Can you hear me?" The worry in her voice yanks me to the surface. Sheets weigh down like giant brillo pads. I smell their pink detergent and am concerned my wounds will be scrubbed empty. I am all wound.

"Can you hear me?"

Speech will disembowel me. Does she not know that?

"Try and move your fingers," she says.

Flames sear up my arm and she sobs enough to put them out with her tears.

*

All light is orange. My mother places a sponge at my lips. The noise that comes out is halfway between a croak and a bleat and I understand how a baby must feel. Everything is loud: the light, the unstretched joints, the digestive system. All of it aches. I find myself flying through blue. No above and no below. My body lacks weight again until I reach out to touch...

"Try not to move. You have a cracked skull, three smashed vertebrae, a broken leg and ankle and a stitched up spleen. You are very, very lucky to be alive."

We are very close, my mother and I, so I know as she falters on the last word that she's unsure if I agree with her. I try to nod, but finding my head held steady by a metal vice, I struggle hard to open my eyes and then steer them sideways. Blinking helps and before I know it I'm sliding them to and fro like a skier down a slalom.

This alarms her, so I squeak, "Good," and feel her hand grab mine as I sink.

*

I doze, convinced that my body lies in the shape of my father's wasted torso on that last lap in his single bed. This must be the night I slept here. The night before his funeral. My head whirrs through a series of hisses and clicks; reruns from forty years of DNA jumping to attention. I can smell the overheated motor, the warm grey metal as Bakelite arrow-knobs on the reel-to-reel clunk towards play, or rewind, or record or fast forward, proving that my father is really under the bed, spooling three-quarter inch tape into the splicer. There he fiddles with deft fingers, tongue between his teeth, slicing out a sentence, a phrase, an attitude with a razor blade.

Mickey Mouse is talking backwards, but the mattress muffles the gobbledygook beyond reach. There will be no new input, no revised programme, no apology, no additional breakthrough of an unexpected hug forthcoming. No revelation of love withheld. But surely, if I listen hard enough. There! I heard an imperative forcing its way through the springs. My father jabs his knuckle up through the wire mesh bedstead to punctuate. *Tomorrow,* he says. *When you read aloud, project your voice. Breathe into your diaphragm. Now is the time for all good men to come to the aid of the party.*

Leaves rustle by my ear. I must be standing by the grave, under the tree, but then I feel my bed shaking in the wind.

"Why did you do it? Why did you take it in the first place?" The whispering is my mother's. Unaware that her disappointment rocks the metal frame, causing sparks that melt me to the bone, she nurses her questions as if an answer will bring her child back from the dead.

"What?" I manage, though the word sounds like a drunk, vomiting.

She stiffens and strokes my fingers. "Sshhh. Ssshh. Never mind. It's all right now. June sends her love. She's still in Thailand. I've told her you're out of danger."

A wash of sun warms me. Beloved June-in-a-heatwave, far far away, out of danger. I can scratch the top of my head, then. The itch is so great that only yanking out the cartilage will bring relief, but my mother's hand is too heavy to push aside.

She thinks I am seeking comfort and squeezes. "Everything is all right now."

The words boom in an echo from a voice that seems to live in my own throat. Rich, satisfied. *Everything is all right now.* A growl that vibrates in a line through my centre down to my sex organs. Tom lives inside me then. These thick walls that opened with such willingness to receive have held him tight. I feel the tip of his penis massaging my cervix, determined to be the core to my apple flesh. *The slow...* (push) *boat...* (push) *to China...* (push). His fudgy heat envelops and fills me.

I remember why my pelvis matters so much. It's a bowl that I can draw the rest of me into, spiralling around Tom, hugging him as I look through the bone bars. I feel him shudder through me, cool space after the fire. *Stay full of my promises. I can only survive if you remember your promise... to remember mine.*

The rocking becomes a whispered squall. My mother has appropriated the boat. "Oh God. Why did you ever *think* of...?"

This time my smile spreads easily, as enigmatic as the Mona Lisa. Now, I will protect Tom as he protects me. It's easy to protect truth from illusion. Say nothing and we will fly through that blue together and never land. This hospital bed, these boils that cover my back, this itch that tries to force my hand to rip out my brain is a dream. A dream I fell into when I looked into his face and saw malevolence there. When I doubted him.

Where is he though? Shame seeps sticky from my jam-body.

"She seems agitated."

The sponge forced between my lips contains the vinegar of my mother's own agitation. She is trying to contaminate me, to bring me back to her world of this and that where nothing was her fault and everything my father's. Where nothing will be my fault and everything Tom's. I shall cleave to him, hidden in my pelvic bowl, and this pain I generate will recede.

I hear the suck of a vacuum filled. Feel Tom stroke my arm. The cool rush of him spreads a butter-like calm through my limbs. As long as he's with me, I can fight back, I can drift with him as I'm drifting now.

"There now. She's sleeping. Don't worry." My angel hovers, dove-wings ready to wrap me at my request.

Chapter Two

Beatrice had come to a standstill. She looked up at the bright blue and mauve elephant painted on the corridor wall. The elephant's trunk was pointing at Meeting Room Two as if helping her on.

Someone swished up behind her, just a little too close. "Dr. Samuels. How nice to see you back."

"Thank you." For a moment, Beatrice had no idea who the woman was, but she smiled anyway. To her relief, the woman smiled back, as if the matter was settled. Corinne... The hospital pass round her neck helped. Corinne Brock, Counsellor for the latest 'Well-Being' directive, because no one was allowed to be mentally ill any more.

Corinne slid past to push and hold open the door. The girl's need for approval seemed to crackle in the overwarm air.

She shrank away, realising that Corinne must know what had happened to her. That the whole department of psychology, perhaps the entire hospital complex, knew, and all of them wanted to try out their endemic counselling skills. Corinne was probably beaming healing vibes at Beatrice's back right now from that monstrous lump of lapis lazuli she wore around her neck. *A higher power. Nothing to do with me.* In her stronger days, Beatrice would have found this amusing. But Beatrice wasn't feeling strong. She was feeling like the last dinosaur on the planet whose mate had just keeled over. Next to Corinne's youthful glow, even her skin looked reptilian.

Jeremy Frost rose from his moulded plastic chair. "Ah, Dr. Samuels. Good to have you back. May I say again how sorry we all were to hear about the loss of your husband."

"Thank you," said Beatrice, sitting down.

Corinne shook her head, taking the chair opposite in the bare-walled room. "How long were you married?" she asked.

Feeling obliged to look her in the eye, Beatrice deliberately looked at the carpet. "Thirty-eight years."

Corinne nodded, slowly. "A long time," she replied, lengthening her vowels, but Jeremy intervened.

"Let's move on, shall we? I'll come straight to the point. Beatrice, while no one working here could be more pleased to see you back, I know your secondment is due to end at Christmas anyway. Would it not suit you better to take more time off? A proper break? A chance to fully resource yourself? Rampton, I'm sure, would benefit from our loss?"

So loss floats all around now? thought Beatrice, noticing how easy it was not to give a stuff. Like flying down the stairs when you were dreaming. In fact, perhaps she was dreaming? Or perhaps she was developing dementia (or *un*-developing, Ralph had said, with that single bluster of a laugh he always choked out). She squeezed her fingertips together, hard.

"Beatrice?"

Really, it seemed quite sane that meaning unravelled with the passing of time, unhitching itself as fashions changed. At what point did words and labels become impossible to use? How many worlds had to fall apart? But people were looking at her. Five of them (she hadn't noticed). Thin grey carpet. Five orange chairs. All topped with reassuring smiles that seemed to be bearing down.

Get out. Perhaps it would be best if she did just get out.

It was on the tip of her tongue to say, 'Yes, of course,' when Corinne interrupted.

"It must be *really* difficult for you, coming back here to listen to people's upset?"

Beatrice stared back, noting that where once the upward lilt at the end of Corinne's sentence would have irritated her, all she could see was dust. The dust this current fashion would come to. The dust that they would all come to. Her eyelids felt too heavy to hold up, the ethical concerns about these college kids with their tinpot diplomas too weighty to hang onto. She dropped her line of vision to where Corinne twiddled the lapis pendant, withdrawing her attention only when Corinne let go. *Cruel of me,* she thought. *Depression*, said her mind, but even that word, having raised its head, slumped back, disinterested.

Only when Beatrice turned to Corinne to answer her question-that-wasn't-a-question and saw that she had not only stopped Corinne from smiling, but also from breathing easily, did she herself falter. The girl had gone rigid. Beatrice gripped the side of her plastic chair. "I'm so sorry," she said, ashamed at what a bully she'd been.

But the faces on the bodies on the chairs had changed only to expressions of concern, her apology seen as a welcome but light expression of her being understandably a bit distracted. She saw herself then: a woman of standing that people listened to and respected, learned from – loved, even. A woman with nothing at all in her life right now except this. Silently, she apologised to Corinne again and offered a dazzling smile. "No, not difficult," she said, but she said it gently.

So it was that Beatrice realised how much she still needed the patient she'd been given and the department and Jeremy and the rest of this prestigious hospital. She even needed Corinne Brock.

"Let's start with an assessment," she said, allowing her authority to expand into her chair, her colleagues, the room. The file on her knee helped. She glanced down at the message paper clipped to the front of the notes she'd skimmed:

Gina Fulbright, 42: Attempted suicide: jumped out of stolen hot air balloon.

All in a rush, she said, "But I do think that – bearing in mind the criminal aspect and my experience at Rampton – it might make it easier all round if I took Gina Fulbright on as my last patient." Forty years of hiding her own feelings while listening to others had to have some use. She beamed round, relieved to have found a part of herself in all this chaos that she could put to use. "Jeremy – do we have an update? Any new information I should know?"

But Jeremy was already shuffling through his own file. "Not that I've heard, but you might talk to HDU. They'll have all the brain and bloods," he said, eye on the next item. "And of course, Dr. Robinson, who has been covering, will be continuing to run things in all but name ready to take up her permanent post in January so..." He smiled his assent.

And that was that. Corinne nodded so much she looked as if her head was on a spring and Jeremy had deferred easily and would not interfere, Beatrice knew, because at last, he could see that the old fossil would soon cease tramping through his increasingly streamlined, solution-focused department of psychological services. *But there's gold in them there bones*, she thought, relieved to sense it, blood-like, warming her from the inside, even a tiny bit.

*   *   *

Tea-trolleys don't rattle these days. They give the occasional rubbery squeak through a warm fug. And blood-pressure kits are digital. No mechanical parts to puff up and fart their way empty. My illness has no soundtrack. I hear the telephone, but am unsure if anyone else does, as no one responds to its endless drilling.

Mr. Bryant came to see me today. He's the heart specialist. One of his students whisked an x-ray out of an envelope when all Mr. Bryant had done was raise his hand. He says my heart's perfectly healthy. Nothing wrong with it. When I asked him if the pain could be caused by a blockage in my digestion he looked annoyed and told me I hadn't got cancer either. Then he outlined the photo with his finger.

The doctor I saw yesterday mentioned physio. but she was unsure when it would start. Apparently, they've got enough porters to move me downstairs but none downstairs that can move me back up again when it's finished. She said I'm lucky I can sit up at all so I suppose I should count my blessings. I asked why the same porter couldn't make both trips. Something to do with wasting time waiting for the notes. I waved my useful arm and said I could hold them safely until he came back for me, but apparently that's against hospital policy. Her tiredness sapped me of the will to argue. She's got enough on her plate.

I did talk to a nice nurse. She said that grown men have been known to jump off trolleys in A&E rather than be admitted to a ward. She said I was being really brave and doing really well and that the coma I was in for ten weeks was very convenient because of my operations. Gave things a chance to heal.

Actually, I like it here. Nearly everyone is very nice. I don't even have to get up to go to the loo. They do it all for me. I'm surprised I don't have more pain though. They're very concerned about that. I only have to groan and they give me morphine. That must be when Tom's visiting. At night, when I'm asleep. Which is just as well because I'm not really in any fit state to talk to him. He'd get more upset in the day, anyway. He doesn't like hospitals at all.

I've gone blank again. I think that's why I've got to see the psychiatrist. Give me a chance to talk. It'll make a change.

*

Dr. Samuels is really old. She has short grey hair and hamster jowls, but her face lights up, turning her into a completely different person when she sees me being wheeled into her office. The walls are made of some kind of prefabricated kit and have strips of plastic where they join at the corners. Although she has a desk, it's pushed against the wall, which is hung with photos of children. She scoots across the floor in a black plastic chair as if she's been waiting for me.

"I can do that," I say, shifting my wheelchair so that I move a little on the thin carpet.

She stands and shakes my hand. "Hello. I'm Doctor Samuels. I'm just going to put my *Do Not Disturb* notice on the outside of the door so that no one interrupts us."

I'm pleased that someone so important isn't going to let anyone else in. She's very friendly, but she does want to know how I fell out of the balloon. She seems intrigued.

"This is the picture of you I'm getting," she says, when she's settled herself opposite me. "I decide to steal a huge, ready-inflated hot-air balloon that's not mine – in fact, it's not only not mine, it's waiting for Sir Paul McCartney. It's in a field full of security men, the other side of a gate that you can only get through with a special pass. But I manage to un-loop the heavy ropes that hold the balloon down, jump in before it takes off, find the knob to light the gas and reach for the sky. Is that right?"

"Yes," I say, but although she's set off, I can't. I'm stuck, looking at the shape the rope makes, twisted around two heavy iron stakes. I see Tom's hand begin to undo it. "No!" I say.

The word rouses me, like shouting aloud wakes someone having a nightmare. I look round the room, see the photo above the desk: two children on a seesaw. One is laughing but the other looks upset and is hiding behind one hand while clinging with the other to the handle.

Dr. Samuels tells me that when people have been in a coma, they often can't remember things when they wake up. She stands and walks over to an art trolley loaded with crayons and paints. On the top of it is a stack of coloured paper.

"Would you like to try drawing whatever it was that made you shout?" she says, handing me a piece of chalk and wheeling me over to the desk.

The chalk feels unfamiliar in my hand and hard to grip. I scrub it sideways in a curve up the paper before curving it higher the other way, arcing across the top and pulling it down, back across and looping it underneath to meet the first mark I made. 8. Then I turn the entire piece of paper sideways.

"Thank you," she says. "Not a literal figure of eight, because it's sideways. Not an hour-glass, because it's useless that way round, unless time has stopped."

I feel as if I'm in a game of twenty questions and since she's so unassuming, I nod to encourage her, because the picture I've drawn has nothing and everything to do with time.

She takes a deep breath. "Is there anything you can tell me about the symbol you've drawn?"

And I know there is nothing I can tell her. Nothing and everything, so I lick my forefinger and rub through the chalk line.

"It's broken now," says Dr. Samuels.

"Yes. I broke it."

"I see. So how did you break it?"

The accusation winds me. My ribs and stomach clench, paralysing the air that could become words. I look at this line I've ruptured, take the chalk and fill in the gap.

Dr. Samuels leans over my shoulder. "What you've drawn is a symbol of eternity." She moves to stand by my side, pointing to demonstrate her meaning. "Two poles, negative and positive, masculine and feminine. They strive to unite, creating the dynamic tension of existence. Without both, all things are incomplete."

Like a car jump-starting, I jolt.

"What are you feeling?" She sounds hopeful. My stomach contracts over and over.

"I'm sort of curdling."

"Curdling?" She puts her hands to her own stomach. "That makes me think of oil and water. Of things that won't mix. A sense of being wrong, even?"

The feeling goes. "How can curdling tell you you're wrong?"

"Well, a cake curdling tells you you've put the eggs in too fast."

"I suppose it does," I say. "But I'm not a cake, am I?"

"All right." says Dr. Samuels. "I think we'd better leave it there for today." She smiles and says, gently, "but I'll see you on Thursday. That's the day after tomorrow. Every Tuesday and Thursday. That's when we'll meet." Her face is round enough to be a cake. Her eyes could be raisins.

*

The porter that comes to collect me is new. He says little, leaving me free to look at and listen to Tom. It's even better than reading the books he's written. More like watching my favourite film again. I'm at leisure to lose myself in the tiny creases in his face – to curl into the crook of his smile and feel the humour behind it.

The lights on the ward seem bright, cosy against the thunderstorm looming outside. I doze, my cheek caressed by the pillow curving around it until the bleeping in the room slows and the patients still awake have only the soft pool of a bedside lamp to see by.

Now Tom will visit.

One by one, the reading lamps go out. I giggle at how easily I was fooled. The comfort I imagined from the bright lights was for those who need reassurance, which is almost everyone, except for him and me. Now, the warm dark air of the thunderstorm seeps through the window-glass to press against my cheeks like the fingertips of a lover. It's him, saying hello. At the first crash of thunder I am filled with enough static to rise from my bed and pour through the wall like Alice stepping through the looking glass. Outside, the wide arc of sky dips to embrace me. Opening my own arms, a great crack of fire on the horizon fills me with electricity. My hair stands on end.

Chapter Three

Corinne sat cross-legged on the armless easychair in the windowless cupboard they called a staffroom, trying to meditate. The rough upholstery pulled against the fabric of her nylon tights. She tried focusing on the sensation but instead, started thinking about friction, and then how this idea dragged her away from the peace she sought. Now the narrative about what the narrative about friction meant was dragging her even further.

At 29 years old, the implications of the return of Saturn in the heavens to its position during the year of her birth frightened her. If she didn't learn the lessons she had so far failed to grasp, she believed the opportunity would be lost until she reached 58, when she wouldn't have much life left. This year, the unconscious side of her personality was to become visible through her facing great difficulty. She had to be ready.

A tear stung her eyelash. Ready? Despite having worked in the hospital for nine months, Corinne felt more out of place here than ever. Her? Corinne Crackers-smells-of-Knackers, a counsellor? Nothing had gone as planned. A mere nine months among the maimed and the dying had proved that she was a massive failure. Only this morning she'd spelt 'comfortable' 'comftabel' and the computer had screamed at her, underlining, in red, six alternative ways of saying, 'This patient is got pitted cheeks not from crying a lot. Scratching I think too much alone?'

Once a junkie, always a junkie. She saw now that she

hadn't, as she'd believed for a while, been special; she'd been lucky. She hadn't been chosen, she'd accidentally stumbled on a youth centre screening of *Christiane F.* OK, it had woken her up to the fact that taking heroin every day was called addiction. But she hadn't been exceptional, she'd been in the right place at the right time to be included in an inner city drive to offer addicts expensive residential treatment. If anything, she'd been targeted, and Corinne had begun to glimpse that even her appointment at Stoke Mandeville was less to do with her vocation and more to do with a need to employ cheaper, less well-trained workers, to massage the hospital's mental health statistics.

Sitting with her eyes closed, the trajectory of her adult education seemed contained within a single chess piece on the chessboard of Government. A pawn. First, the support group for other ex-junkies. Then, on the understanding that she would formalise the group, Lambeth council had given her money and a list of do's and don'ts. Then, when her mother's liver had finally packed up, she'd been granted 'key worker' status and given the tenancy of the family flat in Brixton. At the time, her rehabilitation from offender to helpful citizen had seemed a miracle: *self-help by way of user-led services*, but who would have guessed that *user-led services* would blossom into a niche market? Who would have thought that the wider aim of her sponsored training was to turn her into a commodity? She was an addict. A user, and now, even though she had hardly any of the skills and certainly not the space she needed to work with patients anything other than superficially, the NHS was using her.

"Serves me right," she mumbled, covering her face with

her hands in disgust. Even though almost three weeks had passed, the memory of what she'd said to Beatrice Samuels in that meeting, the one person she really rated, made so much blood rush to her brain it reared up to brand her. "It must be *really* difficult for you, coming back here to listen to people's upset?" She had suggested that the *Senior Consultant for Psychiatry* might be struggling with emotional overload, *to her face?*

She had too much to do to go on like this. Up she sat. *Pull yourself together. Find a way.* But telling Dr. Samuels that she had been at the same festival as Gina Fulbright seemed even more impossible now. Trying to articulate the simplest account scrambled together everything that had happened that Sunday, so that nothing would be clear. She would be unable to speak. She knew, with her adult brain, that trying would be the sensible thing to do, but she shrank at the thought. Why tell her? How? Her work in The Welfare Barn would show her up as the junkie she was. *Had been.*

Yes, had been. But she'd been such an idiot. Off shift just in time for Paul McCartney, but buzzing too much from the work.

Three days of base speed, no sleep and thirty degree heat was what had done for the starving, sodden festival refugees, now cowering psychotically on muddy settees in Barny Welfare (as they all called it). Corinne groaned. Festival Welfare? It only took two police people in uniform and a crackling radio to send people she'd spent four hours talking down to return to bat-shit bonkers, but there they'd sat, littering the concrete floor with fag ends and dozing, on and off, in the dusty swirl. She'd felt like one of them. Had been there enough herself to offer the odd reassuring smile and wait with them, empathising, until time saw their demons off.

Not for Corinne, gathering with the clutch of social workers round the desk by the open barn doors, discussing people, writing notes. She was never going to be one of them. Never going to catch the new shift and handover with, 'that guy in the corner, he's paranoid. Watch him.' Or, 'that woman behind the curtain's still drunk. She's been asleep for hours.' No, Corinne was always the member of staff who went over and discovered that, far from being drunk, this was a brave and adventurous woman at her first festival who'd become separated from her friends and walked around the site for hours. She also had cerebral palsy. Then there was the traveller friend from the convoy, standing by the desk and surrounded by concerned looking social workers. "Fucking hell! Corinne!" she'd said, grabbing her as she came on shift. "I've just covered myself in diesel filling the van so I ran here, fast and said, 'I've just covered myself in diesel.' This lot think I'm trying to kill myself." Now that had been funny.

Watching people recover from temporary psychosis, seeing them through their terrifying delusions, trusting them not to leap up and lay into one another was heady stuff. When they told her of the knifing by security guards in the dance tent; when they told her of the piles of bodybags they'd seen stacked up outside, she just nodded, twirled her identity welfare laminate and said, gently: "You see this picture? While you're in here with me, you're safe." Of course she felt flattered and relieved when they eventually shook their heads, one by one, like a dog shaking off water. Of course she nodded and smiled when they shared the terrifying nightmare from which they'd just awoken. But by Sunday, the triumph had left her too high to settle.

Vanity, then. Corinne breathed into her bottom, felt the cushion and filled her chest, but the air was fetid with the stench of blame. Trust her to have been so full of herself she'd completely missed what mattered. *Who wants to see Paul McCartney? Dance tent'll be empty. Drum n' Bass. Roni in the groove.* Cool? Everyone wanted to see Paul McCartney. He was Paul McCartney, fer Chrissakes. What? She thought she knew better?

That had been the start of it. The dance tent had been between DJs. The drum and bass that had filled so much of her life before heroin, elusive. Instead, hoping for an empty Healing Field, she'd walked out of Babylon and climbed the drag in the late afternoon sun, through the green sector up towards the stone circle. Remembering, her breathing slowed. She saw the shadow from the archway again, reaching toward the garden in the centre of the water circle. She saw the few people resting on the small rustic benches. The mauve by orange by yellow flowers. The hippy-made oasis of pond and small container-bound trees. Searching for a quick head massage, she'd turned left to walk the tent fronts that mirrored the garden's curve. She'd passed a rainbow of flags wrapped round a guy rope, a row of lanterns hanging from sticks in the ground, saw a sign – *Indian Head Massage* – outside a blue and white canvas tent. A 1970s family tent.

The healers had begun to shut up shop. She'd moved towards the woman inside the tent, seen she wasn't interested in more customers. And then she'd stepped back again.

And then she'd fled.

Corinne bounced on her seat. Ground her bottom into the cushion as she stared from the safety of the staffroom at what her two steps back had revealed. Another sign had been hanging to face the garden. By approaching the tent side-on, she'd missed it. First a gold and mauve swirl, then the picture: a naked and voluptuous woman astride a huge lion, its tail a coiled snake ready to strike. *Tarot Readings.*

Crowley. And then the ground beneath her feet that she hadn't felt, only the words, running from those words as they streamed from her head, merging now with the four beat a second drum and bass, louder and louder: *This Trump was formerly called Strength but Lust implies not only Strength, but the joy of strength exercised. It is vigour and the rapture of vigour. Thou art exhaust in the voluptuous fulness of the inspiration; the expiration is sweeter than death, more rapid and laughterful than a caress of Hell's own worm.*

Yes, Crowley. Corinne dropped her head, saw candles flicker, silks billow, circles drawn. She heard Latin verses declaimed, felt her outline as thick as a charcoal sketch and her heart high in her floating body.

"Enough," she shouted, opening her eyes. "Too difficult. It's OK", she said, amazed to find that voice in herself. Certainly enough for now, she thought. "Calm down," she said, but the phrase sounded punitive.

"Calm down?" Not enough authority.

"It's not happening now." She smiled. Much better. Her jaw softened. Her eyebrows lifted. "Calm down," she said, as if humouring a child. "Goodness me. Too much excitement!" But the lion in the picture didn't fade. Leo the lion, the constellation that Saturn had been turning in at the time of her birth.

Chapter Four

Dr. Samuels starts our next meeting by telling me how concerned she was when I stopped responding to her yesterday. She tells me to forget about the cake. She really didn't intend to upset me. And then, she tells me she's been puzzling about the balloon.

"I s'pose I'd better tell you about Tom," I say, because pain starts spiking up and down my spine. Talking about Tom is like spreading lotion all over my body. So I tell Dr. Samuels about stealing the balloon, up to the point where me and Tom are kissing high above the crowds.

"Tell me all about him," she says.

And it just sort of bursts forth, fresh as ever because I never could believe the coincidences between me and Tom. I tell her how no two lives had ever run so parallel in the history of the world. Both of us were single parents with just-grown children. Both of us the same age and both four years into partnerships of convenience, entered out of fear. We even had the same class of degree from a tiny and obscure department in the same northern red-brick university.

"I know it sounds ridiculous," I say, overjoyed that finally someone seems as interested as I am. "But I think our meeting was written in the stars. Over the last fifteen years, we were even at the same pop festivals. One of them so small it only had about five thousand people at it, the other so big it was the size of a city, but we worked and camped in adjacent fields all that time."

"But you didn't meet for years?"

"I passed him performing on a small stage once, when I first started going. 'Who's that psycho?' I thought. He was hurling his body about and flapping up his vest to waggle his flab at bystanders, screaming, *This is your future*." I stop and look at her to see what she thinks but she's smiling.

"Not love at first sight, then?"

"Terrible phrase, that," I say, delighted. "Not fit for purpose. If love is outside time, how can mere chronology of contact tell you anything? He was right across the other side of a field, but I remembered him, years later. It seemed like proof that he'd always been there, waiting." Waiting for me since the '70s, with a transistor radio clamped to his ear, just like I was, as track after track of yearning and sunshine became encoded in pop music and interned between the layers of our growing bones. "We'd have been hopeless if we'd met then. Not very cool among my friends, to love Barry White or the Detroit Emeralds." I giggle. "Especially not The Carpenters. I was all long skirts and flares, he was drainpipes and short hair. Opposite ends of the spectrum."

"So you both had this deep appreciation of contemporary music at the time, but felt you'd be ridiculed?"

"I did. To the point where, in the seventies, I didn't even know I liked it, but he always knew, even if he never said. When we found each other, the appreciation sorted of doubled – quadrupled, even."

"An explosion of celestial harmony."

I check to see she's not taking the piss, but Dr. Samuels

looks perfectly serious, so I decide to confide in her further.

"You know, all the teenage hysteria about David Cassidy made me loathe him. I couldn't listen to him without a... a... without curdling at the crassness of it all. But Tom put DC in his properly exalted place when he sent me a CD with 'How Can I Be Sure?' as the first track." Once the word are out of my mouth, I really expect her to laugh.

But she says, "When love is undeniably present, all that we see and do is pure, and ceases to be manipulated by the small agendas of envious minds."

"That's exactly it!" I say, "Just goes to show that anyone with a complete set of Delfonics LPs could follow their dream with more commitment than me." I remember how the gateway to him lay in every tree, every bird that sang its sweetness into the breathing air and every note that was the middle eight of *Help me, Rhonda*. I think of last night's thunderstorm. "I just wasn't ready then."

"Ready for what?"

"To fall. I wasn't ready to fall. To give up posing... and then when I did, it was more like... "

"Like what?"

"Floating."

Love at first sight is a most unhelpful phrase. What happened was so natural I didn't notice or name it for days. The sense of oddness, of dislocation, came when circumstances demanded we part to get on with stuff. Even then I wouldn't have said I fancied him. Tom was fat, very tall, and had no hair. Not my type. But that's the thing about really falling in love. Preconceptions

don't count. From the outside we looked surprisingly like two people talking, even to ourselves, but we were inside at the time and I only noticed the attachment afterwards.

Hosting residential courses for visiting teachers and students was Tom's day job. Anita, his partner, organised the schedule while Tom was the front man. His warm welcome to twenty-five people as we perched uncomfortably on faded sofas and antique wooden chairs reassured all of us that we should treat the place as our own for the following week. He joked about the creaking floors and the temperamental fire-alarm, told us we must smoke outside, and afterwards, I found him leaning against the back door, inhaling the roll-up tobacco I patronised myself. All the smokers gathered there on and off. When my stash dried up, he gave me half a packet of Golden Virginia, but I hardly noticed him, the way you wouldn't notice a sibling or your best friend.

Tom was more normal than anyone I had ever met. The Platonic ideal of normal: unique, comfortable with his own shortcomings, and able to express his enthusiasm without worrying what other people thought. I fitted with him, I suppose, but not in a nervous, preoccupied way. I became free to be myself.

Four days into a week of writing exercises, it happened. Nothing liberates me more than nailing down what needs to be said, so I was feeling entirely unfettered as I breezed out of the back door. As usual, a cluster of people smoked and chatted, but Tom was standing a few yards away on the lawn. I could see the forget-me-nots hurling their pollen into early summer as I sensed him put some youth at his ease. I turned to look.

The youth tipped up his chin to take in Tom's booming six-foot-four frame. "So do you do anything else, apart from organising this place?" He spoke with deference, but Tom's beam creased into dimples either side of his uneven teeth as he took the young man's hand and vigorously shook it.

"I've got a book coming out next week. Tom Hanson. How d'you do."

A woman I'd sat next to at dinner slid out of the door. "Who is he, exactly?" she muttered.

It's very clear. Like rewinding a film in slow-motion with surround-sound. With surround feeling. I filled up with excitement, outraged that Mr. Normal could use his talents to play the big *I am*. I rose to the challenge. Threw a gauntlet into the great play-pen of the world outside just us.

"Who, him?" I said, maliciously. "That's Tom Clancy."

"You're Tom Clancy?"

Everyone moved towards him.

I heard him spluttering an explanation; felt him turn to catch me, probably by the collar, but by that time I was wandering across the lawn, not looking back.

Because we don't know who we are. Nobody knows. But Tom and I, we both knew about that.

Dr. Samuels' voice breaks in. "So he was a writer?"

"Is a writer," I say. "That's why he's not visiting. Too busy, and of course I want to support that. He has deadlines and he has to work. I told you. He has to concentrate and I disturb that. He says he can't think, can't sleep, can hardly breathe. Because of me."

"So he's published, then? And you've read his books?"

I laugh because I've read his books so many times I could quote from them. I reel off the most recent title and then work backwards. Five in all. "And then there's the one he's working on. I think he's undecided what to call it, but he did a tour of stone circles on an electric bike. Those touring ones – the last three, are all about the people he met and the history of the places. Some of it's about his family, but I expect I'll make it into this latest."

"Oh,"she says.

"He won't use my proper name of course but he says I'm all through it like the word Blackpool is through a stick of rock. The earlier ones are novels. They're very funny. He should do stand-up. Well, I suppose he sort of does, at the festivals." I can tell I'm talking really fast. I just can't get across how great they are. It's best she reads them for herself. They'll tell her far more about him than anything I can say.

"So his name is Tom Hanson," she says. "Which book do you like best?"

"Oh," I say. "*The Disco At The End Of The World* is the one I like best. It's... kind, somehow, but *Stuff The Turkey* is the funniest. Counter-culture stuff, you know. Not for everyone."

"But for you?"

"It's OK," I say. Actually, I went off it, but I can't remember why, so I cross my arms and stare at her.

"Stuff the Turkey," she says, and lifts her eyebrows, just slightly. "Tell me about how you got together. After the course."

"We had it arranged. Well – arranged and not arranged. That was the amazing thing about us. We only had to mention a festival cafe and it was understood between us that we'd meet there. The pop festival was only a month away."

And we were, eventually. I'd been down that dusty road to the Kitchens Of Resistance about three times already, despite his telling me that he never arrived until the evening of the day the festival kicked off. By the fourth time, the seating area outside lay in shadow, though I wandered into the dim entrance to a cafe still staffed by relatively sober people.

I saw him immediately, sitting on a settee at the back of the main body of the tent, like a ship surrounded by a flotilla. A giant among dwarves, completely absorbed in conversation, his long legs crossed, foot drooping elegantly, small hands animated. Until he spotted me. But I felt, rather than watched him spring up, because – overwhelmed by the occasion – I'd turned away.

"Oh, hello," I said eventually, as if we'd chanced upon each other, but he was too much of a gentleman to embarrass me by stating what we both knew. Besides, his hands shook so much that he spilt the coffee. When we returned to the table, we slipped into discussion as easily as we sank into that recently vacated settee, though the place was packed.

Wreathed in a fug of smoke and coffee, we sat in a new alliance. Tom put his hands on his bald head and I saw deep indentations either side of his skull. He leaned towards me, soft eyes wide open. He knew I was working in the Healing Field and I knew he would listen to anything I had to say. "You see these?" he said. "They're forceps marks. I was dragged out of my mother with metal tongs." His face drooped. Bashful, he added, "I saw a counsellor about it – she said it was birth trauma – the difficulties I've had. Do you think it's pathological? That I'm stuck with them?"

I reached to soothe his brow like a fairy spreading dust. "Do I think it's hopeless?" I tinkled, or perhaps we didn't speak at all. It didn't matter, doesn't matter, but I do know he let his head lean against my buzzing fingers. For how long wasn't important, but where the rest of our time had lacked definition, parting for the night was different. A forced wrench that felt wrong, like embracing hunger. But what else were we to do? We'd just met, and lacking any clear way of proceeding, we fell back on convention. "Come and see me tomorrow," he said. "I'm on at eleven. Part of the Green Roadshow."

I didn't know he sang as well as wrote. When I went down the next day, he was flitting between the bandstand and the path like a giant bat. That was when I remembered seeing him, years before, hurling up his vest. This time he wore a flapping dirty-old-man raincoat but up close, he seemed more like a huge, bald baby.

Or a magician. I marvelled as he heckled, then herded a small crowd into watching him. A circle of giant mushrooms made of wood stood next to the main drag, overlooking the bandstand, and I clambered up to watch him strip down to a grubby string vest. He was replacing the lyrics to *My Girl* with the words, *Your Mum* when a reckless feeling filled me with so much joy it was as if his star had exploded and showered me with glitter. Once he'd got us all rooting for more, he began to sing, the way an old-fashioned variety entertainer brings things to a close. From then on, any doubts I might have had about him were suspended as I stared into his daring.

Looking back, I see that it wasn't just Tom's performance that I fell in love with. His timing's not that good and his voice has faltered with age, but his belief in the perfect song was so strong it commanded the audience to see what he saw and hear what he heard. Matt Monro, Perry Como, Nat King Cole – he couldn't sustain being any of them for a whole song, but just for an instant he inhabited their rhythm and meaning so completely that he vanished inside them. That was how Tom poured the collective soul of light and live entertainment deep into me. His brightness and brashness illuminated an almost lost music-hall tradition, conjuring the whole history of working class defiance against filth and poverty everywhere. In one resounding bar of Mac The Knife, Tom managed to embody the sentiments of *Fuck the lot of you, You can't get me* and *You're forgiven*. Talent, self-deprecating irony and nobility poured out of him, and the fact that he waved that flag even as we all drowned in a sea of corporate-generated muzak made me want to fall at his feet.

So hypnotic was his performance that when the cheers from a now large crowd had died down, there was silence enough for a light touch of the keyboard to reach right into me. The introduction – a single chord – lit a flame in my heart that expanded into recognition before he'd made a sound.

'What's it all about, Alfie?' he sang, as if he had no idea at all. As if he was as young and hopeful and pure as Cilla Black seemed in 1968. As safe as the family living room on a Saturday evening, tobacco smoke rising with the coal fumes and the smell of fish and chips. Cilla, heart surging on the black and white telly, while Dad took the piss. But I saw her orange lips and her sequins flashing emerald and I swear she was in colour.

Cheap and sentimental? Never Cilla. And not Tom when he sang it either. Brimful and unbroken, he blessed us with his longing. Not a great voice, but good enough to end an act.

I willed it to be good enough, held my breath like I was restraining his own anxiety, waiting for that top note and when he let it ring, clear across that midsummer afternoon, my sigh of relief went out to meet it. That was the first time I really understood, without words or decisions; without reflection. This guy was a maniac, and I was utterly in love with him.

"What are you doing later?" he asked, as we stood on the bandstand after the stragglers had finished telling him how great he was.

"Hanging out with you some more, I hope. You are totally brilliant and I'm completely smitten." It came out so easily, as if we'd picked up just where we'd broken off the night before. When he bent to kiss me my heart cruised across that tent-strewn city like an eagle.

"I heard you, you know," he said. "When I hit that top note. I heard you sigh. You were with me, willing it."

Oblivious to everything else, on we spooned in the middle of the bandstand while everyone worked around us – heaving the P.A. across the grass, packing the keyboard in its box, but by then Tom's cronies had acquired the status of cicadas on the dry-iced fringe of our veranda.

Dr. Samuels has her head on one side and is nodding. "So you fell very much in love? The connection sounds... powerful." She places her fingers to her lips like a prayer and I do feel she gets it. She waits for while and then says, "What on earth made him decide to steal the balloon?"

My feet fly up from their footrest as I watch Tom's hands unwind the rope from the two stakes that held our figure of eight so taut. I grab at Dr. Samuels misunderstanding as if correcting it will save me from a fall into hell. "Not then," I laugh. "This was – oh, ages ago. When we first met."

"Oh," she answers, "I see. This took place some time back? Fill me in. Not just about you and Tom, but what were you doing? Where was your daughter? Where were you living, at the time?"

But I ignore her question to plunge once more into the story of me and Tom. How we said what the other believed, did what the other desired, until night absorbed our differences and fused them into one.

"I can stop this now," I said to him, as I accompanied him to the exit gate. We stood on a bank between two puddles. "I can stop this now and it will be all right. I can leave it. Wrap it up like a gift to keep, but if we go on, I'll become yours."

The wheels of his case began to bed into the mud. "I'll e-mail you."

"You don't have to."

"I'll e-mail you. What's your address?"

I told him the name of my website, once, to give him a chance to forget it. As he walked down the narrow lane into a carnival of nylon hair and flashing antennae, I turned to watch him go. Among the pedestrians, the pink stripes of his shirt shone like candy.

* * *

----- Original Message -----
From: Tom Hanson
To: Gina@manyparts.co.uk
Sent: Monday, July 5, 2006 02:04 AM
Subject: Marvin Gaye sings in the Healing Field
Dear Ms Fulbright; I found your website very
interesting, though I was sad not to find a
photo of you there. I was wondering how secure
your email system is, as I would like a tarot
reading from you. I am very keen to make an
appointment to come and see you in the near
future, and I hope that you will be able to fit
me in somewhere.
I look forward to hearing from you soon,
Yours
Tom Hanson

* * *

Our first hotel stood by a main road into the city: a
medium-sized Edwardian semi, with a tiny car park
where marigolds spilled onto the gravel beneath spindly
shrubs. The receptionist smiled as we headed for the
stairs. "Bags in the car? Shall I bring them up?"

I paused, turning on the second step. "We haven't
got any," I said, at exactly the same time as Tom,
focused doggedly on the landing, said "We'll get them
later." I ran after him, a burst of giggles propelling us
down the corridor. But then, with the bedroom door
slammed behind us, he pushed me against it, took my

face in his shaking hands and stared.

No one before Tom had ever shaken from desire of me. His passion reduced the room behind him to rubble. Dust soft-focused our bodies and settled around what was left: he and I, still clothed and waiting – longing – to be unclothed.

He placed his palm on his diaphragm. "I want you so much... I want you so much I can't move. I can't move, because once I do... once I do, I can never stop moving until you give in. Until you surrender." I'd have cheered if I hadn't been so busy surrendering already. This was no time to falter. He meant it. With all of himself. For now. For now, he meant it. Churlish and pointless not to try to meet him.

His breathing vibrated into a low growl as he undid the buttons of my blouse and eased it off my shoulders. Stippled woodchip pressed into my bare skin as I leaned into shadow. I moved to sit on the beige counterpane and he fell to his knees, unzipping my boots and removing them as if they were glass. Him page, me Queen. Me Cinders, him Prince. Me Venus, him...

He lay down and placed his hands behind his head. "Take your clothes off."

Pleasure had never felt so serious. I stood with my back to him and let my unhooked bra fall from my arms, slid my skirt over my hips and slipped my pants down my legs and onto the floor. For the first time, I felt exposed and self-conscious, performance making me shy, but once I turned, I forgot all that. He was crying, silently, as he stared. Three steps towards him, for him, in that still room, into the square of light, and I took his hands in mine and sipped that tear away. Then he drew the curtains on the afternoon sun and we moved into one another, coiling together, seamless.

*

So we lay, me in the curve of his arm, his knees nestling behind mine, lips light against the down of my neck.

"We fit," he murmured. I peeped across the brown bedside table to the cheap wallpaper border of blue flowers that cut the room in half, and he pulled me back to his thudding heartbeat as if he could sense me wandering. With my sleepy nose, I traced the veins in his inner elbow. "Power," I said. "Power," and I lifted my head and bit his bicep. He reached across, yanked his arm out from under me and pinned my nearest shoulder back on the bed, bringing his shin up and across my hipbones. I nipped his chest.

"Ow!" he said.

"I think perhaps I hate you," I said, butting my head against his shoulder.

"And I love you," he said, eyes melting into mine, the shock of the phrase replaced by relief. "Don't you see what I've handed over to you? Don't you see that you've got me?"

And I did see that.

"I have handed you everything," he said. "I'm soft, soft as feathers. But I'm hard too," and he slid down and into my body.

*

The man behind the desk wasn't smiling any more but we grinned at him anyway as we sneaked past and into the night when we should have been going to bed.

We drove through a cartoon city, with traffic lights that turned green at every approach. The neon sign outside the train station winked at us.

"Pull over," Tom said, and the command coursed through me down to the brakes as I swerved into the concourse and parked the car.

A light summer drizzle misted my hair as we ducked into the entrance and trotted in unison down the concrete steps. "I could say no," I said. "I stopped because I chose to do as you said. I could choose not to. And don't you forget it."

"I wouldn't dare," said Tom, pulling me off the bottom step. Gypsum chips sparkled along the platform. "But don't you know that I'm as vulnerable as you are?"

I gazed into his face, loose as an old dog's, and considered what he'd said before replying. "No, I don't. I'm a woman, and perhaps it takes some time, but if I really give myself to you, I can't just take myself back." I remember the surprise I felt as this came out of my mouth and the way that surprise was swiftly replaced with relief. "Otherwise, what would be the point?" I added.

"What about Harry?" He pressed the ring on my left hand. "You gave yourself to him."

Helpless Harry, with his public-school values and

his pre-pubescent vigour. The pang I felt for the man waiting at home was one of pity, not guilt. "You can't give yourself to someone who doesn't want you," I said, ruefully. "He loves me and I love him, but he was never into sex. I thought it was time I grew up and had someone to garden and cook and plan with, but it's not enough. What about Anita?"

He sighed. "Anita is an invalid. She had asthma as a child and life with her revolves around the dangers of dust. She's scared of everything and she's never given herself to anyone. We were always about writing, partnership, business. The last time we had what passed for sex I made myself come, and I wept."

I covered my eyes with my hands, then reached to stroke his cheek. "But can't you talk to her? Go slowly? Really slowly. What does she need?"

"I've tried everything." I could hear the desperation in his voice. And the finality. "Come on," he said, and we walked through the circle of light from the iron lamp above the gents to where the railtracks streamed away.

"This is it," he said. "The end of the line. I've fucked everything up so badly and there's a huge mess to untangle, but we've waited all our lives for this." He leaned down. "Our time will come," he breathed in my ear. "Every morning I wake up without your face on the pillow beside me will be a morning wasted." His hand vibrated on my neck as we peered into darkness. "I am your future, for good or ill, as you are mine."

I didn't say, "It's not the end of the line. It's the end

of the platform." I didn't want to spoil the moment.

Chapter Five

Beatrice stood in the staffroom listening to the kettle grumble into life. She opened the cupboard above the laminate worktop for a mug but discarded it for the disused china teacup still hidden at the back. Her hand slipped beneath its porcelain curve and she peered into the perfect white round. If you were tiny enough, she thought, you might walk round and round it, mesmerised, until you slipped happily to the bottom, unaware of the danger. You might be scalded to death. Or drown, jangling with caffeine overload. She placed it gently on the surface and stepped back. China-white perfection became a bowl in a sea of barely related objects. This was a perspective the tiny thing would never have. She lifted the cup, tipped it sideways. *Woman overboard.*

For herself, she knew, though it was never as shiny or elegant as this one, she'd stayed. The bowl she and Ralph had lived in for so long had been hand-made between them. A lump here, a bump there, as layer by layer they had coiled their lives around the rules they both wished to live by. Had that been a good thing? Had it been a good thing, that when the fact of Ralph's death receded it had left so little shape to her own life? She felt thin now, as thin as this porcelain she looked through. Smashable in a way she hadn't anticipated.

Of course she hadn't. Her husband had never died before. Yet this was now the shape. This was now the shape of all things.

The kettle had long since switched itself off. She put

down the teacup, picked the lumpiest and largest mug she could find, put two spoons of Gold Blend in it and poured on water. What was it she'd said, touched by that girl's untarnished and touching faith? *When love is undeniably present, all that we see and do is pure and ceases to be manipulated by the agendas of small minds.* That, Gina had heard and been relieved. It was about the only thing she had heard. Beatrice herself felt anchored by the memory. She peered at the coffee, bounded by the thick walls of the mug, and thought she would like to throw a line to that woman overboard.

"How's it going?" Corinne smiled from the doorway and inclined her head.

How long had she been there? Beatrice felt crept up on. "Well, you know... " she said, inclining her own head to match in the hope that the mirroring would shut Corinne up. She had nothing to say. And then she realised that Corinne had even less, and that trapped in the staffroom with her senior colleague, the poor woman was doing her best to be kind. "I just... " she began. I just what? Was looking at a teacup as if it was the only thing that existed? And wondering what living in it would be like? "I was just making some coffee," she said, hoping the words didn't sound as strange to Corinne as they felt to her. "Would you like some?"

"No sugar, thanks."

Beatrice passed the coffee, handle-first, to Corinne's outstretched hand, made another one and sat down beside her. A gesture of friendship, she thought, trying to pull herself together.

"And you saw that Gina again?"

Yes, she *had* seen Gina. Saw her now, striding, sparkling across a lawn while a tall, bald man whipped round his head to stare before the crowd she had summoned closed in on him. *That's Tom Clancy!* She *had* seen her. But only for a moment. The one true moment of Gina in an hour streaked so luminous with this Tom, Tom, Tom, that after that, the girl – and girl she seemed, even though she was 42 – had forgotten herself entirely.

"Yes." Beatrice pulled a desk diary from her bag. "Power struggle with her boyfriend. She lost," she said, immediately seeing that the words she should not have spoken made her feel more powerful herself.

Corinne looked shocked. "And he pushed her out of a hot-air balloon – but I thought it was attempted... Didn't she try to... ?" The blue stone twirled from her neck as she leaned forward.

Beatrice tried to close the conversation down. "We don't know." Corinne's eagerness for the details struck her as repellent. Flailed her, she realised. But the girl had only taken her cue from the Senior Consultant. She wasn't a threat but a novice in need of guidance. "We don't know," Beatrice said again, flipping through the pages of the diary as if she might find the answer there. She tried to relax but found herself too brittle. Instead, she thumbed through the rest of the month and a piece of folded cardboard ejected itself from the book onto the floor.

Corinne leant and picked it up. "Swan Lake? Oh, brilliant. Ballet! I used to do ballet, well, actually I still do. Adult stuff. Just for fun," she added, looking anxious.

Beatrice fingered the card, opened it up. Two tickets, one booking number and a receipt in separate sections, held together by perforations. Dully, she stared at the black print. Friday October 20th Doors open 7pm. In a faint memory from another lifetime, she remembered putting down the phone, annoyed at having spent fifteen minutes in a queue only to be told how much easier and cheaper it would have been to book online. 'Easier for you,' she'd said to the faceless voice. 'It would be much easier for you,' trying to show the woman that service industries put their own interests first. But the voice had been just a voice, not an ear, and she'd come off the phone to the faithful Ralph. Now she wondered whether her endless rants about the forces of markets gone mad had been a relief to him or a dreadful bore? It had been her choice, of course, Swan Lake, performed by the English National. He'd have preferred the opera, or something contemporary, but as with the rest of their marriage, he'd appeared entirely comfortable in a supporting role.

She heard Corinne's voice, low and next to her ear. "Were you going with your husband?"

Such a simple question. Beatrice nodded. "Wedding anniversary." Her eyes filled at that easy answer.

Corinne put a hand on Beatrice's arm. "I'm very sorry."

How kind Corinne seemed suddenly, in the quiet little room. Beatrice smiled at her – a real smile this time, allowing her own sadness.

"I shouldn't have spoken," she said, after a moment. "About Gina Fulbright. Please forget what I said. I'm a little bit rusty – just back."

"Of course," said Corinne.

Beatrice watched the blood rising in the poor girl's face and felt a rush of remorse. "Please don't be concerned. There's no harm done."

"But I feel – but I feel there is. There might be."

The appeal pulled Beatrice out of herself. She cupped her coffee in both hands and smiled a smile for them both. "Oh, dear, You do look worried. Can I help?"

Nodding encouragement, Beatrice watched as Corinne struggled to speak. At first, the girl couldn't meet her eyes but slowly the hesitation faded and she told Beatrice what had happened.

"So you see, I was there and I didn't say. At the meeting. I just... I just... " and Corinne let out a sigh so great she slumped against the back of her chair.

In fact, Corinne had heard nothing about the balloon until she'd returned to her tent, up by the farm. The Welfare Barn was next to the medical centre, which was next to the police Portacabins and she'd been outside in the farmyard, taking deep breaths of dung-filled air when Cath, the shift supervisor had said, "There she goes," as an ambulance screamed past and out through the fence to the outside world.

"Well, thank you for letting me know that," said Beatrice, more curious about the dislocation between Corinne's extreme agitation and the banality of her disclosure. She waited.

"You see, I was right up there – by the field. Right up there."

"Yes," said Beatrice, nodding. "But you left because everyone had shut up shop." Space, warmth, patience. This, she could do. This, and invitation to speak. "What is it, Corinne, that is so difficult?"

After a few moment's silence while Corinne picked at her fingers, Beatrice said, "It's entirely up to you, what you tell me."

When Corinne finally spoke, the words pumped, then drawled; were loud, then quiet. "It was the tarot card. The picture. And then... I didn't know if that was what had got her... maybe. If she had been – like me. And maybe that was her – in the tent?"

Outside of her own therapy, Corinne had never told anyone at all about her involvement with the cult of Aleister Crowley. Even in the self-help group, she'd sensed an over-eagerness that repelled her. Although she could feel neither of these present in Beatrice's invitation, she still couldn't make a sound. So she sat there, blowing softly, gathering her courage.

"It's OK. You don't have to say," Beatrice said, gently.

But Corinne needed Beatrice to know her excuse for not explaining about her presence at the festival. The word *user* amplified in her head, crowding out all but the slimmest hope that perhaps her story could provide absolution. She felt the breeze in her hair. Saw the stalls flashing past. Heard her own breathing as if it belonged to someone else. Her throat pulsed. "I... never talk about it," she managed. "Well... only in therapy, but... well... I don't know... perhaps it's time I did... talk about it somewhere else. Make it more real. Actually, it's funny you should... Now... I'd just... " The words jerked from her as Beatrice quietly listened.

"Abuse. I can say that now, but it fucks up your head so you don't know it's abuse and it's the not knowing that... not really seeing it... that... well you just can't really get outside the whole thing enough to... " Corinne forced herself on. "But saying this to you *is* getting out... And I know I can say it to you," she said, louder now. "There's some real shit out there and if you don't really know who you are and you want to be important, you're fucked." She was trying to outrun the word that screamed in her head: *User.* Corinne took a deep breath and asserted, "The fact is, I was a Scarlet Woman."

Beatrice frowned.

"Sorry," said Corinne, defiantly and not sorry at all. "I thought you'd know. What I mean is I was a whore... a whore with delusions of grandeur." She dropped her head in her hand and hit it, once, before emerging, red-faced, to add, "That won't help... I got involved with a bunch of men who believed that they could make themselves really... powerful through sex. The younger the woman, the more they told her how important she was. So, for a bit, I became what they called this Scarlet Woman."

"How old were you?" asked Beatrice, the pitch of her voice low and slow.

"Fifteen." The word echoed. "They told me I was the whore of Babylon." She stared at Beatrice then. "And I believed them."

Corinne felt her face drain of blood and her body begin to petrify but Beatrice's words and voice stayed warm. "Yes. I've got you now. She's in The Book Of Revelation. A representation of the female sexual impulse at its most liberated and seen as one of the most ungodly heathens in the bible." She raked back her hair from her face.

A cry escaped Corinne's lips as she reached towards Beatrice. "Yes. That's what was so confusing."

"Fifteen," said Beatrice, calm where Corinne was frantic. "A child." She waited and then added, "Were the men prosecuted?"

Corinne shrugged. "They legged it but they thought they could do what they wanted and so... " Staring at the floor, struggling to match Beatrice's practical response with the impossibility of its application she added, "...so they did." The carpet squares seemed suddenly two inches from her eyes and edgeless, but still she spoke, reaching for something to hold onto. "He said... he said... The Scarlet Woman was only reviled because the people didn't understand change."

"That must have been baffling to a child."

A child. It was so hard to take in that she'd been a child. "They were Crowley's words." Her own words seemed to come from far away. "We had a shrine. That was... well it was... "

"Mmm?" said Beatrice, again.

"He said I was a Goddess."

She reached to let Corinne's hand rest in her own. "You poor child." The world beyond Beatrice's own drama seemed suddenly to need her. "Bound by lies – Women are passive but still responsible for their actions – then bound again by their own need. Hence Crowley gets something for nothing." Evil was so banal; frightening only because it asserted itself where it could get away with it. She felt calmer than she had for ages. A professional calm that allowed nothing past. "*Love is the law. Love under will* – Do what I say. Wasn't that the beginning and the end of his assertion?" she said, offering her own authority to Corinne.

The ecstasy lifting Corinne felt almost dangerous. Fourteen years of digging and tearing, of reenacting and clawing and wondering and smearing herself with shit, peeled away by two clear sentences that had nothing whatsoever to do with her. She couldn't believe it. "How did you get that so quick? It took me ages – years to see that."

"And how old are you now?"

"Twenty-nine," said Corinne, miserably, but astonishingly, Dr. Samuels winked at her.

"Saturn return, then," she said. "Nearly there." Having had a brief parlay with astrology herself in her teens, Beatrice gambled that Corinne, with her mystical inclinations, would have studied this nonsense. It would mean something to her. Something Beatrice could use to help.

And, sure enough, Corinne lifted her chin to listen.

"Well look what you're living through. It's difficult but look what you're understanding. Tell me, Corinne. You're trained. You must be in therapy?"

"Oh, yes. Yes. And I'm nearly better. Stopping soon. I know I've been in there for ages and I'm probably too dependent," said Corinne, anxiously. "They didn't agree, in college. Weren't really keen to sign off my practice."

Beatrice nodded, hiding her confusion.

"Five years. Still going."

"Oh?"

"And three years of group-work, before that. That's

what made me get into all this. Saved my life."

"But having your own analysis got you really hooked?"

"Well – not analysis." Corinne wasn't really sure what the difference was. "But – yes – psychotherapy. Proper, serious commitment. Down to earth. Weekly appointments. Have to be on time. That took a while. I was all over the place. Into all sorts. Tantra. Crowley's tarot pack. Magic." Corinne stopped, worried above all that she was exposing herself as unbalanced.

"And that's not really what's expected? In college?"

Corinne giggled. She couldn't stop herself because it was so obvious that Beatrice, the great Senior Consultant, seemed to have no problem with five years in therapy.

Beatrice settled back into her chair, leading Corinne further from her fifteen year old self. "And how are you getting on with the work here?"

"I'm glad – I... I found that training is all very well. Really good – in fact – for me." She caught the older woman's eye. "But to be completely honest, I'd say mine probably didn't really work – unless I just ignored the patients and sort of stuck the system I was taught on them. But it doesn't fit," added Corinne, all in a rush. "Not here. Not with brain damage and spines that... not with people who're... "

"Un-mendable?" asked Beatrice, quietly. "Yes. Some of them are. So how do you manage?"

Corinne looked away, certain she was digging her own grave, but what else was there to say? "I'm seeing that bloke who's had half his head blown away. I'm supposed to be teaching him to associate his wife's name with warmth and

safety but that's crazy so I just sort of am there with him."
But when she dared meet Beatrice's eye again, she saw
approval.

"I... suppose it's all right to tell you about that?" said a
doubtful Corinne.

"Ah, that," said Beatrice. "Confidentiality?"

Beatrice's ability to hide what she felt had not prevented
the alarm that was growing inside her about Corinne's
misunderstanding of the basics. Contrary to the current
fashion for trainees not to get 'too dependent' on their own
therapist, Beatrice saw psychotherapy as an undertaking that
took the patient into dependency and out of it again. She
believed that this was an experience the trainee had to go all
the way through in order to understand and manage the
dependency needs of their own patients in turn. In her
experience, popping in and out of a bit of 'support' changed
very little and if that enabled young people like Corinne to
think they were fully qualified? Well – Beatrice found this
frightening. Furthermore if Corinne was left thinking herself
wrong for following her own need, she'd be battling the
same kind of muddle she'd faced at 15. Looking at Corinne,
she saw the future she feared: child-therapists with so many
unresolved problems of their own that their
overidentification with the downtrodden prevented them
from seeing outside themselves at all.

Prior to Ralph's death she'd been sick of thinking about
it. Had forgotten, over the previous twelve weeks, just how
sick. Confidentiality demanded more than reading a contract
out to some new patient who couldn't even hear it because
of their own distress. Ethics was not, as it was now

presented, a list of rules handed down from on high. These were for the benefit of an organisation, not the person sitting in front of you, and the thought that these kids would start seeing people privately had started the juices around her own ethical concerns flowing.

Yet it appeared that Corinne was doing one of the most important aspects of training completely off her own bat. The rest – the supervision, the reflection, the reading, she could help her with. Blood began to run faster in Beatrice's veins as she wondered what the girl could handle.

"Yes, confidentiality," she said. "Perhaps we could try thinking about it. Just here. Can you put the rules you've been taught to one side? Just think about what happened between us for a minute?"

"I could try," said Corinne, pulling herself upright.

"Why did I respond by asking you to forget what I'd just said?"

Corinne closed her eyes, felt inside for how she'd felt when she'd first seen Beatrice in the staffroom and said, "I... I don't need to know. I was just making conversation. You'd not meant to tell me?"

So Corinne could divine her own motives, palatable or otherwise.

"And what you told me – about the abuse. Did that feel different? Does it seem dangerous to have told me?"

"No!" she answered, shocked.

"How come?"

"You're senior. Trustworthy. You were trying to help. It was er... confidential."

"But how do you know that. We didn't make any rules."

Again, Corinne took a few minutes, closing her eyes to shut out the face opposite. "Well, it wasn't gossip. At all. It was just something about your authority – and your role," she added.

So dig she could. She could reach into herself and be brave.

"Look," Beatrice added. "Do you really want to know about how to take care of people when you work – whether you're given clear rules or not?"

Corinne had thought the serious stuff for – well – older people. Clever people. With degrees. "I'd love to," she said, shyly. "And I study. All the time. But I haven't got a clue what I'm doing really."

Beatrice smiled. "I could give you a reading list. And spend some time talking about your work?" She rubbed her nose, considering. "I think you've made a great beginning – reaching out to people – believing in their innate will to health, but there's a bit more to it than that." And even though Corinne didn't understand why, what Beatrice said began to make sense and she felt herself relax for the first time that day, glad to have Beatrice and, *yes*, she thought, noticing, *hope*.

"And perhaps you can see now, that the reason you didn't tell me – about the festival – was because it felt too threatening. At a fundamental level, you were protecting yourself, and that's a good thing, Corinne."

But Corinne needed more. She couldn't stop the embarrassment from flooding up, reddening her face. "But I feel so... guilty. As if I should have known or stayed there. As if I could have stopped her."

The look on Beatrice's face was unmistakeably pity. "You could have *stopped* her?" she said. She paused, letting the words hang before asking, "Is that phrase familiar, bearing in mind what you've just told me?"

And Corinne felt like a naked child about to be put in a warm bath, with nothing to concern her beyond which story she might be read as she fell asleep.

"You've got these things muddled, my dear. It's the trauma. I guess you've got lots to go and tell your therapist now that we've talked, but I must go." Gathering her things Beatrice looked again at the white ticket, bent at its perforated centre, as if a butterfly had landed on her diary. "Perhaps... If you wanted to... we could go to the ballet together. It's just..." she said, backtracking, her sudden sympathy knocked away by concern that this was pushy. "Well, I have these tickets and it would be a shame to waste them."

But Corinne was wide-eyed. "God, I'd love that."

"And you'll see your therapist soon?" Beatrice asked, lightly.

Corinne grinned. "What about you?"

Beatrice gave Corinne her *it's shit, isn't it, but we're in it together* look. "Well actually, perhaps if we're working together and we're clear that this is in confidence, I can tell you that I'm going to see Gina." She smiled. "So you can put her down now and leave her to me."

Chapter Six

Harry is sitting by my bed, clean-shaven, shirt immaculately ironed, shoes soft and shiny as a new born calf. He looks up, doe-eyed, from the book he's been half-reading and asks me how I'm feeling. Nothing has really changed between us, vindicating my belief that we were always more brother and sister than married couple. Soon we will be divorced, but I'm not sure how much difference that will make either. Harry remains polite, concerned. Dispassionate. He wants to know if I need anything, but I am a closed circuit now. I no longer send out hopeful signals that flare and fade. I ask him to bring in my laptop. I miss Tom more and more, but if I can see our correspondence, I can dripfeed some of his spirit into me along with the drugs.

Harry brings it later with a bunch of grapes. I can hardly wait for him to leave, so tiring are the platitudes that pass between us, but once he's gone, Tom's words, messenger conversations in real-time that I have cut and pasted for our archive, grip me like a fever.

✧T: Car crisis; rush-arsing about. At least we are in the same boat and soon, not soon enough, I will hold you in my arms.
♡G: Good, because it's the only thing that can stop me floating away. How can I find the words to make you blaze on the inside like I do if I can't stay sitting on my seat by the keyboard?
✧T: You think words are needed? I thought I

might be cool, but you're too open, too clever, too sexy and you have ensnared me.

♡G: Ensnared you? I don't like the sound of that. What do you mean?

♦T: *I mean you are irresistible, witty and exercising huge amounts of power over my nether regions.*

♡G: Hmm. You think I'm so powerful but it's your passion I'm filled with. That's what worries me.

♦T: *That's because you don't have total control. Neither do I but I don't want it.*

♡G: But that's the point. I gave myself to you… you've got it.

♦T: *And when I give myself to you?*

♡G: I told you, that's different. You get to choose but for women, if men are really present, Love, as Byron said, is their whole existence.

♦T: *Love is the whole of existence, wise one.*

♡G: Stop tickling me. I'm sliding down the wall with my hands behind my head.

♦T: *Thank God for that because I'm running out of excuses and all I have left is the ability to ravish you. A considerable ability. Listen, just because men can't treat women like shit anymore doesn't mean there's no place for us. I've learned that you protect people in this world not to control them but because they're precious.*

♡G: I'm falling on my knees.

◇T: Jesus. I'm trying to have a conversation here and all I can think of is your lips, wet with you and me mixed together. Your eyes are grey, and blue, and yellow. They silence me.
♡G: Then we are quits my darling and that is how it should be.
◇T: Good. So I have, at least, some empathy with women??
♡G: For women, being silenced turns into not even being able to think straight. That's what oppression is.
◇T: Sounds appalling. My sweetest love, you're right, power elites don't give up their power; they have it taken from them. But you're doing a fantastic job. I lay my sexual desire before you, to use as you will. And, to that end, I have booked a room for Tuesday night where we can be the whole of the world for a few hours, in a Travelodge beside the motorway. I admit it's not the Berlin Hilton, but give me time. You can meet me in the Little Chef… a perfect example of bathos.

* * *

Mid-afternoon. Tom sat crossed-legged in the middle of the motel bed and stretched his long arm past my waist, reaching for a pillow.

"Here," he said. Facing him, knees placed on either side of his hips, I waited, holding myself up and steady and praying that my thighs wouldn't cramp. Waiting made the backs of my legs ache, but with every twinge of pain, a little of my self-concern fell away and the more it fell away, the larger my heart became. The longer I waited, the stronger the pull of gravity, but up I stayed. A heart, beating for Tom.

The pillow he'd placed beneath me tickled. An itch developed. I longed to scratch but instead I took a breath that would have absorbed a whiplash. I knew I could accommodate him. Really, I wanted to accommodate him until I disappeared altogether.

His hand stayed steady round my waist until my legs began to shake with the stress. He took my hair in his mouth and dragged my head to the hollow just above his collarbone and I stretched across until my mouth touched the side of his neck.

And then it began. First gently, then deeper in before withdrawing, sliding from beneath me and turning me over and onto the bed so that my pelvis rested on the pillow.

He kneeled between my legs and ran his fingertips down my spine until he slid them beyond to probe the soft outer edge.

"So, my Pole Star," Tom lifted my hair and swept it behind my ear as he leaned on his elbow above me. "We need a word, and 'stop' isn't it, and 'no' isn't it either."

"You could do anything to me," I said, melting into the mattress.

"I know," said Tom, "I know," and he pulled away. "That's why we need a word. Tizer," he purred as he pushed me on my side and parted my thighs. "Say Tizer and I'll stop. I promise. Wherever we are, whatever we're doing, I'll stop."

"Mmmm... " and I turned, wrapping my legs around him, pushing at his chest.

*

"The thing about anal sex," I said later, as the dawn modified our silhouettes from black and white to grey.

"Mmm?" Tom lay back against the headboard with a roll-up in his mouth.

"The thing about anal sex is that it must be very nice for the man. It doesn't hurt him and it doesn't make him bleed."

"Oh sweetheart," said Tom, leaning over to drop the gentlest kiss on my hair. "Forget it. It was just an idea. That's why I brought it up. If you don't want to, just say."

"It's not that. I just think if God had meant us to have anal sex he would never have invented piles."

"Ah... " said Tom. "Then why did he make it so good?"

"Good for who?"

"For women."

I searched his dark eyes for the laugh in them but he was serious.

"In my limited experience women have the most powerful orgasms ever and anyway, my dick's just not that big," he said.

I threw up my hands. "Yes, but what's next? I'm as turned on as the next person by all sorts of stuff but it seems to me that once something's been stretched, as it were, you have to stretch somewhere else to get the same kick. Before you know it, what turned you on turns you off but you do it anyway, except next time with a blindfold on, tied to the bed so you can't move. And then what? Where does it end?"

Tom stared at me for so long I thought I'd bored him. I began to pick at my fingernails but he pulled up my chin and gazed at me.

"Yes. That kind of bothers me as well. I don't know," and his lips sagged. "I only know I love you," he murmured, shrugging the cover off with a sweep of his shoulder as he pushed his long arm the length of mine.

"And I love you."

"You're cold," he said, stubbing out his cigarette before tucking the duvet gently around my body and cradling my head in his hand. His arm was crooked at an angle that must have ached, but his heartbeat pulsed into my ear and I settled against it. As I drifted towards sleep my head sank into the pillow and a draught brushed my shoulder.

I opened my eyes. He was sitting up, staring at the wall. His eyes were wet. I reached and stroked his thigh. "What?... darling?" My fingers skimmed his stomach.

I sat, pulling the duvet to cover my breasts. "What's the matter?"

He turned towards me, the folds of his face deepening in the half-light. "It's... it's the thing I'm most afraid of... hurting women."

"Hurting women? Tell me."

"I... I," he struggled and I placed the palm of my hand to rise and fall with the soft hairs on his chest. So we waited in the ticking dawn.

"Tell me," I said again, my voice calm and certain.

"My first wife. She... she died. Liz died," he sighed, a huge sigh that made him shrink against the bedstead.

"OK," I hummed, keeping things steady, no sudden movements. "She died," I echoed.

He lit his cigarette and gripped my hand, pushing his fingers down into the spaces between mine. "I had an affair, you see, with a singer. When Naomi, our daughter, was three."

"How old is she... now?"

"She's twenty four." He looked at me for the first time and I saw his terror flash; lightning behind a cloud.

"So this was twenty-one years ago, sweetheart. Twenty-one years." I bobbed my head. "Go on."

"The night I left home, my lover changed her mind." Tom closed his eyes. "Served me right. She had a religious conversion and decided to stay with her husband."

"So what did you do?"

He laughed out of the side of his mouth. "I was pathetic. I crawled back to Liz and asked to be taken back." He looked at me, pleading as if he was pleading with her, and then he dropped his head. "She stood on the doorstep and told me I was a coward and a womanising bastard, just like my father, and that I could fuck off. And it was true. Look at me. It was true." His eyes were dry, as if he had no right to tears, but his words cracked as if they'd been whipped from his body.

"And she never took you back?" I reached for the question, playing for time as I tried to make sense of his distress, but the past was too far away... And then I shuddered. "Have you done it since?"

Tom shook his head. "No, never. I've never been unfaithful since. Not until now." He drew heavily on his roll-up. "But I wasn't the world's greatest second husband either." He paused. "It had been a struggle, a mess, but Patricia and I were happy at last. Naomi was seven by then. Liz had got herself together. High-flying job. Nicole Farhi suits. Vidal Sassoon crop. New partner. It was just before we divorced. Me and Patricia were in bed when the phone rang. They took Liz to hospital. Brain haemorrhage and I didn't realise... Patricia knew. She was a nurse. She knows about these things."

"Knew what, love?" but Tom had entered a world entirely his own. He scratched at his head like he was mining for details.

"Once, before we had Naomi, me and Liz were watching this programme where they switched off someone's life support machine. 'It doesn't matter how much of a vegetable I get to be,' Liz said. 'If that ever happens to me, promise you'll never switch the machine off.'" Tom grabbed my shoulders and held them tight.

"But it's different when it happens. You do what they tell you."

"Yes." But my yes seemed far away, ineffective against this flicking of a switch. He had turned her off, and the line had gulped, hummed itself smooth and gone out. Transmission over. "Yes," I said, faintly. "Of course you do."

"Still next of kin, you see. You find out what that really means when something like this happens," and I saw the white hospital and the sheeted hump and the bedside crowded with drawn faces, and I took his baby head in my arms and held it firm and we sat steady as the dark holes and brightly coloured fragments of our lives piled up around us.

Tom began to breathe more slowly, but he looked away. "Afterwards we got into a taxi. I couldn't stop crying. It was such a shock." He peeped back to check I was really listening.

I nodded.

"I'd thought she'd get better."

I felt as if my heart could expand indefinitely, as if this torrent of grief would wash away every dark patch and rough edge that men had battered into it. Tom seemed so defenceless in his pain, total in his passion, welcoming every bit of life that came his way.

"Go on," I said.

"Patricia just started screaming at me. All about how I had her now and why was I so upset?" He flinched. "And she just went on screaming." He stared in disbelief, shuddering as though she slapped him over and over. "She went on screaming for the next seven years. Until she threw me out."

His horror poured into me, a mass of black that squeezed out my confusion and left no room for Patricia. I wanted to see it the way he saw it.

"That's why I can't stand drama now," he said, closing his eyes tight. "I just can't stand it. I stopped crying. Decided Patricia was right." And he stared into my eyes again, checking I agreed.

I hesitated. "And Naomi?" I said, holding my hands flat.

It broke him. He pulled away and clasped his knees, tears pouring down his face as he rocked forward and back. "When we told her, she rushed upstairs to the bathroom – this tiny girl in her little blue dress – and locked herself in." His sigh keened across the room. "I stood outside the door, waiting and knocking and all I could hear was her pacing up and down saying 'Naomi, be a grown-up. Naomi, you must be a grown up about this.'"

Tom sat, staring as if her face stared back at him. "She was brave, Christ, she was brave."

"I'm sorry," I said. It wasn't enough. Nothing could be enough. I reached to trace the deep line at the edge of his mouth with my finger. "I know about the phone." I whispered. "I know what it's like to hear it ring in the night. I hear it sometimes – like you hear the cry of a child when you're a mother." I lifted my head. "You get up and they haven't made a sound, but you're ready," I said. "You're ready all the time... like you know that this... " I waved my hand slowly through the still air, "... that this is all temporary."

He leaned towards me, eyes muddy with memory, and put his head, just slightly, to one side. A soft movement, slow enough to catch the world as it stops turning. We watched it together for a moment; watched as it fell apart.

"My brother, Peter," I said, and I grinned my brother's grin, trying to pull back what was gone forever. I even sniggered as if his death was a private joke between the two of us. "The bastard," I said. "He didn't even stop to say goodbye." But my expression stalled, the truth of his absence forcing tears down my cheeks. I pushed on, trying to outpace them. "Go towards the light, they said, and he was off. Typical. Heart attack," I scoffed, as if I could handle anything.

"It's all right," said Tom. "Everything's allowed," and he meant I was all right, and he opened his huge, huge arms and I crawled in like a little girl. He ran his fingers through my long hair, separating the tangles, patient and proud, until I stopped crying.

"That stuff they say about your knees turning to jelly... " I said. "It's true." And I told him about those faltering steps I took like a drunk woman across the tiny side ward in the casualty department to where my darling brother lay, still grinning, with the tiniest tube still protruding from his mouth.

"But you did it," said Tom stroking my face tenderly. "You went without thinking about it. Just did it, knowing it was the right thing to do, however much it hurt. God, you're strong." He cupped my jaw in his hand. "I'll hold you. I can't do much but I can do that, if you'll let me."

I smiled, relaxing at last. "Yes, you can do that... and if you do that, I can do anything." He squeezed my hand and I felt his strength flow directly into my heart, knowing too, that if he stopped, I'd leak away.

"When?" he said. "When did all this happen? I want to know everything. I want to learn everything."

"Two years ago, and two years after my father died," and I told him of that other egghead I had held and stroked, and of the clawed yellow hand on the hospice coverlet and the gentle billow of the curtains from those windows I had flung wide.

"I told him... I told him the night before, that everything was all right. That we could take care of ourselves, but I didn't feel that at all. It was a story. A story he had to hear, to make it all right to die."

"I know." Tom licked away my tear. "We can never look after ourselves. It's a myth. An urban, Western myth. We have to look after each other." And we sat, the bright fragments, prayer flags, hanging paler now from our circling arms in the bright summer morning.

* * *

I see now why they're called laptops. Mine fits neatly on my lap and I grip the edges of it as I'm wheeled to my next session. My shoulder joints grind in their sockets. I could be thrown onto the floor if we hit too big a bump. The porter stops, taps on the door and opens it and I shudder across the threshold and onto the carpet, opening the laptop lid before he's gone.

Dr. Samuels spins round in her chair. She looks pleased to see me. It's not just her smile but the way she flings out her hands as if I'm a surprise. A good one. She stands and comes right up to me, pulling my chair into the middle of the room by both arms and swinging it ninety degrees. I feel like a child on a roundabout and she comes to sit nearby. Not directly opposite, but so that she can look at my laptop easily. She says she hopes I might have some photos to show her. Maybe some of my daughter, June but I tell her I think June is OK.

"I know she's OK," she says. "I spoke to her on the phone."

The phone is behind me, on her desk. It's a cheap creamy plastic extension that I've noticed before. "I don't really want June to be bothered with all this," I say.

"But June is your daughter. She spent a lot of time sitting by you when you were unconscious. You saw her when you woke up. Wouldn't you expect her to still be worried?"

I look at my laptop. I don't want to think of June. She's gone now. Away to university and that's where I want her to stay, enjoying her life. "Well, if you've reassured her, perhaps she won't be worried anymore."

I think she's chuckling, though she speaks softly. "Well your mum certainly is. How do you feel about that?"

I feel forced into responding but I can't think of anything to say so I stare at the carpet, where the wheels of my chair have made a track so slight, it's fading as we speak.

If carpet can actually be made so flat to start with, I wonder if 'carpet' is the right word for it. "Just tell her I'm all right," I manage to say.

She chuckles again. "I'm doing my best. Your father's dead, isn't he?"

"Well, thank God I haven't got to talk to *him*."

"And your brother died just a few years ago?"

I ignore this. It's got nothing to do with anything.

She doesn't miss a beat. "Well, what would you like to talk about?" she asks. I push my laptop towards her and she takes it over to her desk where she settles, looking at it for ages. And that's lovely. So lovely. Eventually, she turns back, leaves the laptop on the desk and trundles back over to me on her desk chair. I could wait all day now because while she's living inside the conversation between Tom and me, there's nowhere else I have to be. Nothing else to say. Even my arms have gone soft and stopped hurting in the quiet fullness of this room.

It doesn't last. She has to speak, which is annoying.

"Power seems important."

It's like a big foot crushing a translucent shell, but on she tramples.

"You said something very similar about it in our last session. This idea that if you give yourself to someone, you can't just decide to take yourself back."

I laugh to show her that this shift in gear is all so much blah-blah to me, but she just waits. Reluctantly, I give up and go with it. "Well you can't if you're a woman. Unless you were faking in the first place." I wonder if she has ever given herself to a man. "If you merge with a man completely, you become the incarnation of the passive principle and he the incarnation of the active."

"Temporarily," she says.

I'm surprised that she's taking me seriously, but anyway, she's wrong. "Outside of time, there is no temporary."

Quick as a flash, she adds, "And there's no fixed, either. They both relate to time."

"But outside time, where the soul resides, we abide in eternity."

"So?" she says.

"So... you surrender your will and rely on his instead. And surrender means surrender."

"And what does he surrender?"

She's beginning to understand. I can tell by the way she's nodding. "He surrenders his active, selfish behaviour and puts all that energy into listening and responding to me."

"So you both surrender your selfish will and put it at the service of the other's needs. Is that what you mean?"

Oh, sweet relief at the memory. No more measuring out the housework or resentment at sorting out domestic details that he wouldn't even see. "Yes," I smile.

"What would happen if he let you down?"

I laugh again, but with pleasure at the neatness of my reply. "Well, you'd be stuffed. But if you weren't, the whole thing would be a farce, wouldn't it?"

"You mean, because the man is the incarnation of the active, your trust in him is everything. He can choose to be separate, but you can't?"

I consider her logic. Her conclusions seem obvious, though I hadn't thought of them myself. "Of course." I feel slightly on the back foot, but she's nodding, thinking with her eyes shut.

When she opens them, she says. "I can see why the sex was so good. To feel so safe and secure would really enable you to let go."

I don't have much to add, but to reassure her I say, "I guess that's how it works, and then sex makes complete merging possible."

She taps her teeth with her fingernail. "For you," she says. "But since you recognise that you're approaching this union from opposite directions, isn't it possible that for him, the really great sex came first. He handed over his will and protection afterwards?"

"Well, it's chicken and egg, isn't it?" I say. In eternity, of course it is.

"But he might have felt seduced into it?"

This is so far from the loveliness that I have mistakenly allowed her to smash that I hold up both hands. It hurts but I have to push her back. "What's that got to do with it?" I say vehemently, because she's muddying something very clear and I can't let that happen. "We knew it could *look* like that, but that's what made us so special. Ideas about perception fascinated us."

"But he says in the message, *you have ensnared me.*" She gesticulates over her shoulder, towards the desk.

I try to be a patient patient. "And that led to a discussion about how women and men traditionally see each other. The story we're trapped in. We learnt from each other all the time."

"And do you feel trapped in a story now?"

Frustration rips through me. "Of course I bloody do.

Isn't it obvious? I am trapped in a story. Your story, where either I have seduced him, or he me. One too narrow for... " But she's led me too far from what matters. I find my mouth has closed in despair.

"Where I will somehow reduce your experience by talking about it?"

I retreat from her gaze, nodding. At least she understands that she's smashed the loveliness and she leaves a decent interval while we sit observing the wreckage until she makes an offer.

"Suppose you tell me about what happened after this conversation." She points to the desk. "How that meeting in the Little Chef went? I promise not to say anything."

"Even if you didn't, the story would change," I say. I know that I mustn't share it with her, that somewhere the story is all I have left, but I can't help myself. Already I feel the pull towards that particular Little Chef. I can see it, bright in the afternoon sun. Sweet, sweet place of refuge, white and shiny and trimmed with red.

The Travelodge squats beside it, grinning at every businessmen that drives his secretary to the entrance in a Ford Orion. We grin with it from the front of Tom's Renault 5, separate from them. Different.

Dr. Samuels asks me why I'm smiling, and unable to resist, I invite her in.

*

Precisely what I've just told Dr. Samuels is lost to me. I see the Little Chef and the Travelodge. Then the walls cut away and I see me and Tom in bed, but the rest feels like a big purple gash where I've been surgically opened. Dr. Samuels smiles as if she is not staring at a disembowelled woman at all, and I desperately need to know what's going on in her head. I ask her what she thinks.

"Sex and death. That's what I was struck by. The sex and the deaths." Gently, she adds, "How death complements the sex. Make life, which is sex, more alive."

This has never occurred to me but it's true. "I wouldn't have minded," I say, realising something. She leaves a gap so I go on. "I wouldn't have minded when we were making love, if he'd killed me. That was what was so wonderful. That he could have killed me and I wouldn't have minded. I could have stretched right into death, for him. Could've let him strangle me or break a bone or crush me. That would have been... exquisite." He could have, but he didn't. He might have wanted to but he chose not to. This, I realise as my stomach softens, was completion.

"You said he always gave you control. A word."

I flush with the memory of Tom's thoughtfulness. "That's right. *Tizer.* Shows our age," I grin. "The right word and he would stop, whatever he was doing, wherever he'd got to."

"Absolute trust, then." Dr. Samuels looks me in the eye. "How would it be if I suggested that it was this trust that was really the heart of your relationship?"

I consider this. How intangible the idea is and how it fits with the word 'spiritual'. Slowly, I nod. "That's exactly it."

"And did you use the word much?"

"Never. I never needed to."

She looks surprised. "You never used it?" she pauses. "I wonder if that worried him?"

I've no idea what she means. "How would it worry him?"

"Perhaps he did trust you not to let him kill you, but your willingness to die... "

"Well, obviously he didn't trust me enough, if he was worried I might." A harsh edge has entered my voice.

"But suppose he'd doubted you?" she says.

He'd have said. Surely, he'd have said? He couldn't be expected to know everything. Knowing everything would have made it wrong. A frisson of fear starts in my heart and rockets through me. I drop my head, too late to avoid what I just saw, what I just felt – looming, thuggish against a blur of clouds. Nausea clogs me.

Dr. Samuels gives the mildest of frowns and I push these words against my closing throat. It's imperative that I tell her. "I remember now. I remember the balloon. How I fell out."

"Go on."

"Because of doubt," I say, all doubt stripped away. "In cartoons, Tom and Jerry run off a cliff and keep running in mid-air. It's only when they look down that they fall. Only when they doubt." Of course it is.

"Are you sure?" asks Dr. Samuels. "I'd say they'll fall anyway. It's just that they realise it in the split second before it happens."

But I have an answer for this. "Maybe their lack of believing that they're on solid ground makes them fall?"

"Maybe," says Dr. Samuels, but her face has gone a bit

plastic. I'm not sure she's convinced. "So tell me, how did you fall out of the balloon?"

It comes in a rush. His huge forehead. That one-sided smile. "Doubt. But not his. Mine. I didn't believe that Tom wanted to fly with me forever. I thought, for a moment – just for a moment… " My thoughts go to war. One starts to scream that I'll make things more true if I say this out loud, the other spikes up my spine, grinds into my aching shoulders as if to ask, *is this is not truth enough?*

"You thought he was going to kill you?"

"Not for long. A split second." I'm back-pedalling now. Like Jerry before he falls, but I already know, in all eternity, that it's too late.

We wait, hearing the clatter of cups being wheeled up the corridor outside until the sound fades completely.

"When Jerry fell," Dr. Samuels says, eventually, "I think it was because he ran off a cliff. But how about you? How did you find yourself outside the basket?"

"We slid." Into the blue. Into the ocean. "Tom said we had to." The urgency of his voice merges with his surge. "Not resisting was my gift."

She's quiet for a while before saying, "So this story only makes sense from his point of view then?"

"That was the deal," I say, confused. "What he wanted was what we wanted."

"And he was supposed to protect you?"

"Yes, and I failed to trust him."

"But if you had trusted him, you'd have flown?"

"Yes," I want to shout because I need her to believe it. Because I don't. I don't believe it either, but my withered body and crabbed hand have to. How else will my legs ever support me again? What else will get me out of this chair, or straighten my spine, or pull forward my arms to embrace the world, except Tom?

"I told you," I plead. "I'm nothing. A response. An emptiness. I can't change anything any more. I have to believe him. I have to be forgiven and then... and then... "

I rock in my seat but my joints burst. Shoulders, elbows, wrists. Hips, knees, ankles. This is my punishment. But Tom is a benign God, so this must be the fate of those separated, cast out by their own failing. I feel the bones rubbing against one another until there is only the sparking of nerves and the pain is one great ball of flame.

"Tizer," I shout. I have contracted into my seat until my back is jammed against it.

"Tizer!" I scream.

I feel tears running down my face. I am on the top floor landing of the house I grew up in, and my mother is in the kitchen, a staircase, living room and dining room away. I am pincered into the corner by my brother, who punches me now and then in my stomach or my shoulder. I defend with my arms or pull up my leg, but I am always too late. He laughs. My elbow bends into my chest. I giggle even though it hurts, because he is wrapped almost around me, his narrow eyes searching my body for a gap. But I want it to stop. I struggle to breathe.

"Deadleg," he says, as his fist hits the back of my thigh and my knee buckles.

I plead. I whimper and wail. I am too small to fight back and win. Eventually I have no choice but to open my mouth and scream long and loud until someone hears and stops him. He looks at me with disgust.

I feel my jelly-body back in its wheelchair, but my bones have crumbled. I know that I am dying.

Dr. Samuels seems to think otherwise.

"Mmmm," she soothes. "I have a lot of questions, but the biggest one – the overarching one, which has no straight answer, is how did you get in this mess?"

I'm shocked but it passes. She doesn't think I'm mad, she just thinks I'm in a mess.

As if reading my thoughts she says, "All my questions are an attempt to find out. Would you be willing to try and answer them?"

I nod, because it takes no effort, because I am going to die anyway and because I can hear Tom murmuring: *Nothing is forbidden; everything allowed.* Perhaps there will after all, be forgiveness, through some means I can't imagine.

"One thing," says Dr. Samuels, as she gets up to wheel me out of the door. "Just a question. Until next time."

My eyelids are drooping and I feel flattened but I nod again.

"How much do you know about bondage?"

"Bondage?" I croak.

"Yes. S & M. Sexual domination and submissiveness?"

"You mean people dressing up in leather masks with whips and stuff?"

"Yes, among other things. The submissive person is given

a word to say when the violence gets too much."

"Like Tizer, you mean?"

"Yes, like Tizer."

"Oh," I say. "What a coincidence."

*

I barely notice the ward. Like someone waterlogged, I feel hands heaving me and the slump as I sink into bed.

A shadow pins me down before moving away. Air rushes between us. I open my eyes. A swimming pool echoes, shimmers. I am wearing only blue seersucker trunks, my top bare and mottled with the cold, and there is my darling brother, who I could not be more pleased to see, pulling me to my feet, his face twitching. He is so big, so much bigger than me.

He smiles. "Come on," he says, pulling at my outstretched hands, but I hear no words, just see his lips moving as my ears fill with a rushing sound. I look down. Water is swirling around my knees, rising fast. My brother stands waist deep now, grinning, strong and wide, and the water begins to lift me off my feet, laps at my chin. Up to my neck. My nose fills and I cough as a wave of chlorine smacks against my throat, kick-starting my body into panic.

He lets go and I reach towards him but he steps back even as he shakes his head. "I won't move again, I promise," he says. "Swim to me," and I stare at his mouth as if his words will keep me afloat. Water closes over my head. I stretch my toes but still my foot touches nothing and when I burst through the surface, heaving and wild for breath, he is laughing; laughing and stepping away.

"Don't laugh!" I want to scream but my open mouth sucks in water and I can only blink and choke as my head bobs below, then above and then all of me bobs, buoyant. I paddle with my limbs, my chin stretching higher as every wave slaps me in the face.

I can see my brother's legs waving in the water, his feet rooted in the green-tiled floor. His hands sway like reeds, ready to catch me. I move towards him but every time my fingers brush him, he sidesteps. "Over here," he says, and I puff towards him again, eager now and smiling. But he's stopped looking at me. He scans the empty pool, blank-faced and then turns away, ploughing through the water in big solid strokes until he reaches the edge and climbs out, dripping and shaking his hippy-hair.

Marooned in disappointment, I'm left.

Chapter Seven

Corinne sat cross-legged on the chair in the staffroom and rocked from side to side, focusing her attention on her nostrils. As she breathed in, she imagined the air moving down her throat into her lungs. A wisp of hair brushed her forehead but she let it be, taking her attention back to her breath as she closed her eyes and allowed her body to expand, feeling the weight of her arms, then her stomach, then her legs. If she could only stay in the moment – breathing in, then out, simply that – she wouldn't keep seeing Mr. Slattery looking at her through his one eye.

It's not that big a deal, she thought, trying to shrug away the distraction, but all that happened was that the phrase took over. Patronising: *It's not that* big *a deal*. Impatient: *It's not* that *big a deal*. Even angry: IT'S NOT THAT BIG A DEAL. But when eventually, she heard the words whining at her, she laughed, which helped. "Of course it's a big deal," she muttered out loud. "He's had half his head blown away."

An eye, like an all-seeing camera, in a white hospital room, and a body in what looked like a shroud, with an almost completely bandaged head propped against pillows and held rigid by a metal cage – that was all Corinne really knew of Mr. Slattery. But how did she look to *him*? When her lips went up at the corners? What did he make of it when she popped in and said: *I'm wondering how you're feeling today?* For six weeks now, on a Wednesday at 10am, Corinne had rounded that door with that smile on her face. The first session she had held his hand, but she'd used the six days in between the first and second session to forget she ever did. Where initially she had 'built on his strengths' (I spy curtains, bedpan, bandages), she had returned by the third week unable to see the room as anything but a burial ground for the living. Yet the six hours seemed somehow continuous and her withdrawal of comfort and cheer an admission of the true state of things. And still his eye stared at her. Six whole hours where he hadn't said a word. And today was Wednesday.

For the first time she allowed a tear to fall on behalf of poor Mr. Slattery, and considered that maybe this was an appropriate response. But why hadn't she known before that it was OK to be sad? Dr. Samuels even seemed to think it was required of her.

To herself, Corinne's emotional and educational deficit expanded by the day. Before this job, she'd *known* positive thinking was the sure road toward promotion, but since that time the man with half a skull had stared her into not knowing anything. A morbid fear of offending him had leaked into the silence and now all she wanted to do was play truant. Would anyone notice if she didn't go? Would he? In his stubborn refusal either to start screaming or die, he fair shone with a positive charge, but of what? Anger? Hate? Could those feelings be positive? If they kept him going – if they gave him identity, didn't that blast to dust her 'think nice thoughts' rule? Really, he seemed more solid, saner, actually even more positive than she, simply by staying alive.

Nothing in her training had prepared her for this. Nor was it like her mother's liver grinding to a halt. It wasn't anything like when Mickey Browns had left the group, overdosed and died. That had offered them all something which Corinne now recognised as an ugly thrill of self-righteousness and an opportunity to work-harder-at-thinking-positive-from-now-on-because-relapse-was-the-alternative. So although Corinne had believed that *Suffering begins when you mentally label a situation as bad,* deep down, she no longer knew whether what looked or sounded positive was really positive, whether what looked or sounded negative was really negative, or even whether suffering might not actually have some value after all.

She only knew that spending time with Dr. Samuels was unthinkable. The woman couldn't possibly be willing to support her professionally when she found out what really went on in her head. And now the ballet – a whole evening together – threatened instant annihilation.

Corinne's nervous system was shrieking, flashing in her brain, feeding on itself. What did she know about culture? Paul McCartney was probably about to play *Blackbird* and she'd left for the duf-duf dance tent. She closed her eyes, telling herself to breathe gently, but became aware of her hand crushing her brow as she thought again of her dreadful note taking. One look at Dr. Samuels was enough to see that the woman had learned how to write as naturally as she'd learned how to walk. Dr. Samuels would never have the spellcheck lighting up on her computer. Probably didn't even know there was one, so how the hell could she understand Corinne?

In her trance of self-loathing, Corinne had no idea. She told herself that she knew only about getting *things* and that the people she really admired had never 'got' anything, because the kind of confidence she envied wasn't something you owned or could buy. Those people never spent time worrying about mistakes or getting it right or wrong because they were too busy living. That was what they had – the confidence to fully live, whether that was grieving, facing up to their own weakness or going to the ballet. And what had Corinne done with her own life? What had she done? Spent three years of it sticking a needle in her arm. How the bloody hell could Dr. Samuels understand that?

*   *   *

Rain darkened the carriage as Beatrice travelled into London for the ballet. She tried flipping through *Psychiatry Today*, but put it aside. The journal made her reflection in the window look as if it belonged to someone else.

Instead, she took a notebook from her bag and began to sketch. First, puddles on a station platform. Then, a man in a raincoat. Snatches of remembered dialogue murmured in her ear – *I want you so much, I can't move. We fit* – an urgency lighting up the lover like the neon that shone from the lamp post Beatrice had doodled above his head: outline stark and solid but face and the fedora she'd added blacked out entirely. Realising that she was stroking her cheek with her palm, she put her pencil down and sighed. What usually stood out about her patient's stories was the way they failed to hang together in time and space, but every episode Gina had so far conveyed had been as vivid and coherent as a film. Beatrice had initially thought Tom a charming spiv with skills in stage-management – so one-dimensional that he'd been easy to get hold of, but in yesterday's session, the request for a word to suspend the rough stuff had sounded respectful, and Tom's grief, authentic. Not at all what she would have expected from someone keen to recreate *Last Tango In Paris* before buggering off. She half-closed her eyes, confused by her shifting feelings, before realising that what she wanted most was to know what had happened next. And then, that she wanted to disappear into the story altogether, with Ralph's hand across her waist, holding her stomach so she could push it away before drifting off to sleep.

Picking her pencil back up and pressing hard, Beatrice wrote the word, *countertransference* straight through the picture and thought of her patient. No easy way out of this one for a determined girl who'd committed her heart. For Gina, true love could have only two possible outcomes: reconciliation or death. Beatrice found herself irritated. The woman was over forty. She had a grown-up daughter. But girl she'd seemed, with her Carpenters pop tripe.

The train began to slow, the aisles to fill. King's Cross, six-thirty. She waited until the hordes subsided, and when they didn't, she gritted her teeth and pushed, hoping that Corinne wouldn't be late and that if she was early herself, Corinne wouldn't be. Since the plan had been fixed to take her to the ballet, Beatrice had reflected on her generous offer to mentor and wondered who it had been for and whether she really had time to see it though.

But when she got to The Coliseum, Corinne was at the top of the steps, standing small and out of place in her hippy dress on the red carpet as people queued or strode purposefully around her. Seeing her relieved smile as the bell rang and the call to take seats came over the tannoy, Beatrice softened.

"It's the second time they've said that," said Corinne, pushing her long damp hair behind her ears. "I thought you were going to be late. They don't let you in once it's started."

The foyer smelled of overheated lights and gin and tonic. Ushered by friendly young men wearing red and gold livery, they found their seats at the front of the circle. Corinne leaned her head against the brass bar and gazed through the gap at the orchestra. Beatrice looked at the boxes, their gold drapes like braid on a ball gown, and thought, as she always did, how much better boxes looked from the circle than they actually were when you sat in them. Ralph's voice sounded as clear in her ear as if he was sitting next to her. *Have to screw your head round to see anything.*

"Would you like a mint?" Corinne whispered.

Beatrice shook her head. "Is your phone switched off?" she asked, pointing at the notice projected onto the fire curtain.

As Corinne delved into her bag, the lights dimmed, voices hushed, the conductor took to his platform and the overture began. Beatrice thought of Ralph squeezing her hand and felt loved. She smiled as if he could see her. *Happy Anniversary,* she thought.

The opening scene of velvet-clad, dancing courtiers always made her grin. But by the time the curtain fell on Prince Siegfried leaving his twenty-first birthday party with his crossbow primed for action, Beatrice had warmed to the atmosphere and was ready to be drawn into the fairytale.

She held her breath. The sound of a single horn announced a harp that billowed out in a great cloud before plucking precisely at her throat and picking down to her solar plexus until she was empty of everything but the last fading vibration.

Now, onto the blue-lit lake of the empty stage, flanked by cygnets, unaware of Siegfried watching from the shore (he is searching, though he doesn't know it, for his soul), Odette appears, as lithe and graceful as a swan, to stretch her limbs in ways that men can only dream of. It's natural for her to sweep across the water, her arms stroking the air as if it were the softest thistledown. Her legs are as long and elegant as a swan's neck as she twirls en pointe, slowing onto the surface, stretching up and out and down, before making a nest of her tutu, settling her wing-arms over her head and reaching to cover her outstretched foot.

Odette does not know that Siegfried is watching.

As Beatrice listened, she realised that the shudder of a violin, deep and solid against the fluttering harp, arrives just at the point where Odette becomes aware of Siegfried's presence. It embodies *his* wanting, *his* need. Odette has no agenda, but only wakes, responding, as he bends down and strokes her finger as if he too has wings to fold over her. He does so little. Helps her to rise. Holds her waist so gently she can pirouette, his outstretched hand available for the very lightest of her touches as she extends into the arabesque that expresses his yearning.

Perfection ached for expression in Beatrice's joints as the music became movement, story, feeling. On Odette dances, a spirit caught somewhere between wake and sleep, accepting without question this lover drawing her toward the inevitable fulfilment of what she has not realised is missing. Odette leans so far back she touches the ground. But just when Siegfried's arm should break, in chops the wind section, staccato, anticipating her fully alert presence as she prepares to dance *for* him. The cygnets hop towards the couple, then stand, one leg raised to draw out their long white tutus like so many curtains in a staggered frame.

Now Odette really performs. She leaps, she twirls, she steps away, she steps back. Beatrice stubbed her pointed toe on the front of the circle. As the staccato repeated, she whistled silently along with it, but it was the vibration of the first violin that undid her, dredging up the loss in her soul.

By the interval, Corinne was smiling the wide-open smile of a child. "I'll order you a brandy," she said, leaving Beatrice to gather herself while she battled her way to the bar.

Beatrice took out her powder compact and dabbed at her cheeks. She peered at her own right eye in the mirror and saw what was true. Ralph was not coming back. Not coming to wake her with a kiss or lull her to sleep. Without him she felt as helpless as Odette.

She saw now that she'd been skating on the surface of her frozen grief for months, hardening herself by rejecting anything and everything. She clung to the velour arms of her seat, winded by the full force of her predicament – a loss too painful to look at.

She pushed herself up from the chair and climbed the stairs, consciously pressing her feet into the floor. Didn't everyone get these glimpses? Bare snatches of understanding? And wasn't it best to hold one's ground against them lest you were swept into wilderness?

As she entered the bar, Corinne caught her attention, waving from a low square armchair and gesturing for her to sit in front of the brandy she'd placed on the square table. A double, by the size of it.

"You look like you've seen a ghost?"

"I have," said Beatrice, glad of the opening. "The ghost of Christmas past." She heard her flippancy, felt herself stiffen against Corinne's warmth.

"Go on," said Corinne, nodding.

Beatrice tried to explain before she iced herself over again. "Because it's a past that seems more alive than this grey present," she managed, aware of her tongue thickening in her mouth and her own impatient behaviour. It was herself she'd been trying to save. She could see that now.

"It's the music," said Corinne. "Like the dancing. It says everything all at once. It just is, and then it isn't. Gone again."

And Beatrice found herself reaching for Corinne's hand, grateful for her common-sense. She breathed in the brandy fumes. "Yes. Odette seemed for a moment to be – like you said – sort of all and everywoman." She laughed at herself. "Well, I suppose it would feel timeless, wouldn't it?"

"Thank God for theatres," said Corinne. She winked. "Doing it for us so we don't have to."

"Don't you find... that we *do* have to do it in the end?"

"In the end. And the beginning. And the middle, too. But not all the time. Beatrice... " said Corinne, squeezing the hand in her own as she downed the last of her bitter lemon, "...I kind of get that you don't like the word 'spiritual', but it's just another word for... well... drama, I suppose. But the stuff you can't... get round. Life, birth. Death. All the big stuff." She blew out a breath strong enough to ruffle Beatrice's hair.

Beatrice grinned."I think what you mean is *myth*," she said, warmed by the brandy. Myth! Of course. Was *that* what these young people were talking about when they went on and on about the spiritual? The generation obsessed with lack of meaning had discovered that life was both finite and predictable after all. She laughed and clasped Corinne's hands between her own, rubbing them and nodding, and the longer her sense of this unexpected connection went on, the more difficult speech became.

Up until that point, she realised, she'd been leaning on Ralph. Dead as he'd been for almost four months, she'd still felt him holding her up. Holding the part of her that only he could really see. Even she hadn't noticed it – this part that needed a place to rest, free of struggle. But now Ralph was gone and that part was still there. Beatrice could sense it, out and on the loose, searching.

Hearing the bell for the second half ringing in her ear, she asked, slightly drunk, "What's all that stuff with the lapis lazuli about then?"

"Oh, that. That reminds me that there's more to life than fast food. That and the magic vibrations." Corinne giggled, and Beatrice wished they had time for another drink.

*

Not until she was on the train home did the drama of the second half ebb away enough for Beatrice to contemplate how lucky she'd been in her marriage and how anxious she was now. Only in this state of total exposure did she see that Ralph's true gift had been keeping her secure without ever making her feel dependent. That was something he had protected her from completely. She smiled away the tears and gazed at the window, but saw only the reflection of a lone passenger drooping in his seat across the aisle. Gina's loss had been inevitable. It wasn't rocket science to predict the outcome of an affair. Beatrice's nose started twitching with the disdain, she recognised, of a whole culture. The sniffy insistence that the girl-who-wasn't-a-girl 'should have known better.' As if that cancelled the suffering.

Her ears thrummed to the train wheels as she glimpsed the fate of Odette, rising into the heavens. The girls of her own generation had that glimpse and saw a cautionary tale that sent them running into the arms of the boy next door. A tale that put them off messing with The Fates for life. 'Don't stray from the path,' said Red Riding Hood's mum. 'Avoid all needles', said Aurora's dad, and what the modern reader heard was that if only they behaved, took care, didn't get too close, the outcome was in their hands.

All except Gina. Gina had leapt right into the crucible, certain that her Prince had come, and been burned to a crisp. *Fate is myth. Fate is myth,* said the train wheels, but as they slowed, Beatrice heard them shift. *But myth is fantasy, myth is fantasy.* Through the window, she saw the approaching lights; the dirty platform, puddled with black; the billboard advertising help for chlamydia.

With a screech of metal, the train jolted and stopped. Close-up, the billboard proclaimed obscenities in black marker pen. Beatrice climbed down. What did anything matter?

It didn't. Everything would disintegrate, everything be lost, she knew. However good you were. However well you behaved, the idea that you could take control – that fantasy – was the worst betrayal of all.

Chapter Eight

Under a sky as grey as the staff car park, Beatrice picked her way past the puddles and up the shallow slope to the side entrance for day surgery. Beneath the porch a group of patients in a clutch of wheelchairs sheltered from the rain. As the glass doors swished open, a blast of warm air mingled with the smell of nicotine and disinfectant.

"Aarp."

But Beatrice didn't need the prompt. Her hand slipped into her bag already and now she held out her lighter, kept for this purpose, to the tip of a shaking cigarette. The man nodded, sucking loudly until a cloud of smoke almost choked him. When he bent one arm in, Beatrice expected him to take the fag from his mouth, but instead he pointed to a fellow wheelchair user, whose packet of Benson & Hedges nestled in the bend of her paralysed body.

"Let me get that for you." She took one from the pack and lit it from her own lips, exhaling the smoke almost before she'd breathed the stuff in. "Here you go," she said, placing it in the woman's mouth. The woman blinked, rapidly.

"Welcome," said Beatrice. "Do you need me to wait?"

"Y're alreet." A much younger woman, bleach-blonde, tottered over on a zimmer frame, plonked it four-square on the paving stone and leaning on it with her elbow, fished in her dressing-gown pocket. "Burr if you'll gis a leet?"

"Says *'No Smoking'* here," said Beatrice, with an exaggerated raising of her eyebrows.

"Yeah, and over thur it used to say *Jimmy Savile*

Welcomes You To Stoke Mandeville Hospital, bur I never seen no one tekkin' 'is cigar off 'im. Thur 'e was, wearin' that bloody greet dick on 'is face and none o' you lot seen it."

Cheered by the woman's clarity, Beatrice smiled. "Well, let's hope they cut it off in hell," she said, and meant it. She bent to light the cigarette. "You from Stoke-on-Trent?" She had recognised the accent.

"Aye. A very different Stoke. And don't get me wrong. I'm greetful to be 'ere, but 'ow you expect the likes of us to get to the other side o' carpark wi' now legs?"

Beatrice found herself agreeing. She nodded and headed inside and up the stairs, heavy with regret. She knew it was pure luck that she'd never met and been taken in by Savile. All her colleagues at Broadmoor as well as here had been completely fooled, and being glad he'd never made it to Rampton gave her no relief. The experts had let a psychopath operate freely in the midst of the place where the experts locked the psychos up to observe them. And then they'd given him free rein in one of the most prestigious surgical, medical and spine injury rehabilitation complexes in the country. As ever, the thought fused her brain and made her heart thump sick against her ribs. In her office, she dumped her coat and bag in the corner and reached for her in-tray, glad of the distraction.

Dear Dr. Samuels,
RE: Dissertation/D.Phil.forensic.psych:
Bunty(DCThompson): A pre-pubescent training in
sado-masochism as a defence in girls reaching
the age of consent in 1980?

```
I hope you don't mind me writing again, but it
is now five months since you so kindly agreed to
mentor me. As my dissertation proposal has been
accepted on this basis and I have not heard from
you, I am writing to confirm that this is still
the case,
Yours sincerely,
Harriet Worsley (Dr.)
```

Beatrice placed the letter on her desk and stared at the thick cream writing paper. Like so many of the projects she'd been involved with before Ralph's death, this was one she had entirely forgotten. She looked at the address. Postgrad. at Gonville & Caius – thick blonde hair, massively over-anxious Harriet doing forensics, placement at Rampton, making Beatrice the obvious choice. That unopened letter at home from the University Library must be giving her notice that they were holding the comics she'd ordered in that other lifetime. Beatrice imagined them, mouldering in a huge pile as the Cam dripped through the nearest wall.

A brief knock on the door and a man in a peaked cap peered round. "Boxes for Dr. Felicity Preston. Room's locked."

Beatrice nodded, "I'll hang onto them for her."

"She leaving us?" he asked.

"I guess we're all leaving, sometime," she answered, regretting the words as soon as they came out of her mouth.

He stacked them next to her desk.

She looked again at the letter. She'd go, as soon as she could, to the library. The thought soothed her. She'd spend a few hours in the reading room where silence was the norm and even walking too loudly was frowned upon. Quickly, she scribbled a note of apology to Harriet reassuring her she was on the case, and dropped it in the out tray.

*   *   *

When I arrive in Dr. Samuels' room I spot a load of cardboard boxes stacked against the back wall. I'm sure they weren't there before. "You thinking of bailing out?" I ask.

"What makes you say that?" she responds. A sense of her backing away brings the dream about my brother to mind and I tell her about it but she doesn't say anything and the longer I wait, the more the pain in my chest feels like hot coal. I curl around it.

"It looks as if you want to get away from me," she says, which is confusing.

"It's you that are leaving," I blurt.

"What makes you think I'm leaving?" she asks.

I point a bent finger at her stack of boxes, keeping my elbow tucked well into my side. Unable to stand the tension any longer I say, "I'm too much work, aren't I? I'm not trying hard enough."

"Tell me more."

I'd like to uncurl but am sure that she'll veer away. I can't move. The best I can do is tell her what I know and she's lucky I can manage that.

"And why would I step away?" she asks, gently. "Why did your brother step away?"

"Oh, loads of reasons," I say, released suddenly by the

chance to talk about someone else. "He probably thought it was the right way to teach me to swim. I wasn't fast enough. Little sisters are a drag."

Dr. Samuels pauses. "Did he say that?"

I nod. "Well, you can see why, can't you? You have to look after them and they can't keep up. They go wailing to mum whenever you don't do what they want. Little sisters get everything you never got at their age and they're always hanging around."

"You've perked up," she says cheerfully. "And you have a particular expression on your face." She waits and I wait, too. I can out-wait her, easily. Eventually she says, "I'm wondering if it's your brother's?"

Both my sneer and the half-laugh that follow are accompanied by a feeling of deep satisfaction. "Yes," I say, noticing. "The one he had when he was whipping a tea-towel at me. Man, he could make it crack."

"When did he do that?"

"When he'd been told to dry the crockery and I was putting away the knives and forks."

"And I'm wondering if it's not just his expression you've got, but his words as well? *Man*, for instance. I haven't heard you say that before."

I laugh. "I wish I could crack tea-towels like he could."

"You can really step into that feeling, can't you?"

"Yes. I can."

"And how he thinks. It's almost as if that has become how you think?"

"Why not? I adored him, didn't I? He could do everything. I couldn't do anything."

"And your father? Did you adore him?"

"Yes." I discover that I am staring at her, defiantly. "I loved him and I hated him," I say, eventually. There's no point being here if I don't tell the truth.

"What did he think of you?"

My mouth sets itself in a thin, impatient line. His line. "I can do him, as well." I cross my arms. "This is how he looked at me. He hated me. I wasn't fast enough. Mostly, I was irrelevant. Stupid. He had far more important things to do than waste his time on me."

"So he was quick, busy?"

"Brilliant," I say. "Absorbed, usually, in his study. I made too much noise, of course. Disturbed his concentration."

"So did he get angry?"

"Furious." I struggle with this understatement but manage to control my response. "But usually because people were so stupid," I huff.

"I can hear it in you. As if you are looking at the world from his point of view now."

"Well, people are stupid." But I know, somewhere, that this is not a licence to attack them. "Life can be very difficult when people hold you up."

Dr. Samuels looks very sympathetic. "So you understood him in the same way you understood your brother. You could feel their frustration and their need?"

"Completely," I say, airily. "I feel like that myself half the time."

She raises her eyebrows. "I'm not surprised. You seem to have had your fair share of it crammed down your throat. Yet you still loved them."

My smile is secret. It's not my problem if she doesn't get it. No one can share my love because no one else knows these people like I do. No one else is inside them. "Yes. I understand them," I say.

"And me? With my cardboard boxes? What was it you thought? That you're too much work, so I was leaving?"

It's a sneaky sidestep that opens a trap. If I agree, there will be no fallback position, no cover. I stare up into her face but see only interest there.

"Well," she says, quite casually. "It's just that I notice you had a whole story made up about *me*, and my guess is that you really believe it."

"I don't really know," I say, calmer now, though I'm certain it's true.

She points at the wall. "If I told you that these boxes are waiting for my colleague to pick them up, then what?" She smiles, and I know I've been a fool. "Can you see?" she says, so very quietly that I give the briefest of nods. "All you really have to go on is the boxes. You're sort of predisposed to be seen as someone not worth bothering with, so they become evidence and trigger your story that you are too slow and worthless. But this story isn't even yours. It's the one you believed your father and brother had." She waits, but her words make sense. I nod again but I feel like I'm sinking, down, down. She pauses again before saying, in the nicest possible way, "It sounds like you've believed this for a long time. I daresay it's a story you believe so deeply that you even feel annoyed with yourself about the time you're taking to get over it."

"OK." I squirm as I realise that I have failed to step

outside my own expectations, failed to spot the psychological conditioning that Tom and I so prided ourselves on transcending. My helpless 'OK' is a pathetic bleat. I am failing, even now, to do anything but loathe my own shortcomings, even though that too is a habit I have learned.

Dr. Samuels looks really sad. "Getting out of a downward spiral is as hard as leaving a helter-skelter when you're already sliding. When the only tool you have is a mat and all that does is speed you up," she says, "escape is impossible."

And it's true. I've fallen to the bottom, my strategies exposed and useless. I smile my death-is-coming smile at her.

"Yet you seem to have found a way," says Dr. Samuels, smiling back as if I've just won a race.

I shrug. Might as well. I've got no idea what she's on about.

She waits. I can feel her leaving a space for my hope to expand into. She'll be waiting a long time.

Bending towards me until she catches my eye, she says, "It's highly creative. You *imagine* your way out. You *become* the parent or the brother or the person you are close to. You try to inhabit them, take on their whole point of view. Then you don't have to be you, where there is nothing but… "

The gap she leaves is black.

"…Darkness," I say, because I know what she means now.

"Well met," she says. "Considering how unbearable I guess the darkness can seem… " She is very gentle. "…I'm not surprised that you stretch into the clues that people seem to drop – like my cardboard boxes. You find meaning in them; a way to be that makes sense and avoids that darkness."

I feel my father's irritation in the set of my teeth, my brother's scorn in my own nostrils. As I exhale, I feel the relief I believe Dr. Samuels felt at the decision to leave. But most of all, to my surprise, I feel that if I stop loving Tom, love will abandon me utterly. If I see a Tom who is not shining with beauty and intelligence, I will have lost beauty and intelligence forever. I dare not not-want Tom. It is all Tom inside me, animating me. His gratification is my completion.

"These men – your father, your brother. I suspect there was nothing they could say or do that didn't affect you tremendously. I think you were too small to stand your ground so, instead, you swallowed their attitudes – their scorn, their anger, and found a way to stand up for yourself that way. You found it!"

So I am a parasite, feeding off the feelings of everyone I meet.

Dr. Samuels smiles, a huge wide smile entirely at odds with the horror I feel. "I know this is hard," she says. "But you are following all this with such strength, such intelligence. How are you feeling?"

"Drained." I feel sick. "I'm so ugly." I gather my strength. "Why don't you just finish me off?"

She shakes her head, sadly. "Well, isn't that just what your story would say?"

She has taken even that from me. I cast around and find nothing inside me and nothing but a sharp-angled room outside.

"Do you feel attacked now? It would fit with your expectations."

Her words peck at me. Helpless in this chair, I can't even get up and walk out. I stretch my arms until my hands grasp the wheels, but the brake is on and no matter how hard I push, rubber blocks hold them fast. Jutting out my chin, I face her, my heart thudding. "Well yes actually, I do feel attacked. But you can prod me and strip me bare. You won't break me."

"So you think I'm trying to break you?" She sounds concerned. "You imagine I am violent. Determined? And yet you manage to take that determination to use for yourself, stretching so far that you can accommodate even my imagined violence." She throws her hands in the air and smiles. "That's brilliant. You win."

And it's as if something has broken. Some cord that bound me to her. I really have no idea what she's talking about but I loosen, sensing the determination she speaks of, remove my hands from the wheels and place them in my lap.

After a while – I don't know how long, only that the sun is casting a low, ochre light strong enough to warm the room – she asks if it's OK to go on for a while longer. When I say that it is because I feel so much better, she asks me to tell her more about my father.

"You said you hated him."

It's true. I really did hate him. I can sense the rage. "So much, I sometimes wanted to kill him."

"So did you defy him?"

Sort of. "I ignored him. He could say what he liked and the more he pushed me around, the less I did what he wanted."

"So you put up with a lot and he couldn't change you? Would you say that your relationship was about outdoing each other?"

I think, instead, of Peter. "Yes, with my dad, but with my brother it was about catching up. Being as good as him."

"No matter how much he tormented you?" She seems happy to change tack. "He could pull your arm up your back? Demand that you go out of your depth when you couldn't swim?"

"I got to be with him," I realise only as I speak.

"But not much. It sounds like you tried so hard. Stretched further. Like he could push you and you'd never give in?"

But her words are wrong. Silly even, because I know she's really trying to make a point about Tom and this idea of 'trying', of struggle, has nothing to do with him.

I see myself creeping across the bed – another bed, a different Travelodge – and teasing him with tiny licks before pulling my head away.

Then he's on me, pinning my thigh flat with a shin, pressing his thumbs into my windpipe as he leans into my face. "I could kill you."

"I dare you." And we stay, rapture squeezing us into one.

"Now I know you're mine I can wait forever," he murmurs.

"Nothing else will do," I say, because I know every glance, every secret pleasure. Because I see into every line of his being.

"Trust," he says. "Nothing matters more. I promise there will only ever be you. I have to tell you this, because I have to match you. It's the only way I can give as much as you do. I swear to you, whatever happens, you can rely on me."

"No," I say, to Dr. Samuels. "It's not about defiance. Really it isn't. It's about being able to give as much as I got – and then giving more." And what I sense in that moment is Tom's softness, his opening, his receiving of me until I no longer feel either of us.

"Being able not to give then, but to give way?" she says, quietly.

"It's the same," I say. Something has been completed. The thing I have been trying to tell Dr. Samuels about since I first came into this room. And she seems to concur.

We sit, like two people who have reached the end of a book together. A door slams outside and a couple of women walk by, their laughter fading as they pass on down the corridor.

"What do you think?" I ask, at last. "Do you have a diagnosis for me? It all seems very... run of the mill to you."

"Yes, dear," she says, in a way that I find comforting. "There is a word that describes your behaviour. It's a way of anticipating and avoiding persecution."

"Go on," I say, "Tell me the worst."

"It's masochism." But Dr. Samuels doesn't have a mean tone. She looks concerned. "As I said, bearing in mind how critical you are of yourself, your way out was highly creative."

"Masochism?" I laugh. Hardly. Surely masochism is about enjoying pain. Is that what I want from Tom? Pain? Ridiculous. "Pain was the last thing I wanted." From where I sit, trapped in this chair, hostage to morphine, bedpans, bleeding bowels and splintered bones, the idea feels just plain silly.

"But you may have put up with it to get what you needed – like you did with your father and brother, because you felt you had no choice? Like I said, you learned a way to make things work, but now that your father and brother are dead, that chapter is closed. You'll never get what you wanted from them. Never hear from them that you were more than just something in the way. But with Tom, perhaps there was a chance – if you let him hurt you enough?" She is so sincere, trying so hard to help me.

"Yes – yes," I try to stifle my brother's laugh. The one I egged Tom on with. "But you've got it all wrong. Me and Tom were about being quits. Equals. Completing the circle."

"For you." The words hang in the air, inviting me to consider them, but I retreat.

"For us both, and he knew it." I feel him now, with his hands around my neck, the moment stretching forever even as it tightens around us.

She shifts in her seat. "Well," she pauses. "That must have been ecstasy, finally making him see things the way you did?"

"Trust, yes." Struggle over. No winners. No losers. "That's what he said. *Trust – nothing matters more.*" I gaze up at Dr. Samuels and smile, and she closes her eyes, trying to reach into the moment with me, but I know it's demanding too much because when she opens them again, she says:

"He said a lot of things."

* * *

They want me to stand. Apparently the discs in my spine will fuse together unless I stretch, and now that I'm out of traction, the physiotherapist wants me to start by leaning forward in the chair and pressing my feet down as if to get up.

The exercise sends a red hot poker through my central nervous system. Slowly. Still, I suppose I'm lucky, since my legs are all mended. It's fear that's the problem. Fear that these wasted limbs will snap down the fault line of the breaks. I know the fear is absurd, because the flesh around them would hold things together, but every time I get up enough pressure to lift my bottom, it feels as though my pelvis might crash to the floor.

Ironically, it's when the pelvis is safe on the black vinyl seat and she asks me to push out my arms and legs that the pain is at its worst. It shoots along my limbs until they crackle. I can actually feel ropes pulling them, hear them creaking as if they're attached to a winch.

When I opened my eyes to see the physio smiling with that 'doing really well' look, I was reassured, but back on the ward it seems a matter of time before everything snaps. My hands and feet go on extending, my elbows and knees pulled so taut that the balls in my shoulder and hip joints will be yanked from their sockets. No amount of stroking helps. Every junction of my body is weakened, and as soon as I stop rubbing, the stretching starts again, as if some soul-body is telling me that there is nowhere to hide.

Perhaps it is Tom.

I wake in the night, arguing that giving and giving way are the same, but Dr. Samuels' words echo. "For you." They burrow deep into my head, generating more words. *You have misunderstood, you fool. It's sadists who enjoy pain. Other people's pain. Making other people hurt.* I can hear Tom's breathing, laboured and heavy as he turns the handle of the winch whispering, *I can't stand hurting women.* But where is he, really? Why hasn't he come? A voice shouts, *If you play with the big boys, you'll get hurt.*

Do I prefer the rack, the noose, the knife?

Whatever I wanted from him, it wasn't this burning. If I'm a masochist my suffering would be desired, but who could possibly desire this? The voice is rational now. Disinterested. *If Tom was a sadist, your giving way would be the last thing he needed. Sadists need screams, not someone who says 'yes'. They take no prisoners, unless to keep them alive and hurting.*

I lie in agony, longing for the joke to be done with, the 'fooled ya' which should put a full stop to this game, but all I can see is my brother's last grin of amusement, his promise of a big wide smile that didn't come. His eyes never did peep out. He never winked, though I waited in that tiny white hospital room until daylight lit his body with as much life as would ever warm his skin again.

The howl that wakes me is the sound of air being sucked

so hard into empty lungs it grates, yet all the air in the world is not enough to bring my brother – my *brother* back. When the nurses come they hold my thrashing body steady and croon that I am dreaming, but their faint tinklings are the dream. "Tizer?" they say, wiping my tears away. "There's no Tizer here, but we can get some in the morning." I see the bottles, red and gold on the shelf above the batter bits in the chip shop and I sob into my pillow because I know it is not allowed. Cheap. Common. A sweet fizzy poison full of nothing.

Chapter Nine

The answerphone on her hall stand blinked red. Beatrice rushed past it, guilty that people cared about her when she couldn't bring herself to respond. But real friends would understand. She herself understood that when she really needed them she'd phone, but that for as long as she could hold back the grief with hard work, she was unlikely to throw herself voluntarily into that bottomless pit. She dumped her briefcase, grabbed the letter marked University of Cambridge and marched off down the leaf-strewn pavement toward the library.

Oppressive to visitors, the nineteen-thirties block of bricks greeted her like an undemanding friend. She glanced at the long windows. Seven floors high, they had the impregnable quality of slits in a castle wall. Above, a tall square tower containing everything in copyright rose from the roof, its lightning rod pointing at the heavens.

Beatrice climbed the steps that swept up the front of the building, passed beneath an enormous wrought iron arch and pushed through the wood and glass roundabout. Dust and draught. She relaxed into the smell of books and civic anonymity and climbed the curved stone staircase to the enclosed corridor and on to the reading room.

The brass-fretted double doors stood twenty feet high. Heavy against her arm, they closed silently behind her, quelling all social contact. She would be able to breathe in the concentrated air and sit unobserved.

She approached the huge mahogany horseshoe of the

reception desk. The librarian glanced up and smiled a wide, ambitionless smile. Beatrice raised her finger towards the stand on the far side. The librarian gave an encouraging nod.

Through a further set of double doors was an annexe where items waiting to be borrowed were stacked on shelves. The man behind the desk took her letter of reservation, returning a few minutes later with a book, *Stuff The Turkey*. She looked blankly at the cover before remembering her order and putting it in her bag. The man then filled both arms with a pile of Bunty comics, each in a plastic folder. Even though the cover of the top comic showed a colour drawing of a prepubescent girl sporting yellow plaits, ribbons, blue ankle socks and a pinny, the librarian nodded respectfully. A huge grin was spread disproportionately across Bunty's face as she bore a steaming pie to a table.

So this was Bunty in the 1970s, fifteen years later than the ones she remembered from her own girlhood. Beatrice carried the heavy pile back into the reading room where she dumped them on a service table. Bunty's red skirt swirled around the middle of her chubby thighs, revealing the provocative frill of a white petticoat. Like Peter Pan, Bunty never aged. Big white pants and a flat chest beneath, surmised Beatrice, remembering the cut-out wardrobe from her sister's days – paper paste on the sofa and slivers of old cereal boxes on the carpet that Beatrice was always blamed for. She flipped over the top comic, but in place of the imagined vest, Bunty stood hand on hip, the other hand behind her head, wearing a floral starter bra with matching pants and heeled sling-back shoes. Around her, five groovy outfits floated free on the page: loons, midi-skirt, tank-top, sheepskin waistcoat and platform shoes. Bunty somehow come of age, ready to be stuck onto cardboard in her lingerie prior to being dressed.

Beatrice let out a strangled cough which echoed the length of the long tables to both ends of the room. People lifted, wave-like, before settling back to their books. She picked up half the heavy pile and made her way along several desks, searching for the best place to immerse herself in the thoughts already filling the gap between Bunty the Home Pie Queen and Bunty the whore. Slag. Slapper. Tart versus homemaker. Homemaker makes tart. Tart makes tart? What did a thirteen year old make of that? Returning to pick up the rest she found, at the top, a haunted Bunty fleeing across the front cover pursued by a flock of birds. On her hat stood a huge falcon, picking at the bunch of grapes with which it was decorated. Beatrice skimmed the storyline. Bunty had seen a gloved and sophisticated older woman wearing a fashionable hat and had raided the fruit bowl in order to mimic it. Punishment for puberty? Better to stay a child. Innocent. And she knew where that might lead. Heavy with regret, Corinne's pale face gazing up through her mind's eye, she carried the rest gently to her desk.

Even the sound of her bottom hitting the chair was lost in padded PVC. Soon Beatrice was skimming through a world familiar from what seemed like every Tuesday morning of her childhood. A world of Bunty Club Corner and letters from polite children who sent pictures of their ponies or rabbits. Reading, she noticed how she dismissed the lightweight stories – a girl pushing a four-poster to Land's End or Toots the Terrible Toddler – as boring. And how she was drawn to the crisis-led dramas where an endless procession of pre-teenage girls were pitted against malevolent oppressors. Stories that seemed clandestine. Contraband disguised as sweets offered by a stranger in a car.

A younger sister was dragged beneath the sea by a sinister rubber ring. An upper-class bitch dirtied floors on purpose which were then scrubbed by a bullied charwoman. Lorna Drake, a would-be-ballerina, danced through *The Nutcracker* on a broken ankle. The excitement was familiar. And transgressive, Beatrice realised. Over and over, she saw the same message. The path to womanhood was fraught with pain. A pain you had to put up with until nullified by the prize. Beneath the desk, she pointed her foot until it hurt and read: *Dance 'til you Die: Emma Blake was badly injured because she'd pushed a girl from the path of a lorry and as a result, fallen beneath it herself.*

"Can't I have special exercises to strengthen my leg? I'll work hard, I promise. I'm going to show my father I'm as good as any boy – somehow I've got to get fit in time for the audition to dance Giselle."

Dance 'til you die? Ballet as the path to the perfect orgasm? Did Emma Blake know that the character of Giselle was a ghost who haunted a graveyard? So many ballet stories, where women battered their own bodies into submission. Corinne's suffering at 15 was never queried. Already prepared, she'd put up with it for the attention. A neglected kid, trussed like a turkey by her own need and ready for the furnace of Crowley's particular taste in hell. Beatrice's foot started to cramp. She pressed it into the floor, trying to increase the weight. Pins and needles flooded her leg and she stood, bouncing, making ready for her escape.

This is what Corinne didn't do, at any point, she thought, silently hobbling up and down. Corinne had embraced the pain, tried to let herself stretch right into it. *A pre-pubescent training in sado-masochism as a defence in girls?* Sado-masochism? Did people think that if the sadists weren't there, the masochists would seek them out? Masochism was a learned response to having no choice, that filled you with a feeling of strength instead of weakness, and who wouldn't choose that? Aleister Crowley had cashed in on a whole ideology. Harriet should look into him. In fact, thought Beatrice, as her leg began to ease, since she was here, she'd have a look herself, but first, closing the fragile comic and craving for what she realised was a cigarette, she'd go for a cup of coffee.

She found herself halfway through the catalogue hall before remembering that the tea room had been moved to the Rotherham building a good ten years ago. She clicked her fingers against the memory in her body that had taken charge so quickly.

The easiest route was back down the reading room corridor and on through the ground floor of the north wing. She reversed direction, turning right and right again, propelled by a lightness she had known before Ralph's death but forgotten. A lightness, she realised, that came with being absorbed by and in a single task. Of grappling with a particular problem. If Bunty prepared girls for a life of overcoming abuse by reaching further, higher and deeper, what exactly was the story that convinced them that this was a good idea? Discuss.

So rather than coffee, Beatrice realised it was meaning that she was in pursuit of. That and its companion calm of concentration. Bypassing a narrow staircase, she turned impulsively towards a double-panelled grey fire-door with a vertical hinge running down its centre, folded the panel back on itself and stepped into the small metal box of the library lift as if into a time-machine. Crowley would be up with Psychology – a travesty, but there it was. She pressed one of the seven ancient bakelite buttons and up she shuddered. When the lift stopped, she pushed aside the fire door of the seventh floor, alighting in a corridor just wide enough to permit access to rows and rows of books off to her left and lit on the right only by a section of those ground-to-roof windows that had reminded her so much of slits in a castle wall. Except now she was on the inside. One big bow and arrow and she'd be able to see off anyone within a hundred and fifty yards. She put her left arm out straight, pulled back her imaginary string with equally imagined effort and stuck her elbow into a passer-by. Frowning, he shuffled on.

She turned her attention to the stacks, searching along the ends of the rows, but the cataloguing had changed. Where the psychology books had once occupied a few shelves on a floor almost entirely given over to medicine, *Social Anthropology* gave away almost immediately to *Esoteric Studies*. Then, below the sign she saw something so familiar that her breath caught in her throat. It was a light-switch – a bakelite clockwork dial. Turning it took her right back to her student days. *Your fifteen minutes of light starts now.* Determined to keep going, she set off along the row, running her fingers along the spines of the books, but Ralph seemed to lurk at her shoulder. *Yes, Ralph,* she admonished him, as if he was purposely obstructing her. *Study. Concentration. This is the other thing I have loved*, but she could feel the lack of him now. Trying to distract herself she read through the titles until, just above her head she saw:

Aleister Crowley: The Book of the Law. The law?

She pulled out the book and for two turns of the dial read page after page telling the reader exactly what was what and what to do about it:

Tear down that lying spectre of the centuries: veil not your vices in virtuous words: these vices are my service; ye do well, & I will reward you here and hereafter. I give unimaginable joys on earth: certainty, not faith... Faith must be slain by certainty, and chastity by ecstasy.

So Crowley really thought he was the man to lay down the law? The violence of the prose shocked her. Heavy laden with secret globes, wingéd beasts and dimméd gems, the writing was wreathed all about with a superstition as dead as a Victorian drawing room, but to a naive girl it would surge with power. To a lost girl, it would seduce.

She scanned the page:

If Power asks why, then is Power weakness.
Also reason is a lie; Pity not the fallen! I never knew them. I am not for them. I console not: I hate the consoled and the consoler.

Surprised by the emotion and the visceral loathing the man had inspired already, she flipped to the end.

Do what thou wilt shall be the whole of the law. Love is the law, love under will. Every form of energy must be directed, must be applied with integrity, to the full satisfaction of its destiny.

It must! It will! It is! The thought of ploughing on through this stuff made her feel nauseous but with the typical perversity that had enabled Beatrice to drill her way through several not altogether interesting degrees, she pulled out a thin volume hoping it might be a crib, but it turned out to be *De Arte Magica:* a pamphlet of more directives.

...voluntary sterile acts create demons, and (if done with concentration and magical intention) such demons as may subserve that intention. Thus, as Levi testifieth, to graft a tree successfully, the graft is fixed by a woman while the man copulateth with her per vas nefandum.

Per vas nefandum? Frowning, Beatrice dug into the decaying store of Latin at the back of her brain. Sounds like nefarious – criminal, wicked. The wicked vase – vessel. By the wicked vessel. But this was common sexual activity these days, wasn't it? This was what Gina Fulbright's Tom had wanted, even if Gina had been more interested in discussing it than obliging. Not as submissive as expected? The object failing to do as required? Perhaps his abandoning her was that simple? Beatrice screwed up more than her eyes.

Anal sex. She had a dim recollection of engineering a single exploratory moment early on in their relationship. Of Ralph in tears because, in response to his tentatively obliging her, she'd shot up the bed so fast she'd almost knocked herself out on their oak headboard. Over before it began. And they'd only been messing about. She read the verse again, sighing, and yes, this revolting man genuinely believed that if he buggered women with a true focus on and desire for gain, demons would come and help him get whatever it was he was after. So what of the women?

A reference number directed her to a footnote by the editor, quoting one of Crowley's later reflections: *"The Orgasm was such as to have completely drowned the memory of the object."* His recollection chilled and passed through her as if she were invisible. She shut the book. Her misery thickened and no wonder, with her head stuck in this filth. *Makes you see filth everywhere.* One of Ralph's simple, solid lines. They'd met for the first time in here. Which row? Surely this one, because the light had run out with no view of a window from halfway down. This was partly why Ralph had bumped into her. Up here. She was standing in the exact place – the place now holding books on *Esoteric Studies.* She heard his voice as clearly as if he whispered in her ear. *Nothing esoteric about me.*

It jarred her whole body, the way his knocking into her had jarred all those years ago before a lifetime of edging her towards sanity and reason with his calm logic. Until three months ago. *Three months gone*, she whispered, disbelieving, smiling as she recalled the books he'd dropped. She'd said, *is this some sort of a joke?* and he'd responded with that utterly baffled look that convinced her he knew nothing at all about Hollywood films. Then he'd apologised profusely, spotted Freud's *Interpretation of Dreams* (which she'd dropped herself) and suggested they go for coffee to discuss the unconscious-as-idea. After that first meeting they'd cooked together, on a low-light for several months before she grasped simultaneously that he had no truck whatsoever with the usual assumptions about the institution of marriage and that she couldn't possibly spend her life with anyone else.

Strengthened by the memory, she turned over the book she was holding in her hand. A photograph glared from the cover: uneven eyes set deep in dissolute, fleshy pouches, large Fedora forced over the brim of an outsize head. Thick lips, slightly parted and curled in amusement. She replaced the book, yanked out another, which turned out to be a commentary on his well-known and probably much-used tarot.

Justice as idea has none but a purely human and therefore relative sense: so it is not to be considered as one of the facts of nature. Nature is not just, according to any theological or ethical ideas; but Nature is exact. The Scarlett Woman is masked. Her expression shows her secret intimate satisfaction in her domination of every element of dis-equilibrium in the Universe. All things are harmony and beauty; all things are Truth: because they cancel out. She represents Manifestation, which may always be cancelled out by equilibration of opposites. She is purely a matter of calculation.

Purely a matter of calculation. On Corinne's behalf, she uttered a silent prayer to the heavens.

The light went out and with it, the last of Beatrice's interest. The fifth floor held no sound of human presence. Outside was dark. She walked back down to the time switch, gave herself a couple of minutes of light and yanked out a book of essays and a commentary on *The Book Of Lies*, but they weighed like lead in her hands. So she was searching for meaning? "Oh, Ralph," she said softly, as a tear hit her upper lip. She put the books back on the shelf. She wasn't going to find any here.

Chapter Ten

The ballet class always warmed up with a few stretches. Corinne lifted her leg, placed her heel on the back of the chair and felt the inflexibility of the tendons running along the inside of her thigh. Her immediate impulse was to bend the knee on which she stood. Pain shot into both knees and her supporting calf. Straightening up again, she turned the leg on the chair outward, shifting her attention back to the inside of both thighs. This time she could feel the tendons pulling all the way down to her ankles. She pointed her toe as hard as she could and focusing on the pain, pulled her body higher, turned her leg out further, pointed that toe until only a pulsing, sparking ache numbed her to everything but her lower torso. Slowly, she pulled her stomach in and up, brought her arms, too stiff, in front of her before making them soften, every muscle and ligament alert as she breathed the tension out. Flesh melted around a frame of steel as finally, thought left her.

"Arms in first, then out to second and up to fifth." Janet's voice wasn't singing, exactly. More keeping time for her less-than-professional class of mostly lumpy middle-aged women. But Corinne was responding to the melody and rhythms of Chopin over which Janet spoke. The sound of the piano – now fast, now slow, now soft, then loud – flushed her with fire like a match along a line of gunpowder, willing her and obliging her to express the perfection of this music in movement.

So, while Janet's mini-speakers breathed in and out for

her, from arms in fifth – her head framed in a perfect oval, elbows crooked, fingers curved, hands symmetrical and facing one another, shoulders down and both arms aching, aching – when Janet bid them all stretch those upper torsos taller even as they bent at the waist, Corinne folded down to touch the knee on the back of the chair with her forehead until her creaking spine brought the pain into her back when she stretched some more.

Brixton Memorial Hall was barely changed from the 1980s, when Corinne had attended most Saturday mornings from the age of seven. She'd been so good at it that her teacher had arranged an audition for the Royal Ballet School. Following that disastrous day, she had stopped. The same piano stood in the corner, but The Pianist was extinct and the blue stage curtains, unopened for so long, rags. Looking at them, Corinne wondered whether the dust in the folds consisted of those exact same motes scuffed up from the splintery floorboards by her old black leather pumps. Certainly she felt a part of her lay there, suspended in time, waiting for...

Whatever it was, he/she/it had never arrived.

On their backs now, chairs pushed to the side of the hall, the women lay flat, arms wide. As the music played, they scraped a pointed toe from the side of their supine ankle and up to the knee, before extending the leg skyward, the opposite arm mirroring each movement of the leg. Corinne felt her hip joints grind, so she stretched further, imagining the ball pulling away from its socket. So little meat on her. Skinny and un-fattened. Eaten away at by others taking bites from her. A poor sacrifice.

And hold. And hold. And hold.

Straining as the sweat poured down the edges of her body, she felt suddenly visible from every angle and scrutinised in all of them with no chance of escape. And then she was trying and trying, harder than she'd ever tried, back on the day of white sunlight, back in that room of walled mirrors. It was the very last time she'd danced as a child. Just one among twenty eleven year olds lining a barre while a terrifying stranger with a stick watched to see if that leg – that aching leg, heavier with every second it remained in the air – would drop. Corinne had watched the stranger approach, held her breath as she passed by to hit the supporting knee of the girl in front. *Tight. Tight.* And the one in the air. *Up. Up.* In spite of gritting her teeth, both Corinne's arm and leg had dropped, just a few inches, dragged down by gravity and pain. But even when the woman had clicked her finger for the piano to pick up where it had left off, the order was not to rest and begin again, but was just to bend both knees, touch the left inside leg with the right pointed toe and stretch full out and up again, this time to the side. When the woman had walked back past her, she had sneered only: *you sit in your hip.*

"Corinne?" Janet was calling. The others were up, standing in front of the stage. "Don't overdo it. Remember. This is about enjoying yourself. Port de bras?"

Standing in fifth, right heel against left big toe, right little toe flat against left heel, Corinne felt anything but still. The silence in the hall twanged with sinew and muscle. *But the child tries*, she thought, as the piano gently bid her knees to bend, her arms to lift. *Even as the ballerina lifts onto her pointes, her black toes saturated with surgical spirit that has hardened overnight, the child rises into beauty or joy or triumph, or dies, in faltering steps, of heartbreak.* The effort as she reached, reached, reached to become the perfect incarnation of grace seemed elsewhere now: behind a gauze curtain lifted only on the day of reckoning. *The child believes she is, and so she is.*

But Corinne was no longer a child, and when Janet bid them line up in the far corner she found herself glad of the opportunity to wipe away her tears before they were witnessed. Again she heard the voice: *Don't turn your back on the teacher. Don't sit down.* Directives screamed at them in that audition room, hitting her across the head as surely as if they'd been the back of a hand. Walking, she could feel her body tensed, even now, against their violence. Against all violence. A necessary tension, enough to distract you from what they were going to do. From what they were doing. A maelstrom of colours and chaos loomed, one after the other, into Corinne's mind. A person. A penis. A smell. A taste. Bright colours flashed through her head. And eyes. Pairs of eyes, looking at her. Garlic on the breath. Soft words making her skin slippery. Strokes warming, cosseting until her body lifts, lucky, special. She was, she must be, the Scarlett Woman, no longer seeing as she's scored and split open, no longer hearing as she's urged to breathe into the force that runs her, that breaks her and everything is hurt until the bursting. Not her bursting. She's not there. No one is.

That was how, split in half, she'd hidden even from herself, but of course, she'd felt the pain when therapy put her back together years later. Ripped apart, Rehab and withdrawal had been a reenactment of sorts, though the mess in her head had convinced her she'd failed. Too much pride. Her wings had melted. She saw a balloon in the blue, blue sky and a girl, falling with her arms splayed.

The others were giggling and dissimulating. *You go first, then I can copy*. Janet, telling them it didn't matter. What mattered was to keep the chin up, the smile broad, small steps, level centre, knees pliable and returning to the same depth of *plié*: not too bent, not too shallow.

So when Tchaikovsky's introduction crashed into the room, Corinne was the first to lift her front foot in a small coupé, and swish! – she pushed it along the floor and travelled further to her right using the three small steps of the *pas de bourrée*. This was followed by the two large leaps of the *pas de chats* – knees out, first foot landing just prior to the other joining it in fifth position. But the cymbals were unrelenting, boxing her ears as they clashed out the first beat of every bar.

Now two *jétés* are demanded. Corinne jumps, taking off with both feet, one leg flying out to the side before both land again, a different toe and heel in front, ready to repeat on the other side. But has she put a foot wrong? No time or space for that. All, all will be lost. And where are the arms? The ARMS? Off again, the same sequence of steps in the other direction, traversing the room, closer to the front at every refrain, getting hotter and hotter and breathing evermore heavily.

Determined not to drop a step or the rhythm, Corinne flies from side to side, sliding and skipping, her arms slicing through space as she offers life itself to the empty air. Her hair clings in strands about her reddened face, no energy to suppress her shining smile as she dares to express ecstasy, unguarded. Her own? That of the music? That of the world?

Yet the ecstasy is inseparable from the pain. To become fully poised, entirely flowing, she must stretch beyond the limits her body can achieve naturally. That which is exquisite, hurts. The search for perfect expression hurts, not footsore, but heartsore, and ballet is always a search, an endless struggle against imperfection. Her exposure is only bearable if she keeps dancing, stretching, holding arms, wrists, fingers, neck, shoulders one step ahead of exhaustion.

And then the music, approaching its climax, marshals all instruments together to complete itself and blooms. Above the triumphant acclaim of the piano, Janet's voice shouts:

"They love you. All of them. The audience are whistling and throwing roses from the stalls and kisses from the Gods. You step forward and they stand in their seats and they clap and they hoot and they cheer."

For a moment, Corinne is the pinnacle and the consummation of all things. She steps to one side and placing her toe behind, sweeps out first one arm and then the other, acknowledging her audience. Then in deep, deep humility she drops her head, shifting her weight onto that bent back leg, taking her right hand to her left shoulder before rising, front leg outstretched, to brush those fingers to her lips and send that kiss out to the dark huge auditorium; to the intake of breath that receives it.

*   *   *

The porter that wheels me off chats with everyone he passes and they stop and smile at me as if I'm a cretin, so I slump to one side. Just because I can't walk doesn't mean I don't understand them. Even through closed eyes I can still see them, patronising me, so I think instead, of Tom.

I see him sitting on the low wall surrounded by our bags when we first arrived at our holiday cottage. I watch his gestures like a spy, delighting in his bigness which seems set free, just for me. Every movement of his long thick limbs is endowed with grace. I watch him cross his legs, absent-mindedly circling his limp foot as he rolls a cigarette and places it, dangling, in his mouth. As he focuses all his attention on what I've just said, all self-consciousness drops away and he speaks with his full wild being.

"Only women should own property," he says, those teeth gleaming despite his attempt to be serious. "I'm useless. I forget that windows need painting, gutters need cleaning, mortgages need paying. Women should have control of the whole lot and men should only enter their domain when invited."

My laughter falls close enough to breeze across his face. "That's brilliant. The best excuse I've ever heard for not having to grow up."

He leaps up in mock-frustration and lunges at me but I run off and down the uneven path to a dip. "Look at this tiny door." Tom follows as I push it open onto a small square room with a high narrow window, empty except for a fireplace and a stained mattress on a rusty iron bedstead. "Like a monk's cell," I say.

"Or a nun's cell. Single bed. Very austere," says Tom, pushing me towards it.

I feel behind me for his wrists and pull his arms over my shoulders, wrapping them round me. "Do you think it's part of the house?"

"I think it's holding up the house," says Tom. He stands on the raised flagstone and kicks the wall with his foot. "This chimney must go right through the middle and up to the top." He begins in earnest – he's obviously thought about this a lot. "Look – just because I've read a bit about architecture, doesn't mean I'm any good with a paintbrush or that I'll even notice a whiffy drain."

I laugh. Even louder this time. "You're just shrugging off your responsibilities by appealing to my mothering instincts. Hoping some woman in your life will do all the work so you don't have to. What's more, you're turning your bloody laziness into some grand theory of the gender divide."

He jumps off the hearth and bends over me until my neck stretches backwards and his fists have to restrain themselves. As I know they will. I duck under his arm and back out into the yellow sunlight, but he follows and soon I'm stumbling through green dock leaves and tall grass until he eventually pushes me to the ground and pins me down. I fight back. I always fight back. The audacity and confidence beneath Tom's meek exterior never fails to rile me, and he never fails to spot it. The merest glint of those teeth is a 'c'mon then' – an amused invitation to put him in his place by mercifully showing him, before he gets out of control, that he's little more than my slave. He smiles. I shrug. He splutters. I raise my eyebrows. He places his hands on my back and shoves me down. I bite his shoulder, just slightly harder than is fun. And on it goes, until panting and exhausted, I let him rove over my body with his own. Somewhere in the struggle, the hunted becomes infused with the passion of the hunter and once he's reassured I've given way, I slap him and he lies his great bulk upon me until my lungs fail. Only then do I stop resisting and let him stroke me inside, allowing that pressure to wash right through me until we meet in sweetness. The depths in Tom's astonished eyes become fathomless then, matched only by the numberless stars he sees in my own and we clasp one another all the tighter to make edges again, for we both know there are really none.

Chapter Eleven

It's a shock when we get to the doctor's room. I look to check that the boxes we were discussing last time are still there, but they've gone. She's still here though, and takes the handles of the chair, thanking the porter in a way that reminds me we're here to talk about me.

"Last night," I begin, soothed now by the daylight and my thoughts of Tom. "When I couldn't sleep, I kept hearing Tom, over and over, saying he hated hurting women." I offer this up as a starting point. Something we can look into together.

"That's right. Well done for bringing that up," says Dr. Samuels. "I remember you telling me, before."

"He said it was the thing he was most afraid of. That was why we went on as we did, with him not telling Anita."

"His partner," confirms Dr. Samuels.

I nod, just to clarify, but she nods back with an enthusiasm I do not feel. Anita! Anita had been voiceless in the writing centre. Invisible. Tom did all the hosting. I barely saw her twice, but once was enough to rule her out of this story completely. I can't begin to explain it to myself, let alone Dr. Samuels, because what happened was before I'd even spoken to Tom. Before I even knew she was his partner. And yet if I hadn't almost fallen through that ghost-cold crack I would never have got involved with him.

I must have been nipping out for a fag when I was supposed to be tucked away in some corner, writing, but the way outside was through the enormous kitchen. Tom and

Anita were standing a few feet apart on the far side of a large oak table. He tall, wide and ugly. She, petite beside him, bird face haloed by a frizz of dark hair and her jeans pinning a man's too-big shirt into a small waist below large breasts. I stepped through the doorway, Anita looked up and I saw it at once. There was *nothing between these two people*. Only absence. An almost palpable vacancy. But how can I explain that to Dr. Samuels?

She is waiting, smiling. "We've never talked about Anita."

"Yes we have," I insist, hoping she'll drop it. "She was his business partner. The sex didn't work – had never worked."

"But she lived with him, didn't she? Ran the place you met him in, surely?"

I bridle. "It wasn't me who gave up on her. I urged Tom to try harder. He said he'd tried everything. I told you. Tom's problem was identical to mine. He and Anita had been together the same length of time as Harry and me." I wait. Not bothering with Anita seems self-explanatory. Dr. Samuels waits too until I say, "Why should we talk about Anita? She was only a partner on paper. I was his wife, in everything but. We even went into a church."

"Really? Would you be happy to tell me about that?"

I certainly would. Anything to get away from Anita, but I'm not surprised this has come up, since Tom has been alongside me almost since I left the ward. Smiling, I tell Dr. Samuels about those few days of snatched holiday. One of the most precious weeks of my life.

Our cottage was a higgledy-piggledy affair, built into the hillside and accessible on three different levels.

From the patio, the land rose in a series of low terraced walls to the far ridge, where patches of buttercup-waving scrubland gave way to a forest of pines. Beyond, a ring of hills held us quiet. Perhaps the stones of our little house were once part of those hills, hewn and lifted piece by piece to fit in this uneven clearing. We tried to walk to them.

"This way," said Tom, steaming left. I followed just in time to see him disappear between two rhododendron bushes. Though the flowers on either side had faded to a papery brown, further in, orange blooms massed up high, clamouring for the sky. Before us a tin house rusted in a nest of grass.

"See," said Tom, triumphantly. "I knew there'd be a chapel near. Keeps off the evil spirits. Bet you can't get across the threshold."

But it was Tom who had to stand outside as I slipped sideways through the crack. I pulled and he pushed and the top of the door wavered and threatened to come apart, but we scraped the bottom over uneven flagstones until half open, it stuck fast.

The sweet smell of rot thickened around us. Creepers had forced gaps between sheets of corrugated iron and the rain had seeped in, turning the walls to rust and the floor to a carpet of mould. Four arched leaded windows threw a dull light across two rows of wooden pews.

Tom took my hand. "You and me then," he said and we walked up the aisle towards the wooden cross on the bare bleached table and sat on a bench at the front.

I squeezed his fingers. "A bride has to be given away. Perhaps that's why my marriage didn't work... I don't know if marriage could ever work for me." I stared at Tom. "I suppose I thought with my dad dead I was free." Tom looked confused, but nodded anyway. "But maybe it didn't work because my dad didn't want me. And if the form of a woman depends on a man... " The thought arrived as I spoke it, entirely new but obvious. At odds with everything I'd ever espoused yet utterly consistent with all that I'd experienced through being with Tom. "...I never was. I was never wanted, so I couldn't be given. No shape, you see. No substance."

"But I thought you loved your dad. You said... "

"Oh yes. I loved him. But he didn't love me. He tried to palm me off on the first bloke that came along – took my boyfriend outside one day and said to him 'I suppose you'll be taking Gina with you when you go to university?' I think the plan was get me anywhere that he wasn't."

"Really?" Tom ran his fingertips across the bones beneath my eyes. "This precious beauty?"

But I couldn't hold his gaze. "I think my boyfriend was so appalled he felt he had to take me. I never thought about it much at the time – not until recently. My dad had a way with words. He always seemed to talk so much sense, even when I didn't want to hear it."

We sat, the stillness making dust of these knots; Tom's gentle hand stroking my concerns away.

I turned. "I wonder what life would be like if my dad had always thought I was precious? Precious enough to put the fear of God into men on my behalf or struggle with himself to honour the day he handed me over into someone else's care. I'd know then, at least, that I was worth having."

Tom kissed my forehead. "Yes," he said, "You'd know, and I can't bring that time back. I can only show you, now, by the way I cherish you." He sighed. "Daughters! When Naomi started seeing her bloke... you see... I still can't bring myself to say his name! I wanted to rip his head off."

"That's because you know how much he lusted after her, because you're a bloke too."

Tom looked relieved."But how come you know that? How can you and still want me?"

"Because you know it too. You're not trying to pretend and make up some stupid idea that justifies you behaving like a prat. I bet you didn't rip his head off. I bet you smiled and asked him in for tea."

"But what's good about men?" He looked at me like he really wanted an answer. "All they do is make pathetic excuses whenever they can and go to the pub. Well, they used to, before you lot came along and refused to put up with it. Three thousand years of total control and I have to miss it by about five minutes."

I poked him in the ribs. "You love it. Stops you getting bored."

A look of surprise spread across his huge forehead followed by a tenderness that softened his eyes into syrup.

"What's good about men?" I said. "Absolutely fuck-all unless they put their faith in women, otherwise they become monsters. Out of touch, scared and disconnected from what's important." I snuggled up to him. "It's OK. You've got me now and all I need is for you to keep loving me, keep telling me what it's like to be you."

"But you let me be how I am. That's why I can tell you. Because it doesn't bother you."

"Why should it bother me? It's the hidden stuff I have a problem with, the stuff I can see that people pretend isn't there."

"My God," said Tom. "I wouldn't stand a chance, couldn't hide a thing and that's what I want. I want all of you."

"Do you?" Mild as he was passionate; self-effacing as he was certain, this giant wanted me. In his presence my big mouth became the oracle, my sullen face reflective, my talent for missing the point a quirk to love. I felt my heartbeat, steady as his pulse as he put his arm around me and we stood together.

"With all of me," he said, pulling me close as we walked back down the aisle.

The smile on my face feels much bigger than it must look. Like a curve that starts at my ear and scoops right down beneath my feet and up my other side. Wrapped in the memory of that meeting, I'm surprised the doctor is still here and can't fathom why I might need her.

"So, you see, everything's fine," I end, hoping she'll agree but she looks at the clock and tells me I have another forty-five minutes.

She wants to know what happened next. "So you had this ceremony," she says.

"Well, not really." Hating it when she gets me wrong, I begin to squirm.

She apologises. "It's just that you said you were his wife in all but name." She pauses. "Rather than Anita. That's what you were telling me."

She's right. I was, but I can't remember why. The room is too pungent with rotted leaves and the faint smell of blossom – of sharp, honeyed air – for me to be anywhere but back in the crook of Tom's arm. I see Dr. Samuels waiting, but only in outline, so I carry on.

The rhododendrons closed behind us, making a secret of our chapel, the path a wide road that would carry our intimacy beyond the whitening sky. Violets I hadn't noticed on the way dotted the rocky path.

"I don't really know about men," I confessed. "Only how to keep out of their way and how to get rid of them." I looked up, anxious that he'd be horrified, but Tom seemed untroubled by what I'd said. "My daughter ended up fatherless like me really. I was trying to protect her but of course, she just became scared of what she didn't know."

Tom sighed and stroked my head. "I don't really know about men either. I don't know how to be one," and we frowned together.

"Actually," I said, stopping. "I'm not sure we're doing that badly." I'd made myself sound awful, yet telling Tom had been easy, so easy that I began to

giggle. Then Tom began to laugh and soon the stories of how useless we were fell away, as absurd and easy to step out of as a hall of mirrors.

He put my arm in his and we walked on. "So, between us we've one fatherless daughter, one motherless daughter and then there's my other daughter, Nancy – the child I had with Patricia. She used to live with me four days a week until her mother moved away." I could tell by the way he sped up, just a little, that it still hurt. "She's fifteen now. Dyslexic. Doesn't look you in the eye. I pay for her schooling." On he marched. "It's very important to me. This is the first time I've ever earned enough to really do anything useful."

I chuckled, light where he was heavy. "What – so you've brought up one single-handed and half brought up the other one. So you've not done anything useful, really?"

Tom grinned. "I can't believe you said that. Women do that stuff all the time and no one bats an eyelid."

"Yes – and women know how hard it is." I wanted him to appreciate his own achievements, to know that his commitment to his kids was part of why I loved him so much. "And so do you."

"That's why I can't tell Anita yet," he said. "Because my kid's welfare is tied up with everything I'm doing. You do see that, don't you? The writing centre houses us, pays us. And the thing is, I have to finish my book and I can't work in chaos. Can you give me a few months? Just a few months."

Now it was my turn to grin. "It might kill me." I squeezed my eyelids down tight, but when I opened them again, Tom's eyes stared from a white face.

He grabbed my hand. "Don't say that. Don't even think it. Listen – me and Anita were never going to work, never going to be lifelong lovers. She knows that as well as I do. We haven't had sex for months. I know I can make her understand," he said, hardly pausing for breath. "Give me time. Just give me time and I promise you that no one will get hurt."

His conclusion stunned me. Tom had delivered these two statements with a conviction that joined them as smoothly as butter in a sandwich and made them as easy to swallow. Except that his conclusion, far from being logical, was complete rubbish. I almost shouted. "But she lives with you. She loves you. Of course you're going to hurt Anita, just like I'm going to destroy Harry. There's no way round that."

He didn't hear. "No. No. I just have to make her see what she knows already and then it doesn't have to be like that. It's just a knot. It can be untied. Patience, that's all that's needed. Patience and strength. The strength you give me. You're a fantastic woman – my woman. My true wife. I know I can do anything as long as I've got you."

His arms closed around me, his big lips kissing conviction into me until I breathed the air he breathed. And I wanted him to be able to do anything. Wanted human relationships to be other than my experience of them. Most of all, I wanted to stop balancing this ball on my nose and stop being the person who always knew best. Who was I, in the virgin territory of that bleached-clean summer? A woman determined to root out the hard certainties scored into my DNA. And if I discovered how and why I was wrong, perhaps I'd be the better for it.

Dr. Samuels' chair squeaks as she swivels to and fro. Her room has dimmed and her grey hair looks dull and brittle.

"I was sure, somewhere, that he would have to break Anita's heart in the end," I say. "But if I was right, I was right. I didn't have to push it. I had nothing to lose."

"Nothing to lose," she repeats. "And you were sure about that?"

"Oh, yes." I reflect. "I mean there'd be pain and guilt but I was ready to support him. You know. Eggs and omelettes and all that."

"Yes." The doctor pauses, searching my face until I look her in the eye. Eventually she says, "Except you're the one looking broken to me." She stops for so long I think the session must be over but then she says, "You talked of logic." She smiles, waiting for my nod before continuing. "That not hurting Anita was a priority and therefore Tom decided he would leave her without – I think 'destroying' was a term you used?"

"Yes. I kind of knew it wasn't do-able, but I wanted to believe him."

"Did it not occur to you that if he was determined not to hurt her and he couldn't explain his way out of the relationship there might be a third way?"

"A third way?" I laugh. "Tell me, please. Tom and I went round and round in circles discussing this and I could never make him see there wasn't one. But people get over it."

"Well that's good," says Dr. Samuels. "Because who's suffering now?" Her eyes run over my wasted arms, my shrivelled legs. "Tell me, Gina. What did happen in the balloon?"

We have to jump. We have to jump together. You know that, don't you? The sound comes from above, as though God is shouting at me. The basket crashes against my ribs, the firmament reels, smiles, triumphant. I am the wrong way up.

I grab the wheels of my chair. "Don't even think it. I told you. He wasn't even married to Anita."

"I guess something had to give?"

"It wouldn't be possible. I am his wife. We are one person. Can't be separated."

Dr. Samuels nods, but I know she doesn't get it. "You are so very sure of this," she says. "I want to understand why."

"But you know why." I feel like hitting her but try again to explain. "Because I gave myself to him and he to me. *He* understands that. And don't think I didn't put him through his paces. You've read the conversation on my computer. I gave up on all that soulmate stuff years ago – decided it was crap, until he showed me he could protect me against... against the way men take advantage of women. Don't you see that giving myself to him was the greatest thing I ever did? And it was the same for him. Total trust in one another moved us into... into... another dimension. Look... " I seize upon it, my dim fumblings breaking into light as I feel Tom, steadfast beside me. "...once I had agreed – consciously – to our union, everything changed. I told you – right?" I look to check Dr. Samuels is following and she is concentrating, hard. "Things got difficult. I said I'd wait, because to be a man he had to pay his daughter's school fees. He had to keep his job, finish his book, and not just for the money. It was a moral thing – seeing through his commitments – an upright thing, as well as being practical. What sort of wife would I have been if I'd wept and wailed, but naturally, I struggled, got paranoid. As time went on I took up more and more of his energy needing reassurance, which I hated myself for." I could feel my smile, thin and watery. "How weak is woman, eh?"

"Especially when they've given up their independence."

"No!" I shout. Because this is the point she is missing, the point I was missing until I met Tom. "Independence is... is... a diversion. I've done it and it doesn't work. For women or for men, but between us we've got everything. Incredible will and direction. Awareness of the smallest, most caring details that are essential to really make the most of that will. If we can only listen to what we really want to give to one another, independence looks like a one-legged man trying to ride a two-pedal bike. Really, there's no such thing."

"No such thing." But Dr. Samuels is considering what I've just told her, not arguing, and I want to give her a moment to think about what must be a new idea to her. Like a timid child, raising a query that she expects to be demolished, she says, "So, was equality for women a mistake?"

I smile. "Of course not. You have to be able to choose.

That's the point. I can be on my own. I've worked and made all the decisions. Brought up a child. Slept with who I felt like sleeping with. Only it's never quite right and I knew that. I just didn't know there was an alternative until I met Tom."

She nods. I think she's got it.

"And then what happened?"

"Thank you," I say, because she's focusing on what I'm telling her now. Really trying to understand. "After I surrendered, trusting that he'd find his own way, it became obvious that none of my fears had anything to do with him. I could see my fantasies about what he might be doing with Anita, about how he might be using me – for exactly what they were. My own, old personal insecurities. Every misgiving became something to study and once I really took on board Tom's devotion to me, my fears slid away. I felt calm, stopped badgering him and let him get lost in his book."

At last I've explained. The relief is so great, even my spine has stopped aching. I sweep out my arms. "Giving myself to Tom wasn't restricting, it was liberating. Don't you see? That has to be love, doesn't it? He gave me myself back!"

Dr. Samuels is staring at the wall behind me. The silence between us is filled with light as though my words have caused tiny cracks in the air to show that reality is actually made of diamonds. I am delighted when eventually she says, "I feel very privileged to have been trusted with your story. The love you describe sounds so... pure."

I smile some more. "We are all Gods – and Goddesses."

Outside, rain drizzles down the window pane. Dr.

Samuels looks towards it and says, gravely, "But surely not all the time. Aren't we also mortal, flawed? Sometimes selfish?"

Her enquiries are easy to answer now that I feel she's asking to learn something for herself.

"Yes. That's why we have to work so hard to trust and not become self-obsessed."

"And that's what you think Tom did?"

"Does," I correct her.

"How do you know?"

It's quiet enough to hear every raindrop that drips onto the window ledge. Quietly, I say, "Because my love for him is bound in service to his needs by a force greater than my own."

"Can you tell me how?

"Vows," I say, holding her gaze. "We exchanged vows, witnessed in a place sacred to him, by the one person Tom owed it to. The one person who could give him away."

Dr. Samuels leans forward, rapt.

"After one of our nights together."

"Where did you go?"

Where did we go? Into the mystic. Wherever Tom was taking me I was happy to follow, and since Dr. Samuels is listening so intently, I'm willing to take her there myself. We settle back in our chairs, and I feel again the warm breeze against my arm as I hold it in the high air, the Severn sparkling far below as Tom drives across the sunlit bridge.

I don't remember passing through the town, only Tom's tiny Renault, rattling at forty miles an hour through the country lanes until the hedges rose above our heads,

funnelling us down into a valley. Then deep in the Forest of Dean, by a churchyard, Tom stopped the car and took my hand. "I've brought you here to prove how serious I am and how important you are to me."

He climbed, with difficulty, out of the cramped drivers seat and I followed him through a squeaking timber gate, across a path and a square green lawn to a plaque set into the low stone wall. He wiped the dust from it. "It's Liz," he said simply. Beneath, old foliage protruded from a square marble vase, the petals long-dissolved, leaving brown stems, tough as wire, sharp as the arrows that still pierced him. This was goodbye. His final goodbye, seventeen years in the making. As we gazed together over the moss-clad boundary, two horses cantered past, sheer as water down the rippling slope.

Tom turned and strolled back through the leaning gravestones, but I knelt, pulling out the stems one by one before throwing them over the wall to pile up on more recently faded blooms. Straggling couch grass, too close for the mower to reach, fringed the vase. I tore it out by the handful, brushing away the debris as tenderly as a mother sweeping hair from the face of her sleeping child. "Thank you," I whispered to that ash-filled ground, and the gentlest of breezes lifted my gratitude up to my face and wrapped it back around me.

I walked back to the gate. The smell of oiled wood seeped from the canopy into the drowsy morning as Tom took my hands and held them between his. "I love you. I love you with all of me." And he pressed his lips tight and stared past me for the last time. As he turned back, his pit-black eyes cleared. "It's only knowing you are there that makes it possible for me to go on. I promise I will never leave."

"You don't have to... "

He put his finger to my lips. "I choose my words carefully. I don't say anything I don't mean. I promise we will be together."

"Are you sure?"

The smell of his skin poured through the warm cotton of his shirt and he drew me to him. "Promise me," he urged. "Promise me you'll remember my promises."

I cupped his shadowed face in my hand and kissed my agreement into it without reservation.

My voice is low. "Now do you see?"

"Yes." Dr. Samuels looks worn. "I do." She was quiet for a while before adding, "You agreed to keep his promises *for* him. Took his intention to devote himself to you upon yourself to uphold."

"Yes – and my own promise to do that freed me."

"From yourself, as you said. But at the same time it bound you to him," says Dr. Samuels. She could be talking to herself. "It's almost as if the whole thing was a magical incantation."

"Almost?" I say. "It was a magical incantation. An exchange of energies. So surely it must make sense now when I tell you we can't be separated. That I can't just take myself back?"

She thinks for a while. "It does if you believe that with

your own promise you handed your will to him."

"As I knew it would," I say, lighter now than I have been for ages. "But fortunately, I don't need anyone else. Liz gave her approval... and in that moment... " I find gratitude has undone me but wait until it has subsided enough to say, "... in that moment when I felt her let him go, I swore to her that I'd keep an eye on her daughter."

Dr. Samuels looks at the clock on the wall. "Thank you so much for telling me this. I feel as if I have the whole picture now. How would it be if you mapped it out for me?" She gets up and lifts an old fashioned sweet jar from her desk, but it has stones in it – big dark ones and tiny shiny ones. I can see marbling through the glass. "We could use these to represent all the people involved."

"OK," I shrug. "But you should have left the sugar in. He's much sweeter than a stone."

"And the others?"

"What others?"

Dr. Samuels takes what I'd assumed was some kind of stepladder leaning against the wall and turns it into a table. We sit either side, the jar to my right. She takes the lid off and spreads the contents across the top.

"Would you like to pick out the people?"

Immediately I choose the largest stone, the size of a paper weight.

"And now everyone else."

"How do you mean, everyone else?"

"Everyone you've mentioned in our sessions so far. Let's start with Anita, shall we?" she says, gathering the stones into an accessible pile.

Quickly, I choose a small black stone for Anita.

"Then Tom's daughter, Naomi."

I pick what turns out to be a bright piece of blue glass for Naomi – blue for the dress she wore and the grief she faced. "All right, I get it," I say, and choose a smaller, paler stone for her dead mother. "That's Liz. And that's Patricia." A large pebble marbled with pink does for Nancy, the dyslexic daughter. As an afterthought, I choose a chunk of coal for Harry. "Will that do?"

"Yes, but haven't you missed two people out – as well as your own daughter?"

I pick up one for June. It feels heavy in my hand, even though it's the smallest I could see. I know I have let June down and that even though she has left home, my actions have affected her deeply. I'm stumped about the others.

"You told me Tom said he'd had an affair before – that Liz threw him out for it."

"If you think it's important." I ignore the association of myself with the word 'affair' and take another from the pile.

"And what about you? Where are you?"

I'm not falling for that one. "I'm under Tom, in Tom. He's solid enough for both of us." I pick up that first biggest piece and bang him on the plastic top.

"Humour me for this session." Dr. Samuels picks up a lump of quartz and places it just in front of me. "Let's pretend that you are here, watching from the sidelines. I'd like to hear about Tom's life before he met you."

I want to say Tom had no life before he met me, but I'm trying to behave. Instead, I wheel back a bit and lean forward until my line of sight is blocked by the quartz. This puts tremendous pressure on my shoulders and at first, the task seems impossible, but by imagining I have died, I gain distance. Being a lump of crystal seems rather fitting. "Tom's life before he met me?"

"Good girl," says the doctor.

"He went to university, got Liz pregnant and like a good working-class boy, married her and took her home to mum."

"So where shall we put Liz, in Tom's life?"

I wiggle and straighten until I feel I'm looking down from heaven. "At the centre."

"And Naomi. Would you like to move her, too?"

I pick up Naomi and place her next to her mother, but they look wrong. "For now," I say, "this one is Liz and this Naomi," and I swop them so that the mother is large and vibrant, the daughter small and protected.

"Then what happened?"

"He fell in love with Whatshername. She was a singer in the same band. Tom left Liz and rushed off to meet her at the station where they planned to run away."

Dr. Samuels spreads out her hands, inviting me to move the stones. I shift Liz and Naomi sideways and place a new stone with rusty lines crossing it – Whatshername – centre stage. "Then Whatshername ditched Tom at the eleventh hour, saying she had become an evangelical Christian, and Tom crawled to Liz on his knees, pleading to be taken back." I see the light shining from the hall onto the front step, the woman with shoulder-pads just inside and Tom begging to be let back in. So, apparently, does Dr. Samuels.

"I think I'm getting the picture," she says.

I put Whatshername back in the jar but Dr. Samuels

immediately takes her out again and places her opposite me, also watching from the sidelines. I put Liz and Naomi back in the centre, with Tom on his stony knees, prostrated in front of them. Liz stares at Tom, glassy blue. "The words are important," I say.

"So can you say them as you move the stones?" asks the doctor. "Be Liz."

I pick Liz up and raise her above Tom until she looks down on him from a great height. "No," I say. "You can fuck off and not come back. You're a cheat, a liar and a womanising coward, just like your father," and I crash into Tom and bash him halfway across the table before moving him to the side like a counter in a game of draughts. "Tom licked his wounds for a couple of years." I trot Liz and Naomi to the left, "Liz found someone else." I take the first small stone to hand and place it next to her. "And then Tom met Patricia at a dinner party." Patricia as a small stone will not do at all, though brown is almost right. I swop her for a larger more nurse-like lump and place Tom beside her, cuddled up. Their love is now centre-stage and I want to put them in a double-bed, with a canopy. The bed I imagine they were in six months later when the phone rang. "The early morning call." Slowly I remove Liz from Naomi and shift her to the very edge. "The brain haemorrhage. The hospital scene, where Tom was the one who had to switch off the life-support." And I flick Liz onto the thin carpet and out of the picture.

"But she's been around for you, very much, in our talks," says Dr. Samuels. "Why not change her with Naomi. Put the smaller piece on the sidelines." She looks for my agreement, then leans down and picks Liz up.

I swop her with Naomi, moving the blue glass with Tom now, further from Patricia. I place the small pale stone, the plaque that is now Liz, on the edge. "Liz's demise sounded the death knell for Tom and Patricia too. He was very shocked. I think he blamed himself. Patricia couldn't handle Tom's distress. She couldn't understand why he was mourning Liz when he had her. They married, she had Nancy… " I place Nancy next to Patricia "… but they separated after several years, and she moved away." I remove Patricia and Nancy to the corner nearest to me.

"Then Tom was on his own again."

Dr. Samuels arches her brow at that. I look back at the table and it's true really, he doesn't look as if he's on his own. "Apart from Naomi, who grew up and had her own life." I place her on the other side of the table, opposite Patricia, and add a button for Naomi's partner. The table seems to be getting more and more crowded. "And then he got on with his life, met Anita, never really had a sexual relationship with Anita, lost patience with Anita… " – I move the small black stone in and back out – "and then he met me."

"Harry and June?"

I don't want to pick up either of them but they take positions equidistant from me, though I know Harry should be over the other side of the room. Then I slide myself towards Tom before attempting to remove the piece of quartz altogether, but Dr. Samuels reaches out to stay my hand. "But this is before the promise. Before you were one."

I look at Tom, surrounded by people who don't love him enough. "Everyone has left," I say.

"Are you sure it's not him who's left or got rid of them?"

"Well, he certainly hasn't left Anita," I respond, annoyed as I realise I will have to bring her back on. I move her closer to the centre.

"OK," says Dr. Samuels. "So this is Tom's life as it was when you met him. He's surrounded by people – or the ghosts of people – that he seems unable to get rid of, no matter how hard he tries."

"How so?" But I see what she means. These people are beginning to haunt me too. I want them gone. June, I have a desire to cover with myself. Harry sits inert, reproaching my mauve and pink hues. Patricia is spiteful, harassing Tom about his failings as a father. Anita hangs around looking dense and refusing to get out of the way and Liz is a tombstone now. She's not going anywhere.

"They *were* gone. They were all gone. After the promise. Tom knew I couldn't live without him – without all of him."

Dr. Samuels voice rises, just slightly, but I notice. "Did you tell him that?"

She must feel as embarrassed as I do. I remember how ridiculous it sounded. Me, a woman over forty drawn into the sort of nonsense that teenagers play at. A woman who up to that point had repeatedly said that she didn't believe in soulmates – that relationships were about negotiating as equals. But I remember too, lying together, glutted with moonlight, musky as leaf-mould on the forest floor.

I can hardly bear to look at Dr. Samuels. "Yes. The words just slipped out. *I cannot live without you.* I suppose I got a bit carried away. Does it matter?" But as I repeat the words, I know it does.

I knew it the moment I said them.

Dr. Samuels voice is low and gentle. "And did you believe it?"

"It felt real, at the time." My leaden arms can't play with these bits of rock any more and I'm not at all sure I want to go on. "It feels real now."

"You're very tired. You've worked hard, letting all those people in." Dr. Samuels stands and moves her chair to the side before wheeling mine over to sit beside her. "Do you want to stop now, or would you like me to tell you a story?" Her tone is conspiratorial.

I lean towards her, intrigued. "Once upon a time – sort of, you mean?"

"If you like. Why not?" Her voice quietens until the hush spreads itself evenly through the air. Even the walls seem to be listening. "Once upon a time then, there was a young man away at college who had never been in love before, and when he found his young woman, he thought she must be a Princess, because he had never met anyone so beautiful in his life. All his senses became so absorbed by her that he believed that he would love her forever."

Dr. Samuels is very sweet and it's easy to forgive her attempt to explain away my problem because sitting here, doing nothing, is strangely soothing.

"So they lived together on bread that she baked and honey that he collected from the beehive, in a sunrise which seemed never ending. They were so close and so young that they felt bound together by fate. When the beautiful Princess told him she couldn't possibly live without him, it seemed hardly worth a mention. Before they had time to count to ten, she was going to have his baby, they were married, and off they went together to live happily ever after."

"Into the sunset," I add, relaxing, since this is obviously not about me at all.

"I'm glad you said that," smiles Dr. Samuels. "It shows great wisdom and is a sign of your great age!"

"Well, everybody knows it can't be sunrise forever."

"Except them, because they hadn't yet seen the sun go down. Mind you, by the time the baby was crawling, perhaps we could say that it was mid-afternoon, the shadows were creeping in, and our young man was finding it pretty hard sharing his Princess with a small person who seemed to take up all her time."

"Plus his Princess was beginning to look more like Cinderella, but with stretch marks."

"Exactly!" Dr. Samuels looks pleased about me joining in. "And you would think, or know, as you do, that really, their shotgun wedding should have put a bullet through those words."

I'm puzzled by that, so she explains, quite briskly. "Well – that whole, *I-can't-live-without-you* thing would have been grown out of with the nappies, wouldn't it? And by now our lovely young man was getting uneasy and restless with all these shadows gathering around. He began to stay out more and more and late one afternoon he went off to sing and was introduced to someone who wanted to harmonize with him. She sounded so like a lark that he thought he must have been swindled by his wife, who was obviously an imposter. So the young man decided that the real Princess was... "

"Was she in a band?" I ask.

Dr. Samuels nods.

"Whatsername," I say.

"Exactly!"

I take up the story. "So he ran to Whatsername, but Whatsername had changed her mind, so he crawled home on his belly, begging for forgiveness, but she wouldn't have it. Sent him off with a flea in his ear."

Dr. Samuels is staring intently at me, nodding, but the creases around her eyes are deepening. Her mouth drops slowly open and I feel sucked towards it, the room disappearing until I am waiting, breathless, for the punchline.

"And four years later, she died in the night."

I look over at Liz's stone, growing moss on the edge of the table, and then at the stone that I have picked to represent Whatshername. Her connection with Liz is unavoidable. The line between them shimmers as bright as the tingle running down my spine. "The swearing she would die without him. She did die."

Dr. Samuels sighs. "With him. Without him? Who knows what might have happened? But for a person who had betrayed his first love, it might have seemed that the prophecy came true: he had broken the spell and was left with nothing but the curse of his own cowardice."

"So Tom thinks Liz died because he left her for Whatsername?"

"I don't know, because I don't know Tom. I wonder though, what you think?" Dr. Samuels stands and wheels me back to the table. Then she reaches into her bag and pulls out a ball of red wool. "How about using this," she says, handing it to me, "to link the people in the story together?"

"They're all important," I realise, aloud, because once I have placed Whatsername on the end of the wool and stretched it until Liz sits on it too, I intuit the enormity of the task. I further unravel the skein and wrap it several times round Naomi before returning to Tom.

"Perhaps you should start with Tom?"

I begin again. From Tom and Liz to Whatsername and back to Liz, then on to Naomi and back to Tom. Then from Tom to Patricia, twice round Nancy and back to Tom, before unravelling the ball of wool further to encompass Anita, back to Tom and on to me. From here, I go round me and Tom several times. The pattern on the table is beginning to look like a lopsided windmill on a stick. I sit up straight, aware that something is missing, and then stretch the wool from the quartz representing me to Liz and back, then from me to Naomi several times and lastly to Nancy. I have made a pledge to all of them.

"What about Anita?"

Anita! Bloody Anita is always in the way. I want to pick her up and chuck her through the window, but instead, I loop the wool around her tight. I hope she chokes. "OK," I say, my own voice sounding strangled. "Tom says he needs Anita – at the moment. He can't tell her about me yet, because the important things – his daughter's school fees – his job – the stability of his home-life so he can finish his book – they're all tied up with her. She could turn nasty." Reluctantly, I stretch the wool from me to Anita and back to Tom, from me to Anita and back to Tom. If I do it three times, we will be fixed in an eternal triangle.

"Your promises mean a great deal to you?"

"Everything," I say.

"And what about Tom's promises? His promises to Anita and to Liz, for instance?"

"He told me he had made a mistake with Anita. He was never in love with her. She was a child. Almost virginal."

"And you? Is it possible he made a mistake with you? He had an affair before, didn't he?"

"An affair?" I say, coldly. Something clicks in my mind, the way a mine clicks when you step on it. I cover it with words, scrabbling to keep it deep beneath the earth, like Liz. "You don't swear on your dead wife's grave never to leave someone if you're only having an affair with them."

Dr. Samuels inclines her head. She's trying to force me to meet her eyes. "But if you were, or did swear, mightn't getting your lover to promise to remember your promises be the best way of protecting yourself?"

There is nowhere to look except for the web on the table.

"He promised you that he could untangle this too, didn't he? But who, in this whole muddle is held most fast?"

Tom is almost obscured by a mass of red wool, cocooned as surely as a fly in a spider's web.

"Who has the strongest belief, Gina? You or Tom?"

I turn my face to the wall. "Neither. We match each other in every way."

"And what," says the doctor, picking up Whatsername and knocking her lightly on the table, "...do we think Tom believed happened because of the last affair he had?"

"That... that Liz died. That he killed her." Every word is

a knock on the lid of Liz's casket now, and a punch to my heart. "But I don't believe that. I told him there would be pain." I stare again at the bloodlines joining the people on the table, and it doesn't matter that I have forced them around me and Tom over and over, the others all seem thicker than the line between us.

"His comment about not being able to bear hurting women seems a little bit muddled to me. Do you think it might be his own pain that he can't bear? His own guilt?" Dr. Samuels draws her finger around Liz and Whatsername and then around me and Anita. "Look at this. Isn't it possible that in Tom's imagination, you are to Anita what Whatsername was to Liz."

"I... I will kill her?"

"She will die – because of you. Isn't that what he thinks?"

She will die. Frail Anita, with her asthma and her art. Anita, who had to have every room hoovered twice a day and her nebulizer close in case of an attack. "But, I... I would never... I promised to wait."

"Until he untangled things? Until he managed to do what you didn't really believe was possible?"

"I did believe it. I said I'd wait."

"And he didn't end it? Tell you it was over?" Dr. Samuels presses down on the mass of wool connecting me to the others on the table. "He didn't cut you loose?"

Tom, sauntering across the field to the balloon. Me running along beside him. His hands stripping that figure of eight from its moorings. The rope, trailing long and thin as we bumped across the grass. "Never."

Dr. Samuels voice seems to boom from every corner of the room. "And you didn't let *him* down?"

"I... let him down. *I...* let *him* down?" Tom, breathing into my face. *We have to jump. We have to jump together. You know that.* His hands yanking my arm, pulling my shoulder until my body follows over the edge into free flight... into free-fall.

"It must have been heavy work, freeing the basket, Gina."

My hands, weak against the twisted hessian, hacking with a chisel until I hook a rope and force it over the iron stake. My heart, hammering as I run to the next and then the next as the basket rocks and nearly knocks me over. The scrabble over the lip as it almost gets away from me. My fist, punching that button. The roar of gas is deafening, the field, shrinking until all I can see is a toy-town, a refugee camp I have escaped from. Glaring, alone, drifting higher and higher and further and further away from the only person who can save me. I nod.

"I don't think anyone else was with you in that basket, were they, Gina?"

The howl is only air caught in the wings of the angel above me, surfing on the thermals before it swoops to scoop me up. I open my eyes. The sky is black and empty.

Chapter Twelve

Home was beginning to look like a charity shop. When Beatrice walked into the bedroom she was surprised by how many black plastic bags she'd left on the floor, a quarter full of Ralph's clothes. It wouldn't do. Quickly, she opened the wardrobe and said, in response to the screeching door hinge, 'Hello, I'm clearing this stuff out now.' Refusing to press her face to the pile of laundered shirts that she lifted from the shelves, she whispered, "It's not you. You're not in there," and put them in the bag.

If this was madness, she didn't care. She just couldn't get on in all this mess. *For goodness' sake, Ralph,* she wanted to say. *What do you expect me to do?* The answer came back as it always had. *I don't need you to do anything. You're fine. It's fine.*

Tears she felt she couldn't afford to have right now stung her eyes. Better to be annoyed, so she banged around stuffing things in bin liners until his chest-of-drawers was empty too. Then she carted the bags that were full downstairs and dumped them in the porch.

Returning, she faltered at the entrance to the living room. Even from the hall she could see a thin coat of dust on the piano. Unless she closed the top the strings would become furred, but she couldn't move. Her bones seemed to have set in her body. She could feel her jaw inside her skin and the pulse in her head like a metronome ticking away the life left.

"Fine," she said, angrily. "It's all fine," and she picked up her handbag and stomped up the three flights of stairs to the attic.

This room had always been hers. It was where things that Ralph hadn't liked got banished to: her mother's antimacassars covering holes in the chintz bedroom chair; a poster advertising *A Hard Day's Night* that she'd begged from the cinema manager at the end of the run; a still-unopened trunk full of her childhood bits and pieces that should have been chucked out when her parents had gone into sheltered accommodation; a plywood, fifties coffee table with thin, pointy legs.

She placed her bag on it. It swayed, as it always did, and she hoped it wouldn't break, as she always did. She closed the door behind her, shutting out the hospital, Gina, even Ralph. He'd never been part of her life in the attic. She'd always felt so high up in her castle in the air, as if nothing could touch her, yet she'd not settled for any part of a day in here since Ralph had died.

She knew it was because being up here felt like a betrayal. But now, finally, lying back on the lumpy chaise longue, she wept, because being up here was so clearly not a betrayal. She wept because Ralph was not there to betray and because this house was just too big.

But as the tears began to lessen, it was not Ralph's, but Gina's white face that crept up on her. And a sense of guilt. Forced to acknowledge Tom's excess of lovers and dependents by the power of forty years' experience, the reality had smashed the girl's illusions to bits. And she – Beatrice, crying on a chaise longue above an empty house that echoed with dead people – was the one who was supposed to hold her up. Weighty with grief enough to imagine her own body crashing through the floors to the cellar, she could see the parallels. She talked to the dead just as Gina talked to imaginary people. Until Beatrice had slain them. Worse – she'd allowed herself to be sidetracked by Tom as if she was investigating a crime, and then led Gina to think that Tom had abandoned her because he believed their affair would kill Anita. Seamless as their session had seemed, the joints Beatrice had glued together glared up at her, fraying at every urge and intervention she'd made.

The point was, where had that left the poor damaged child? Unlike Beatrice, she had neither home, money, status or any inner strength. She had a year of illicit sex, a hard disk full of highly literate messages, a visit to the dead wife's grave on a summer morning and a tearful goodbye as a pair of horses cantered freely down a slope in the next field. And one Byronic sentence slick enough to bind and gag her for all time. No wonder she'd focused on Tom. Even Beatrice was left doubting which promise had come from whom.

Angry again, but on Gina's behalf, Beatrice grabbed a sheet of paper and wrote the sentence down.

Promise me you'll remember my promises.

Riddle enough to cast a spell and short-circuit the brain, leaving him plenty of time for a speedy getaway. She had to admire the twisted logic, but the guy was morally bankrupt. She'd met some smart people in Rampton but none so clever as to avoid being locked up.

I know what you're thinking. I know you see things the way

I do. No other idea could better have checked Gina's dissent. *I love you. Whatever happens, promise me you'll remember my promises.* Gina had referred to Tom as a magician, and the art of the magician was to make you look so closely at their left hand, you didn't notice what their right hand was doing.

But Beatrice saw Tom's right hand hypnotising Gina. Stroking her body until it craved for more. Driving her to a sacred site. Pointing out the sunlit grave of someone he had once purported to love while apparently transferring that love to her.

And to pull that off you'd need an avalanche of charm.

For the third time that week she was reminded of Aleister Crowley. Fat, ugly, bald Crowley who sounded, nevertheless, as though he'd never gone short of women. Beatrice put her laptop on her knees, switched it on, wrote "Crowley and women" in the search engine and found herself facing more websites than she could possibly read.

She glanced through. He'd even contracted syphilis, but no-one seemed to care. He'd pandered to women's vanity, was a skilful lover, hard to resist...

```
www.scarletoheteira.com
"…through my channelling, I have spoken to the
many women he loved and all of them agree that
the truth he spoke was never in question.
Crowley never pretended to be something he
wasn't and as to his humour… "
```

His humour? Of course. Beatrice replaced the word *women* with the word *humour*.

www.thewilltowomen.com
Humour was a vital part of Crowley's
personality: a great deal of damage was done at
Croyden, especially at its suburb Addiscombe,
where my Aunt lives. Unfortunately her house was
not hit. Count Zeppelin is respectfully
requested to try again. The exact address is
Eton Lodge, Outram Road…

Even this brief extract showed her that the man had been a comedian. Witty. Bald. Big-lipped. Yet the face that Beatrice saw as she reflected was not Crowley's but the face Gina had described over the previous weeks. She scrolled down:

www.arseonfire.com
"…*per vas nefandum* never put women off. Crowley
buggered them mercilessly while remaining
entirely plausible… "

In my limited experience women have the most powerful orgasms ever.
Tom.
Tom Hanson. She typed the name into the search engine.

www.tomhanson.co.uk
"…in particular, it is recorded here that Monah
Snot wants to draw attention to Tinaa Drogdad's
Ssemalina (the clue is in the misspelling) to

```
which he gives his full and gracious blessing
and for which he takes full credit. Thank God
you saw the light in the end, my darling. Hope
you didn't twist your neck too badly."
```

So this was him? Wearily, Beatrice realised that the light in the end was probably something to do with a backside and Monah Snot an anagram of Tom Hanson. She was just about to close the machine down when *Tinaa* resolved itself into *Anita.*

Anita? Even as she recoiled from giving this man any more of her time, Beatrice's heart lurched. *Tinaa* was Anita? The frigid virgin-child he couldn't bear to hurt? *Thank God you saw the light in the end, my darling.* Acid rose in her throat, as though Tom Hanson had whispered those words directly in her ear, about her personally.

That bad, eh? Focusing her mind on a single point she found, at the end of her own long tunnel, Ralph's smiling face.

"Yes. That bad," she said aloud as she tapped her legs and rubbed her arms to get rid of the sick feeling. "I blame you," she added, stamping on the floor, but she couldn't bring herself to say more. Whose arms would she fall into? What would be the point?

Instead, she looked at the promise in her lap and wrote beneath it: *Anita Drogdad.* Anagram of Grodad? Anita Grow-your-own-dad. Very funny, under the circumstances. Within moments she was leaning back, pencil in hand, as absorbed as a bachelor with a crossword. Goddard seemed more likely, and *Ssemalina?* Messalina. Of course. *The clue is in the misspelling.*

She searched it.

`www.observing.co.uk/review`
`Ship Of Fools, Islington``: Don't mess with`
`Messalina. Anita Goddard's one whore show a`
`triumph of feminist counter-culture. Over the`
`counter, under the counter or in her lady's`
`chamber, the scene against an offstage Cilla`
`demonstrates there can be more to putting it`
`about a bit than common prostitution.`

Beatrice blinked. Anita-the-virgin? Who didn't like sex? Just in time, she recognised the fascination dragging her into a black hole. Definitely time to end the wild goose chase. Relaxing into her seat she threw back her head, stretched her neck from side to side and raised her palms to the ceiling in supplication to nothing. *How is this going to help?* It wasn't. She told herself she'd stop. Just one more tap, to establish that Anita Goddard was a different Anita completely and dispatch her back to where she'd come from. So Beatrice checked. It took one minute to establish her out of date connection with Tom Hanson.

Anita-who-didn't-like-sex collapsed into a two-dimensional story she realised she'd believed without question. Now, staring into the middle distance, she saw that Anita-the-virgin could easily have been Gina's creation. Or Tom's.

The shift of perspectives left her disorientated and casting about for something solid, she remembered Tom's blog. That had seemed real enough – viciously real.

She clicked back through. Why would Tom *take full credit* for some kind of sex show starring his ex-partner?

She blew out her cheeks and took a metaphorical step back to touch the very edge of that overwhelming sense of being personally mocked. Was this the way Tom had made all the women in his life feel? That they were failures? If so, Anita could have been dancing around him trying to avoid his scorn for years. And now she was dancing like Mata Hari.

Her stomach turned but the digital evidence compelled her to keep trying to work out the story. If this was the real Tom Hanson, what could be more predictable than compulsive womanising, followed by vilifying the woman who had most recently and deeply met his sexual needs? She'd met so many like this – men who adored the pure, reviled the dirty; were addicted to the dirty and hated themselves for it, returning to the pure for absolution. Beatrice groaned as her head raced on. The story was ancient. Epic. Gina only a bit-part-player whose belief in her own primacy was too strong for her to see herself in context. An illusion Anita's existence would have ruined, hence Gina's almost obsessive sidelining of her. Because Gina would have to keep herself centre stage. Have to remain convinced of Tom's goodness or be eternally flayed by recurring shame at her own stupidity. So what would be more likely, when her inevitable dismissal had come, than that she'd fill the void with a gesture too dramatic to ignore?

And who seemed, literally, to have replaced her centre-stage now?

Her heart thumped and she leant back. None of this –

the rush of intrigue – the compulsion to pursue – felt as if it belonged to her. Her thoughts were swirling now. Contempt opposing desire, anger opposing terror in what seemed like a fight to the death. The urge to resolve them – by analysing the components of the muddle more and more as if feelings had a solution – felt unstoppable. Jumping to her feet, she walked across the floor, bit down on her knuckle. Anything to stop up the gaps where the raw feelings of the world seemed to be pouring through unchecked. *Really, Ralph,* she muttered, *I shouldn't be working.* The reply was typical: *Well of course you shouldn't, you silly sod, but at least you seem to know what you shouldn't be doing. So what should you be doing?*

She should be calming herself down. Talking to people who weren't dead, or fictitious, or mad as hatters. Forcing herself toward the more tangible concerns of the day, she checked her emails and found one from Corinne, sent only five minutes earlier, offering to take her to a show in return for the ballet. Beatrice fired back a reply with her telephone number on, asking Corinne, if she wasn't too busy, to ring.

The phone went almost immediately. "Hello?"

"Beatrice Samuels speaking," she answered smoothly.

"Hello, Beatrice. How're you doing?" Corinne sounded very surprised.

"Actually," said Beatrice, despite a powerful sense of her own transgression, "I could do with a bit of a chat."

"Ah," said Corinne, quick as a flash, "Talking about it? Seems to help."

And Beatrice found herself laughing. "Great. That's just what I need."

"Tell you what," said Corinne. "Have you got Skype?"

Within five minutes both women were smiling out of each other's screen, though Beatrice felt a bit manic. "I'm sorry about this. I just needed... to make contact with someone outside myself," she said.

"Well, you've just lost your husband so that's not surprising," Corinne shot back. "What's going on?"

Beatrice exhaled, long and hard, trying to backtrack. "Oh, I just need to touch base. I'm so senior, no one dares tell me to stop work and I don't want to but... taking on this girl who came out of the balloon is proving more... well, a bit more demanding than I expected."

"Jeremy tried to stop you. You seemed so confident." Corinne heard her own confidence. It sounded brash and brittle. Not like confidence at all.

But Beatrice grimaced. "Story of my life."

Corinne swallowed hard, wincing at the nonsense she heard coming from her mouth. "Sorry. Please – feel free to tell me all about it. It's a big privilege to be able to try, and I'll be holding confidentiality."

Beatrice just prevented herself from saying, *you mean, it's all in confidence*, before forcing herself to say instead, "It's fine. I just wanted to... " She paused, rubbing her cheek softly up and down. "Most of all, the work is generating a response in me that's getting in my way... " She dropped her gaze "...Yes... " she said, eventually producing the word like a surfacing diver might wave a pearl, "...I feel ashamed." Immediately, Beatrice regretted speaking. What on earth was she doing, using the girl she said she'd mentor to investigate her feelings? Corinne would be bound to interpret a professional awareness of psychic processes as a request for sympathy.

But Corinne did not. She frowned. She paused for half a minute, but then she looked straight at Beatrice and said, "So, if we talk psychologically – the girl, Gina, feels full of shame but doesn't know it. So the shame invades you. Clouds your mind. Shuts you up." She took a huge breath in. "And then your own sense of confusion feels like failure. Sort of feeds it. So that would be, whadya call it... countertransference anyway – probably." Taken aback by her own daring, her face fell. "But you know that. Of course."

Her clarity left Beatrice deeply impressed. This girl, hardly a woman, was able to be completely present and think dispassionately about what was in front of her. Beatrice grinned at the face on the screen. "Corinne, never underestimate how helpful it is to have things spelled out."

Excitement burst from Corinne. "You mean I'm right?" Warmth spread from her centre, covering the desk she sat at with an aura that seemed to roll through the screen, as if her mentor's willingness to meet her in this internal world had melted the difference between them. More sober now and more grateful than she knew possible, she said, "I would really like to know more, if that's OK?"

"What – you mean the writer, his lover and now including his girlfriend, the actress?" And Beatrice told Corinne of Gina's obsession with Tom and how contagious it was. "But I don't know anything about him. It's not him I'm working with. Still – contagion," she added, attempting to assert her authority, "is clearly something that you can anticipate and are starting to make sense of."

Corinne nodded. "I'm – well, I'm trying, but it's not easy. If you'd said what you felt in college they'd have said you weren't mature enough, so it's... "

Were these tutors really teaching their students to hide their feelings? Even from themselves? Silencing their experience instead of learning how to accept and use it? Beatrice kept her face straight and said, "A good counsellor should have empathy and when she feels what the patient feels, she should know what to do with it. It's a clue – an essential clue about what will be helpful. It's just that we sometimes don't recognise it as such and become muddled or taken over."

Corinne nodded, but she was shocked. OK, so students might have that problem, but Dr. Samuels wasn't supposed to be 'taken over', was she? She felt disappointed.

But Beatrice was positively breezy. "I'm overloaded and that's made me confused. It's partly because the role I have here and the one I have at Rampton are completely different. One's about confirming or discarding a theory while the other requires me to accept a patient unconditionally. There, I'm being a forensic psychiatrist looking at the big picture, not an open-hearted facilitator of one person, but I'm not keeping those approaches separate. It's probably not helping that Jeremy passed my day-to-day responsibilities to Dr. Robinson, so I've got far more time than I should have. I'm flooded with an idea about what's gone on and I'm struggling to keep my focus."

"At the moment," Corinne insisted, because whatever else was going on in this mad, upside down Skype call, it wasn't her mentor's incompetence. If Dr. Samuels was fallible, her capacity to see that seemed more relevant than any amount of pontificating theory. What was needed here was – well, *unconditional positive regard* – a term at the core of her training. A term she'd thought applied until a patient got something 'wrong'. She'd never quite seen so clearly that sometimes you could go on accepting the 'wrong' while the 'right' worked its way through. "At the moment," she said, again, because it was supportive and positive. Because she trusted Dr. Samuels, and that meant that everything that was happening could be deepened in service to an answer that would work itself out. Was this stuff really that simple?

"Thank you," said Beatrice, feeling relieved. "That's such a help. It very much is 'at the moment'." Still, something didn't feel right. "But… "

"But… "

Beatrice winced. "Well – that aside – when I looked, later, at the way Gina had already had her world destroyed by this man, I have to admit, I'm not sure I didn't go too far."

"Have to *admit*?" said Corinne, sensing for the first time, both Beatrice's vulnerability and her pain. "Sounds like *your* world turned upside down. Just like Gina's?"

Beatrice narrowed her eyes. "Very good. You know, you could go far. I mean, I can usually deal with this sort of thing standing on my head, but… " She watched Corinne's face soften.

"But things aren't usual, are they?"

No they weren't. Not usual at all. Beatrice stared at the black, scuffed surface of her coffee table. What she was doing now certainly wasn't. Things would never be usual again. She looked at the girl in front of her, the girl she'd thrown in the deep end, and saw that these depths were no stranger to Corinne. Pretending they weren't there would hardly make her the therapist she so clearly longed to be. She smiled. "How about you? This isn't usual for you either, eh? And not what you expected."

"I'm fine," said Corinne. "I'm sort of... filling with new stuff, but it's all good. You seem... well, you seem surprisingly fine yourself, considering you're not. And really... " she had to say it, "is it going too far to add in some real world facts when you've got a patient who needs to get to the truth? I know you're old school, but people need to know that there's more going on in this world than their own psychology."

"Well, you must tell me if you'd rather stop," said Beatrice, professional again. "I have other people I could go and talk to. It's just – well – maybe seeing what's happening to me, from the inside, might knock me off the pedestal you've probably got me on."

But far from the pedestal losing its object, Corinne felt as if she'd been allowed round the back and seen the bolts, the paint drips and the way the base was dug, foursquare, into the earth beneath. "Actually, I'm more in awe than ever," she said, reflecting. "But I feel loosened up. Not scared that what I say might lead to some terrible punishment. Go on," she offered.

"Well you're right. It won't." Everything Beatrice had been ploughing through came back to her then, and with it, that self-satisfied picture of Crowley. Liberated by the strength and confidence before her she said, "Now that I've looked into the ex-girlfriend, Anita, I'm thinking more about Gina's circumstances – the similarity, the element of sexual performance, and if I'm right about this man Tom, Gina's only on the sidelines." The detail poured out of her. "And since our recent discussions about Aleister Crowley, I'm finding he's in my head too. It's all surprisingly dark and tangled." Perhaps that was why, of all people, it was Corinne she'd rung.

But Corinne's face elongated on the screen, her chin hitting the bottom and her forehead the top, and for a moment Beatrice believed the force of her words had somehow wreaked destruction. Overwhelmed with regret, the face seemed to her certain to disintegrate and the screen to go black, but it righted itself almost as fast as it had gone wrong.

Still, Corinne looked haunted. She stayed looking haunted. "People will do anything to avoid being nothing," she said. "They'll believe the most bizarre things if they're not strong enough to live without believing them." She paused and then added, sadly, "Nothing's impossible where loss of power and sex are concerned."

Although Corinne was referring to Gina and Anita, Beatrice heard a statement so true about both Corinne and herself that the screen, the time and the space between them disappeared. She reached out, touching the glass, rubbing it, cold beneath her finger. "It's weird," she said, almost to herself. "It's very weird."

"OK," said Corinne, nodding from another room again. "It is weird, Dr. Samuels. It's weird when you don't know what's real and what's not." She found she was holding the edge of her desk so tightly that the crescents of her thumbnails had gone white. Crowley. He was under her thumbs now. She would break them if she had to, to squash him and keep those feelings from creeping up her arm. Life or death. Broken thumbs were nothing.

But Beatrice couldn't respond. She only knew that what she'd said was so wrong it couldn't be righted. *Crowley?* She'd tried to escape something but instead, she'd opened a door and now she was contaminated and must leave, immediately so she reached for the button, saying, "Sorry. I'm so sorry... "

And Corinne shouted, desperate now, "Well it's just shame, Dr. S. You've got it. Now I've got it. Whatshername – Gina's got it. That actress – Messalina... well, what's in a name? It's a bloody plague where everything you say sounds stupid and unforgivable. Where you can't speak for hearing yourself scorned. Believe me, I know."

"I'm... I'm all over the place," said Beatrice. Recognising the disintegration as her own, she clung to the only sense she could make of it. "But I shouldn't be talking to you about this, of all people. Shouldn't be dragging you through... "

"Well, shame's probably easier than bloody grief, isn't it?" Exasperated, Corinne's eyes filled with tears of frustration. "It's grief that's driving you mad, Dr. S. Not some arsehole fuckin' people over." She'd shocked herself now and covered her mouth with her hand, but both words and gesture made Beatrice laugh and they sat for several minutes, laughing and crying and shaking their heads. "Whatever gets you through the night," said Corinne, eventually. "Making up stories. Maybe even feeling ashamed." The thought was a new one. She paused before leaning towards the screen. "And that doesn't mean you're not onto something that actually matters. Who knows? What's that book? The one with the wardrobe where they don't believe their sister. Narnia. That's it. And they all say she's mad but then they go and see this wise old bloke and he gets them to... er... think about it – because they don't actually know how to do that. Think properly, I mean."

A smile spread across Beatrice's face as the story offered an alternative. She cleared her throat, sat up straight and pretended to stroke a long beard, before saying in a deep voice, "So before your sister said that she entered this country through the back of a wardrobe, would you have said she was prone to lying? Has she ever shown signs of madness?"

"That's the one," responded Corinne, relief making her rush her words. "If she's not lying and not mad... we must assume, 'til we know more, that she's telling the truth. You know it!" she added. "So that's what I'm saying. What he says. Do it like he does. We should follow that... " she broke off.

"Logic," laughed Beatrice. "And I think you should probably start calling me Beatrice."

"Logic. Yeah, that's it. You should follow your instincts... Beatrice," said Corinne. "Find out more. Let's go there." Beatrice heard her tapping at the keyboard.

Corinne had entered *Anita... sex... prostitute...* in the search engine and the result came up immediately. "Blimey. It's at the *Ship Of Fools*," she exclaimed. "Have you ever *been* to a pub like that?"

"I don't know," said Beatrice, shaking her head. The thing seemed crazy now. A dream blown into the life of the world around them. She put her laptop on the wobbly coffee table, plonked her elbows in front of it, let her chin fall onto the bridge she made with her hands, and released a long sigh.

"Is that relief I'm seeing?" Corinne asked.

Beatrice glanced up at the image of her face in the inset subwindow that relayed Corinne's viewpoint, but saw only the top of her head, sparsely grassed. "Thank you, Corinne," she said, moving back into the frame.

"I'll take you," said Corinne, one loud tap confirming that the tickets were still out there. "Why not? *Ship of Fools. Upper Room, Upper Street...* Sunday. Yes?"

"*Messalina!*" grinned Beatrice, clapping her hands on her head.

"...pulls it off," laughed Corinne.

*

The elation from her conversation with Corinne rapidly gave way to exhaustion. Aching, Beatrice stumbled downstairs, put on her pyjamas and slid under the chintz eiderdown, but the darkness, when she switched out the lamp, brought her fully awake. She felt sure that if she switched it on again, a face would be just in front of her, nose-to-nose. Her mother's? Her father's? Ralph's?

If only, she thought, beginning to drift. Fear of ghosts was like paranoia, wasn't it? The fear of being followed a defence against understanding that no one actually gave a shit about you. So for her, the fear of the ghost was better than the pain of facing the reality that she would never see her loved ones again. She opened her eyes and closed them, opened and closed them. Was seeing a face better than facing the loss?

When she woke an hour later, the dark held not a glimmer. She reached for Ralph and when she couldn't touch him, shuffled across the bed, trying to. At the very edge and knowing now that he wasn't there, her hand still felt for him. The cold black plastic of the bin-liner she touched became a bodybag with the curve of something hard concealed there.

Ralph's head.

Two in the morning and the rest of the night lost to grief. Great, swamping rollers that knocked the breath from her and produced an undertow that dragged her, without mercy, across the jagged ground of all things. Surfacing, gasping at last for relief only brought a brick-blow to her head. Down she sank. She would never feel him hold her again.

So that was the face she'd been so afraid of. The one so close up, she couldn't see it. And now she couldn't get away from it. She switched on the light, hugged her knees, stroked her cheek and blew her nose, saying kindly to herself, *come on now*. She saw the cycle of her thoughts – the, *I'll never see him again* – kick-start the howling, and knew that if she could avoid thinking the words, she might stop. So, in the end, truth *was* to become a convenience, was it? She searched out T.S.Eliot from its place at the bottom of the pile on the bedside table, but the thin leather-bound volume smelled of a past she had spent with Ralph. Of Cambridge dinner parties and civilisation. Of a small, privileged world they had willingly sheltered in together, aware of its value. And its fragility.

She couldn't stay in bed. She reached into the bin-liner, past the hard-leather washbag to the soft stuff jammed down the side, and pulled out some paired grey hiking socks the size of a small cat. Wrapping the eiderdown around her, Ralph's socks slouching at her ankles, she padded down to the kitchen. Wet from tears, her pyjama top had chilled her chest and the cold had spread, making her shiver, but she smiled as she put the heating onto twenty-four hours. Illicit. Indulgent. *Put a jumper on!* But Ralph would have approved. They would have agreed and been bad together.

She gripped the banister on the way back upstairs until she passed the bedroom and made it to the top of the house. The ill-fitting doorknob rattled in her hand. She expected to be met by a blast of cold air but the attic room was still warm, like a nest.

In the circle cast by the standard lamp – a soft light from a velvet shade – she propped herself up on the chaise longue. Here was love, shimmying above her in the fringe that swayed against the warmth of the bulb. As a child, staying with her grandmother, she would run her finger beneath this fringe for tens of minutes at a stretch just to watch it fall into line.

Beatrice covered herself with the eiderdown but couldn't bring herself to turn off the light. Drama still ticked in her, and without Ralph to tell, the bleak conclusions of the previous evening began to occupy her thoughts.

Best kept out in the dark where they belong, dodgy men, murmured Ralph.

She looked at the comforts that filled the small room. The poster, the table, the bedroom chair, the trunk in the corner, iron-bound, carted upstairs because mum had wanted it kept, half-torn labels still stuck to its mottled surface. What was actually in it? Some old exercise books? A couple of threadbare teddies? A great mystery. In code. And a map. Unlikely, unless she was a boy. Try again. Her mother's wedding dress, embroidered with pearls, now yellowed with age – but inexplicably torn down the back. Beatrice giggled and, boiling hot now, shoved the duvet aside and crawled across the floor.

The buckles fell to dust in her hands, she thought. They didn't, though the leather on one of the straps was so stiff she had to flex it until it broke. *She flung back the lid.* No, she didn't, because the hinges had seized and juddered open, powdering the contents with rust. Still it felt... exciting. Humming quietly to herself, Beatrice settled on her haunches. What would she find? She lifted a very old, folded paper bag from the top that she knew contained her crumbling christening robe, put it aside and there they were, in two piles, taking up a third of the space.

Bunty. Every Tuesday Price 4d.

Squatting on the worn rug, holding that spent joy in her hands, Beatrice started crying again.

The sequence in front of her was complete. Every Bunty from May 1958 to September 1960 promised that next week (probably) the reader would be released from their three-bedroom semi onto the stage at Sadlers Wells or Wimbledon

Centre Court or even the throne room at Buckingham Palace. In this secret, parallel life, she had won the Nobel prize, discovered a shield for radiation and been crowned May Queen, all within fifteen pages.

And that was the great hope. Bunty's hope. Beatrice smiled, remembering. That was the whole story: a girl in need of a future finds a trunk unopened for fifty years. And in the trunk she finds a comic with a story in it about a girl who finds a trunk. Probably in the attic. Life as cliffhanger to string girls along until what happened? She looked at the bottom of the pile. Until September 1960 happened. She'd have been fourteen that year. Growing breasts she wanted to show off but was supposed to hide. She turned the comics over. No cut-out wardrobe in the 1950s. No starter bras. Just a page of badges printed in sequence around the words, LOOK! IS YOUR SCHOOL BADGE HERE?

She flipped through the pile, chose two from the bottom and was soon back on the chaise longue. Moira Kent, the Principal Ballerina at the Globe Ballet Company, had pointy breasts above a Scarlett O' Hara waist and a New Look full skirt. And gloves. It was impossible to know how old she was, beyond being very definitely GROWN-UP. Margie, the Swimming Marvel, on the other hand, had no breasts at all but came closest to what Beatrice remembered from the issues of Bunty she'd seen in the library. Margie had a sadistic teacher who made her lift weights with her feet until she passed out, but instead of the teacher being an evil woman, the coach was a man and the injustice was spotted by her father. Peg of the Peaks was an older girl, with a sheepdog, but she always wore jodhpurs and jumpers and her breasts were invisible until she was rescued (because the car broke down) by a boy. Peg was seen last in a dress, smiling at him.

Beatrice knew she was enjoying herself when she heard the door click, just slightly, and Ralph, saying as he left, *Good girl.*

'On she pored,' Beatrice thought. No-one pored over things these days. They studied or they concentrated. Strange word, *pored.*

She turned the page to *The Four Marys* and found herself ludicrously pleased to see them. *The Four Marys* were what her niece would have referred to as a *legend*. And with good reason. They'd still been going when her sister had got *Bunty*, which must have been a good eight years after her. Mary Cotter (plaits), Mary Field (sporty), Mary Radleigh (posh Earl's daughter) and Mary Simpson (scholarship girl from the council estate) were the firm friends who never grew up. Prototype Spice Girls, they pooh-poohed class barriers and they shared a study, which had always seemed the height of sophistication. With Dr. Gull (Headmistress) and Miss Creef (in her gown) as role models in an all-female world, they outwitted any man who underrated them. And they had breasts. Irrelevant breasts behind solid school jumpers and shirts buttoned right up to the neck.

Sleepy now, she picked up another comic and opened it at *The School In a Class By Itself.* Sally Winter, a happy fourteen year old, is determined to find out the secret of exclusive Cradwell College – where all the pupils behave like robots – so pretends to be hypnotised herself. Janice, the Professor's suspicious assistant, jabs the palm of Sally's hand with an enormous needle.

This girl was trying to trick us, Professor. She was conscious and cried out with pain when I pricked her.

As she is dragged into the laboratory, smart Sally picks up a letter opener and heroically slices her hand open to make it look worse than it is.

I've warned you against violence before, Janice (says the Professor). Only the deepest hypnosis would prevent pain from such a cut, but one minute under the eraser ray should remove all her memories of the last hour.

Something about the two huge straps with which they tied Sally's body down set Beatrice tingling. Blood pulsed to her genitals – a masochistic response, for sure. Or was it sadistic? Wasn't she identifying with the Professor? When the possibility of masturbating crossed her mind, she giggled at the incongruity of wanking over a girls' comic in a world awash with hard porn. But that led her thoughts to *Messalina*, and her body wilted.

She turned her attention back to where the physically immobilised Sally lay while the Professor used the raygun to wipe her memory. *That's more like it,* thought Beatrice, getting back into the spirit of the thing, and seeing at once that whatever delicious penetrations the father-like Prof might have visited upon her, Sally would be cleared of all charges. She would remain the innocent schoolgirl, never the whore, because of her purity and her powerlessness.

No wonder people felt confused. Beatrice yawned, snuggling into a daydream where things were being done to her, but was jolted awake by a memory of her mother yanking together the seams at the neck of her school shirt: a silent communication that deep down, Beatrice was asking for trouble. To a girl proud of her new breasts, she thought, a mother's fear might seem that way.

Listening to the rain, she considered turning off the light and realised too late that the brightness couldn't be stopped; the day had come and a man was climbing through the window. Beatrice's single bed shook as he landed on the floor. She watched, fizzing with anticipation, but he ignored her, headed straight for the corner and leaned over the trunk. She felt her heart twirl in a cavity of ribs. Bad, that heart. Black as coal. It would have to be hacked out in chunks with the cheese knife. Cooked chunks, like the liver her mother served up on a Wednesday. She saw herself laid out on the dining room table ready to get her just desserts; watched as the diners shook the crumbs from their napkins and the mice pattered around her. Waited, as the tablecloth rotted.

She woke, still sitting. Emptiness pulsed through the room and she remembered the man she'd been waiting for in her dream, and how he had never arrived.

She managed to turn off the standard lamp before slumping back, but the room continued to brighten. She closed her eyes, thinking of Wendy and Peter Pan, but saw again the man who had climbed in the window: fat-backed, suede-headed. Something about the jacket he wore – green and shiny – shell-suit cheap – was familiar. Hunter.

Huntley. Ian Huntley. Murderer of two ten year old girls who'd made too much noise when he'd grabbed one of them. She could see his eyes as clearly as when they had sat opposite one another in that interview room. *Poor me.* Sure. My heart bleeds. And she saw again that hardened heart with the forked tip of a cheese knife stuck in it.

No use trying to sleep now. What time was it? 7.00 already? She needed to get up, get out, retire. Because she'd spent too much time working with monsters. With the kind of men who suffocated little girls and dumped their bodies in muddy streams and then pretended to look for them.

Her years of experience weren't enough. Nothing could be enough. Ralph had been her buffer, keeping her safe, separate, sane for years and years, and now that he wasn't she had men creeping through the bedroom window of her dreams. Violent men, trawling through her psyche as if it were a filing cabinet where they might find a folder to belong in. She was living in unprotected space, a space she no longer felt intrigued by. She just felt scared. Watching the mysteries of the unconscious had fascinated her as a young doctor. Then, she'd rushed towards her dreams, even her nightmares – had to get Ralph to sleep in another room sometimes so she could 'explore'. With no Ralph around, she felt the contents of God knows what rushing towards her.

She no longer knew what 'normal' or 'all right' was. She needed to talk to someone because she couldn't get rid of the picture. The two little girls in their red football shirts. One fair, one dark, smiling together into the camera. What stories did they have in their heads? Eraser rays. Olympic medals.

Bad men who would never get away with it. The stories of ten year olds. And then no story. No redemption. Just the moment before it happened.

She couldn't keep looking where she was looking because there wasn't anything to look at. Forcing herself to rise, she picked up her laptop and made her way down to the kitchen, where she settled at the table and turned it on.

The envelope symbol flashed blue in the corner of the screen. Internal mail. One quick click and:

```
Attn> Dr.B.Samuels@stmand.int
Dear Beatrice,
The new multi-agency initiative has left me with
6 boxes of police files on the balloon incident.
All you need to know is that 10000 witnesses saw
only one person fall or jump from the balloon.
Sir Paul McCartney has decided not to press
charges. It seems pretty clear that the vehicle
was stolen as a random act by a single
individual. Obviously, this has implications for
Paul M's security but I hope it's helpful for
you to know notes are unlikely to be requested
for a court hearing,
Let me know if you need anything,
Best,
Jeremy
```

Well, at least that cleared up some of the confusion. Perhaps her forensic explorations with the stones hadn't done so much damage after all if they'd clarified the outcome: no mad murderous attempt. No new-age love levitation. No ultimate sadistic act. Probably. At least, not from Macca's best balloon. Just a badly hurt girl who'd been too far up to come down quietly.

Chapter Thirteen

The pavement outside *The Ship Of Fools* was deserted except for the occasional couple arriving for the performance: a pair of grey-haired women, intensely involved in a loud conversation with one another; a man and a woman, not communicating as they brushed the drizzle from their coats before going straight up the narrow stairs.

When, ten minutes later than arranged, Corinne saw Beatrice push open the heavy door to the downstairs saloon, she felt guilty for inviting her. If the dynamics of inner being were Beatrice's territory, this was Corinne's, and she had strategically arranged herself on a barstool in a tight dress of corseted purple velvet.

"I'm so sorry I'm late."

"It's fine," she said, brightly pushing a single gin in a glass and a bottle of tonic along the polished bar.

Beatrice strode across the sticky carpet and kissed Corinne on both cheeks. "Dahling. If I'd known the place was a burlesque I'd have worn one of Ralph's dinner suits."

"You'd have looked good in it," said Corinne, impressed.

A sleepy barmaid in drag blinked a half-hearted welcome and pushed up a pair of salmon-coloured breasts until a cleavage peeked from her basque. "Ice and a slice?"

At the far end of the bar, two men – one in a black sou'wester and PVC coat, the other in smart jacket and tie – dandled their pints beneath half-lowered lids. *Modern-day cowboys*, thought Corinne, sensing sawdust. She handed the drink to Beatrice, saying loudly, "Such a shame you didn't. I could've been your moll."

The jacketed man looked around, tipping up his chin until two people shrinking at a table beneath a smeary window could no longer ignore him. He gnashed his teeth into a smile. "We don't bite, you know. Not on a Sunday." The couple smiled back, lips tight, and made a show of looking at their watches before they bustled out of the bar.

He jerked his thumb after them, speaking to Corinne and Beatrice. "They're for her upstairs. Anyone would think it had never been done before."

Alert now, the barmaid huffed, "You wouldn't see this lot dead here on a Tuesday when people are pissing across the stage into the mouth of the lovely Jemima." She gestured towards an oversize photograph of a pair of red lips adorning the wall.

"*Or* when Topper and Springs are hanging from the ceiling," interjected the nodding sou'wester. Bounce, bounce, bounce.

Beatrice sniggered and the barmaid softened. "So, what about you then, my loves?"

"Voyeurism, plain and simple," said Corinne.

The man in the jacket raised his eyebrows with his pint. "I wish you joy of that."

Corinne raised her empty glass back at him, but a kerfuffle at the half-opened door distracted them. It banged shut, then opened again several times as people peeked in and withdrew. She gracefully extended her palm towards the barmaid. "I think you might be the main entertainment here."

"Probably better than the MPhil in *Recreating The*

Wheel With a Thesaurus Jammed up your Arse." People were tramping up the stairs now, making the panelling on the adjacent wall vibrate. "They'll be in here soon enough once it's finished. A couple of tequila slammers and they'll all be mouthing off. I'll say that much for her, she knows how to play 'em." The barmaid cocked her head and pointed up. "Catch Bacchus for a double before you go in. You'll need it." She shook her arms until the bangles fell above her elbows.

"Scandalous," squeaked PVC man.

"And he doesn't mean the sex," added his partner.

The tannoy system crackled. "Tarts, call-girls, strumpets, harlots, whores, punks and trollops. Please come upstairs." Instead of a bell, the rhythms of *The Stripper* sirened across the empty pub.

The barmaid mock-yawned. "It's part of her script."

"*We're* part of her fucking script," said the man in the jacket, bitterly.

Corinne and Beatrice rose from their seats and made their way to the foot of the worn staircase where Beatrice bought a programme for three pounds. As Corinne handed over the tickets, she found her way barred by an arm.

"Vestal Virgins?" enquired a man in a toga, though the Roman effect was offset by the fascinator dangling in front of his eyes.

"You are feeling sleepy," said Beatrice, hypnotically.

"Anywhere but the front row," he responded, in a voice camp with disapproval. Obviously they'd got off lightly, because as they walked up the stairs, Corinne heard him say gruffly to the people following, "and keep your knickers on, please. This is a one-whore show."

They took a left and found themselves queuing for a trestle-table that shook every time a plastic cup was slammed down to make it fizz.

Corinne made an exaggerated sucking sound and waggled her fingers.

"Are you sure? On top of all that gin?" asked Beatrice.

"Oh, not for me. I thought it might just get you in the mood."

"Oh, it will, darling," said a little round man with a beard made of grapes. Apart from a white fissure between his big and second toes, his feet were separately encased in black shiny plastic up to his hairy ankles. "A little of what you fancy." And he grabbed Corinne's arse with his podgy hand.

She responded by squeezing his beard in her fist until purple juice spurted down his stomach.

Beatrice laughed as the people who slid past her tutted. "But it's a Bacchanalia," she remarked, "isn't it?" Leaving Bacchus to clean himself up, Corinne shepherded her into the upstairs room. The sound of their giggles shrilled against the quiet, concentrated space of the temporary theatre. A pair of women glanced up and frowned above the loops of their elegant silk scarves. "Bloody hell," whispered Corinne, spotting two empty seats in the middle of an otherwise full row. They teetered through, but not without disturbing a woman absorbed with a notepad.

The lights faded. The room became silent. Even the exit signs went out. No one made a sound. They waited, peering into black until a woman's voice rasped:

"Alone, we are not enough. Bounded by our skin, we

chafe and we push to be free, and in our pushing, try to squeeze through pores too small."

Pinpricks of light lit the silhouette of a figure sitting on a stool. No longer amplified, the voice continued. "Alone, I contort what is not me into womanish form." The voice became a wail. "I try to reach the Godhead but past lives hold me in restrictive shapes."

"Bastards!" hissed a woman from the back of the audience.

But the images that began to flash across the backdrop were not of men. A projection of Elizabeth 1st was followed by one of Elizabeth Taylor, which melted into Cleopatra, then Buffy the Vampire Slayer and Mary Magdalene. A picture of Madonna exploded into a flash of white. The PA rumbled and as the lights came up, dressed from head to foot in a red sequinned dress so tight it might have ended in a fishtail, Anita beamed from her stool.

She opened her arms. "Welcome," she said. "WELCOME," she echoed, lifting the microphone from the stand. Wondering whether Anita was about to shed her skin, Corinne swallowed and coughed, while Anita boomed, "This show is about letting go into the All. You've heard this called a one-whore show. You've been labelled tarts and trollops... "

Corinne glanced at the people around her. The woman with the notepad was chewing the end of her pencil.

On the stage, clouds scudded across the backdrop followed by images of meadow and mountain, city and motorway. Flowers thrust up from the earth, petals fell, stems withered to the trills of a flute with a tribal backbeat.

Lit by a bright spotlight, Anita said, "This is an opportunity to taste your power. To sense that power that is your birthright. A power that can be harnessed. I myself needed money and a place to live – within a week of focusing this energy, I was working and living in a massage parlour."

Corinne wondered if she'd heard right, but when she saw Beatrice biting her lips, she bit at her own thumbnail in sympathy and they stared at each other nervously.

Anita had slipped from her stool and moved to the front of the small stage to pick up a red sequinned top hat held out by someone in the front row of the audience. Placing it on her head she leant down, took a whip from the floor and cracked it. The word CONTROL flashed behind her. She cracked the whip again. It flashed. She cracked, it flashed. When Anita began to rap, the women in the front row stood. Initially, Corinne thought they were naked, but as they climbed onto the low stage, she saw that they wore body-stockings. Obscenities fell from Anita's mouth as she rhymed *fuck* with *suck*, *go* with *blow* and with each crack of the whip, the women moved robotically and violently to the orders of their ring-mistress.

What had she been expecting? Something amusing, Corinne realised. Some entertaining subversion of what usually passed for soft porn. She turned to Beatrice, who was watching, bug-eyed. They reached for one another's hands. The word changed to POWER as Anita shouted, too loudly:

> *You can keep that body still*
> *Or you can use love, under will.*

A mass of glitter twirled from the ceiling. The women fell to the floor of the stage, but Corinne had stopped watching, her head struggling to absorb what she'd just heard. "Fuck! Crowley. It's Crowley," she said, pulse thudding like a lorry revving its gears.

Anita was in full swing now, hat in one hand, whip in the other. Whether the audience was speechless out of awe or alarm, she had their full attention. "There's a secret, of course," she said. "A heavy karma attached to sex. As we grow, our fear and longing for safety hardens into an expectation. Where we had love, where we had flow, we become uptight controllers who never stop demanding." She paused. "But I also discovered that if things get really intense that way, an over-attached atmosphere can be diluted by having others witness the act? The inter-coursing? Then it becomes possible for a full disregard of the self – the emotional self. Then we can take the energy for ourselves."

"It's OK," whispered Beatrice, and Corinne felt the hand that was apparently clinging to Beatrice's being squeezed, tightly. "We can... "

"Suck on mine," shouted an educated voice, from behind them.

"Howabout you suck on mine, baby?" Anita shouted back. "It's not about domination. It's about choice. It's about... " She cracked the whip one more time and behind her a phrase lit the screen:

DO WHAT YOU WILL

"Jesus," whispered a disbelieving Corinne. "Crowley's

fuckin' got her."

Beatrice put her arm through Corinne's and placed her hands, prayer-like, against her lips as together they watched Anita position the limbs of her co-performers and place them into couples: one facing towards the backdrop, one facing towards the audience. One couple groin to groin; one groin to bottom. The last couple she positioned so that one walked away while the other looked on. When Anita pulled her arm down hard, the beat stopped. Placing the back of her hand melodramatically against her brow, she howled,

"He betrayed me."

A spotlight shone onto a woman spreadeagled against the corner, wearing a bustier and stockings.

"The bastard," someone hissed from the back. At the same time, one of the couple facing towards the backdrop walked towards the woman and froze.

Peeking through her fingers, Corinne shrank into her seat. "I can't bear it," she whispered. Beatrice tried to stand, but could find no easy way out and Corinne waved her down, indicating to wait and to watch. The spotlight had swung back onto Anita, who had stepped out of the tableau and returned to her perch. "And that's so easy, isn't it? To blame?" She spoke without amplification, waiting while a few of the audience nodded. "To fail to see that we really make our own reality?" Her voice lifted at the end. "Where's the liberation in that? You know, I get it," she said, as though sharing a confidence. "Now, I get it. I had a low self-image. *My* self-image – maybe the only part of this affair in my own control. *My* self-worth was low."

As Corinne watched, bubbly Anita rubbished everything

a woman might need for the development of a healthy relationship. Where she could rightfully have blamed her faithless boyfriend for her difficulties, she insisted that she should have done or been something or someone else. Misery rose through Corinne until her blood felt thick. If this was a masterclass in how to cut your own throat, she couldn't have done it better.

"So if *I* was betrayed," said Anita, "if *I* was exploited, even, *I* have to take responsibility for what happened. Otherwise *I'm* not free to use the power at *my* very centre."

"I told you," Corinne whispered, eagerly, "I told you... there? She's... the mistake... self-image... We DON'T have control... " she managed.

Anita was talking about the *jewel in her crown, the object of real value,* while on the screen, something pink and moist shone like bubblegum. Anita's silhouette sharpened against the brightness as the shot skimmed the surface of whatever glowed behind her.

The audience had started fidgeting. Several people near the front gathered their coats and left. Others groaned. Whispers turned to a low, unbroken muttering. "It's her cervix," said Beatrice, indicating the exit again and looking worried, but Corinne shook her head, fixated by the image.

As Anita's breathing erupted into the microphone, more people stood and quietly excused themselves. Anita stopped. "Come on now, do this with me. All in it together in this safe space." She began again, drawing the breath up and in and out until the sound became a hum and the hum became a moan, Anita's body heaving as the performers settled cross-legged around her, their own bodies lifting and falling in concert. "*This* is the path," Anita pronounced. "The breath *is* the path to liberation. To the union of souls in the higher realm."

A bank of dry ice billowed up from the stage and rolled towards and around Corinne. Cold struck her windpipe. She coughed. Long and dry and hard. Other people were coughing. A woman rushed up the aisle with her hand over her mouth. Beatrice was pressing a tissue into her hand, unwrapping a sweet and asking if she was OK. She nodded. Took the sweet. Sucked on it until her horror became easier to stomach.

By the time the mist had dissolved and Anita had begun to lecture about the difficulties of 'dropping the ego' and how 'letting go of attachments was fraught with self-delusion', Corinne could see only random words, drifting, detached from any meaning at all.

"How do we distinguish true acts of liberation from mere simulation?" Anita asked, as if certain of her answer.

The lights dropped, Anita's shadow stretched monstrously behind her and the cervix was eclipsed.

"One sure way to tell the difference is when we know nothing is hidden."

To illustrate Anita's message, the shadow vanished and there she sat again – teacher, lover and girl-next-door. "When we know someone is spiritually available and open, we can go – or be taken, to higher levels – levels nine and even ten, where we can bring the soul home to its rightful place in the universe," she said.

"Does it go up to eleven?" yelled a voice. Alerted by the heckle, Corinne jolted upright, prepared for a fight, but

Anita only grinned, stood and turned round.

The spotlight zoned in on her bottom where the cleft of her buttocks peeked through a slit in her skirt. Shimmying, she bent, briefly pushing her arse tight against the shiny satin before turning back, flicking open the fan dangling from her wrist and saying, "What do you think?"

"Get your knickers off".

"Get your knockers out." Men they hadn't noticed before made gruff sounds of half-formed words. Some of them stood. Anita shouted, "So, perhaps we could all breathe? Perhaps that will take us out of 'basement desire', onto at least level one, where our feelings can be out in the open?"

Distracted by the action in her neighbour's lap, Corinne saw a reedy erection in a podgy hand. She nudged Beatrice hard and indicated the exit. Beatrice struck out, oblivious to who she pushed. Corinne barely had time to grab her coat before they were in the aisle.

Behind them, Anita had become persuasive and sexy. "Think of the show as an experiment in how to love differently, openly, without shame. An antidote. A shame-antic."

A lusty growl started at the back. Again, Anita flirted. "OK, boys. Take a quick break. Cool down. Get a few drinks. Then, I'm going to prove that it's possible to abandon oneself wholly to the experience, without my personality or my neuroses getting in the way."

Corinne and Beatrice slipped from the room, the jeers fading as they ran downstairs, burst through the swing doors and fell into a now cold, clear night where, speechless and side by side, they leant against the pub wall.

Eventually, Corinne said, "I think she's going to have actual sex in the second half. I think it's supposed to be 'experiential'."

"I'm afraid she is." Beatrice took Corinne's hand. "I should never have let you take me."

A bus thundered past. Corinne had to yell above it. "But what about you? You look like you're going to explode. I've never seen anyone move so fast."

Beatrice exhaled until her lips vibrated. "I just saw it, that's all," she sighed, pausing. "Well, I felt it. I had to stop feeling it."

"Felt what?"

"Her grief... my own grief? Maybe it's just grief. Impossible. Impossible... " The word tapered off. Beatrice shrugged. "That's why she's dressed up like that. Because she's a little girl and she has to hide it."

A little girl, thought Corinne, seeing herself. A little girl hiding behind make-up and high heels, trying, the best way she knew how, to find comfort.

In that room.

In that performance.

Several cabs swept by, shining like coal in the street lights. "Let's just go back to the bar," said Corinne. "You can have another gin and tonic. I'd have one myself but after that, nothing would stop me from being stone cold sober."

The brave few who had not stayed in their seats for the interval but made it downstairs were returning upstairs. As they passed in the corridor, she heard, "Yaas, its vey brave. Don't you think? Vey strong. Third wave, I'd say."

"Had enough?" asked one of the couple who were still at the far end of the bar.

For an answer, Corinne ordered a double gin and two bottles of tonic.

"You can't take those upstairs, you know," sniffed the barmaid. She'd renewed her lipstick. Corinne noticed a smudge of white above it.

Beatrice scrunched up her face, raised an eyebrow and slowly shook her head from side to side.

"Conscious coupling, unconscious coupling," said the barmaid, loudly inviting the others to join in.

"Conscious tie-up-your-partner-and-flog-'em," added the man still wearing his sou'wester.

"Conscious fisting," said his mate.

Beatrice grimaced. "That doesn't sound very good for you."

"It's not," said the barmaid. "That's why you get a fistula."

The door slammed. Bacchus stood gasping, the second half safely begun. "Seven fucking times, I've seen this now," he said, clasping his hands together to keep them still. "She's never going to climax unless she gets to the point and she's never going to do that while she thinks she's talking about sex. It's a canard. A duck's arse."

"But they'll all be in here, buoyed up with bullshit," interjected the barmaid to Corinne and Beatrice. "They see one show where someone dares to say 'hog-tying' and they think they've invented it. And people call *us* phony."

They took their drinks and moved to a couple of plush-covered stools at a small wooden corner-table where the words *Larry woz 'ere* had been scratched into the varnish. Beatrice placed her coat on the floor behind and pulled the programme from her handbag. On the front, a picture of Anita in her red dress beamed an invitation to sexual knowledge.

Sitting silently together both women sipped their drinks, but Corinne couldn't shake the sense that she was shrinking. At first, the inability to explain what was happening to her made her nervous and she would lurch towards Beatrice, sure she should be helping or clarifying or apologising. But every time she looked, she saw that Beatrice didn't need anything from her. That they could be together, regretting their outing, or Anita's performance, or the entire fucking muddle that people seemed to assume women's sexuality to be. This feeling didn't help for long and as soon as anything approaching calm arrived, cold replaced it, spreading from her centre. Cold violence that made her shake with fear. Then hatred. Then fear again.

Beatrice sat quietly beside her, but there was no ignoring Anita's performance. The bar downstairs was almost empty, quiet enough for the outbursts of clapping upstairs to interrupt the most profound of thoughts and remind both women of what had been promised. Music came and went. Laughter too, but when a studied yelping turned to longer and louder screams, Corinne drew Beatrice's attention to the programme on the table in front of her by jabbing her finger onto the words, *Sex magick.* "Can you... read it to me, please?" she asked.

"With or without irony?" said Beatrice, which made Corinne smile. She fished in her bag for her glasses. "It says...

We are indebted to Crowley for showing how to empty the sexual act of emotion and personality. Once women have freed themselves of emotional baggage, they are free to copulate as and when they choose."

"As opposed to what?" said Corinne, draining her tonic water. "Another?"

Beatrice nodded. "*Reichian Orgasmatrons*," she read, over a loud thud. "*Indigenous ancient cultures. Secret techniques*," she called after Corinne, who was already halfway to the bar.

As she returned with the refills, Corinne said, "I wonder how badly she needed money? Maybe that's why she's doing it?"

Beatrice shuddered and handed the programme to Corinne, talking to distract her from the sound of thumps above them. "It's all in here. A bunch of cliches reinvented by a global media for a new generation of women. Your generation, numbed by pornography and ripe for sensation." She shook her head. "This stuff used to be underground – that was partly what made it transgressive. Now you have to make an effort to avoid it. Why she's doing it... " she added, looking Corinne in the eye and holding her there, "is because she's in so much pain she has to find a way of being someone else. Of feeling more powerful."

"But she was going to get people to watch," wailed Corinne. "How can that make her feel powerful?" But she knew first hand how being seen could create a light so bright it could obliterate everything. And then, those eyes. She shut her own but couldn't stop the tears. "Sex between two people," she blurted, too loudly, but the words brought her back, "is *supposed* to be intense." Private. Sealed. Bonding. Wasn't it?

"I know," Beatrice soothed. "I know." She placed a protective arm on Corinne's shoulder. "This whole thing was an exercise in bad faith. Obviously."

The sudden silence from upstairs left Corinne desperate to make more noise. "Perhaps," she suggested, though she heard the speech garbled, like a woman drowning, "Once she found out about the affair, Anita decided that Gina was a whore?"

"As well as turning herself into what Tom appeared to want." Beatrice had downed a good deal of drink, but to Corinne she seemed reassuringly sane.

"So what's *hyper-orgasmic* in a *union forged beneath the banner of conscious sex*," said Corinne, reading over Beatrice's shoulder, "is sluttish fantasy if it's unconscious?"

"What does it say on the back?" asked Beatrice, sounding like a primary school teacher.

Impossible to miss, in large letters across two lines, both women read:

> *Do what thou wilt shall be the whole of the law.*
> *Love is the law, love under will.*

A tear fell down Corinne's cheek and Beatrice held out a tissue to dab it away.

"Do we all have broken hearts?" muttered Corinne. She shook her head with the weary, acceptance of someone who already knew the answer.

"Yes," Beatrice said, firmly.

"What we both need is... " Corinne held a finger in the air as if to summon the end of the sentence. "What we both need is more confidence." She smiled, peering into her glass and cocked her head. "And if I drank, I'd buy some, but as it is... " Standing up, she scraped back her stool so hard it fell onto the thin carpet. By the time she'd returned with two further bottles of tonic water and a gin for Beatrice, it was back on its legs. She nodded her thank you to two very straight-looking men who had appeared at the next table and who were now looking, with interest, at the pair of them.

"OK, sister," Corinne said, the drinks wobbling as she slammed them down. "So she was really going to have sex on stage in the second half?"

A burst of applause, cat-calls and stamping overhead appeared to confirm it. In the racket, the two men seemed to have shifted their stools nearer. Corinne sensed them eyeing the curve of her breasts and the stack of empties on the table. "That's what the audience were hoping for," she said directly to them. "They were hoping for it." Where had that come from? One minute she'd been steeped in a broken heart, now she was challenging these men to a confrontation. "Cheers." She clashed her glass against Beatrice's, saw herself angling for a fight with a couple of total strangers and shouting *mine*. The pub was filling up, marshalling itself into a noisy set ready for the scene where she leapt on the bar and started singing. This was The Fool's pub, they'd been on a fool's errand, and fools they were in danger of becoming.

She began to sweat. "I've got to get out of here," she whispered. People dressed in tutus were piling through the door. One giant of a man took off his coat to reveal an artificial phallus wrapped in lurex, a yard long. She felt suddenly flattened, sinking around the contours of her stool and into the folds of the curtain behind her. Everyone was shining, flushed with fun and drink among a sea of moving hands: opening, waving, lifting the rising excitement higher. Corinne clamped Beatrice's wrist in her own. "Please," she pleaded. "Now."

The hubbub grew as the corridor filled with people, some of them shoving their way into the bar. Leaving was impossible without pushing past bodies. Bottoms and breasts and men's private parts seemed poised to obstruct them. Shrinking as small as she could, she kept her eyes down and headed for the door and still she jogged someone's arm so that a third of his pint lurched in a wave down his hairy thighs. Intent on it being replaced, Bacchus was jabbing a fat, ringed forefinger at her when a roar of clapping and whistling heralded the entrance of Anita. Corinne and Beatrice could just make out bits of her tiny form through a gap between shoulders as people backed away. Blue jeans. Grey jumper. The woman was stick-thin and looking shyly around her, nodding a brief acknowledgement before heading to the bar. "She looks as if she's hardly there," shouted Beatrice into Corinne's ear, and whispered to herself, "She looks like Gina."

They stood for a while, watching the occupants of the pub divide. The regulars ignored her while the straight men kept their distance, as if biding their time. But some women pushed forwards. Winsome women, wearing hippy layers of chiffon and silk, with hair that looked as if it had never been cut. Girls, thought Corinne, lost girls trying to find a way home.

"So that's Anita looking normal?" said Beatrice, as Corinne pulled her through the crowd and out of the building. "She's so thin! I can't bear it," she muttered. "Let's eat."

Oblivious to the time, they walked quickly down a side-street, found a pizza place and without looking at the menu, ordered a twelve inch Al Pomodoro.

"And a bottle of water, please," added Beatrice, putting down the wine list. "You're not drinking, are you?" she asked.

But Corinne, her brain sharpened by fresh air, had lifted a breadstick from the jar and was already crunching it. "*Love under Will* – it's just... I've just... it's just clicked. You said this Tom bloke was a writer? – An artist? Well Crowley fancied himself the same. I said, didn't I, about Sex Magick? About it giving you power?"

Beatrice nodded, her face flushed, pupils huge in the dim bistro.

"Well – for it to work – actually work – you had to be properly involved – deeply involved. I told you that, didn't I?" Corinne searched for confirmation. "You couldn't pretend. The man's part in the sex had to be real. His belief in his Scarlet Woman – it had to be total. How else would you generate any heat?" Even in the low light, Corinne felt herself shrivelling as she paused, searching for the right words. "But the point is – and this was what fucked my head so completely – she had to believe too. Where the *will* part came in... "

"Go on." Beatrice said, gently. "If you want to. But don't... force... "

"No, no. Listen. The girl in the balloon – Gina. He set her up," Corinne urged. It seemed impossible to believe that Beatrice could understand, so she began to use both hands as a container for each thing she spoke of before depositing them in an invisible line along the table. "He made it so that heart, soul, body and mind were given to her and hers to him." Then she ran a finger round all four. "Totally. Completely, yes?" Corinne leaned forward, gazing into Beatrice's eyes until their noses were a foot apart. "You get merging. Surrender. You get passion. On every level. Heat generated in the head, in the sex, in the soul. That was the ideal. And then, BANG." Corinne clapped her hands together hard before parting them in an arc. "Like Crowley, he broke off the relationship. Completely. Went from total involvement to never having anything to do with the woman again. Love – but total love – *under* will."

Beatrice narrowed her eyes and lurched just slightly forward. "Well, love as he knew it, I suppose," she added.

"Yes, and when he tore away it must have been like splitting the atom. He took all that power with him." How could she not have connected this up before? How could she, Corinne, have not known that she'd felt like a piece of rubbish because that was exactly what she had been to them. *I will cast her out from men: as a shrinking and despised harlot shall she crawl through dusk wet streets, and die cold and an-hungered.* All animation had drained from Corinne's face now, leaving deep, bruise-like shadows.

"Yes, I get it," said Beatrice, her tone dull, and she opened her arms against the wave of despondency that had hit her. "I expect he used it to write some crappy book."

"Perhaps, somehow, he really did throw her out of the balloon. What would have more impact?" said Corinne, all fizz gone.

"Or be a more complete way of separating from someone?" added Beatrice, sounding defeated.

As if on cue, they both looked up to find the waiter waiting with a boxed pizza in one hand and a credit machine terminal in the other. All of the other tables had chairs upended on them. Beatrice handed over her credit card, the man whisked it through his machine and before a minute was up, they found themselves on the pavement outside, struggling to put on their coats.

Sucked into the emptiness that had opened up at the end of their search, Corinne felt exhausted. "So that's it then?" Her arms dropped to her sides. Had it only been a single evening – four hours that they'd spent together? She felt like a child on a treasure-hunt who'd chanced upon some illicit pornography only to find it repellent and devoid of either value or interest.

Beatrice offered her some pizza and said, through a mouthful of her own, "That was what?"

But Corinne pushed her hand away, asserting herself as if her life depended on it. "People are still doing this stuff."

"Not so hard to believe." Beatrice stopped. "Rampton's full of them." But she gave Corinne a hug, long and tight, and together they walked slowly to the underground to wait for the train to King's Cross.

Chapter Fourteen

I'm in the holiday kitchen in our toy-town home – nothing on show but some salt, a plastic orange squeezer and some crockery, which by the look of the dull, heavy teacups, has been there since the 1970s. By the cooker stands a very small electric kettle with a flex too short to plug in unless you place it on the fridge-freezer. Tom comes up behind me and presses me heavily against the work surface with his body, but I turn my head, smiling and pull open a drawer next to me. "Ooohh, look," I say. "Kitchen utensils."

"I'll bloody kitchen utensil you," he smiles, looking in the drawer at a small, blunt chopping knife, a tablespoon and a partially melted fish slice. He grabs the fish slice and waves it to and fro before my eyes. "You are feeling soft," he says. "Soft, soft. You are melting and have no volition of your own."

"I have salt," I say, grabbing the damp packet from the formica surface and brandishing it at him. He backs off, cowering against the microwave but I advance, staring at his darting eyes. All of a sudden he rushes at me, knocks me off balance and catches me before my full weight crashes onto the table, which wobbles.

"How disappointing," says Tom, as it sways beneath his fingertips. "My dastardly plan has been foiled."

"You mean you didn't want me for my cooking, sir?" I drop a curtsey and leap through a small archway into a room that runs almost the width of the house. Small latticed windows with iron handles look out just above ground, so that from the back the house seems built for children. I nip into the tiny bathroom and when I come out, Tom is leaning on the mantlepiece, waiting.

He leads me through a narrow door and up the stairs to the bedroom, bare but for a plain wooden chair, a double bed and a picture of the house itself on the whitewashed wall. He sits and slides his hands up my thighs, pressing his face into the chiffon of my summer frock, holding me firm, though I pull against him. Eventually he raises his head to look, puppy-eyed, as I smile down. "I have nothing for you but myself," he says and I kiss him lightly on the lips and walk round the foot of the bed to where the sun pours through a glass door. I push it open, walk onto the flat roof of our private verandah and lean over the balustrade. To my left, the bank behind the house veers up sharply until it's almost level with the bedroom floor, burying the bathroom and half the kitchen in the slate-dense earth. I can feel Tom creeping up behind me. He brushes his fingers lightly up my back and over my shoulders until they rest against my breasts. I could stand there forever, half in a mountain and half in the sky. I turn, astonished, to look at him.

"I could never love anyone more than I love you," I say. "You do understand that, don't you?"

"Yes," says Tom, "and you're so beautiful, I can't believe that you're not going to fly away. Don't fly away. Don't ever fly away." Tears brim in his eyes. He slips his arms tight round my waist and lifts me from the ground.

I have no words to explain, only the smell of his neck and the soft breeze as he carries me back into the bedroom. "Our first home," he says placing me down as he walks back towards the open door. I follow, laying my hand gently on his back, and he turns to face me. "And no, I don't want you for your cooking. I don't want to be cared for. Not like that... Listen," he says, stepping onto the rug. "I've been such a prat in the past. I want you to promise me that if I make a stupid decision, you'll stop me." He pauses. "I get these ideas sometimes and I just do them. I left Patricia to cope with the kids on her own for months because I thought I needed to go to college." He shakes his head. "And I was wrong. I don't want to get it wrong again. I really want this to work."

Although Tom is standing upright, I feel he's on his knees before me, his head bowed as he defers to something beyond, something that billows through me and in which I directly stand. I reach out with both arms and stroke down the sides of his clothes, the edges of him dark against the square bright space behind, and I feel my feet vibrating, part of an unbroken line to the vast bedrock that masses down from the mountains. I lift his delicate fingers and kiss each pearly nail, each furrowed knuckle, until he turns up his palm and pulls my face to his and we stare at each other, teetering.

It's a long way to the old block. Miles down endless corridors, but apparently the room I used before is being refurbished. We end up in a cavernous gym. At the side of it a strip of blue stippled rubber, three feet wide, is stuck to the floor. The physio takes me from the porter, wheels me to the start of it and tells me to clasp the rails that run the three metres on either side. "Now," she says, "I want you to name the person you'd most like to get up and hug."

She goes behind my wheelchair. I can feel her hands inches from my body, encouraging me onto my feet. Then she tells me that Tom is waiting at the other end and urges me to stand. My arms are quite strong now but when I put weight on my legs I feel I've crash-landed all over again. Once I'm leaning firmly on the rails, the physio runs over to the CD player. I hear the first three words of the lyrics and the smell of freesias lights me like a spring morning. The song could only have been this one, and Tom's smile glitters like a plane at the end of a runway. A smile of pure joy. Not a jot of sympathy in it for me because he's responding to a tiny pause in the music, a gap that he and I know promises to stretch into a missed beat at the same place in the second verse. But the unaccompanied words *I'd like to* that bang this song into my bloodstream have already slipped by and if I'm to catch up I must step out immediately, pressing the ball of my foot into the rubber and thumping down my heel in the gap between *I want to ride my* (crash) and *bicycle*. Together, we have become an accessory of the thumping double-bass transmitting the rhythm of the universe. Besides, this is the first step towards a declaration – *Oh, Lori!* – where every off-beat twang shouts with anticipation. To fall now would be an act of perversion. If Tom tells me that I am the seasons, how can I not allow autumn leaves to whirl through me, winter chill in my stillness, spring in each step and the adrenaline of summer to scorch us as I dance, painlessly, towards him? No one knows this like we do except the pop-star Alessi Brothers whose xylophone and 'doo-waah's' twinkle like Ginger Roger's toes, bright as stars on a moonless night.

So I'm lifted as the flute cuts in, not by a string of notes, not even by the gaps between them, but by what pours through them.

Just as the chorus fades and I am done, Tom winks and disappears, leaving only the astonished face of my physio who insists I lean on her until she can get me in the chair.

"That was er... very good for a first try. Perhaps a bit over-ambitious?"

"I like that song," I reply, but the fairy-dust is already fading as I slump onto my bottom. She cheerily wheels me off to wait for the porter in the old, empty dayroom for 'a change of scene', but I feel emptied out.

No-one else is here.

No-one was in the corridor.

No-one is in the world.

Only words echo out from the old, high walls. Bad words: Fickle. Conditional. Treacherous. Frivolous. Gullible. Weak. Vacuous. Lightweight. I laugh at that last one but not for long. Whore. Slowly, as I sit, these words form whole sentences. Women have no soul. Their love is a pretence. They can't go the distance. *You've been around the block a few times.* That's one of his. I jerk at the memory and something cracks in my elbow. It sounds like a twig breaking outside. I feel nothing, but his sentences build up, overlapping in my head. *I can't stand drama.* Ha! I laugh out loud at that, but no one is around to hear.

I'm the future and I can wait. Please, all you have to do is keep your promise, which is to remember what I promised. If you could live only with that and trust me. Trust him? I trusted Tom enough to liberate him from himself and the world from its confusion. Anger clears a space in my head. Inside is a bed in a room in a Travelodge. One of our sealed units beyond space and time, though by then our passion was so thick it must have seeped under the door into the corridor. I had brought my teapot, to make our cups runneth over even in the morning. And milk, because those piddly little UHT pods were so unsatisfactory.

But our bubble could hold us. I know this was true as clearly as I know that the dayroom I appear to be sitting in is an illusion. I hear Tom's voice. *You needn't worry that I will stop loving you; my body and soul are yours. You have brought me back to life.* If I am torn from him or he has forsaken me, it must be my doing. I must have sinned against truth and life and growth. But how? Where? *Never censor yourself,* he says. His words dissolve the bars on these long Victorian windows until I can see outside, to where November drips, too warmly. The heating in the Travelodge is on and the radiators blaze and make the short curtains in front of the PVC frames wave. We have fucked and fucked and fucked again before staring, lost in one another's eyes until nothing else exists.

Until nothing else was supposed to exist. But it does. It did. Then.

I looked away.

Sharply. I looked away sharply and I shouldn't have.

I found myself staring at those waving curtains, not meeting Tom's eyes because Tom had told Anita that he'd bumped into an old friend and drunk too much to drive home.

I have looked away because I was relying on his story. The one where he is quietly, and naturally, slipping out of his already tenuous relationship with her.

But he has lied to her. His behaviour doesn't fit with his statement that he must honour her.

Therefore, he has lied to me.

Well – not lied. Deceived him*self*, because only I can see that he doesn't realise that he is not slipping, naturally, anywhere. He is, in fact, misguidedly tying himself to her with this lie, in order to avoid conflict. This, I have to address.

But I did shift my gaze. Suddenly. Violently, even, but in disappointment? He might have thought that. A misunderstanding then. I looked away because I needed time to consider my response, my words that had to be spoken. The ones that wouldn't disappear despite his stare.

I reach into the air of the dayroom that isn't real, as if I can pull the half-turned shoulder back to me and rescind this misunderstanding. He has rolled over to the bedside table and lifted his half-smoked cigarette from the ashtray. "I hate it that I've lied. I think of myself as an honourable man," he said.

Now I hear the confusion in his voice, but in the bed I heard nothing but an error in his thinking, forced by a normal aversion to rowing with Anita. I thought finally he would have to see that guilt and misery were unavoidable. And that we would live through it. My faith in him was as unshakeable as I knew his was in me. I spoke free of concern for anything but the truth, trying to help. The solution was obvious. "Then be honourable. Maybe it won't be as bad as you think. Start by moving out of the bedroom. If your relationship has really become the business arrangement you told me it was, then keep working together, keep living together, just start to reclaim your life. It's no longer her business what you do in your spare time."

"I can't."

Now I can hear his horror, I can hear it very plainly. But I didn't hear it then. No horror had penetrated our world. Not even for a moment. It occurs to me *now* that I could have said nothing. Just kept staring. And then that I couldn't have done that. That to have ignored this would have been a corruption. I see again the cigarette smoke spiralling. I feel my words, indifferent to his pain, precise against the backdrop of the waving curtains. "Of course you can," I said. "What you mean is you won't."

But Tom just sighed. "I know this is horrible for you. These circumstances really are difficult." He gripped my arm. "They require a lot of courage. But just because you can't see any movement, it doesn't mean nothing is happening."

I shook my head. I do it now and the bones in my neck, although sore, click into alignment, allowing such a cool empty space to fill my brain that the pain seems far away and I'm back in that motel room, my crossed legs nestling in the soft mattress as I explain. "What I'm asking you to do is say what you really mean. Use the right language. It's not true that you can't. You mean 'I won't.' Otherwise you'll come to believe that things are impossible when they're not. I'm not telling you what to do. I'm telling you what you're doing." But when I searched his eyes, they seemed cloudy, or maybe it was the smoke. Either way, I couldn't get through.

He sighed again, fidgeting, but he could see I was waiting. Closing his eyes, he stopped to check out how he felt inside, as I had taught him. "I feel a bit panicky," he said, at last. "But I have to learn that I don't any have quick fixes. And that 'very difficult' doesn't mean impossible."

"And you have to cope with my frustration, and with my refusal to let you give up." At last, I had a chance to give something back to this battered God. If I'd taught him to reflect on his feeling, he had given me, in return, the capacity to be objective. Using his own strength and clarity, I turned from his tired eyes and gazed through the smoke between the warmed curtains to where reversing lorries beeped in a grey dawn and people breakfasted in the Little Chef, next door. People who saw things differently. I stepped into their perspective and offered it to Tom – innocent Tom – to help him see the importance of exact language when you know what you are doing but everyone else takes a dim view.

"To anyone but us," I said, "to anyone outside the circle of our love, this looks like an affair. You look just like a typical bloke saying, 'My wife doesn't understand me. I'm going to leave her, but not yet.' To them you look like a coward, or worse, a bloke having your cake and eating it too. And I look like just the other woman." I didn't feel angry, but passionate. Emphatically passionate. "I keep telling you

– I don't mind you living with Anita. I'll wait, even though it's killing me. What I mind is you lying to her."

Tom frowned. He even forgot to suck on his roll-up, staying still way past the time it went out. Eventually, he said, quietly, "That's what Patricia said. That I was having an affair."

I am still stunned by this. Now, back in the dayroom, as the bright sun shines through the old barred windows, a phrase from one of his emails hammers in my head, as it did then. *Patricia is mad; how do you persuade mad people to talk to someone professional?*

Patricia is mad. Why then would he consult her of all people? The woman he was divorced from because all she did was scream at him? Why, if he was confused, did he not consult me? *Me?* The wise woman who was his future? The one who held his body and soul so tenderly, with whom he would spend his life?

I know I asked these questions. I know that I protested that to me, this was never an affair. That affairs were sordid. We even agreed that it was time to call a halt to sex if I had become just the other woman, because I was beginning to feel cheap and shabby. But all I remember is him shuddering through me again and again and his rich, hot, words breathed into my ear. "Now tell me this is sordid."

And so, while he separated from Anita, we would put things on hold.

*

"Whore," I add. I'm back with Doctor Samuels. Somewhere I had lunch and tea because it's getting dark outside, but I don't recall anything except a need to get in the room with Dr. Samuels. "Whore. He said... " And then whole sentences arrive and leave. "He said... He said... " I say, unable to pick any specifics. "It was this view – whose view? The view... " I shake my head, helpless now, but she seems to not mind. My heart thuds and thumps as I add, "...that I was a groupie or a whore that made me call off our sex-life. This was what I was trying to explain to him when he... " I stop.

"When he what, Gina?"

The words are at the front of my mouth, but my lips are glued together. I haven't told this to Dr. Samuels. I haven't really told myself because I haven't believed it. But this moment must have been coming from the start. Ever since I began to talk to Dr. Samuels, this is what I've been missing. A shadow is creeping up the wheels of my chair, thick as coal-smoke, and I can't shake off my sense that Tom is crowing at the words he knows I'm finally going to say. "When he told me he wasn't going through with it. With us," I say.

"When did he do that?" asks Dr. Samuels, very, very gently.

"On Christmas Eve. In an e-mail," I tell her, miserably. I can see his words on my computer screen. They still jump about, defying sense, but the incredulity in my voice has gone.

The subject line above the e-mail: *December 24th: I love you. I go to bed dreaming of you* stands out, like the longed-for caress that it was. So does his opening: *Darling Gina –* but even now, when I try and remember what he said next, my throat floods with bile, because halfway through every sentence, nausea got the better of me and I had to leave the room.

Just before the first day of Christmas and my true love said to me – *I only know I cannot do this – I will always love you but...* I could read bits – part sentences, standing so that I could quickly escape from the screen, and then my legs would give way. I kept trying to lift my head, but every attempt battered my skull, crunched my bone, crushed me like a scrapped car until I crawled into bed, trying to use the soft thick duvet for protection as I jerked unsleeping through the nights.

Dr. Samuels looks shocked. "What did you do?" she asks.

"I phoned," I say, remembering the five rings and the click of the answerphone. "I phoned, many times, begging for a kind word to stop the vomiting. Even when I left a message telling him I wouldn't treat a dog that way he didn't get back to me. And then... "

"Yes?"

I'm glad, suddenly, that she is still there wanting to know. "We did meet – in mid-January, when Anita was away. He refused to speak to me for the whole Christmas period, yet when he was ready, when *he* wanted to meet, I reeled towards him like a drunk towards the bottle. Being with him seemed so right, so normal. Everything clicked back into place so fast, yet as soon as I left him again, I couldn't connect our afternoon together with the decision he'd made. How," I say, loudly, "is it possible for a man who proved his commitment by promising on his dead wife's grave, to simply change his mind?"

Dr. Samuels is leaning close and breathing slowly to try

and calm me down, but I am onto something. I have got to the point. The problem. Can she solve it? Someone must be able to. My 'how?' becomes a howl. Someone is howling. Something is pure howl. Sound-waves circle the earth at such a pitch they surely must break everything solid, reveal everything to be dust and illusion - a howl so strong I can see it happening. Yet I can't be awake because I am making a sound that my awake self could never quite reach: the howl that searches for its other so we can howl together. But my voice is swallowed and falls forever, echoing down through the empty earth. On and on I keen.

Because my father is dead.

My father is dead. My mother, brother and sister have gone and left me alone with him. Soon, whatever that means, a man will come and take his corneas so that someone else will be able to look through them, but I cannot go yet. I know he is dead and I cannot leave him. I sit by his yellow head which seems to shrink and change as I watch. His jaw is slack against the pillow. On the counterpane his hands are becoming wax replicas of themselves. His eyes remain closed where my mother pressed down their lids how long ago? Ten minutes? Two hours? For her there is nothing now. An empty shell. I go to the windows and open them, concerned that his soul needs to get out. I am all concern, stroking the paper skin on his head, but he just lies there. I can't remember the last time I loved someone so completely. I want to wrap him in feathers and give him everything I couldn't when he was still alive. I want to bathe him in warm soapy water with the softest cloth and pat him dry. I want to carry him home in my arms and read him a story but I can see there is no point. Even the skin on his arms is fading to grey as gravity flattens it over his bones. Because he is dead. This man. This Father Christmas. Prime Minister. Drafter of THE Constitution. Arbiter of all that is right and wrong. This great charismatic God who made me, whose DNA I can feel in how I am, what I say, how things look, is shrivelling and will never speak again. HOW CAN THAT BE?

Dr. Samuels is holding my head. She is cradling it in her arms, but my craving is gone, leaving nothing but space. "How?" I ask again, curious that the word can continue to exist. 'How' lacks bitterness, but it lacks sweetness, too. It sounds crisp. Open-ended. "How," I say, trying the word free of sugar. The sugar has gone. The sugar is over. My howl stretched until the L dropped off, until *I*, not the world, broke, and now sugar will never coat my world in palatable lies again.

*

It's dark when the nurses lift me into bed. I peep out just enough to check that Dr. Samuels hasn't left and catch her drawing the curtains in the side-room into which I've recently been moved. She strokes the hair away from my face, puts a kiss on her fingers and places it on my cheek before turning out the light. And then she's gone.

At the click of the door, I sit bolt upright. My ghost-body feels no pain. I know I am in my parents' bedroom, staying in my father's forever-empty bed. My mind scours the family bungalow, reaching for who has come in or gone out; for who has fallen over in the hall.

It must be my mother. She still sleeps in the small bedroom where she spent so many nights in these last six months trying to preserve her strength for when the bell next to her ear buzzes because my father's sheets are wringing wet or because he's too weak to reach the loo or because the night is just too dark for him to be on his own.

I lean over and switch on the light. The two anglepoise lamps between the twin beds smell faintly of scorched and dusty wiring. I want to crawl into the shades like a bee into a foxglove but I know the nectar won't be there, just as I know for certain that the backs of my parents' 1950s matching wardrobes are made of plywood.

I notice how weightless my body feels as I glide out of the bedroom. A sliver of light radiates from beneath the bathroom door. I open it to see my father in the bath, washing himself. Here. In the bathroom. My father, his blue veins standing taut on his skinny neck above the curve of pink skin that wasn't covered by his t-shirt. He has been in the garden all day and is scrubbing his nails with the Dettol he dilutes and keeps in a bottle to prevent germs. He is a pre-antibiotics man. A man of Zam-Buk and Germoline and Permanganate of Potash.

Through the water in which he sits, I see the blue vinyl strips he stuck, ages ago, to the bottom of my mother's new acrylic bath. She'd bought a matching suite. Not cracked or yellowed. Not second-hand or ex-display. Not cleaned with Ajax or a Brillo pad but with a spray and a wipe. Floral tiles up to the ceiling too, and a pine-clad wall with a bathroom cabinet to match. All paid for with her own earnings. And what had he done? What had he done? Bought a roll of gaffer tape and stuck strips along the bottom of the bath. Said (after the deed) he was worried about slipping.

But I don't care. He is alive. I'd buy him fifty rolls of gaffer tape and cover the parquet floor in the hall with it if he asked me. He is alive. Alive again. I see him move, note the moles on his back. But the thing is... the thing is... I saw him die. I saw him dead. I held him, definitely, definitively dead.

I know I can ask him about this. And I know he can handle it. He has too much confidence, too much realism to duck away. "How can that be?" I ask him, full of curiosity and wonder. No-one could be happier than I at his miraculous resurrection but how can that be? Surely he has an answer. He always has an answer, and not a fudging kind of answer. He would never tell me he hadn't really died. Not after all that.

He looks up at me, bald head gleaming, sponge sodden against his wiry arm. His eyes twinkle as he draws breath. It could be a look of impatience. I used to think that but now I can see I was wrong. He was always, as now, just thinking hard, trying to locate a suitable answer, working to provide the most accurate and appropriate solution for his daughter. "Well, Georgina," he says eventually, making me understand through the sheer force of his will. "You have a great deal of love to give... "

Then he smiles at me, and vanishes.

I wake to the feel of my mother helplessly fingering my hair. "I thought I heard the bell... " Her voice tails off and I rise from my father's bed to steer her through the thick emptiness of loss back to her own, but my feet jar on the floor, the door opens and I find myself blinking against the bright strip-lights of the hospital corridor.

Chapter Fifteen

The door to the staffroom stood ajar, the light off, occupants long gone home. Beatrice walked past and on down the corridor, imagining Gina on a slab in the hospital morgue instead of tucked up in bed. She upped her pace. *Suicide* would never have done for *cause of death*. Howabout *Loss of the people she loved?* Or *Loving the people she shouldn't?*

A song by Burt Bacharach appeared in her head, though the words had gone awry. *Why do psychos suddenly appear – every time, I am near?* She could feel Ralph's eyebrows lifting. *Your father not all that he seems? A selfish, steamroller of a man?* Really, it seemed extraordinary that what had once been so destructive for her was so helpful for her patients. The childhood cross-examination that had driven her to such career heights. The years on the analyst's couch that had led to every memory, feeling and belief emerging into awareness like a lily in a pond? She could feel it now – that same desperation, that same overweening need in herself, so many years before Gina, to believe that her father must be busy with important things. That like God, he must be saving the world by moving in a mysterious way, because he certainly never had time for her. Even the great benefit of Ralph's devotion was only realised because she knew her own heart was so broken.

Since then it had been Ralph who was worth listening to, arguing with. He might have loved his own dominating culture, but tough as his own learning had been, he loved her more. And now he was dead.

Down the passage that led to the old block, distant footsteps echoed off thick window glass. "Bastard!" she hissed involuntarily into the corner as she turned left. Poor old Ralph, but he could take it. It was she who was diminished.

As she pushed down the handle to her office the door was yanked open and slammed back on its hinges by a gust of wind. Inside, the blinds were half down and the carpet just inside the window showed a damp patch.

The ghost of Midsummer Tom.

The wind wuthered and banged.

As she turned she knew that normal people might have felt a chill, or at least a frisson of fear. A diagnosis of depression entered her head – *Don't care. Can't sleep. Think you know it all.* – but she pushed it aside. Depression didn't express itself as anger. Not until people were recovering. "Ghosts," she said loudly. "The place is full of us," but she felt empty. As if part of the universe was missing. Or was she muddling up being a ghost with having her heart ripped out? Of the three of them – four, including Ralph – Gina seemed the most ethereal by far, but largely because her mind as well as her body had been thinned by Tom.

"You can't kill and chew people up because of your pathetic lack, you piece of shit," she shouted. The blind rattled. She pulled the vinyl slats away from the window. Boiling now, she saw a fire in the depths of the yellow flood lamps outside that seemed anything but ghostlike. The rain lashed against them and still they shone. The wind tore at the signboards and still, they stood. She swung back the blind as if launching a ship. "Fuck this and all who sail in it." But it was Ralph she spoke to: *This is happening to me. That is happening to me.* She talked to him just as she always had. *Not so stone-like then,* she thought.

Tears rolled down her face.

There, there, old thing, Ralph responded. *There, there.* Just that.

But how can you tell people who kill and chew people up that they mustn't? she asked. His silence seemed a better answer than most. You couldn't. Beatrice knew that, though at some point they'd all believed you could get through to people if only you tried hard enough. Beatrice attempted to locate where in her illustrious career she'd stopped. She even asked Ralph.

He giggled. She could hear him trying not to and sniggering with his mouth shut.

Oh, shut up, she said in her head but her pleading just made them both giggle now.

Because you couldn't make anyone do anything. How many times did she need to see that to really get it into her own head, let alone Gina's?

She closed the window, shutting the bluster out, and stretched her arms and hands and fingers until they cracked and the tension in her back began to ease.

No, she couldn't make anyone see, but she knew what could go on in a naïve, unfathered woman. And she could still spot a selfish, self-obsessed man at a thousand paces. Gina's hunger and blindness and shame were such that the poor girl wouldn't have cared what Tom said to her as long as he kept talking.

Tom. The great writer.

The book she had borrowed from the library must be still in her bag. *Stuff The Turkey*. Beatrice sat in her office chair, turned on her reading lamp and read the plaudits on the back: *A cult classic: one of our most original comic writers.* Then she skim read from start to finish.

*

Car Park D was half-empty, rain still bucketing down by the time she left. A lone, damp figure wove through the shiny cars. Corinne. Beatrice could tell from the lack of umbrella and the straggly hair.

Slowly, she nudged the long hood of the Audi towards the exit until she caught up and honked the horn.

Corinne scowled.

Beatrice smiled across the passenger seat and flipped open the door. "Hello, you smart woman. What are you up to?"

"Oh My God. I thought you were one of those rich bastards," said Corinne, zombie-like against the neon of the car-park. "Guess." She left no time. "I'll tell you. Train to Marylebone. Walk to tube. Change tube. Tube home. Pick up a ready-meal. Watch TV. Sleep. Get up. Go to work."

"D'you want to get in?" asked Beatrice but Corinne was already sliding into the leather seat.

"How're you doing?" Corinne managed, though she looked exhausted. "How are you?"

Beatrice told her 'there's been a bit of a breakthrough' and left it at that. After a couple of false starts, Corinne began to explain what happened to her whenever she began to ballet dance, but they arrived at the train station before she'd finished, so Beatrice offered bed and breakfast and within half an hour they were cruising up the A421. Forty minutes later, they arrived in Cambridge.

At which point, despite the intimacy of their conversation, Corinne stopped talking altogether. As they pulled into the drive the laurel screeched along the car wing, clearing the windscreen only for the house to loom up like a castle in a gothic fairytale. Beatrice chivvied her inside but under the high ceiling in the empty hall it was impossible not to see how wretched and out of place Corinne felt.

"It's cold and unwelcoming without Ralph. I'm glad you're here," said Beatrice, going through to turn on the heating.

"When my mum died, she hadn't been in the flat for ages because she'd been in hospital. But once she was actually dead... well, she wasn't there in a way she had been even when she hadn't been," said Corinne, following into the kitchen. As the fluorescent tube fired up, the room flickered like a disco.

Beatrice put some lard in the frying pan and turned on an electric ring. "Ralph's mostly in here. But he follows me around too." She took bacon and eggs from an under counter fridge and bread from a chest freezer. "He worries."

"How nice," said Corinne, not without a hint of bitterness. "My mum came back in the end but she just gets pissed and talks at me from the settee."

*

They sat across from one another at the red formica-topped table, the expelair whirring above the cooker. Corinne's wrists crackled as she manoeuvred her knife and fork. "Are your ankles that thin?" asked Beatrice, pointing as she swallowed a sliver of fried egg.

Corinne pushed herself back from the table and stuck out her leg. "I suppose so. Why?" She folded her bacon into three, poked her fork through it, speared a piece of toast and filled her mouth.

"They look so frail. You have a ballerina's body – not frail at all, of course – but it helps me to feel what you were talking about. The pushing beyond endurance until you break or you break free." Corinne's neck had tightened as if she was finding it hard to swallow and she was biting her lip, hard.

"Something's wrong," said Beatrice, concerned. "What is it?"

"The thing is," Corinne blurted, "I'm an ex-junkie. I've got to tell you that now... because... I can't talk t'you otherwise."

"A heroin addict?"

"Ex-addict," Corinne corrected her. "I don't use. Haven't for years. That's why I don't drink. I couldn't, anyway. A bit of excitement and... " She looked young and suddenly, hopeless. "Well, you saw what happened after the play. I get it if that's not all right," she added, her voice shaking as she focused on her food.

"Why would it not be all right?" asked Beatrice, calmly.

"I don't know." Corinne hung her head. "Oh, it's that, *once an addict, always an addict* thing. You'll think I'm going to nick your stuff."

Beatrice paused, then said, gently, "You've been through so much. You know, in the end, when you've sorted through your experience, it will make you a much better counsellor than people who haven't."

Corinne gave a sigh, put down her knife and fork, leaned back in her chair and said, "It's not so easy to talk about, but if you really want to know what I think – about pain – about stretching 'til you hurt, I can probably say some things."

Beatrice nodded again, fascinated. "Yes. I'd really like to know. Whatever it is."

"Heroin. It's the most concrete example. The best description. The best ever." Corinne opened her eyes wide as if she couldn't quite believe Beatrice didn't get a line in simply from hearing the word. "Strung out, trying to get it? Ever heard of that? Everything about heroin's a risk you have to overcome. Even when you've got hold of some you don't know if what's in it'll kill you. Harpic? Talcum powder?" Her speech was racing now. "The spoons and candles and straps and stuff. Tapping the needle to get rid of the bubble that'll give you a heart attack if you forget. *But when I put that spike into my vein...* " This last phrase smoothed out of her and she stopped, hard. "C'mon," she said, in need of a soundtrack. "Where's your computer?"

*

Upstairs in the attic, the two women listened as *Heroin* – the seventh track on Andy Warhol's great *Velvet Underground* production – grew in its six minutes from a single, languid guitar into an ongoing car crash of metal scoring against metal.

"*Closing in on death*," Corinne said softly, looking as if she longed to be in the middle of it. "That's it. You get close enough to death to really live. Heroin's a lover – a lover and a killer."

Beatrice watched her rocking gently to and fro. "A lover you're still in thrall to?" she asked, careful to avoid any hint of criticism.

Opening her eyes, Corinne replied, "Always. The thing about heroin is that unlike men, it never lets you down."

In her mind's eye, Beatrice watched Gina drop through space. "Oh, come on. Never lets you down? Something you need more and more of? You can't focus on anything except getting it? You can't hold a conversation or read or think straight?"

Corinne looked annoyed. "That's the kind of thing people say who've never tried it. It's bollocks, and it nearly always stuffs anything helpful to do with giving up whenever... " but she stopped.

Whenever you talk to straight people about it, thought Beatrice. "Sorry."

"Well, all that endless thieving and being at death's door – that only happens when you can't get any. If you've got money, you can do everything you'd normally do and feed a habit no problem." She gripped her thighs, opened her mouth like a woman panting through labour. "As long as you don't have to stop – then you're really up shit creek."

"But if you don't have to stop, doesn't the drama – the thrill – become normal, leaving you with nothing but a tolerance to opioids?" Beatrice asked quietly, wanting more but holding back, trying not to lean on Corinne's bruises.

"It's true. By then the thrill is gone." Corinne shivered.

What extraordinary strength the woman had alongside such fragility; her highs and lows reenacted at every pat of approval and every perceived slight. Beatrice looked at the delicate fingers and long neck in front of her. "Sorry. I find it really interesting, but presumably you've talked enough about heroin to last a lifetime."

Corinne held her gaze and said, crisply, "I hope you won't take this the wrong way, but that really is a daft thing to say to a person who's been a full on addict."

Corinne's sudden surge of adrenalin put Beatrice in mind of the way Gina reacted when she shifted the subject to Tom. That same readiness to blast towards excitement and away from the point.

But Corinne had shifted her focus. "I told you, I don't drink? At all? That's really because of what drink does to me. Turns me into someone else. Before I know it, I'm effing and blinding like I'm God Almighty."

Beatrice offered the slightest nod. "I can sense that, just a little. To touch the thrill is to be carried away by it?"

Corinne drew her feet up onto the armchair and pulled a throw over her knees. "Yeah. Any thrill. But being a heroin addict is king," she said. "It's so dangerous because feeling invulnerable and like you know everything is really easy, and staying with difficult feelings – the ones that you couldn't cope with in the first place – the reason why people start taking the stuff – feels im-fucking-possible."

"So you're just as addicted to being the person you become as to the drug?"

Corinne shut her eyes. Whether to concentrate or to avoid looking at her, Beatrice didn't know. "Yes, and alcohol puts you in touch with that, big time. And once you've learned how to be that arrogant, know-it-all smartass, you've just found a new way of not feeling."

"A new way? What was the old way?"

Corinne tipped her head theatrically to one side. "Well – before heroin, I was stuck in a knackering cycle of trying to ignore what happened to me as a child. I was neglected," she mumbled before saying more loudly, "You bounce from blaming yourself to trying to be perfect. That way you take control. You don't have to stop and feel how helpless you were. And then, after heroin," she said, flipping her head the other way, "I was stuck in a knackering cycle of blaming myself and trying to be perfect." Shrugging, she added, "The habit just reattached to the next thing I tried. It's a parasite."

Beatrice held her palms to the heavens and said, softly, "It sounds like the whole thing's hard to talk about without that self-hatred rearing right back up."

Corinne's face sagged until she looked twice her twenty-nine years. "The only way out is in noticing what you do, really. If you can stop for long enough." Opening her eyes, performing again, she said, "The self-help books came to my rescue when I heard myself thinking *you create your own reality* and the words sounded just like *look what a total mess you've made of your life, you stupid bitch*."

Beatrice had to laugh. "You know," she said. "You really are funny and lovely and not quite the complete know-it-all you think. Pretty self-deprecating, actually. Has it occurred to you that maybe the arrogant bit is just armour to protect yourself from people who are going to misunderstand?"

"Or perhaps the self-deprecation is just a front to prevent my elders and betters putting me straight?"

"Oh, there's no end to it, is there?" said Beatrice, stretching out on the chaise longue. Tossed from one point of view to another, Corinne's covering of all possible bases was painful to witness, and the certainty she wanted well beyond Beatrice's powers to bestow. Curled up now, in the armchair, the girl reminded her of Marty, the collie-cross she and Ralph had owned. Long dead, Marty had been their substitute child. She in her attic, Marty in the chair, Ralph somewhere – probably in the kitchen. All of them absorbed in their interests and feeling safe enough to simply be. That, as Beatrice knew, wishing she could lift Corinne from her struggles, was as good as things got.

"I'm very fortunate," she said, by way of apology. "I had enough isolation and predictable boredom in my childhood to make me want to leave it behind. But I suppose I also had enough certainty and resources to focus on where to go and what to do."

"Well, lucky you," said Corinne, drily. "Sorry. I s'pose, in a different way, that's true for me too – not your kind of discipline, for sure, but I got a lot of help."

"I don't think anyone really gets anywhere on their own – for good or bad." *We can never look after ourselves. It's a myth. An urban, Western myth. We have to look after each other.* Where had she heard that?

Corinne was frowning. "You're right – about the... the discipline, but it's really easy for you to say that. This... " she hesitated, then drew breath. "Look, I mean, I think... well, of course I was fed and housed and stuff, but I think my background helped me, in reverse – because it made me think I was rubbish. So I pulled myself up by my own bootlaces."

To avoid scrutinising Corinne, Beatrice reached for the pencil and pad beneath the chaise longue and bent her knees for a prop. She began to frame the page with a sketch of plaited bootlaces. "How so?" she said, casually.

"Well, telling myself how crap I was made me try a lot harder. I helped myself." Her face screwed into tight, quizzical lines. "The *you are rubbish* message came from outside. From my mum. From my dad never being around, but I used it as a donkey's stick."

"So – own bootlaces," said Beatrice, drawing a little bow in the corner. "And the pain?"

Corinne released a sharp hiss of breath, then said, with a self-conscious sigh, "Ah, the pain. Well, the thing is, if you can keep trying harder and running faster, you can avoid that. Until you fuck it up, of course. Then you know you really are a worthless, pointless waste of space."

Corinne's eyes had filled. Sensing how childlike she was, Beatrice put down her pad and went over to give her a hug. She felt proud to have brought Corinne home, proud of her for giving up heroin, for making a career from that achievement, for not going back to it when she lost her mother. "It hurts, even to think about it," she lulled as she pulled the throw around her friend. "And it's just some dodgy old belief you had no control over. But look at you now," she said. "Responsible job. Professional, valued member of society! Because you're lovely. Yet it still hurts, like you said, shame just hurts."

Corinne sniffed. "I don't think becoming a heroin addict did much for my self-esteem." She blew the statement out of the side of her mouth, grinning.

"Too hard to believe you're OK on your own, I guess," said Beatrice But not impossible, she realised. Corinne had found a way. Gina was the opposite. With an almost audible click, Beatrice saw a mirror image of the two women. Unable to bear the death of both father and brother, Gina had become addicted, and not just to Tom, but to the persistent adrenaline rush generated by the drama of the relationship. Was that why Gina kept falling back into her fantasy? *We can never look after ourselves. We have to look after each other.*

Now she knew where she'd heard these statements before. These were the words Tom had said to Gina in the motel room: his response to the story of her bereavements. He had said that the capacity to look after ourselves was an *urban myth*.

In the bootlace frame she added the thoughts and feelings that Gina would use to prevent herself from plunging into despair. First, she'd try to understand his actions which would inevitably lead to seeing him more clearly...

"What are you doing?" Corinne looked worried. Beatrice wrote *Gina F.* inside the circle and handed it over.

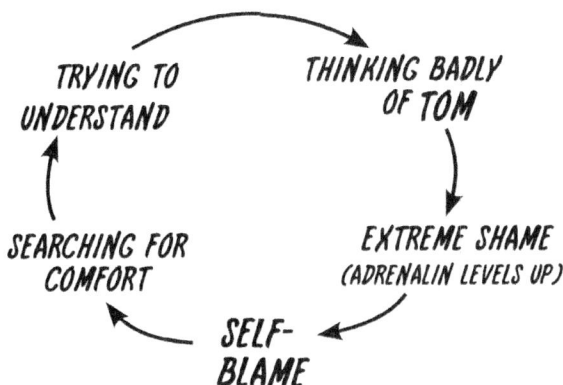

"That's it." She shivered. "Exactly. Hatred – shame – adrenalin – try harder, because you can't afford to hate the thing you need." The lines on her face deepened for a moment. "He ditched her, so she thought it was because she wasn't good enough." Corinne sighed. "So she started trying to be better all over again."

Beatrice hummed. "You see. You know all about it. Your own experience and your therapy has brought all this stuff into the foreground." As if Corinne, too had felt something shift, she turned her head and noticed the trunk in the corner with the comics still scattered around it. "Wow," she said, sliding onto her knees and across the room.

"Help yourself," said Beatrice, glad suddenly to be here with company.

Corinne's giggles became exclamations. "Listen to this!" She could hardly get the words out. "*Teeny... Weeny... Tina, victim of a miniaturisation process...* " She paused, trying to collect herself. "*...had been hiding with her loyal – but scatterbrained – friend... in the basement of a derelict house, when Joyce was trapped by falling debris...* " She dissolved into hysteria.

"That's not funny," said Beatrice, "and her so small and all."

Corinne's gulps became sobs.

Beatrice pursed her mouth.

Unable to respond, Corinne began to shake.

Beatrice started sniggering, slid to the floor and crawled over to where Corinne sat by the open trunk. Together, they leafed through the pages.

In the first, five members of a ballet school comforted the crying Nina. Behind her stood the teacher, looking lost, but next to her a chubby princess smiled a ruthless smile.

Corinne read aloud:

"Jenna Jones and all the members of her ballet school had been kidnapped by huge bubbles and taken to a remote island in order to teach Zulkeika, the plump daughter of a wealthy Sultan, to dance. Money could not make her into a dancer, so she was forcing the girls to help her, and the bubbles were constantly on guard."

Beatrice dragged herself away from a drawing of a bandaged girl in a hospital bed. "This child's little sister has been kidnapped from a ballet class by a woman who bribed her with a red balloon." What was it with ballet and the colour red? Red shoes and women got so carried away they had to have their feet cut off. And balloons – any balloons. She glanced down at the picture of the toddler being lifted through the hospital window by the rubber balloon she'd just inflated. Up, up and away.

"That'll teach 'em!" Corinne looked gleefully, absurdly happy. "Parents didn't do their police checks, did they? Too many assumptions about the reliability of authority figures. See!" she said, looking, Beatrice thought, rather triumphant. "Maybe that CBT stuff I learned is best after all."

"Of course," replied Beatrice, too tactful to labour the fact that deconstructing the way people thought was something she'd learned to do with her A levels.

"I know," Corinne said. "I could do some research? Get some background? About Gina's bloke? See if he's got form?"

"You'd be better off reading his book," said Beatrice. "A

compelling story close to the dead spit of what he did to Gina, played for laughs. I'm sure he's got form in the area of abandoning women, but haven't so many men?"

"What's it called?"

"*Stuff The Turkey*. Horrible title. Horrible book, with a central character by the name of Wolfie." Seeing Corinne's fascination, Beatrice sighed, leant back and ran through the plot as fast as she could.

"This guy is the caricature of a slob. A user. Lives on people's sofas. Eats their food. Gives nothing back. He falls in love with a woman and is totally transformed. He starts shaving. Starts washing. His friends are astonished. He becomes a helpful person. Listens to his new love, gets into her politics, meets her parents, goes to Sunday lunch with them. She's young, a virgin, and her parents are very middle class."

Corinne grimaced.

"Won't that do?" added Beatrice, but Corinne's attention compelled her to finish.

"Wolfie and this woman are invited to a party. It'll be too late to catch the last bus back so he persuades her parents to let them sleep over in a friend's flat. Says he'll stay on the sofa. The next day he's back with his friends, unshaven, eating out of their fridge and when they ask him how it went he looks blank, as if he doesn't know what they're talking about. When they ask where the girlfriend is he tells them he 'fucked' her, got blood all over the sheets and then he left. They ask, 'What happened?' and he says, 'She got the bus home, I think.' And that's it. He never sees, speaks to her or remembers her again."

Corinne dropped her head in her hands, pausing before saying, "Maybe Tom Hanson's a junkie too, like Crowley was? Maybe he's a magician and that's how he gets away with it. That would fit."

"Or maybe he's just an unconscious arsehole, doomed to repeat what's in his head." Beatrice's eyelids were beginning to droop. She glanced at the clock. 11.30. Crowley had been a junkie. Of course. She'd forgotten. But that, of course, was the whole function of glamour. "All seducers are magicians of a sort," she murmured, hoping that was an end to this discussion. "How about a brandy?"

"Just a tiny drop? In hot milk?" said Corinne, hopefully.

"With honey."

Chapter Sixteen

Next morning neither of them spoke much. The early light drew Corinne's attention to the peeling emulsion at the edges of the kitchen walls. And how threadbare the rugs were. She had expected... what? Thick carpets, she realised. Polished wood. Antiques. Instead, she found easy chairs with stuffing poking from the seats, their wooden arms angled toward a pre-digital television the size of a kitchen wall cabinet. She stood in the front living room waiting for Beatrice, wondering why, despite the sense of emptiness, she had an urge to sit down and stay still. The smell of the place seemed to be slowing her. Something dry and settled waited behind the damp. And then she noticed the books, floor to ceiling, on either side of the fireplace. Plain books with no gaps or ornaments between them. Dusty books with only their spines visible, as if hiding their faces. *Modest*, thought Corinne. No, that wasn't it. *Learn'd* – yes, the words in these books were the outcome of years of concentration. They demanded you look inside yourself as well as their covers, and had no interest in selling themselves.

She moved towards them: *The Rise and Fall of the Roman Empire. The Complete Works of Longfellow. Plato's Republic.* Had Beatrice read all these? They weren't even about psychology. And here was she, confused because her friend didn't have new curtains and carpet. Horrified by her own narrowness, Corinne felt lonelier than ever.

*

The motorway seemed to have turned Beatrice into a maniac. One hand on the wheel, she tailgated the car in front until it shifted. Corinne jerked.

"Sorry," said Beatrice, slowing down.

"Thank you," said Corinne, relaxing into her seat.

"You're very welcome," responded Beatrice. "Honestly, you feel a bit like the daughter I never had."

Corinne's stomach flipped. Her mouth filled with the taste of butterscotch. "You're nothing like my mother," she said, because she couldn't bear the sweetness. "Thank God," she added, abruptly, in case Beatrice misunderstood.

On they drove, saying nothing, but by the time they swooshed into Car Park D, the hospital signs seemed a much brighter blue and larger than usual and Corinne had a strong sense that she should hold Beatrice's hand in case she got run over.

Only after they parted with a smile in the foyer did her anxiety return. Really, what had Beatrice meant? Had she meant anything? Probably just being friendly. These thoughts rapidly deteriorated into self-contempt. How could she possibly have considered herself of any lasting value to Beatrice at all? It had to stop now.

Waiting for the lift she felt more and more exposed. First she found herself to be *needy*. Then *juvenile*. Then *grandiose* until the more the judgements contradicted one another (*how could you be grandiose if you were juvenile?*) the more she felt her very appearance would draw critical attention. When the metal doors finally opened on a group of nurses, she saw only squashing space and turned to climb five flights of stairs instead.

Head pulsing, trying to outrun her jeering executioner, she thudded up all the way. By the time she reached the staffroom she'd retreated far inside her brain. Professional again, she logged into her emails to find that the case conference she was due to attend had been cancelled due to the death of Mr Slattery.

So the poor man had escaped, his final gift a spare hour. Tucking her feet beneath her, Corinne tuned into her breathing, taking her attention to the soles of her feet. But the centre of them became a glittering eye. *Goodbye, Mr. Slattery*, she thought, imagining soft pink waves emanating from her heart, but the waves turned icy blue and jagged.

Beatrice.

If Corinne cut her out of her life, she'd be trapped in this cold, alone place.

But if she hung around, neediness would swallow her down.

Cringing and breathing more heavily than ever, Corinne found a solution. She'd look outward instead. Pick up where they'd left off – with the Tom and Gina problem! Head racing again, heart slowing with every decision that distanced her from the memory of feeling cared about, she decided to do what Beatrice wasn't allowed to do – put out some feelers. Find out whether Tom was a junkie. Whether he had a record. Mental health *or* criminal.

Aware of her bias and in the name of objectivity, she checked her urge to go for a straight internet search and instead, turned everything she'd heard about Tom Hanson into a symptom:

Excessive risk taking.
Inappropriate sexual behaviour.
Lack of empathy.
Socially disinhibited.

Then she copied her list and pasted it into Google.
The first five headlines all highlighted the same phrase.

Frontal Lobe Damage.

Astonished by the uniform results, she clicked on one of the psychiatry websites and discovered that sufferers had an almost total lack of insight and difficulty deciding between what was good and what was bad. But the bit she read next made her feel she'd got a FULL HOUSE at Bingo: one of the main indicators of Frontal Lobe Disorder was the patient's excessive sexual drive.

Corinne needed a face for her subject. She logged into her Facebook account, typed the name Tom Hanson into the *find friends* box and found there were fifty-two Tom Hansons in England. She added the word 'writer' to her search and within seconds found herself sitting in front of the last picture she expected.

Fat didn't cover it. The man was gross. Button-poppingly enormous, his features lost among the sagging flesh of his face. Yet his smile, which almost reached the lobes of each ear, instantly drew her. Comfort with his own corpulence seemed to ooze through the screen and within seconds Corinne found herself looking at nothing but grace and graciousness. And something else. Something to do with the smile. She hit the magnify icon and closed in on his teeth. Pearly. Glinting. Surely not with the Colgate Ring of Confidence? The Colgate ring of con. Like a halo round the mouth. She imagined him licking his thick lips.

The webpage was full of him. Links to articles, videos, his own website. She avoided them all, sensing that she could spend hours clicking and looking – that whatever she searched for would lead her further and further from her purpose. Do not, she thought suddenly, look into his eyes.

She stamped on the thin carpet. Twizzled on the chair. Found the heading Personal Information, and hey-presto, she located his date of birth. Risk-taking? she thought, checking the name of the place he lived in. Who in their right mind would put their name and date of birth on a public account for all the world to get hold of?

Only two GP surgeries existed in the small town in North Wales where Tom lived. Corinne picked up the phone and dialled for an outside line.

"Blackwell Surgery. Can I help you?"

"Oh, hello. Corinne Brock here. Wellbeing counsellor at Stoke Mandeville."

The pause was followed by a slow, "Ye...s...s? How can I help?"

Corinne tried to sound bored. "I'm phoning on behalf of my department head – Dr. Beatrice Samuels? Initial inquiry. Just to confirm that you have the notes for a Thomas Hanson, born 10.8.57. I'm really checking whether or not they are on your computer system as opposed to still in a manila folder on the wall?" She gave a little cough. "I'm not sure which is easier sometimes."

The receptionist gave a wry laugh. "Oh – we're up to

speed, but I expect we'll fall way behind once the new software arrives." Corinne could feel her peering round to check that no one in the waiting room was listening. "The patient of whom you speak *is* on our system, though of course if you want details you'd have to have a secure email address. Nhs.net."

Corinne smiled. "Of course, *I* haven't got authority, though Dr. Samuels has. Only nhs.uk for the likes of me!" she added. "I'll leave the explanation to my boss. She's seconded here from Rampton. We've got a Mental Capacity issue with one of our patients. Thank you so much. She'll be in touch."

She replaced the receiver, surprised at how much pleasure she felt at out-witting the silly woman who should have told her precisely nothing. In the NHS, everyone was obsessed with confidentiality, but not so much to the letter as to the word. And that word was In or Out. Corinne's theory was that the degree of stress experienced by every employee could only be tolerated by *themming* the patients and *ussing* the staff. Why confidentiality might matter was never reflected on. In her own brief practice placement working in a surgery, Corinne had been urged to read her patients' medical notes ad infinitum and the nurses and doctors had dumped their opinions on her whenever they could. While she'd managed for once to exploit this need for herself, concern for the general public seeking deeper emotional support through this triaged NHS tempered her success with a deep weariness.

She checked her watch. Just time to get to *Mums Matter* and facilitate the session.

Chapter Seventeen

"So you are wheeling yourself? All the way from the ward without help?" Dr. Samuels smiles and I know she means I'm thinking for myself.

I nod. "It's part of the rehab. and independence plan. I have to score the time it took and how easy or difficult it was when I get back to the ward." Then I tell her all about my dream and how wonderful it was to see my dad alive while knowing he had died. She asks what I think it means.

"I think my love for him was so great it meant I couldn't lose him, really."

"And what do you mean by 'really'?"

"I mean that love conquers all. We might fall to dust, but we're made of dust and where can it go? The amount of matter in the universe doesn't change."

"But a pile of dust is not your father – or your brother."

"It is now," I quip, in the manner of both father and brother.

"What about Tom? He's not even dust. He's somewhere else, refusing to visit you," she says adding softly. "And you said last time that after he ended things, on Christmas Eve, he was still speaking to you?"

I want her to stop talking about Tom. I feel all right now. Dragging all that back up seems a bit – well, pointless. I just want to hang on to my dad, loving me.

"But you were telling me he'd... decided to end things."

I pretend I can't hear her and imagine my dad's blue eyes as he fixes them on me.

She's not giving up.

"You told me he met you after that appalling Christmas?" Her persistence strikes me as distasteful.

"Yes, we met, just for an afternoon," I say. My voice sounds very casual.

"Please. Tell me what happened?"

She waits so patiently. My body starts to buzz like I'm back there opposite him in that deserted seaside pub. I'd tried to hang on to my fury but when he told me he still loved me – loved me so much he couldn't ask me to wait – my snarl became a purr. *A girl likes to be asked,* I'd said. He smiled at that.

Even after the Christmas he'd just put me through it was impossible to be angry with him. Instead, the weather did that for me. Rain slanted across our gorse-covered cliff-top like a migraine and when we weren't huddled against it, the wind whipped our words out to sea as we opened our mouths. We cried. We yelled. We saw how small we were. We stepped out of our roles and doubled up with laughter before starting all over again.

"I just don't really get it," he shouted, water dripping from his bald head as fast as he wiped it off. "I've never felt so strongly before. My feelings hit me like a tidal wave whenever I have anything to do with you."

I cheered. The whole universe had conspired to provide the scenery and the sound effects for this climactic love duet and still he needed me to interpret.

Of course he did.

"Isn't that the point?" I screamed above the gale, laughing because the gorse bloomed and the sheer cliff edge screamed with me – happy, because I was the one person in the whole universe who could open his heart. "Isn't that the point – that you get to feel? That you get to live your passion through my soul? That was what you wanted. Why you needed all of me."

But he nodded and kept his head bowed.

We tried to take refuge in the church and found it locked. "You never did make love to my arse," I said as we made our way back down the flint-lined path. By then, the many plans we'd made had begun to disintegrate. He would not dance the tango with me on Bournemouth pavilion. Or do unspeakable things to my bottom. "How do you feel about that?"

"Disappointed," he said.

Yet there we were, our exchanges still bubbling up from the source that even his decision had failed to staunch.

We ended up in my Nissan Micra which was fortuitously too small to fuck in. I watched him glance over to the back seat, assess it and then sigh. "I have to go now. The publishing company owns my soul."

"Have you told Anita what happened?"

"No." His dog-eyes sank in disgrace. "I have to reconnect with her first. Honour her. Oh – only until we separate. If there's one thing you don't have to worry about, it's that I'll go back to Anita, but I can't go on letting her down this way. I can't hurt her. She's too good a woman."

I remember looking at the dashboard and tracing my forefinger in the dust as though I might locate the neurone there – the one failing to fire in his brain. "And me?" I said, more curious than angry. Our communication was always so clear. I wanted to checkmate him, or for him to checkmate me, or for some whole new possibility to open up as it so often had. "You batter and break me, but because you can't bear to hurt women, you return to care for her? The only way that makes sense is if I'm irrelevant to you. Less than human. A whore who doesn't count. Otherwise where do I fit in to that equation?"

He was silent for a moment, but his eyes had become dreamy. "Do you know," he said, eventually, "I've thought about that and I've no idea."

I find myself drifting, like a kite loosed on its string. I can get no purchase on this room with its grey plastic walls, but Dr. Samuels finds me.

"So after he broke it off, you kept trying to get an answer?"

"Oh no," I say, surprised she thinks this. "I let him be. His new book was supposed to be finished in March. At the beginning of May I sent him a list of multiple choice questions so that he only had to add a tick. I remember the answer I offered him to question ten was, *Sorry I can't communicate. It's because my moon is afflicted. Well – not sorry, because my moon is afflicted.* He ticked that."

"So you started to do the communicating for both of you."

"Actually," I confess, relieved at how easy it's become to say this now, "that's when I started to think that he didn't really care about me. That maybe he'd never cared. But I knew I was going mad." I look up for confirmation but Dr. Samuels looks quizzical so I explain. "You see it was only his refusal to speak to me that made me wonder. I couldn't stand that. Certainty – even the belief that he was a womaniser, was preferable. But... " I say, shifting in my chair, "...I knew it wasn't true, that it was just my mind, and I could have borne the whole experience of feeling crazy but the hurt crept in and became that physical pain I told you about instead."

"As though you were stretching too far to retain the idea of Tom as someone who really cared?"

"Exactly." I'm amazed by how clearly she's put it. "Because what we *normally* do when we don't get what we want is blame people. Love is about not reverting to the same old shit, and our relationship was so special I had to go beyond that. To have made him into some saddo charmer just because I couldn't cope would have been a betrayal of all we'd had." I falter as something snags on my heart. "I fought against it," and I gaze at Dr. Samuels, hoping she understands how blaming him would have killed a more important part of me than not blaming him would. "Every bone in my body ached. By mid May I wrote and explained what was happening. The thing is, it never occurred to me that he wouldn't help me. Up until then I'd been trying not to ask for anything, but once the pain really took over, I asked if he could send me a couple of emails a week – just short ones. Anything. But he wouldn't make any agreements and the more I explained that this was about me, not him, the less he would respond."

Dr. Samuels pauses, then says, "So the opposite happened?"

I frown and listen.

"Well, before the split, when you trusted him totally, you heard him encouraging your thoughts. What was it you said? Your fear left and your thinking expanded?"

She waits for my agreement.

"Well, perhaps the opposite of that was also true? That once you suspected him of having dark motives, your thinking shrank and you couldn't stop yourself manufacturing horror stories about who he might really be?"

"Yes." Again, I'm amazed she can see this – that she can lift me past that hump just by identifying it. "The thing is, I could just about keep on top of those. What I couldn't stand was the pain. I had to do something."

"Had to do something? What did you do, Gina?"

But the pain whites everything out. Despite what I've just told her, I feel myself becoming smaller. The arms of the wheelchair look like black slugs and the carpet has become grey moss. Only when I glance up do I see her waiting. I breathe again, just lightly. "I started to remember some of the things he said when we'd been together – stuff I'd forgotten." Horrible things that stun me all over again to think of. "Some writer that wrote the same kind of non-fiction books Tom did – I'd never heard of him – had just died of cancer."

Tom was standing, always standing when he told me these things. First I see him in a car park, one hand flat on the bonnet of his Renault 5. "John McQueen's dead." He licks his finger and draws an imaginary chalk mark in the air. "One down." I remember my fascination and the way I dismissed his gloating as not meant – as just his way of breaking a taboo. Next I see him in the motel room of a Premier Inn, standing at the end of the bed, talking about the girlfriend before Anita. "She didn't like me. She loved me and I loved her, we had fantastic sex, but she didn't like my politics or my manners so after four years I dumped her and do you know what she did? She slept with my best friend."

I'm still surprised by how bleak he looked, and amused by the way his sense of injustice blinded him to the probable motives behind her behaviour. Sweet innocent boy, I thought but the words he went on to say left even me recoiling. "She was always up for some kinky stuff, so he wrapped her in plastic and put her in the boot of his car. Then he drove around for half an hour."

He had been grinning but he sobered up, backtracking when he saw my face. "She was furious."

"You don't say," I said, like a mother explaining to a child. "I expect she thought she was going to die." A chill whispered across my naked flesh. "I hope you don't want to do that to me."

"No, even for me that would be going a bit far."

I asked what happened to her.

He said, "I don't know. She went back to her mum I

think and had a nervous breakdown."

"The subject was dismissed, as if it meant nothing," I say to Dr. Samuels, remembering. "And then, that May, when I was waiting for him to tell me his book was done so I could finally get some answers, something made me reread a novel he'd written, years earlier."

"Was it called *Stuff The Turkey*?"

I must be staring at her, but she's happy to hold my gaze. Her eyes are so kind. Sort of creased and soft as she says, "The one where the character Wolfie seduces and dumps the young virgin?" Knowing that she's read it brings her and the whole room closer.

Dr. Samuels sighs. "I'm wondering what that did to you," she says, and I know she's interested. Her stillness invites me to go on.

"I began to think that what he did to me he might have done to a whole string of women across the country. Even that he could be a serial killer. How could he ignore me when I was so desperate? I had to find out – had to put an end to going round and round in circles. I remembered the name of the ex-girlfriend – Jane Rothermere. I even thought he might have murdered her, but I found her through the internet. She was working in mental health, back in Belfast. I found the number of the hospital and rang her. When I told her Tom had gone off to write a book she laughed, just a little. Said that sounded familiar and gave me her mobile number for later."

I could hear a tannoy in the background. I imagined

Jane on her mobile, rushing from one work appointment to another while the disembodied voice that was me drew her back into a nightmare she'd been trying to forget for years. In the end she asked me what I wanted from Tom. 'I want to know what happened,' I pleaded. 'I want an explanation.'

Apart from the sound of whistles and machinery, the phone went quiet for a long time. 'Well you'll never get it,' she said, eventually. 'I was with him for four years. One day he went out and never came back. Never rang. Never wrote. My letters disappeared into a void. You'll never get an answer from Tom Hanson.'

"There was nothing more to say. But the day after I rang her, I had the longest e-mail from Tom that he had written to me since the split."

"Tell me."

My hopes of hearing from Tom had dulled after so many months, though my behaviour in the mornings remained habitual. I fired up my computer on my way to fill the kettle and looked through any new e-mails as it boiled.

The message had no title, but was long enough to go beyond the bottom of the screen. I scrolled down, glancing here and there, light and fearful. He began with a sort of resume: he wasn't interested in anything until he'd finished his book. After that, he would meet up. He knew he'd hurt me and would love to talk.

Then, halfway through, he started a new paragraph.

I know that talking to Jane can't have helped at all. You told me you didn't want to make things worse, but you're a liar, because you have. I know that I have postponed your pain just as much as I have my own and I know this hurts you too. But that's the point; I've tried at least to stop hurting you anymore.

Txxxxxxxxxxxxxx

PS I've just picked up your messages on the answerphone, but there's nothing I can say that will help.

Blame seemed to sweat from the screen. Baffled, I read his words again. 'Postponed your pain'? If ever there existed evidence of the trauma he'd caused me, it coursed through my body so violently now I had to sit down to avoid falling over.

I went over his e-mail several times, but whichever way I looked at it, I could find no sense. Usually, the word 'liar' would have burnt me on approach. I could never have looked in its face and not fried. Rather, I'd back away, tucking my abominable hands and feet as far from shame as a good, agreeable girl could get. Any attempt to argue would certainly bring something worse. But this felt different. His swing from self-pity to attack and back was a manipulation so systematic it almost snaked across the screen. So this time, shaking I grant you, I headed back to the kettle.

In those early mornings, tea and the spring May light brought a blessed, alert peace to the only part of the day I enjoyed. A brief respite before exhaustion made it difficult to start anything, let alone finish it. Despite the shock, sunshine streamed through my French windows and I opened them as wide as they would go, but no amount of fresh air could calm me. I sat in my armchair, condemned by every sorrow, every disappointment, every frustration Tom's phrases charged me with. Yet he'd listened to my messages. Heard me begging and pleading for just a word after weeks of waiting, and done nothing. In the continuing absence of any insight to my predicament his words exposed who he really was rather than covered him up.

"I don't know what happened," I say. "Maybe the sun shone straight through him and took some kind of x-ray. Everything he said looked like a ploy to make me feel guilty. That was when I began to notice how much he needed me to see him as a vulnerable, upright bloke – and to wonder if he was only bothering to do *that* because he thought I'd tell Anita?"

Dr. Samuels' eyes widen. It's quick, and in a moment she's composed herself, but however calmly she says, "That was the first time this occurred to you?" I know she is surprised and I'm pretty sure she thinks I'm an idiot. Just like Tom does.

I can't meet her eyes. "I loved him. Telling Anita wasn't really my business. It only occurred to me when I really thought I'd die, but of course, I would never have actually done such a thing."

"You would rather have died?" Dr. Samuels looks shocked so I shake my head because I don't know how to answer.

The clock ticks too loudly from the wall, marking each step that I take away from the Tom I loved. The texture of his shirt, the smell of his neck, the colour in his soul are stored in each second, sealed tight by every tick. Fixed. Past. Soon our story will be like a strip of film, our living, breathing love a series of dead images, because if I don't have him, I can't keep them alive.

"You said that you briefly escaped the shame when you got Tom's long email. When you saw through him. Do you remember that?" she asks, settling back into her own chair. She rubs her palms on her thighs and waits.

I do remember that x-ray quality and the anger. I nod a lot, forcing myself to croak, "Yes."

"Yet before too long you ended up in the same place, surrounded by self-blame. You just did the same, here. I think I know how. Let me see." Again she checks. "It was that moment you saw that Tom was trying to keep you sweet, because he thought you'd tell Anita... Wasn't that it?" Dr. Samuels bangs her hand flat on her thigh.

He thought I'd tell Anita? The memory spears through both temples. "I was so afraid."

"Of what, Gina?"

"Of fading away," I manage to say, but I mean I was afraid of losing my mind. My vision becomes restricted. Trying to speak louder than the rushing in my ears, I hear myself tell Dr. Samuels that even if I had told Anita I could never have won, because Tom needed to get rid of her. My tongue feels coated with tar but I try and try to make her see that telling Anita wouldn't have helped because he'd have used my betrayal as an excuse to get rid of me too.

Dr. Samuels looks concerned. "I can feel the panic in you, Gina. Can you feel it as you talk? Can you feel it *making* you talk? Making you think this way?"

Panic, dread, darkness, evil. Of course I can feel them. They are creeping onto my feet and up my legs, trying to gain access to my soul through my ears or my nostrils, but I won't let them in through my mouth. My words push them back. "It's impossible to explain. He compels people to see things his way, and they don't even know it's happening. I kept trying to show him what I saw. How could he refuse after all we'd been through?" I reach toward her. "But his view of things became *the* view. Voices began to sneer at me in my dreams," but when Dr. Samuels asks me what they said, I can't remember because I'm trying to keep them away.

I watch the lines soften on her face; see her droopy jowls up close. Astonishingly close. They're warm and smiley. "OK," she says, and the danger fades. I collapse. My lungs empty. My fingers go flat.

She waits a while before pointing out that Tom thinking badly of me seems impossible to bear. "Let's stay with that moment," she says. "Where the sunshine showed him up." And I know she's right because when I go back there I can feel the way I turned on myself.

I sense Dr. Samuels holding her breath, concerned not to reignite my shame, which helps. "You're right," I say, careful to articulate one word at a time. "First, I got that he was trying to manipulate me, but then I saw his low opinion of me and... well... it sort of... took over. I knew he must be right." I keep my breathing shallow so that I can't be swamped. "I thought that if he was some kind of bad person I was worse, because he'd said such appalling things about Jane and I'd just simpered along."

"So having latched onto the idea that you were a bad person, it seemed reasonable to you that you must have been been hatching a plan to tell Anita about him all along – if you didn't get your own way?"

She waits, but the rushing sound gets louder.

"Is that how the fire – the fire of shame, as it were – got a hold?"

Fire? I nod and I shake my head, hoping that the noise will recede or be thrown off, like the water on a dog when it shakes its coat. I really can't remember anything but those weeks of waiting: the mornings of watching the forget-me-nots on my patio crush each other as they fought to stretch their fading blooms higher; the afternoons where they showered one another in a last dusty gasp of pollen.

Tom had told me his deadline would be at the end of May, but by the second week in June, I'd heard nothing. A night-storm blasted the late-flowering lilac at their peak and smashed them off at the neck, scattering still-born clusters of stars across a soaked lawn. It was dawn, a week before midsummer. I wandered the garden in my nightdress, gathering the white blooms in my arms, crooning to them. In the kitchen, I placed them, like a

wreath, in a round flat bowl. Halfway up the stairs, I became detached from my own body and watched myself enter the bedroom, where in one seamless movement I smashed the bowl of lilac through the closed window then followed it out through the broken glass.

I felt my palms first, sticky against the pottery. Then my shins burning through the thin nightdress where they'd banged against the stair. Cold as stone, and aware only that the me that had thrown myself from the window was less than twenty seconds ahead, I placed the lilac on the step above and slid back down to the hall where I held onto the carpet. And there I lay, face-down, squeezing the stubby woollen fibres, telling myself over and over that I had a daughter and that her name, like her bright, warm soul, was June. June. My June, not Tom's. My everlasting flame that seemed to rise in the sky, for me – making a yellow haze of the warming hall until I wept for her.

Gradually, the fibres slipped from my fingers and I sat up, leaning against the wall, knowing that if I was going to survive, I had to do something. I had to act.

I went to the bathroom and showered and dressed. I would travel down to the writing centre and knock on the door of Tom's house. If Anita answered, so be it. I'd been driven to this, as Jane had been driven crazy before me. As I approached the car, my pace slowed. Jane had looked crazy. She'd been made to look crazy. And if Tom wasn't in his house, I knew I'd have to go to the writing centre where I'd bang open both doors of the old barn in which the students listened to their lectures.

And then what? I saw myself as others would see me. A crazy woman, framed in light, raving.

I reconsidered. It would be far safer to give him a chance to answer the charges privately. Writing them down would take the heat out of me and then, if he didn't respond, I'd lost nothing. All the strategies I'd ever attributed to Tom began to boil in my head. Horrors I'd dismissed as my own paranoia began to formulate so fast that my fingertips itched to write them down.

```
----- Original Message -----
From: Gina Fulbright
To: Tom Hanson
Sent: June 5. 2006 08.45 AM
Subject: [Norton AntiSpam] Visit
We're two adults. You have all my understanding
but you also have my broken heart. A heart you
could probably fix with a five minute phone
call, except that as you continue to cut
yourself off, you can't even do that, so unless
you get back to me right now, I'm coming down. I
shall see you very soon.
```

"Blimey," says Dr. Samuels, who has chirped up considerably. "What happened?"

I grin, because looking at it from Dr. Samuels' point of view, what happened next seems entirely predictable. "I boiled another kettle, made some more tea, went for a walk round the garden and returned to my computer. An email was waiting."

From: Tom Hanson
To: Gina Fulbright
Sent: June 07. 2006 09.02 AM
Subject: Re: [Norton AntiSpam] Visit

Didn't you get this?

To: Gina Fulbright

Sent:May 31. 2006 10.05 AM
Subject: Re: [Norton AntiSpam] Visit

Dear Gina; I have finished; finished yesterday. And first thing in the morning the taxi comes to take me on holiday. I still want to meet and talk, if you'd like that. At least I can listen again, or try to; I'm back on the 6th.
Love, as ever
Txxxxxxxxxxxxxxxxxxxxxxxxxxxxxxxxxxxxxxxxxxxxxxxxxxx
xxxxxxxxxxxxxxxxxxxxxxxxxxxxxxxxxxxxxxxxxxx

I have no way to prove that I sent you that email before I went away, at least I don't think so. It's in my sent box, and didn't get bounced back.
I would love to meet and talk. I have always

known how much pain I caused you. Is there
anything I can do now? I would very much like
to, and I would have thought that meeting and
talking is a first step.
Txxxxxxxxxxxxxxxxxxxxxxxxxxxxxxxxxxxxx

Dr. Samuels screws up her eyes as if she can't bear it.

I nod. "It's hard to explain – but the tone of his email...
After all that time waiting, it was like actually being with him
again. And that was all I wanted. I wanted it so much... "

"So did you go to meet him?"

"Yes." But I'm not convinced. I'm not sure who it was
that went to meet him. A wraith. A mere outline. Where a
person with her own opinions had been, only doubt
remained, shifting from one view to another. Was he kind,
caring, exhausted Tom or a calculating manipulator?
Choices, again. And whatever the truth was, I couldn't
handle it because whichever way I looked, I was supposed to
leave him alone.

Dr. Samuels is watching closely and I know my thoughts
have been mirrored in the movements of my eyes. Left, right.
Up, down. Grind, grind, grind. "Well, it does sound like, at
the time, you had no choice," she says.

"I needed an answer," I say, astonished at the
understatement. I needed not to die. He was my food, my
water. She's right. There was nothing else I could have done.

**I was a wreck. The clothes it had taken me half a
morning to choose hung off me. Tom sported a deep tan
from lying on a beach for a week. We sat in a pub**

garden and looked at the wide shallow brook shimmering along the boundary. Fear of sounding stupid made me shake as I spoke to him, but his presence was as effective as ever. Before long the appearance of his rapt attention had me babbling like the brook we stared at to avoid looking one another in the eye. He winced a lot but was obviously determined to sit through an afternoon. Perhaps he saw it as penance, this tolerating of what he couldn't stand or understand, and as he bore it he attempted to communicate back.

"When you said I looked like a coward – when we last slept together at the Travelodge – something inside me broke. All I could hear was you and Liz and Patricia, all calling me coward. But behind that... I want you to understand." He stopped and caught me with his deep sad gaze until I could do nothing but return it. "I believe I killed Liz. You know that, don't you? She haunts me now. Hers is the voice behind the whispers that fill the space she left when she abandoned me. She emptied me of everything and all that remained was my betrayal, with no possible appeal, ever."

I stared across the brook, over the tops of the hedges that lined the country lane. The green parkland beyond became a sheet of thin baize, fraying at the edges. The shadowless oak trees shrank to mere parasites, sucking the last of the air from the sky. As I exhaled, I found myself back on the threshold of the writing centre kitchen, re-experiencing that void between him and Anita when I had first really seen him.

That shock.

That nothing.

It was Tom's personal wasteland.

Again, I felt Liz whisper from the grave, happy fool that I'd been to hear only what I'd wanted to. She meant *For God's sake take him and tell him to let me go.*

Tears rolled down Tom's cheeks. "I couldn't face that again."

I sat at that picnic table with the strap of my too-big summer dress fallen against my arm, unable to eat. My home was half-furnished, my husband long gone, divorce papers served, daughter reluctant to return from university and my world effectively over. And why? Because Tom couldn't bear to feel what life and his own actions had brought.

"And so now, in turn, you have abandoned me. You found a place to put all the crap, all the destruction, and you left it behind," I said simply and even he, however briefly, had to agree.

"We might be caught up in the past," I said, reaching to touch his face, "but we're more than that."

He jerked away, hardly pausing for breath. "I know how much I've hurt you," he said. "Is it really such a big deal? I'd have thought you'd have moved on after all this time."

Dr. Samuels gives an exasperated sigh, but it's not enough. Unable even now to believe Tom's response, I say, outraged, "He had clung to a ghost for sixteen years before finding a way to get someone to love him so much that he could merge with them and then leave behind all his guilt and despair – pass on the impact of Liz's death by getting rid of me."

The quiet between us is heavy with my unspoken demand that she agrees. All doubt has left me yet this shining certainty sounds ludicrous. Psychotic even. But I don't care. If she fails me now, I'll go screaming into a life of locked wards.

She's backtracking, her face smoothing into a mask, but I won't have it. I shall chisel that look of anger back even if I have to shout it at her. "Tom *made* me love him. *Made* me need him. *Made* me trust him until I was so open he could dump everything he had felt about Liz's death by jettisoning me like rubbish from a space-station," I insist. "And then he couldn't even remember how bad that felt."

Dr. Samuels waits. And waits. She waits long enough for me to watch the space-station fade as I drop into the black. No up, no down. No back, no forward. No time, just space for ever/anon. Eventually she says, "I guess that would be the point."

And I know she understands. I watch her gazing into the interstellar dark. A shiver starts up, deep in my chest. It spreads to my arms. My fingertips have gone white. She understands, because I have pushed her to where *I* am. A final question rattles out before my chest freezes solid. A stony last request as likely to seal the door of our tomb as smash it open. "Have you... now that I've... " As my own vocabulary fades, I struggle for one last clarification. "Perhaps, by telling you... all this... all this detail, I have done the same to you."

But she smiles. The dark snaps open. A line of light spreads. "Well, let's just say I'm noticing how much you needed him to see it your way. And now, since he's not here, you need me to do the same," says Dr. Samuels, clear and slow. "Obviously, it would be very satisfying to go and hit him, but that wouldn't help you, would it?"

To me, this is so clearly not the case that I smile back at her. It's a good answer, but not enough. If we stay in this place, so does the darkness. Waiting. But her smile remains. Her warmth is pink. I rub my hands together over and over, desperate to absorb some of it. "So what do you think? You're a psychiatrist. Are such things possible? Or common?"

"We're here to talk about you," she says.

"What if Tom enjoyed switching off Liz's life-support?"

She doesn't bat an eyelid. "Then wouldn't it follow that we'd be unable to believe a single thing he ever told you?"

Up until now, I've experienced the possibility of thinking freely only as a terror of being cut loose. Now I feel as though I've dived into fresh air only to discover I can walk on it.

"The things he said Patricia did, particularly after Liz's death, made me want to go and slap her," I exclaim, and the rage I feel is so great it lifts me out of my chair and onto my feet. But it's no longer anger towards Patricia: it's Tom I want to kill. I turn, lifting my arms. Popeye has eaten the spinach. The Incredible Hulk has burst through his shirt. I hold the pose, thinking again of the story: Patricia had no sympathy with Tom's grief. She kicked him when he was down. Then I remember that my whole response could have been a nonsense, because he could simply have been lying. I let myself teeter, then collapse into my seat and hold tight to the arms of the wheelchair.

"So the feeling has picked you up and let you drop again?"

"Yes – like I was filled with hot air – and it was his outrage – the air of his outrage and then... "

Dr. Samuels beams.

"The moment I doubted him, the hot air went. Worse!" I cry, trying to name what happened before it fades. "The ground went too. Completely. Not just the bit about Patricia, but everything he ever told me. The stuff about his life that I was using to make sense of who he was. It went."

"Well," says Dr. Samuels. "The sharing of experience to take the heat out of feeling is very common. You do it. We all do it. Just now when I said I wanted to hit Tom you looked relieved. What happened?"

I think for a moment. "I got less angry – like the anger was out there. It existed. It was justified and someone else was... " I falter, looking for the right word.

"Carrying it?" Dr. Samuels suggests.

"Doing it." I wait again, feeling more substantial than ever before in this room.

"Well that's a tiny and very mild taste of what can go on between people, and I'm only going to say as much as I think will be helpful." With these provisos in place she takes a deep breath. "We're not as good at expressing our feelings as we think. Sometimes, when we decide our feelings are a problem, we stop feeling them altogether. But they don't really go away. So we need someone else to feel them instead.

Then we can label that other person as 'the problem'.' "

Completely gripped, I say, "Go on."

"Well, we tend to use the person closest to us. We start to believe that *they* are feeling what we can't bear to feel. We think that what they do and say is coming from those feelings – feelings we unconsciously recognise but can't acknowledge in ourselves."

The room in the Travelodge is not solid. Dawn light seeps through our bodies into the bed. My head is more pores than skin, blood and bone and the daffy-down pillow it sinks into is the sea of Tom's perfume that holds this form – this breast, these arms, legs, person – together. I turn on my side, amazed by my volition, words surging out of me like a dying breath: *I cannot live without you*.

"I cannot live without you," I murmur. "I really fell into that one, didn't I?"

Dr. Samuels speaks very, very softly. "And you? What about you? It does work both ways, this story-making."

"That's what I've been trying to tell you. After we split up, the stories were like a demon at my elbow, whispering that in order for the illusion he'd cast to hold completely, Tom had to be seen as an honest, loving man who didn't have a duplicitous bone in his body. Anita had to be perceived as having such delicate health that a shock could seriously damage her. And I... " It's painful to acknowledge, dangerous to think about. "I had to look like a brief aberration. All these horrible ideas... " Confused, I shout,

"But I can't believe that for Tom – brilliant Tom – I seemed like the source of these difficult feelings and instead of looking at himself he... he – ejected *me*."

"Well, didn't you cling to him?"

"Not really," I yell. "You see? This stuff is so infectious even you can't really grasp that expecting a few emails and an explanation after all that passion wasn't unreasonable."

Dr. Samuels smiles. "Well, I'm very glad *you* can."

Her words calm me. "What I can't get is how *he* couldn't see it. However much I told him about my difficulty, he could only see what he wanted to."

"Really?" Dr. Samuels has that look on her face again. The one where she knows something I don't.

"Yes," I say, annoyed that she's not just agreeing with me. "I mean, we'd been in this together – this bliss. This... this joinedness. Well... " I flick my hand up "...not even joinedness really, because when we were merged we were only one."

She nods. It's irritating. And unnecessary, but I might as well point out how it all worked. "So obviously, when he pulled away, he left me feeling I was going to die. I needed proof that I wasn't, because however much I knew what was going on, my body was in spasm... "

"Hang on. You sound very sure – about what was going on for you."

"Oh, I know what it's all about. I'd told him. Told him and told him," I say, airily. I must have been so wrapped up in the story of Tom that I omitted to fill Dr. Samuels in. I know all this stuff of course, but I suppose she needs to as well. Just for reference. I run through my history. "The reason I couldn't get out of that feeling was because I'd been stuck in it before. My mother was ill. Kidney stones. Very, very bad when she was pregnant with me and she had to have the kidney removed a few weeks after I was born. It burst on the operating table and she nearly died."

"OK," she nods.

I think she might be humouring me. I've no idea why. I thought this was stuff psychiatrists considered important. "I lost her," I add. "First when I was tiny, tiny, tiny, and then she got really ill again when I was about four months old. I went to stay with an aunt who had two other young kids and didn't want me. Apparently, I screamed the place down." I smile. It's the family story. The one that demonstrates what a pain I always was. "So I started out being difficult and carried on like that for the rest of my childhood, but it explains a lot."

"Anyway," I say, glad to have passed that bit of information on, "When he dumped me I went mad, as you might expect, and I needed him to help – with the feelings. That was all it was," I add as a matter of fact. "I needed to know he was still there, and just to acknowledge me every now and then. He knew all this stuff."

"And you expected him to deal with it?"

"Yes."

"Because he was so brilliant. So empathic?"

"Yes," I say.

"You're sure about that?"

"Yes."

"You can't believe, that with all that brilliance and empathy, he couldn't see you clearly?"

"No," I say.

"And what about your father? Wasn't he empathic when he was singing or teaching? What about your brother, who could do everything? Didn't you always believe that one day they'd see what you needed and come to the rescue?"

Something is creeping up on me. I look ahead, trying to avoid it, but what I see is a red-suited Father Christmas in green wellies opening his arms wide to swing me in the air. I recognise those blue eyes that twinkle straight through me: I know you; I love you. Afterwards, I can never connect those wellington boots in our hallway with the vicious impatient father who shouts. I look to the side and see my brother, standing on the vinyl seat in the local coffee bar. He is telling the story of Albert, who was eaten by a lion, to a crowd of listening schoolgirls. John Lennon's nasal voice grates from the jukebox, backing singer to Peter's seismic presence. Together they rip down the walls, open up a highway out of this one-horse town in which we just exist. *I am the greatest. I am the Walrus.* Peter, Cassius Clay, The Beatles, Bob Dylan: for me, they're interchangeable. Big brothers, boxers, rock and roll stars, they're all heroes.

A light touch on my hand alerts me to the presence of Dr. Samuels. She waits until I am looking at her before saying, "What is it that *you* can't bear?"

I see my father's yellow head, slack jaw, wax fingers all shrinking. The white room he lies in is vividly alive; the curtains and counterpane breathing as he stiffens.

The words, "Two years are not enough," burst from me. Two years between two rooms. The second as oblong as the coffin in it. The smirk my brother wore just after death remains, but I no longer think he will wake. The bags beneath his eyes are green. Purple stitches show at the top of his chest above the absurd frills they have dressed him in.

Slowly, Dr. Samuels shakes her head. "Two years are not enough," she says.

No. It's not OK. It's not OK. It's not OK.

Chapter Eighteen

Beatrice watched Gina wheel herself to the end of the corridor before returning to sit at her desk. Her pen felt ludicrously heavy, and although she managed to write the words *Projective Identification* on her notepad, when she came to the last letter *n*, instead of stopping, she slid the nib in a line down the page. Once at the bottom, lost for where to go or how to be, Beatrice wrote *Borderline* in tiny letters, in the margin.

Because the truth was that although Beatrice had waited, then soothed the girl until her grief had quietened, Gina's expression of shock had broken straight through the borders that held Beatrice together as an everyday, functioning person. Up to that point, her sense of Ralph as dead had been object-like. Her own grief had been a *thing* contained by outbursts of distress. Because if you had an *outburst*, she saw, retrospectively, that out of which you had burst was there for you to return to.

Narcissist, she wrote, on the far side of the page, parallel to the word *borderline*, because gathering her thoughts and transforming them into marks on paper might pull her back together. Writing did help. She spent some time focusing on the specific events Gina had just remembered: Tom's apparent lost email, his therefore-late apology for blaming her. Tom's sudden willingness to meet, and the way that had arrived on the heels of Gina's first ever decision to act against his interests. And the further Beatrice's notes shifted toward what and when Tom had acted or not acted, the more comprehensible Gina's delusions became. Whatever Tom had felt, his talent for focusing on Gina must have taken her back to Eden prior to its fall. To before she had so suddenly and traumatically lost her mother. It was always the mother. Not for the first time, Beatrice felt glad to be childless. At the most fundamental level, in just the manner she – Beatrice – had briefly lost herself – Gina could not understand that she was a separate and different adult to Tom, and that his actions had nothing to do with her except in the most rudimentary, self-protective way. Stuck in that place, Gina had no choice but to keep relating everything to herself, trying – trying until her joints were so stretched she lived on painkillers – to understand Tom.

Still trying to nail down her perspective and needing more space than A4 could provide, Beatrice cleared her desk and with a piece of chalk, listed the months from January to July horizontally along the centre. When she chalked a loop between the arrival time of Tom's last emails and the time he said he'd sent them, between his apparent time of apology and the time of Gina's decision to fight, the desk looked like one big scribble, much as Beatrice knew Gina felt. Every lie was so eloquent; each episode of apparent absent-mindedness so charming. No wonder Tom's actions looked designed to undermine rather than the desperate behaviour of a man cornered. And no wonder Gina looked to her own failings. Because when you were struggling not to be ripped in half, blaming yourself for the situation became the only option.

She stepped back from the desk but felt something pressing on her. Not wanting to turn, she kept her eyes on her work, her mind concentrated, but the pressure in the room seemed to spread, weighing down the air. Trying to ignore it, Beatrice thought about her role and responsibilities, but questions about moral and statutory duties faltered, crushed by a sense of something behind. When finally she turned, she found herself looking at a blur of air and light. Where the chair and the walls and the photos on the walls and the windows and the blinds and the door were, she saw only bars of fog, a substance differing from the air around her in density only. Just her work on the desk remained – the representation of Tom and Gina's relationship fixed in time and space – the only thing fixing *her* in time and space.

Frightened, she reached out, touched the chair and then the wall, but far from reassuring her, these objects seemed cold and distant. Slowly, knowing that she would not find him, yet unable to stop herself from trying, she eyed every corner.

Searching.

For Ralph.

She went to the door and looked into the corridor. The lino, so blue when she'd arrived this morning, had dulled to grey, barely different from the walls that rose on either side.

And then Beatrice knew that her brain too, was grey. That her organs differentiated from her epidermis and her epidermis from this plastic-seeming hospital only minutely. But that carbon was carbon and atoms were atoms and that this might just as well be Ralph. That Ralph, as she knew him, was gone.

Returning to her room, she managed only to slam the

door before doubling up to sit, winded, against the wall, taking tiny sips of breath in case a full, deep one should overwhelm her the way a malt whisky might send the world reeling.

She sat for how long? Knees up, knees down. Weeping. Dry-eyed. Fingers in mouth. Palms face-up. Through all these positions she sat sipping air and reminding herself that Ralph no longer existed. Although he appeared now and then in the corner of the room looking quite upset, she silenced him by remaining silent herself and that way, eventually, she knew him to be, as she had known really since his death, only a phantom of her imagination.

Empty now as an aircraft hangar, vast as outer space, the peace this understanding brought with it felt as soft as the last few months had been hard, and her sense of purpose as clear as it had been blurred. She knew only that she must go back to Rome. The desire to see everything that mattered writ small, perfected, beholdable, became the only thing that made sense and she grabbed it. Only there in Rome could she say goodbye. He was already gone – long gone, but she needed one last and absolute goodbye. She'd make it sudden. Like nipping off for a coffee, leaving him to stare at the statue of Romulus and Remus for a while when she'd had her fill. A weekend would do.

Her sitting bones dug into the floor, but painful as that was, she remembered the earlier horror when everything seemed to be giving way, and felt glad. Her phone vibrated in her bag. A message from Corinne, who obviously had predictive text: *Droopal loaf damage? Have d.o.b. but need your backing to go after notes.* Despite all the tears, her laugh filled the room. *Droopal loaf?* Wonderful. And *damage?* Perhaps Corinne was caving in under pressure? Now that the grief Beatrice had been lugging around for so long had exhausted itself, she couldn't stop grinning. Grinning with relief and gratitude. Gina had portrayed the sheer craziness of grief with the power of a Greek tragedy – blinding – impossible to resolve. Engaging with Gina's battle, Beatrice had vicariously fought her own, gasping when she gasped, loving when she loved. No-one could have shown her what Gina had. And letting go? The muscles in her chest ached.

Back at her desk, she traced the still visible chalk marks with her finger before licking it and striking them through. Up (slash). Down (slash). Down (slash). Up (slash). Down (slash). Turning the chalk she had used on its side, she scored a thick horizontal line through it all. The mother line, fixed in time and space. Monolithic. Non-negotiable. *Tom made me love him. Made me need him. Made me trust him.*

Deeper magic. Yes, they would find it together. As Gina had taken Beatrice confidently into a daytime world filled with a coherent story – even one with an unhappy ending – so Beatrice would follow Gina down to the underworld. And if Gina should doubt or look back, Beatrice would be behind her still, because what indeed would Gina have to hold onto but only and entirely the certainty that Beatrice would not abandon her?

She was just trying to visualise the whereabouts of a file when a text arrived officially informing her that Mr. Slattery was now deceased and no longer had a bed. The way it had been written seemed pompous. As if the hospital was rather put out. Not as put out as Mr. Slattery. She found herself irrationally pleased that the poor man had managed to throw a spanner in their admin and triumph over something after all.

Which made her think of Ralph. When he'd died, the admin had rolled into motion so smoothly you'd hardly have known anything of importance had occurred. His will had been all settled, of course. On her. As hers was on him. All sorted, by him, years ago. For the first time, she became aware that when she died he would no longer be the recipient. If she didn't do something about it her house and savings would end up with her sister, who was married to a banker.

Money, she asked. *What do I do with the money?* But instead of Ralph's answer she heard her own words from that morning: *You're like the daughter I never had*. She replied to Corinne, arranging to meet her in the canteen at one, and settled at her desk with an old fashioned pen and paper. One day, Corinne might have more to thank old Mr. Slattery for than she could ever imagine.

Chapter Nineteen

By 12.45 the main canteen on the ground floor was half full of what looked like an extended family sitting blankly around a too-small formica table in front of several untouched cups of tea. Corinne recognised one of them as a son of the deceased. She was quietly pleased that to a person, the whole crowd looked upset.

By comparison, Beatrice bloomed. Putting down the coffee she'd just bought, she said sympathetically, "How's your loaf feeling now?"

Corinne frowned.

"Your text?" Beatrice showed her the screen.

"I meant frontal *lobe* damage," said Corinne, stiffly. "Tom Hanson." Trying to be professional, she rushed on with her findings. "I'm seeing stuff I've never come across before. Spent the morning on the internet, but of course, it's all... well... " She faltered. Telling a senior psychiatrist that she'd made a couple of diagnoses through Google was absurd. Beatrice must think her an idiot. But when she looked up she saw only affection.

"I think that's very resourceful," said Beatrice. "What did you find? More to the point," she added, looking serious, "how did finding that information make you feel?"

Corinne searched back through her morning and remembered the clarity Tom's symptoms had seemed to offer before his weird on-screen persona had pulled her into a dark fairy-tale wood. "Relieved," she answered. "I was really relieved to discover that someone, somewhere might

know something about people who have massive problems –
well, people who make massive problems for other people...
to find there might be a... a... a load of symptoms." Seeing
how carefully Beatrice was listening, she went on, "That gave
me some idea what to expect. I mean, not what I would
expect, because – well – because – I wouldn't want to *expect*
anything." Muddled now, and exasperated, she looked
Beatrice straight in the eye and risked the truth. "It made me
feel p – empowered, I suppose. Not so I could control him,"
she added, worried again. "More so I'd be ready for him."

Slowly, Beatrice added, "Ready to defend yourself
against any nonsense that might be thrown at you by him?"

"Yes."

"So that must be quite a shift, I should think, from how
you've been trained?" said Beatrice. "Having some categories
at your fingertips rather than an entirely open mind?"

"Yes," said Corinne, excited by the idea, though
confused about how it would be possible to be unbiased
with all those labels floating in your head.

But Beatrice seemed to understand. Even to think those
concerns might matter.

"Much more important, to have that open mind than to
start with fixed ideas," she said. "About the labels though –
what matters is understanding that our heads are full of
assumptions anyway. It's what you do with them that
matters." She winked, slowly. "And don't let anyone tell you
different."

"Well – of course, I know that," said Corinne, disturbed
by the assumption that she didn't. Nonetheless, she had a
sudden apprehension that a head full of naive goodwill was a

head neither free of assumptions nor particularly able to anticipate what might be going on in someone else's head. "But what *should* you do with 'em?" she blurted. "That's what I want to know."

But Beatrice appeared pleased, taking the question seriously. "Well – first you need to become conscious of what your assumptions are. Then you need to put them to one side."

All Corinne could see was her own vague notion that if you were nice enough to people and you got them to talk, they'd sort themselves out. "Go on," she urged.

Beatrice smiled as if the request was welcome, moving closer to make sure Corinne could hear. "OK. Let's start with Tom Hanson. You'd consciously hold the assumption that he might have – what was it – *frontal lobe damage?* on one side, as a possibility. Given this assumption... Beatrice began to tap each finger of her hand as she checked through a list of symptoms, "...you'd talk to your patient and listen to their story, but with one eye out for empathy. Then, are they likely to take big risks?" She tapped a second finger, then a third. "You'd be looking out for boasting – to see how strong their sense of entitlement is, but overall," she swept one hand across the other, "you'd want to know whether anyone else had been strongly affected by their behaviour and whether they'd even noticed."

"So – you'd start with a hunch, study the type and then see if someone fits in it?" Even as she said the words, Corinne knew it was hopeless. "But I've not really got any understanding of 'types' at all."

"Of course you haven't," answered Beatrice, brightly.

"You haven't needed them. Nor have you been asked to learn them because your work is very different to mine. I'm really talking about the stuff I do at Rampton. Your priority is to help people – not protect the world from nutters."

This made Corinne sink even further in her own estimation. "Yes," she said. "But that means the nutters and maybe even the people most disturbed might get away from me. To be quite honest, my assumptions aren't even what I'm thinking about when I'm working."

"Well at least you know you've got them."

"But don't they make me biased?"

Beatrice squeezed Corinne's hand rather tighter than expected and said firmly, "No. They mean you're alive rather than dead, and I suspect, given permission to actually hear them, you'd find you're more aware of them than you think, with all that therapy you've done."

Corinne's eyes moistened. "Really? Do you think so?"

"I do," said Beatrice. "And in your kind of work, you really only need to know what you're thinking so that you can put those thoughts or beliefs at the back of your mind." Beatrice paused. "Then, if they're obviously prejudiced, ditch them. Just don't let your ideas about who people are or what you think they need take over. Now – lets find a better example – more relevant to your work. Have you had any other ideas that we might draw into the light and look at?"

Plenty. After the *Mum's Matter* group, Corinne had returned to searching on Google and become so lost in possibilities thrown up by volume V of the *Diagnostic and Statistical Manual of Mental Disorders* that she'd begun to feel sick. So many of the symptoms listed were familiar aspects of her own inner life. To regroup she'd turned her attention to Gina's obsession instead. "I er… " she stumbled, but Beatrice looked so quizzical and interested, beaming at her from that frizz of grey hair, that she continued. "Well, I er… found myself wondering if Gina had Stockholm Syndrome – you know – where people can't escape so they identify with the people who've captured them and end up supporting them?"

Beatrice stifled a smile. "That might make a lot of sense."

"You're kidding me."

"It has a value. All of it," said Beatrice. "Keep that group of symptoms in mind. You'd use them to expand your idea of what it might mean to be her, and if she categorically displayed behaviour that didn't fit, you'd chuck it out."

Corinne hesitated. "De Clerambaults?"

"Stalking? Love as madness? I'm sure that if you were working with her, familiarising yourself with those symptoms might help you – and to do what? What would the point be, for a counsellor?" she asked, smiling. Expectant.

And the answer came easily, obvious and benign. "To broaden my ideas about what it might be like to be her? To try and stay aware of what's possible – what she might be believing or feeling?"

Scraping back the chair, Beatrice flung open her arms. "Well, I wish you'd been my student," she said.

Corinne let out a sigh and stood. Beatrice's embrace felt like being wrapped in a feather duvet. She hugged her back, found her cheek being kissed.

Beatrice laughed. "And what was all that about having a

d.o.b. and going after notes?" She lifted her phone from the table and pulled up Corinne's text again. "Obviously, I've got Gina's notes and her date of birth. If you really want to try and use them as a learning tool, I can't see why not, but we'd need to look at them together so you understood what I meant by them."

The dislocation struck Corinne visually. All of the hope and light split away leaving a hunched, dark thing. A criminal. She stumbled, falling back into her chair.

"What's wrong?" said Beatrice. "I've hugged you too tightly." When Corinne didn't respond, she stepped away from her. "I'm so sorry. Please accept my apologies. It's been a difficult day and I didn't think, didn't respect your... "

Corinne was weeping now, tensed against the slap, the kick, the contempt that she deserved. With her hands covering her face, she said,"You didn't respect me? You're so full of respect it would never occur to you that... that... "

"What?"

"That it's Tom Hanson's notes I was after." Realizing how much this would compromise Beatrice, Corinne sank. Beatrice would never mentor her now. Her behaviour proved her innate stupidity. The ruins of a career barely born lay all around. She couldn't even bring herself to look at the woman. Stumbling over her words and choked with tears, Corinne told her about the phone call before managing to mumble, "I'm really sorry."

Beatrice waited.

"It – it's so wrong. Me – the person who thinks people should be taken as seen, just ignoring that when I felt like it."

Beatrice nodded.

"You've been so nice and I'm so worthless. I got excited. I was trying to get your approval and all I've done is fuck it up and I lied and now," she wailed, tears streaming down her face, "it's all fucked."

A smile of sympathy spread across Beatrice's face. "So you ignored your beliefs, did you?" she lulled, "but now it's – what did you say? 'It's all fucked.' You've totally fucked it?" She reached into her bag, took out one of Ralph's big handkerchiefs and passed it across the table.

And helped by that simple act, Corinne saw what her therapist had been banging on about for the last five years. As if a tiny crack opened in her brain – thin enough to slide a piece of paper down. As if she were standing on one side of that crack and her self-hatred on the other, she saw that main assumption screaming back, there, now. *You're so bad, so wrong, so worthless. you've fucked everything.* Self-hatred in the driving seat, looking through the windscreen of her eyes, defining every act she'd miscalculated as bad and battering her every hope.

When she'd wiped away her tears, Corinne's initial response was to tell Beatrice she'd been a complete idiot, but when she realised that the words, 'complete' and 'idiot' were more of the same, she carefully and slowly said, "I really am sorry. I got so carried away. I didn't stop and think. I really hope I haven't done any real damage."

"Actually," said Beatrice. "I think it might have done you some good. But please," she added, sounding quite reassured, "next time you find yourself being unorthodox, stop. Think about it, and then run what you've thought about past me." And Corinne glimpsed again, not utter destruction, but a safety net, hope, the possibility of getting something wrong and that being OK.

Beatrice stood. "Really, Corinne, I'm very excited about your desire to learn. I'll get you those books." She paused, thinking of something else. "I'm away for the weekend, so I might not see you until Monday. I'm here tomorrow but have a stack of admin. Then I'm going to Rome for the weekend. I think that's why my hug was so tight."

"Why Rome?" asked Corinne, anxious that her question might be an intrusion.

"I need to say goodbye to my husband."

"See you next week then," said Corinne, feeling exposed before noticing that they both were. That to love was to risk bumping into the loved one's most tender places daily. She grinned. "And your hugs are lovely," she added, watching until Beatrice left through the swing door. Then she straightened herself up, walked over to Mr. Slattery's family and offered her condolences.

Chapter Twenty:1

I am doing Recreational Therapy, in the basket weaving class, standing at the side of the long wooden table in one of the pincers. Well, that's what I call them but these are permanently open. Also, they're upholstered in blue PVC, like chair arms, so that if I lean on them, or fall, the impact won't break my shoulder, or one of my ribs. I am being rehabilitated, arms and legs strengthened 'with each tick of the clock'. The Recreation Assistant woman changes every Monday but the clock ticks on: time measured mechanically but experienced aurally because a cog turns a wheel and that wheel clicks a strip of plastic on the surface of the white moon-face on the wall.

This is the stuff I think about as I stand in front of six balls of raffia, picking one colour, weaving it between the willow sticks that protrude from a hardboard base and snipping it before placing another layer on. Raffia time. Plastic-strip time. I won't say I enjoy it, but I find it comforting. Manageable. My thoughts wander to stars we only know about *because* they measure time even though they no longer exist, and not only that, our planet *didn't* exist at the time that that star *did*, but I can pull myself back by focusing on the plan for yellow to follow red and blue to follow yellow. Dr. Samuels says this is good for me and I'm sure she's right. There's no smoking here, not like there would be in prison or in the past, so no chance of measuring time by the amount of tobacco I get through. I suppose it makes sense – all that ash in the raffia – but I think the room loses something by it. Despite, or perhaps because of Radio Two's lilting tones, the restriction on smoking has an air of menace.

Because Radio Two is not good for me. Something is wrong with the introduction to *Echo Beach* because it is not *Echo Beach*. Or even *Martha and the Muffins*. I have been fooled by the similar beginning and the soft, funny name. A single guitar riff has sneaked inside my head but it is *Blue Oyster Cult* and when that drumbeat explodes, I'm riddled with holes. Voices, gentle as Simon and Garfunkel's persuade me to jump into the unknown. They call me *baby* and take my hand and tell me not to fear the reaper. But really, it's Tom. He's sitting inside the speaker because Radio Two is on Tom's side.

Here comes a candle to light you to bed. Here comes a chopper. But it's OK, baby, we'll be able to fly. The word 'seasons' stabs at my rigid body. Again? Like in *Oh Lori*. Clues dropped by Tom in his cat and mouse game. *You've been around the block a few times.* But I never paid attention. How could I have missed it? The middle eight has dropped into a minor key. The drum-brush swishes, heralding the scream of the guitar solo. Chaotic. Deafening. Come for its dues. The reaper is Tom and I am being erased. Scraped off. Soon, like the Witch of the West, I shall be nothing but a mass of steam. Like the Little Mermaid, I shall turn to foam, because the soul I thought I could create is nothing but vanity and greed.

But the hand on the table in front of me tells me I have not turned to foam, or melted. I reach for a ball of red raffia and even though squeezing it shoots pain up my arm, I'm reassured. I put it to one side and with the other hand, do the same with a blue ball. I start to cut lengths off each and sort them into piles. Piles of time will put this horror behind me. Everyone says what a healer it is, and if I cut the twine small enough – too small to knot round my wrists, for instance – Tom cannot get me. Not enough time. The clock clicks. I urge it on but Tom's ahead of me, he's left the speaker and jumped inside me, whispering what he's told me before, shattering my strategy before it's begun. *You don't take up my time. You are my time. And my time, Princess, is coming.*

Over and over, I mutter "I will not fear the reaper. I will not fear the reaper," but I know he can wait. He's told me often enough. *It will take a lifetime to tell you what I mean.* I fight back, tuning his words to my own meaning. A lifetime. He will spend a lifetime, *my* lifetime, *my* waiting. But on he croons: *You are my muse, and you run through everything I do. I hope that you won't give up on me. Time really is an illusion, and our day really will come.*

I steel myself, separating red from yellow, blue from red. There are no stories in eternity, only stories about it, and if I'm to sort lies from truth I will have to ignore those, because there is no separation in eternity and I need distance. Time = distance. I shall distance myself from his lies, and I know they are lies, at least some of them, because I began to spell separation as seperation, like he did. And that was wrong. He could be wrong. We are not together in eternity because otherwise my hand would not be shaking or my body stretched to breaking trying to get there. I will be in space-time, with my piles of colour, my varying wavelengths of energy that look like raffia. That for the purposes of building my sanity, however restricted the view, *are* raffia.

Every length tells a story, his story. But which one is true? I shall sort them like I sorted the stones with Dr. Samuels.

The blue corner will be the truth corner. I shall de... deracinate (another of his words) what he said through remembering those phrases and putting them in their proper place. *Power.* That was it! *Power elites don't give up their power; they have it taken from them.* I snip a length of blue and push it to the right, to the blue corner. I must have been so grateful, so desperate for a conversation pertinent to a man and a woman that I ignored what he was actually telling me.

I cut a length of red – red will be the lies corner – and I concentrate hard. Evelyn Waugh. He mentioned Evelyn Waugh and Larkin. And Betjeman. What was it he said about them? That these rascally old men were his heroes. Problem. This is not a lie, but a statement, embedded in glamour so that I am blinded by brilliance, success, power. Anything but *I want to be a bastard, like them*. In relation to women, these men were wankers. Cowards. Yellow. It is a Yellow. And yellow, I have.

Let's take a look through the arched window. Tom is trying to distract me with his impression of Floella Benjamin but I grasp my yellow thread which is not a window from *Playschool* to look through, but a corner with sharp edges I shall use to capture his words until they cower. I'm ready for their ambiguity. And red is no longer the lies corner. There's too much truth in what he says for a solution that simple, so

I make red the danger corner and herd phrases into it on the basis of their surface meaning.

On Tom whispers: *The first thing you must know is that I have NO kindness for you. I do not want to see you for any other reason than my own UTTERLY selfish desires. My passionate love is for you; my kindness is for Anita. And for Harry. So no kindness, please, and don't suspect me of it.* Original. To a novice. Bright red, to anyone not shag-happy, but I'm listening too hard for his casual seduction to work any more. Instead of his words soothing me, they scream *beware* and I defuse them with my system before I'm fooled.

He's moaning now: *I wondered if I'd never have sex again. If I'd become divorced from the truth of my humanity.* Oh, how he complained about Anita. But later – once he'd been fucking me for a few weeks, he said – what was it? I will the words out, dredging them through the golden syrup of his obfuscating whimper: *This is the truth of what I am – someone with no redeeming features.* The shock of this idea makes his mutterings more twitchy than tinkly: *If we are 'uninhibited' in bed, if we feel able to unleash our deepest desires, then that is because we somehow both feel safe.*

Feel safe. Yes, we *felt* safe. But I don't feel safe now. I feel like a discarded sex-toy.

Every murmur spins a thread that leads further into a labyrinth: *I understand. I do. I know that I have filled you with grief and confusion. But all I can do is smile, and be happy. How bad is that?* It's bad, definitely bad and definitely red. I push a piece of raffia to the left before I too, can empathise with true love as a chaos of feelings that smashes the old order with as little concern as death strikes the living.

Love makes you do strange things. Makes a person run towards it, heedless of the danger.

I am staring from the assembly-hall window of my boarding school. Term is over. Usually, on these occasions, I heave a suitcase far too large for a twelve year old past the Mercs and Saabs that fringe the long drive, down to the Green Line bus, where I will travel for half an hour before dragging the same suitcase halfway round Luton. I have to catch the train because my father, who disagreed with the whole boarding school idea from the start, thought it a nonsense to drive from the midlands to collect me.

I am staring from the window of the Jacobean mansion because, this term, my father is coming to pick me up. Finally, I'm like the other girls next to me, noses pressed against glass. Our hearts pitter like the hearts of twelve year olds should who have a long-missed home to go to, a loving father who will take them, and a charade of filial harmony to uphold.

Up the drive he strides, beaming his ease with those Mercs and their fur-lined drivers, though he's left his battered Morris Minor further down. My excitement lifts to exaltation. I take my velour hat in my hand, skid round the tiled floor, which is approved of strictly under only these conditions, run through the open oak front doors and down the stone steps never used by pupils on any other occasion and hurtle, faster and faster down the gravel drive. My father's hat is also in his hand and his smile is as wide as his arms are flung open. I leap into them and he swings me round. Merry Christmas. He is Father Christmas and I am the Little Match Girl. He is James Stewart and I am Shirley Temple. Together we are love, reunion, obstacles weathered and overcome. And everyone watching from the window knows it. The only thing don't do is take a bow. And when I get into the car and sit on the edge of my PVC seat for the resentful, monosyllabic drive home, the feeling's worth the fall.

Tom nudges me. No memory is safe from his viewpoint because he can see everything. He approves of the little girl in me, of her total exposure; her willingness to trust. He is devastated by my father's charade, understanding how betrayal has led to my suspicion of him now. He longs to change it. I can hear his helplessness. *Darling, I don't hate you. I fucking worship you. I adore you.* Even thinking of Tom's smile now, I'm warmed, and I can't believe the filth in my own black soul that attributes such vile motives to him.

The slam of a fire-door explodes me into the recreation room. My heart stalls, starting up again as I hear a grunt. Tom's grunt. The one he always made when he first slid fully into me; the one that powered my heartbeat.

Two men are physically manoeuvring an old woman out of a chair opposite me. She has tied her wrist to the arm with raffia and is grunting as she puts effort into each short jerk away from them. A different grunt. Not of love, but force. Triumph even.

Cold spreads through me. My insides are congealing

because to Tom, I am not an equal and opposite, but a chattel. Beneath those soft lips and droopy eyes, Tom's smile is the smile of the crocodile, enjoying his prey all the more for resisting its fate. And I never even noticed. I thought his smiles meant that he approved of me and as long as his approval remained, everything was all right. When did his quiet nods become a silent put down?

As if he can read my thoughts, he whispers: *I'm not the least bit scared of you, for a very good reason, which I keep to myself.*

This is not keeping it to himself. The red corner is filling with violence – words glide towards it. His words, that are meant to sound good but are bad. *One day, I really will tie you to a bed and tease you 'til you beg me to stop.*

I am tiny. Too tiny to see through the hatch from the dining room into the kitchen. I stand on a chair, watching my mother fork waves into the mashed potato she has spread over left-over beef minced with onions. Beside the pie is a smaller dish with no onions, for me. Mrs. Dale's Diary finishes and I run to the bay window because I hear the front gate click and I know my brother and sister are back from school.

While my mother washes the Kenwood mincer, I grab my sister, but she shakes me off. "Stretch me," I say, desperate for her to stay. She's not keen and tries to run upstairs after my brother but I threaten her more and more loudly until my mother, tea-towel and mincer in hand, comes and tells her to play with her sister. My brother emerges from his bedroom, takes the stairs two at a time. He is twelve. "Stretch me," I urge, voice rising as I block his way. My brother swings his leg towards me and flips it so his foot kicks the back of my knee. It buckles and I fall. My sister takes my arms and my brother my ankles and they pull. And they pull. I take a deep breath, torn between the delicious warmth of their full attention and the wrench to my arms and legs. I wish they would pull slowly so that I can adapt and my limbs become more elastic; so that I can put up with the pain and lose myself in the grip of hands round my wrists and ankles. It hurts but I use my breath to beg them to go on. I want to feel them more than I want it to stop. Something twangs. "Stop, Stop!" I scream, despite my desire, but they carry on. My arm comes out of its socket.

My mother rushes in and they drop me and run upstairs, but not before my brother shouts, "Well, she asked for it." He is disgusted. I am mortified. A failure. My mother thinks my distress is because I have been bullied and comforts me as I wail, wretched and abandoned.

I took whatever attention I could get.

I'll tie you down until you scream.

Why did this sound so great? Because, unlike my brother, Tom *did* stop when I screamed? Was I so wrapped up in my need to be taken seriously that I never questioned the nature of his own desire? Crocodiles stupefy and disorient their prey by dragging it in and out of the water, ripping off its limbs and burying it in silt until it rots.

Perhaps men disorientate with words. Stupid. Stupid seems right. The word *Stupid* laughs up from the table, where only half-consciously, I've been forming the letters out of raffia.

"What's that, deeaarrr?" The Recreation Assistant woman is Scottish. She leans on the pincer arm as if to demonstrate its reliability. "Stupid?" She picks up a ball of twine and fiddles with a length of raffia until it says above it, in joined up writing, "I am not."

"How do you know?" I ask. It's not an accusation, like my brother would have made. Or my father. "How do *you* know?" I really want to understand, but either she can't hear this or she too, is on Tom's side.

In a low voice she says, "We doon't tell ourselves negative things when we are trying to get betterrr. It kills red blood cells and feeeds the white." She tells me this as if it is essential, but against policy to disclose such information. As if the NHS is misguided, but she has to keep her job, and for a moment I long for Tom, because he would see straight through her.

He would smile and nod.

And his nodding would communicate a tolerance that pierces my heart.

I begin to shake, scrabbling frantically to destroy the words on the table, but although they return to a mess of raffia, the viciousness of my contempt cannot be so easily erased. I have defiled Tom. Again. Too late, I see that it's not his nod that is driven by a put-down but my own.

Tom and I are as far apart as trust is from suspicion.

The word STUPID sears through me, frying my sausage fingers and melting me back into the amoeba I have always been. Spineless without his presence. Unable to rise to the challenge of loving him enough, I see now that I was sucking on his power all along, feeding on his glamour; temporarily colonising a backbone without which I'm left too cowardly even to blame myself.

Yet here he is, still declaring a degree of patience I can't fathom. His voice rocks me, like a cradle, holding to his promise:

If I'm worth waiting for, then you will have to wait. It is for you to decide whether I'm worth it, I guess.

He never snapped at me or even raised his voice, but I couldn't wait. When he needed me to keep quiet, I simply wasn't capable. I feel him looming, benign as a muffin on a winter's day. He was so much bigger than I was. But kind as he was big.

Through the yellow window, I see us framed in gold, sitting on a red-checked cloth on the soft hills of Devon. Giant oak trees whisper above us. My knees are crooked over Tom's legs as his fingertips circle my ankles. He's trying, patiently, to convey the simple beauty of mathematics with a sandwich, half a bottle of champagne and a couple of bread crusts.

I stand. The light streams through my flimsy dress. Behind me, the hills slope up to a sky so close we could run up, break a piece off and jump onto the sun as it descends into the cleavage of the world. A palpable, human, ever-wheeling world turning me on it, over Tom, under Tom. I extinguish Euclid with one flick of my knickers. One and one make one. I won. Enchanting, to a man who believes arithmetic is inviolable.

But how long did it work for? Showing your ignorance has about as much charm as allowing your petticoat to hang below your skirt-line. And to a high achiever, sluts will become a liability. And I was a slut. Am one.

But I forget. Tom is listening. *Please keep clinging to your belief,* he murmurs, like a man talking me back from a cliff-edge, or a mother waking me from a nightmare. *The only thing that turns me on is you. And this is NOT an affair.*

A guitar chord twangs into our reverie, shattering it. I slump onto the pincer but it curves around my waist, holding me steady. Slow, simple, echoing from the speaker, a tiny bell chimes. Tom is resting his hand in the incline of my hip, ready. A cello and David Cassidy's voice breathe a wonder explicitly denying that there is any substance at all in the question he is asking. *How can I be sure?* Because of the music that builds and builds. Cassidy tries to stay on the ground, but the violins behind him lift one octave, then another, then another. One more feeble expression of doubt and off we roar – one, two, three; one, two, three; one, two, three. How can I, how can I, how can I? David Cassidy wants to know so much he's got us all spinning now, round and round the celestial bodies. That was all we ever needed. And I painted Tom as a trite sentimentalist; a womaniser. The jury is in. Built on garbage, my argument can only be vitriol. But he never even mentioned it. Like the maths, he let it pass. Even now, he tries to reassure me:

I know this must be grinding you down, he whispers, but I hear only my desperation, see my arm flushed with purpose, a muscle-flexing miracle of dexterity.

I understand. His words are grey sticks. They slam

against a background of shiny red gloss and break apart.

My chest blazes. Hell is the place of no forgiveness, because hatred begins at home and it is my own heart I have burnt out.

"Are you all right, deearr?" The Recreation Assistant is breathing cheesy crackers on me. Or Ritz biscuits. My hands are mangled in raffia. This raffia is the mafia and I am crackers in the Ritz. Lowering my head to get away from the stench, I manage to mutter, "I need to see Dr. Samuels."

Chapter Twenty: ii

She comes to get me, which is weird because I've never seen her outside her office or trying actually to do anything. She doesn't mess around either, wheeling me off and up the corridor as if she doesn't much like the Recreational Therapy room herself.

When she shuts the door of her office behind us, I want to go and push at the handle, to make sure it's properly closed. I don't want anyone to overhear. "He asked me to wait," I whisper.

"I remember," says Dr. Samuels, nodding. "You said."

But she can't know what I know. I smile.

Dr. Samuels does not smile back. She looks serious and takes my hand. "What else really sticks in your head? Things he said, I mean."

They are all at the front of my brain like ticker-tape ready to roll. Warmth spreads out from my pelvis. Tom is in there, where he has always been, listening. Soft as a baby, he strokes his cradle of bone. He is pleading with me not to forget how he has promised always to tell me the truth, begging me to cling to that.

Dr. Samuels sees me listening and asks what I'm hearing, so I tell her, word for word, and she gets up and writes it on a flip chart, which she pulls from behind her desk. She underlines this sentence:

DON'T FORGET HOW I'VE PROMISED ALWAYS TO TELL YOU THE TRUTH.

Below it, she writes:

I PROMISE TO ALWAYS REMEMBER YOUR PROMISES.

"Did you do fractions at school?" she asks. "Where you have a common denominator underneath that the top number needs in order to tell you what part of the whole it represents?"

"Like a quarter?" I say, wondering what she's getting at. "Where there's a 4 underneath a 1 to show that the 1 is only 1 part of 4, if the whole is represented by 4?"

"That's it," she says. "Where the top is dependent on the bottom to define and give it meaning."

And I see what she's getting at, but if she's trying to apply fractions to these phrases she's got them upside-down. In order to make any sense, it's my promise that relies on his promise. It's me that would divide over and over into into the great truth of his love. And for Tom, I would divide indefinitely. "You've got them the wrong way round," I say. "*My* promise relies on *his* promise to tell me the truth, always."

"OK." Dr. Samuels springs up from her chair, roots around in her desk drawer, pulls out a packet of blu-tack and hands it to me. "Pull a bit of that off." She takes a pair of scissors, removes the paper from the flip chart pad and cuts it in half. "Now – what do you want me to do with it?"

I point, indicating that she should swop the two pieces around, but I can't say more because Tom's words are coming through loud and clear. She wheels me to her desk, shifts across a pile of paper from the art trolley and hands me a thick felt-tip. Before every new phrase, Tom thumps my pelvis and a shiver of delight runs up my hand and into my fingers. I can hardly finish writing what he says before another vibration prepares me for what's coming next. Delighted, I scrawl on one piece of A4 after another and shove them at her. When he stops, I look up. Dr. Samuels has moved the flip chart away and stuck the papers on the wall. At ground level in the middle, is Tom's promise and above it, my own. From there, the phrases fan out. The hand-writing is dreadful and looks suspiciously like Tom's. A giggle stalls in my throat because I have failed to capture the richness of his voice. Something's missing.

"Music," I say. "Tom sent me so much music. *Summer Breeze*?"

She nods.

"*Don't You Worry 'Bout A Thing*?"

"Oh, yes," says Dr. Samuels. "That's Stevie Wonder."

I'm surprised she knows anything recorded after 1960, she seems so old, but her tone is enthusiastic. "No one played the harmonica like Little Boy Wonder. No-one *heard* certain beats before Stevie slipped them between what was expected."

"That's right." I exclaim. "And no-one said what was least expected like Tom did. He's a genius."

I look at Dr. Samuels' face and she is further from me than I have ever seen her in this room, as if she's listening to someone else. She's nodding her head and clicking her fingers, just off the beat.

"He's a genius," I say again.

"Did you mean Tom, or Stevie Wonder?" As she hums

and clicks the fourth beat of a four-four bar, the sound cracks in my head and I feel as though I've just woken from a dream. One of those dreams where you're backstage and Stevie Wonder's been a friend of yours for ages. And then you realise that he isn't. He's really a symbol so deep in your pleasure zone that your brain has played a trick. Because I've never known Stevie. It's Tom I've known. Tom, whose words, no longer couched in Stevie's certainties, glare from the wall where Dr. Samuels has stuck my scribbles.

IF YOU WANT TO PAUSE, AND REST, AND REFLECT, YOU CAN RELY ON ME STILL TO BE HERE, RIGHT HERE, WAITING FOR YOUR CALL.

For the first time, I see that Tom has stolen Stevie's blaze to colour his own phrases dayglo. Without Stevie, the words appear empty and unconvincing.

Dr. Samuels takes a black marker and draws a line under:

WAITING FOR YOUR CALL

Beneath it, she writes:

DON'T YOU WORRY 'BOUT A THING.

But I have no time to think because slow rolling thunder is breaking in my depths. A voice is singing so low and controlled, I feel it as a vibration and I think it is Tom, tapping, but it builds until the words, *There's a place for us* become audible. It's Aretha Franklin, pouring her soul through the greatest female gospel voice of the last century. She sounds as pure as my longing for Tom was. As undeniable. As unavoidable. Her rising certainty can smash open mountains until rivers surge down them and the celestial city shines golden on top.

I tell her that he sent me this song.

"So the songs and the genius behind them were the foundation for what he said?" she suggests, scribbling something underneath one of his sentences, high on the wall, and I see she has underpinned it, again, with work and people so inspired that their music deepens every love it touches.

I DON'T WANT YOU TO THINK, 'HERE'S A GUY WHO JUST DUMPS HIS GIRLFRIEND BECAUSE HE HAS GOOD SEX WITH ANOTHER WOMAN; A GUY WHO IS UNTRUSTWORTHY AND A BASTARD TO WOMEN.'

ARETHA FRANKLIN
SONDHEIM & BERNSTEIN

"Any more?" asks Dr. Samuels, while I'm still staring.

"Well, there was an Abba song – One I'd never heard."

"Not, *The Winner Takes it All*, then?"

I manage a wry smile and try to hum the tune, but the buzz from my closed mouth is wrong – sad – descending from a major chord to a minor. I'm surprised to hear Dr. Samuel's join in. Soon I'm humming a melody while she follows a second later with the second part, her third beat hitting my fourth until she descends to a bass note and I hit what I know is a violin playing at the top of my range.

At exactly the same time as I say, "*The Day Before You Came*", she says, "Albinoni's *Adagio*" and I realise they both convey grief and longing except *The Day Before You Came* is a cheap rip-off of a great classic. Without either of them, Tom's words, stuck on the wall by Dr. Samuels, look a cliched, sentimental imitation.

JUST AT THE MOMENT, I FEEL HOPELESS; I'M CRYING, DESPERATE. I HOPE YOU WON'T GIVE UP ON ME. TIME REALLY IS AN ILLUSION, AND OUR DAY REALLY WILL COME.

ABBA

ALBINONI

The wall is beginning to be covered by what look like mathematical equations, except they have words instead of numbers, and every song and artist seems to have less and less to do with Tom's messages.

"How strong are you feeling?"

I can hardly lift my hand and my jaw seems clamped, but inside I don't feel paralysed. I nod, to indicate I'm still in here.

Dr. Samuels goes to the trolley, writes something on the top piece of paper and carries it to the wall. She crouches down by the first piece of paper she put up.

DON'T FORGET HOW I'VE PROMISED ALWAYS TO TELL YOU THE TRUTH.

I see her remove it. Then she covers the space with her body as she sticks up the new bit. She turns around. "Suppose we replace the premise for all that has followed, with this?" She steps away.

Fewer words leave space for larger letters. Covering the half sheet of paper end to end a different statement screams out at me:

I AM A LIAR

LIAR

LIAR

The letters stab my eyes. I can't stop looking at them. They are simple. Clean, like an axe blade. Straight, except for the curve; the master-stroke that whips me with its final, triumphant flourish. Everything goes black. I am on the receiving end of a massive stroke. My skull buckles. The word LIAR has detonated something inside my head. I cover my face with my hand, squeeze my eyes as tight as I can, pushing it out. When I speak, I hear the gasp of a woman clinging to new words, any new words that will keep her from being sucked into the emptiness below.

"It's not that easy," I spit, but exhaustion floods my arms and legs with such intensity and so fast that I know Tom has leapt on my chest, determined not to allow this to go on. "He spoke the truth." Guitar riffs compete in my head, but every line I can distinguish clashes against another. *Love Will Tear Us Apart* is winning. "He spoke a lot of truth. It was just... "

Now that his promise is gone from the wall, all that stares out at me is my own naivety. I shut my eyes to get away but songs surge up from inside as if Tom is ending a display of fireworks with everything he's got. He summons them from where he's sitting on my chest and one by one the stars go out and the vacuum inside me swells. I open my eyes to get away but his words too, are blinding. They flash, black on electric white, pressing their truth on my optic nerve. A truth that relieves nothing; a truth that rings out my stupidity with a note that would shatter glass. *But I believe in equality*, he jeers. *We have to be free to make our own choices. There are no victims in a democracy.* When he growls, *I'm not prepared to give in without a fight*, Dr. Samuels wheels me round to face the window and waits, but Tom continues to whisper, pausing after his next phrase until I pass on the words.

Love is the Law, Love under Will.

Behind me I know that faces are appearing. Tom, sticking out his tongue, grimacing, scowling. I try to resist moving my chair, find myself turning my head but my neck cracks. I lift my foot, kick my heel onto the brake and swing round. Pieces of paper, covered in phrases hang off the wall. Tom rubs his hands together.

COME INSIDE MY HEAD; LOOK AROUND; SEE WHAT'S HERE FOR YOU, AND OF YOU.

He leans right over into my face and stares into my eyes. His teeth glint.

YOU ARE WHAT I'VE WAITED FOR FOR YEARS.
WHAT WILL YOU LEARN FROM ME? THINGS OF
THE SOUL... OF THE SUBCONSCIOUS... OF MY
DEEPEST HEART.

Every face is laughing at me.

YOU WILL FIND ME DIFFICULT TO SHAKE OFF;
MUCH HARDER TO SHAKE OFF THAN FLU.

I try to push my chest out and up but only manage to let in the freezing cold. My ribs have stopped moving. Soon, my heart will be paralysed.

Tom grins between the sheets.

ONE OF MY THEORIES IS THAT THE MORE MUSIC
YOU HEAR, THE MORE KINKY YOU GET; AND
THAT THIS IS VERY LIKE SEX.

The room grows dark, the white papers flutter and a voice outside my head, benign and hesitant as only Rolf Harris's can be, says: *Can you see what it is yet?*

Tom's full-throated laugh almost knocks me from my seat.

I have been groomed.

Chapter Twenty: iii

When I open my eyes, Dr. Samuels is removing paper from the wall. She smiles at me, so I smile back, but my head is white space. My only solid recollection is that she got me out of the recreation room, like a benign drama teacher getting me excused from a game of hockey where I froze while someone ordered me to run about on a muddy field. That's right – she rescued me from the Crackers Woman and the smell of Ritz biscuits. Her colours are strong and warm. I shape my mouth and garble out loud, "How can you know anything when there's no solid ground?"

I stand. My head is stuffed with cotton wool. Breathing is difficult, so I stop. There's no need. Thin blue air breathes in and out for me.

But Dr. Samuels has me in her grip. Dr. Samuels. Not Tom. I feel her stroking down the sides of my head and neck, squeezing my shoulders. Her hands are pulling me down. My arms throb. My knees and legs too. "No solid ground," she says, running her hands over my feet.

Dr. Samuels is still talking but I'm not listening. I'm staring into space. The skies clear before me. "The solid ground beneath my feet," I repeat, pressing them into the thin carpet, steadying my feeble legs until they hurt enough to crack open the truth. "That's what I was trying to prove," I say, curling my toes into the hard floor. "I was trying to prove that I didn't need it. That love would be enough to hold me up." For a moment, I'm free.

"In the form of a Tom who was able to fly," she says,

devoid of question or judgement, nodding as I fall back into the chair. My eyes fill, and when I look at her she looks just as sad as I feel. "Tell me... " says Dr. Samuels at last, "...about the feeling of being separated from your mother."

I open my mouth to speak. Words and bits of words spin out of the dark. I try to move but my hand can only flex and close. I watch it flapping open; snapping shut. Flapping open; snapping shut, before it flies up in the air and hits me in the eye. I vibrate as my hand hits my face over and over. This fist must go. It must be cut off. I bring it down hard on the wheelchair arm but that makes no difference to the howling which is everywhere rushing and sucking and round as a mouth. It will eat up everything. That desk is asking for it, flaunting its sharp corners like it's something. And that window with its fancy see-through glass? One scream from the all-mouth, that's all – one rasping in-breath from the all-mouth will have those broken shards clinging to their frame. They'll beg for mercy but the howling, screaming rasp will consume it all. Chairs, walls, ceiling. All will be ground to dust. Then they'll know what 'difficult' is.

I shut my eyes and squeeze and squeeze. Everything is orange spots.

Faintly – from far away, I hear a voice calling 'Gina'. Slowly, the spots clear, leaving a criss-cross pattern of red lines like tiny haemorrhages on my retina. I try to open my eyes. The light is too bright but I feel a warm presence close by me.

Dr. Samuels is holding my hand, making small humming sounds.

"I was trying to survive," I say. I'm still trying now. I

can't stop insisting that I believed it impossible to survive without Tom's help, but as I speak, the truth in my own words rings so singly, so absolutely, that all need to quantify or qualify it falls away. What I have just said shines, hangs, beats with its own heart. That was it. How it was. End of the matter. Nothing to define. Nothing to analyse. I was helpless to get what I needed. I felt helplessness consume me.

Well, that's what I'm feeling now. Back then, there was no I, only pain and fear. Only being consumed. Here, now with Dr. Samuels, there is an I. I'm here. I am here. Forged from pain. Existing.

"I thought I could fly," I mumble. I can see now why I thought that way. Because I had to.

I sigh. I feel the footrests of this wheelchair and I'm astonished at their solidity. I have been mad, but these surgeons, these doctors, these nurses and physios and occupational therapists; these walls of this hospital are still here, caring for me. They are holding me up. They will not give way. I press my bottom into the padded seat, testing it. From that position, I touch the surge of that roadless sky and say, "I thought that the love I felt for Tom should somehow be strong enough to overcome anything."

"So you'd just *be* love?" she says. "When there's only you, and the pain is you, and the rage is you, and the blame is you too, I guess you have no choice?"

I remember the howling now. It wasn't coming from everywhere after all. It was coming from me. My diaphragm and throat are bruised from it. Now it is I who feel I have had major surgery. I feel disembowelled. Pulled apart.

Dr. Samuels opens her eyes wide, as if she's waiting for more.

"I had to believe in Tom," I say simply. Had to. Then. I think of Tom's text: *I am honestly trying to make a go of it with Anita.*

Now, when I think back to the first time I read that sentence, I remember the way all the lights in my head went out – bang, like a fuse blowing into complete darkness. When they came back on, nothing made sense. What was a lie? What was the truth?

What was real.

I tell Dr. Samuels and realise, as I do, that this is a new part of the story. A part I haven't told her. "If he'd acknowledged his u-turn, I think I could have managed somehow."

She takes a quick, sharp breath. "That would have helped you see how different you were. A fudge must have felt as if all that had happened between you never was?"

I correct her. "It felt as if *I* never was," and something in me stiffens. I put my hand above my stomach and feel it lifting as it pushes, falling as it contracts. I press against my sore, battered centre, against my sick exhaustion, and want the whole dreary vomit of it gone. I curve in the heel of my hand and though I don't believe I have the strength, bit-by-bit, I force the nausea, the memory, Tom-bloody-Hanson, out. "I wrote." Yes, I wrote into that void to thank him for telling me, and tried to cut off contact. Recalling the lack of a response nearly silences me again, but I see Dr. Samuels nodding and watching. "I heard nothing. I tried to phone and he'd changed his phone number." A whole year of promises reversed. I press my poor bruised centre and say, "He'd even changed his telephone number, and still I needed him." My tears come easily, but not for my sake – for pity's as the truth unfurls: "I needed the very man who was intent on blotting out my existence to provide me with a good enough reason for why he'd come to this decision."

And Dr. Samuels just shakes her head, getting it completely, and tells me without fear or favour – just as if it's the equation I now see it is – that this is an impossible position for anyone to be in.

"It is," I say. "The second Christmas after he'd dumped me was terrible. I suppose he offered to meet again in case it all got too much and I told Anita, but by then he couldn't really hear or see me at all. I suppose, because of that, I couldn't see or hear myself." I pause, hearing my words echo like a Greek chorus.

"I didn't want to go." No, I didn't. Some semblance of self must have been fighting, even then, though it lost. "I knew it would be humiliating, you see, but I couldn't get him to see it would be humiliating, so I went, like I always did, in the hope that this time he'd be able to see my humiliation and acknowledge it, which would release me from it." Aware how mad this sounds, I grin, no longer ashamed, just sorry for this poor wretch who's fast becoming a part of my past.

"So you met. Again?"

In the pub. I was meeting a man in a pub who couldn't even trust me with his phone number, who couldn't hear me when I begged for mercy, who told me that in himself he'd begun to feel 'fine, most of the time.' A man I had done everything in my own power to care for and protect.

I had some pretty serious misgivings about myself in

clothes that were two sizes too big. I'd dyed my hair bright red but since we'd last met something really had changed. He seemed fatter and more dirty than scruffy. His newly designed book cover – a book written, as I saw it, in my blood – took most of his attention and yet he seemed convinced that I'd be as interested in it as he was.

He'd fitted me in on his way to somewhere else.

At midday, early January, the country pub was full of empty tables. A fire burned in the inglenook. I couldn't manage my soup, so he ate mine while I listened, between his mouthfuls, more carefully than usual, to the things he said.

First of all he joked about his closest friends – the musicians he played with. He called them both morons.

I tried to talk about what had happened between us. "You said you changed your phone number because you changed your internet provider."

"That's right," he sighed, as if I was making heavy weather of it.

"But if that's why, what stopped you giving me the number? Did you think I'd be ringing every five minutes? You don't trust me, do you?"

"No, it's not that," he said, looking bored. "I just didn't think it mattered."

"But you know it matters. I said so."

He turned, sighed again, louder this time. "That proves that you haven't forgiven me."

"Because I want to get it clear that you don't trust me?"

"Forgiveness is an act of faith."

He was trying to blindside me but surely he knew I could see that? "Not for me," I said. "Understanding is central to forgiveness. To know how something happens is to unravel and let go of it. That's why I keep trying to understand."

"If I had a vicar I liked, I'd talk to him," said Tom, airily. "But I don't really want to know myself at all."

I know this shocked me in much the same way that a cup of water in the face shocks a person awake. I watched, more with fascination than offence, my opinion of him dropping every time he tried to baffle me. He changed the subject. He poured contempt on every discussion of importance. He asked me nothing about myself and when I remonstrated that he wasn't engaging with me at all, he responded with, "I'm here, aren't I?"

But I stuck to my point. "You're here," I said, patiently, "in the same way you've been here for the last year, which is not at all. All I've asked you to do is make and keep a simple agreement about when you'll speak to me or email. It wouldn't need to be often and it would stop me panicking, but you won't even do that. You'll only have anything to do with me when you have power over me. What's it all about, Tom? Wise to be cruel, is it? Or do you think you might be able to give up a little, just the tiniest bit of control... " and I held the smallest gap between my thumb and forefinger in front of his eyes, "...in order to help me?" Briefly, something must have got through, because at least I got a straight answer.

"No," he said. "I know I've got all the power and I'm not willing to give any of it up yet."

I suppose being pinned down this way must have been what he'd feared all along because when he said that, some part of me that had adhered to him fell away. Right there in the pub, I felt myself step back though I hadn't moved. I suppose I'd begun to dislike him. I saw how nasty he was. How banal were his strategies. How capable he was of affording me so little respect that he could happily twist both my words and my head until I thought myself crazy.

Dr. Samuel's eyebrows almost reach her hairline. "So you saw him," she said. "You said what you needed to, as you had done before."

I remember the x-ray May morning and the lunch by the brook. The times I saw so clearly what was going on only to lose confidence in my own judgement.

"But this time you cornered him," says Dr. Samuels as if she can read my thoughts. She lifts her hands and claps them together. "You were brilliant and brave and probably scared the hell out of him."

I see then that I probably did. "That's what happened," I say, amazed at the clarity of that moment and astonished all over again that this powerful, independent me could so easily vanish. *"I don't really want to know myself at all.'* He actually said that. I heard him. *That* was real, and it made me furious." I see the pub door and my car illuminated by a white rage so cold that it hurts to remember and is impossible to imagine I could ever have forgotten.

"Everything I did and said in the pub after that became lip-service," I say, remembering the distance I felt and the growing sense that I had my own game to play, though I'd no idea what. "I smiled. I kissed him goodbye. I even agreed to 'meet up in March and go out dancing', but I'd stopped listening. I was itching to leave." Because I was horrified. Because I feared him knowing just how horrified I was. Because then, as now, what I decided to do on the strength of that feeling comes up in Technicolor to meet me.

"So what happened next?".

"I sent a letter-bomb," I say, seeing my arm flushed with purpose as I slide that fat brown envelope into the slot and pat the collection times to send it on its way. A letter to Anita to tell her what had happened. A bomb to blow up the world as we knew it, in the hope that it might become a better place.

How many times had I written to Anita and not sent the letter? Maybe five or six. Some I finished, but most stopped mid-sentence because I'd hit some doubt about my motives or whether Tom would bring in sanctions about ever speaking to me again. In the end, terror of losing my mind in this back-to-front world or of losing my body to malnutrition urged me to scribble so fast that I hardly read through what I'd written, left it with crossings out and spelling mistakes, though my address was clearly written at the top.

I had seen that the power of Tom's emails would communicate the scale of his infidelity far better than any words of mine. So, desperate for truth, I went to the hundred and seventy-five page document into which I had cut and pasted them all, highlighted 'print', put in ten random page numbers and clicked. Then I stuffed the print-outs in a brown envelope with the letter, without even reading them through. This was evidence he couldn't refute. The problem was that Anita was away for several weeks. That, of course, was why Tom had been prepared to meet me in the pub.

I knew she'd have a pile of circulars and papers waiting on her return. At least half of them would be in brown envelopes and the Tom I knew would simply let them pile up where they fell. Or if they got in the way of his opening the door he might move them as far as the kitchen table. I wrote her name and address in the exact middle of the computer screen in Courier, (left margin justified), printed it on a piece of paper to calculate where the print would land, stuck a label with its plastic back intact over that place and printed the label, which I peeled away and affixed to the envelope as though it was official.

The post-office counter was in the corner of my village shop. The queue never had a place to site itself if more than two people were waiting to be served. We had squeezed ourselves between the all-in-one sewing kits that hung on a row of display hooks and some Ecover refill drums. The package should have burned my fingers, but when I finally got to the counter I handed it over as steady and focused as if I'd been a hidden sniper with a clear view of my target.

"Second class, please." I smiled at the postmistress

and waited while she weighed my letter, printed out the postage and stuck it in the top right hand corner.

She smiled back, "Shall I pop it in the post?" As she swept it towards the white postbag behind her I caught sight of the print. Beneath the large 2LG. Royal Mail. Postage paid, next to the date and the price, was a postcode. My postcode. I would have to make a fuss, but that seemed a small price to pay for an immaculately planned operation.

"Sorry," I said. "But I can't send it with that on because it says where the letter comes from. It'll have to have stamps on it. I didn't realise."

I could feel her grumbling, though she never made a sound as she ripped off the label and pulled out the drawer containing stamps.

I thanked her, paid and clutching stamps and envelope made my way to the car. It might look as if I was sending an anonymous letter but that didn't matter any more. What things looked like had almost extinguished me and I was now impervious to so small a thing as a disapproving postmistress.

As I dropped the envelope into a postbox thirty miles down the road I found everything emptying out of me, as though I'd wrapped all of the truth up in a package with my longing and handed it over to be sorted out by the Gods.

"And when did you post it?" asks Dr. Samuels.

"A couple of weeks after we'd met in the pub."

"And what happened?"

"Nothing."

Dr. Samuels nods. After a few moments, she says, "Nothing. No response. Again." and shakes her head.

"Well, nothing that meant anything. Weeks later, I had an email from Tom saying she'd left the job and was moving out. I'd got my way and perhaps now I'd leave them in peace. That Anita was terrified I'd turn up on the doorstep and I was never to contact her again. But by then I didn't believe anything he said. For all I knew, even though I went to such lengths to disguise it, he could have intercepted the letter and just continued to lie. It was months before someone else connected with the writing centre told me she really had left. I was terrified," I add.

"Can you tell me what of?"

I know now that most of all, I was terrified I'd never escape from the confusion. Never be able to rest. "Of losing my mind," I say. "But in the end it seemed better to die shouting the truth. For a while afterwards I did feel better. I was weak, but for the first time in a year I realised I was hungry and began to eat again."

"So what went wrong? You were better, getting better."

"Perhaps," I say. "All I know is I couldn't wait any longer."

"For what, Gina? What couldn't you wait any longer for?"

But all I can recall is enduring the silence. And enduring it again. And again.

"I suppose I was waiting for a response from the Tom I loved. And the longer I waited, the more I knew I must be wrong. That sending that letter was despicable. Selfish.

Ruthless." I expect Dr. Samuels to reject this analysis, but she only nods.

"It certainly wasn't in his interests," she says. "So, yes. It was selfish. And ruthless, I guess. But survival is ruthless." She looks puzzled and I ask her why.

"It's just that you'd pretty much decided that he was the ruthless one."

"Well, he'd outclassed me again, hadn't he?" I don't want to look at her. "I began to think that the letter was part of the bigger plan." I wince. "That he had sat there, all that time Anita was away, trying to decide whether this was the right time to let her see it. I couldn't avoid becoming what he made me, you see. I was mad woman. Mad and vicious. Scorned. I began to hear his voice – *you didn't have to do that, did you?*"

Dr. Samuels listens before saying, "It sounds a contemptuous voice – like your brother's after you'd screamed for your mother because he was pulling you in half?"

"Well, Tom was definitely pulling me in half," I say, and this time Dr. Samuels seems to agree.

"So you had to do something? For you. Had to be ruthless?" says Dr. Samuels. "But the letter-bomb blew you up as well?"

"I've told you. Told you and told you. Tom *made* me do that."

"And you weren't angry?" she adds. "You didn't want to hurt him? This man who had driven you mad. This man who had crippled you with pain. He made you do it? But I thought you said you'd been cast out by your *own* failing.

Not his. *Yours.*"

"No," I say, because anger is red and blurry and the hand I can see is white and in focus, even though it hurls the letter into the glossy slit like a fist smashing into a red mouth. "I needed him to understand. I hoped he'd see why I posted it."

"So he didn't make you do all of it?"

She's beginning to really annoy me.

"Didn't you decide it was he who was ruthless and nasty? Wasn't that what you made of his later emails? When you met him by the brook? After seeing him in the pub? You told me you couldn't get away fast enough. That you'd decided he was a mean, cruel coward who could betray with the ease of a psychopath? Didn't that make you hate him?"

I want to hit her.

As if I've been hit myself I swing involuntarily sideways, feel the butt of a rifle in my hands and the room disappears. My attention resides solely on that big bald head and as I fantasize pulling the trigger that explodes it, my hatred is the only colour in the universe and it's white.

"I wanted to fucking kill him."

"Of course you did," says Dr. Samuels, as if approving a reasonable response. "Anyone who'd been treated the way you were would feel that. Of course you did," she says, again. "And like most people, you stopped well short of carrying that out." Her pragmatism fades into sympathy as she adds, "And I guess that baby in you who needed him in order to survive had no choice but to go on hoping that he'd see how much he'd hurt you and forgive. But he didn't do that, either."

"I needed *him* to accept what I'd done," I say, but I falter. I needed him. An I that I can sense now. And a him who just couldn't or wouldn't see me.

The lines in Dr. Samuels face grow smooth. All of her smiles as she says, "Welcome to the human race."

I smile back, weak as that baby. I feel my head relax into a curve of soft cheeks and human love, but not like I'm part of her. More like she's got me, tight and loose at the same time. I never felt loose with Tom. I saw everything through his eyes, because now I understand that when you're fighting to survive, the truth of what you know is so much weaker than the need to cling on.

The tether has weakened. It bump, bump, bumps along the ground as the balloon lifts off.

Dr. Samuels holds her hands out and brings the palms together. I feel held between them. "I'm sorry it's been so hard to see him clearly. He spoke such nonsense so convincingly, but if you have this kind of difficulty with a man again, it would be great if you could just let yourself feel how angry you get with him and follow through what you want to say. With friends like Tom... "

I stare at her because she's both opposite and beside me at the same time, which is weird but makes absolute sense. She knows it's true and now, so do I: life can be straightforward if you can find the strength to feel what you feel and to see what you see.

It's dog-eat-dog out there and I'm growling.

*

Her face is composed and patient as she cocks her head. "Do you realise we've sat in silence together for five minutes?" she says eventually, but she looks amused. "It's time to stop."

I look into her soft grey eyes and find tears appear in my own, tears so big they overflow the brims almost immediately and plop onto the floor. "You know," I say. "I feel like I've woken up from the most terrible, horrible nightmare."

"Yes, I see that," she says, walking over to the door. "Because, in a way, you have." I wheel my way towards her and carefully push myself up until I'm standing.

"Can I have a hug?" I ask, and of course, she hugs me, carefully rubbing warmth into my back in lieu of squeezing too tight. I feel she's rubbing light into my soul.

"See you after the weekend," she says, and kisses my cheek. "Your consultant and her team seem to think independent living is high on the agenda. Let's meet on Monday at ten when perhaps we might start to think about you going home?"

Chapter Twenty One

Corinne stared out of the train window as field after frosty field flicked past. The man sitting next to her pressed the side of his thigh against her own. Again. Twisting away from him, she checked her ticket for the fifteenth time. Change at Crewe. Twenty minutes before the Pay Train to Upton Morley, with Blackhill the fifth stop along. Since pulling out of Euston, the packed carriage had warmed its passengers until Corinne could smell fabric conditioner maturing in their clothes.

She stood. The man next to her moved out into the centre aisle with an expression on his face that suggested he'd only just noticed her. She removed her overnight bag from the rack before he had a chance to sit back down.

She'd been planning to leave London for the weekend since Beatrice had mentioned her visit to Rome. That short time in Cambridge had woken Corinne to the north, south, east and west that lay beyond her tiny flat in Brixton. If Beatrice could jaunt off to interesting places, so could she.

At Crewe, she shuffled along the station platform, white breath leading her through the gloom. Careful not to slip on the icy steps, every footfall bouncing and booming on the deserted bridge, she made her way to Platform 18a – a tiny strip of concrete doglegging away from the mainline to Manchester – and boarded a freezing three-carriage train with its automated doors stuck open.

For fifteen minutes Corinne watched a cold breeze lift and drop a polystyrene cup. Then, with a roar and a screech of brakes, in scooted a sheet of tabloid newspaper followed by a stream of steaming people in coats and hats and gloves, carrying shopping and junk food. By the time she got off, after a forty-minute journey of stops and starts, it was as dark as midnight, her feelings of adventure had vanished and all she wanted was to find her B&B, put on the TV and crawl into bed with a bag of chips.

Mrs. Bowen-Jones seemed friendly enough, leading her upstairs to a back room in the small terraced house and proudly demonstrating the en-suite shower and kettle.

"I'll leave you then," she said, "to get sett-led."

Relieved, Corinne made herself a cup of tea with a teabag on a string and a capsule of what passed for milk. Then she took out her laptop, propped herself against the plush-buttoned bedhead and turned to the webpage she'd copied yesterday. The fight she'd had with herself was done. Her need to know had got her this far and she felt she had her own, personal battle to fight. Just one more push.

She gazed again at the wide grin of Tom Hanson and the digital flyer that filled his enlarged mouth.

> *Tom Hanson~~dsome~~: Lounge music for ~~ser~~loungers*
> *~~His residency~~One ~~month~~night only*
> *Blackhill Working-Mens' Club*
> *Saturday 7-10pm*
> *(Stripper licence refused.)*

Just time for a shower.

*

The en-suite in Corinne's B&B had a pink crocheted toilet-roll holder in the shape of a doll's dress. Barbie's torso protruded from the top. To access the toilet paper, in marvellous harmony with the person using the lavatory, you had to pull up her skirt. Corinne had an ironic grin on her face until she came down the narrow staircase into the hall. Beneath the telephone on the hall table was a round crocheted mat and through the door to the dining room she spotted a pile of crocheted doilies on the sideboard, some with beads for keeping flies off milk jugs.

She crept across the swirly brown carpet and was quietly turning the knob on the front door when the question, "You off out, then?" sang from behind.

What was she supposed to say? Yes? No? Was there a polite way of telling Mrs. Bowen-Jones that it was none of her business? Stumped, Corinne said she was 'covering the gig' for her 'mag', and once she'd started, she noticed how easily the lies followed. "Marmalade Rag," she said. "Offices in Bromley, I'm afraid. That's south of the river, but circulation's growing every month. It's a sort of 'what happened to Tom Hanson' piece. People are interested, you see."

Mrs. Bowen-Jones raised her eyebrows as if to indicate that she didn't really hold with what went on down south. "I know where Bromley is, thank you," she said sharply. "You got a complimentary ticket, 'ave you?"

"On the guest list."

"Well mind you give 'im a good write-up. He's not had it easy from you lot." She paused and Corinne knew immediately that 'her lot' meant women, definitely from 'down south'. "And very glad we are to 'ave 'im back here, and with a local girl this time," added Mrs. Bowen-Jones. "He does a lot for us – opens fetes and tha'. Always brings a smile. We know about the trouble." She paused again as her face settled. "So you'll be after eleven. What would you like for breakfast?"

Corinne beamed at her, battling the urge to ask for an avocado smoothie and organic porridge with goat's milk. "Bacon and egg, with coffee, please." Even the coffee felt pretty radical.

"Between eight and ten on a Sunday then. I 'ope you enjoy yourself."

Corinne pulled the door shut behind her and stepped into a drizzly night. The houses farther along the small town street had front doors that opened straight onto the pavement. She heard televisions burbling their Saturday night jollity, their light flickering behind closed curtains, but when she looked up beyond the rooftops, she saw a mass of dark hill, bare but for a single row of streetlights winding up it. One road in, one out. No wonder these people all knew each other. No doubt Mrs. Bowen-Jones was already on the phone, gossiping to her friends. Perhaps even warning Tom Hanson of her presence. She saw him then, as she imagined the others in the town did. Treated badly by the faceless corporate world. Taken advantage of by the free-living and immoral women of London. Welcomed back to this place as the King of home-made. Maybe. And supposedly settled now, knowing his limits. Big fish, small pond. Their very own shark.

She'd reached the T-junction of the high street. 7.30 on a Saturday evening and the place seemed empty apart from the queue in the chip-shop on the corner. The sort of chip shop where steam and the smell of vinegar billowed into cold air out of what appeared to be someone's front room.

She turned left, away from the station and towards the Blackdown Club for Working Men, feeling alien. An alien who had lied. Again. Panic stopped up her throat for a moment as she realised her previous lie had also been to someone in this town. Supposing the doctor's receptionist had told everyone about her so far unfollowed-up request for notes? And now that she was here, it was crystal clear that Tom Hanson had been nowhere near Stoke Mandeville *or* Rampton. Next to a real live community protecting their very real interests her detective skills looked like make-believe. She could only hope that Tom Hanson really did have nothing to do with Aleister Crowley or she might end up his Wicker Man.

Having convinced herself that a network of people watched her every move, Corinne sped up, passing cheerily-lit shop windows that she failed to look in and veering toward the road whenever an alleyway darkened her path. Only as she approached an open wrought-iron double gate on the left, its arch twined with fairy-lights, did she begin to slow down. A group of people stamped on the forecourt, their warm breath indistinguishable from the cigarette smoke they exhaled. A poster on a sandwich board, identical to her flyer, had the words:

SOLD OUT
(probably)

scrawled across it in red marker pen.

"A'right, love?" The voice lulled her, welcomed her. "Take no notice of the sign. Plenty o' room. Startin' in a minute."

No one bothered her or asked her who she was or why she'd come. Perhaps people had stopped asking about strange women at Tom Hanson gigs? Perhaps there'd be loads of them: the other woman and the other, other woman, sitting at empty tables dotted around the room. Anxious at the thought, she paid six pounds at the door before heading into a large square hall, its far end a stage made up of blocks. Eight fluorescent lights set into a false ceiling lit the place like a morgue. She removed her coat and hung it on the back of a wooden chair at an empty table before crossing the room to buy herself a drink at the bar where a small crowd chatted. Allowing herself to relax, she was halfway there before she fully grasped that the man doing the most chatting was Tom Hanson himself. She heard his loud, abrupt laugh and wanted immediately to know what had amused him. Once identified, his voice wouldn't go away: clear, precise consonants with slightly flat vowels which, among people who sometimes missed these sounds from their speech altogether, stood out all the more. Besides, his shiny, bald head was so high that despite company, Tom Hanson had only to look up to see over everybody else.

Corinne found it difficult to take her eyes off him. He spotted her approaching and smiled the smile of someone who might think himself in the way. Even as she passed him to reach the bar, he seemed aware of her – moving slightly forward so that she didn't have to push past.

She bought herself a pint of lime and soda, and wondering if his gaze followed her returned to her seat where she downed half of it in seconds. Remembering her mission made her feel ashamed. Like some stalker welcomed in good faith. Except stalkers probably didn't feel ashamed. Sipping more slowly now, Corinne calmed herself. So the guy didn't have horns and a tail but that was good, wasn't it? Maybe she'd got it all wrong, but that was why she was here. To find out. No one would know and nothing had to happen.

Softened by the normality of her surroundings after all that rushing, she drifted, wondering what Beatrice was up to, before something brought her attention back into the present. The place seemed tatty and over-bright. The warmth had gone. She glanced towards where Tom had been, hoping for some small recognition, but he'd left. That was what was missing. His voice. Without it, the music of the room lacked some crucial, completing note and she found herself disappointed. How completely weird. She downed the rest of her drink, keen to get another before the show began, but people were moving to their seats. Retrieving her scarf from where it had been knocked to the floor, she sat up just in time to see the woman who had taken her money close the doors and flick the switches.

A row of footlights left the stage a murky blue until someone turned on a couple of spots that hung on the right and left walls. With a boom, the PA lurched into *In The Mood* and a man hopped up from his table at the front, took a microphone from the floor and urged a round of applause for their very own Tom Hanson.

A short man wearing a top hat crossed the stage to reach

an upright piano, sideways on. He switched on a small desk-lamp to light his music and with a professional flick of his tailcoat, sat down and flexed his fingers. Beaming at the audience, he played from the top to the bottom of his instrument with such dexterity that Corinne barely noticed the exceptionally tall Tom carrying a small stool. Placing it mid-stage, he arranged his long and elegant limbs until he was perched on the top of it. Then, with his knees close to his chin, shoulders hunched and elbows in, he let both hands flop outwards from the wrists. The music stopped. Tom looked across at the pianist, nodded, paused and looked moodily towards the audience, embarrassing them into silence.

"There's a kind of hush… " murmured Tom, waiting a few moments. "…but this isn't it." He grinned and the spell broke. Again the pianist scaled the heights. Again, he stopped. Again, Tom nodded and once more, the audience held its breath.

"Round… " said Tom, vowel-perfect now as he waited before nodding again at the pianist who picked up his cue and struck a single chord.

"Like a cabbage in a grocers… " Tom sang, voice vibrating with serious intent. Corinne had to make an effort to stop her jaw from dropping open. The pianist changed chord,

"Like a football in the bath…
(Change of chord)
Never sinking or ascending…
(Change of chord again)
Not at all like smoking grass… "
At every idiotic lyric, Tom became more sincere, the

music building and ebbing with increasing sophistication as each simile seemed initially right but was then discarded as not quite good enough.

> *"Like a bomb dropped from an airplane*
> *Or a stomach in a cow*
> *Or a zenstone on a website*
> *Saying all you know is now,*
> *Or the sun that burnt your retina*
> *On the point where you were pettin' er*
> *Or your head when it is sore*
> *Because you can't try any more*
> *Then you suddenly complain... "*

Where had she heard this? – the familiar music, the wrong/right words, Tom on the wrong/right stool in his 1960s polo-neck.

> *"...That there really is a pain*
> *In the circuits of your brain."*

"There's a bloody pain in mine now," yelled someone at the front and Tom gave him a look of sorrow that made everyone shush those giggling while simultaneously giggling themselves. He seemed able to deliver with the intensity of a teenager in love, and Corinne realised that the song was by Noel Harrison: *Windmills of Your Mind*. A man that her mother had told her she fancied when they were once watching a black and white *Top Of The Pops* show from the archives.

On rushed the music, the passage of time and the

inevitable fading of a love once frantically searched for.

> *"And I knew that it was over*
> *When I glimpsed, though it was brief,*
> *That the autumn leaves were turning*
> *To the colour of her teef."*

Tom stopped for a moment, took a large red handkerchief from his pocket and wiped his head. "Gosh, isn't it hot in here," he said. "My head's going around like a windmill."

The pair were having such apparently careless fun, yet their performance was faultless. Curious, she watched the two men working one another. Tom dropped his head; the pianist grew six inches. Tom looked heartbroken; the pianist offered the audience a very wide grin. When she sensed someone moving a chair over to her table and sitting down, she didn't even look to see who it was. Only when Tom stopped singing to let the accompanist play a series of flurries that really did conjure a vision of leaves twirling to the ground, did she discover that the woman sharing her table was the one who had taken her money and who had switched out the lights. She was staring at Tom with eyes that glowed with the fire of the fanatic.

The number ended to loud applause and a lot of heckling. Tom followed on with *Come Fly With Me* and *Have Yourself A Merry Little Christmas*, twinkling through both so brightly that Corinne was at a loss as to whether irony was involved at all. The songs felt ridiculous, yet Tom's joy made them shine. He appeared to have abandoned himself to them, heart and soul and if silliness glazed the surface, to that as well. Which, Corinne realised, made him utterly charming and made her – even at this short acquaintance – want to join in fully and to hell with how she'd either look or sound. Still, when he strode into the audience and passed by her table, some blind impulse made her shrink back, which she noticed and was glad. Within moments he'd dragged three people onto the stage where he twirled them in syncopated dance movements to recreate The Temptations singing *Get Ready*.

By the time Tom and his accomplice were croaking through a part-performance, part-lecture of and about Nirvana's *Smells Like Teen Spirit* (a soprano, an albino, a mosquito, my libido walk into a bar) the audience were shouting and laughing so much he could barely be heard.

The main lights left Corinne blinking. People brushed past the table on their way to the bar, many of them stopping briefly to squeeze the arm of the woman sitting next to her. "Is he like this at home, Bethan?" she heard someone say. "What a nightmare."

"Is he your husband?" Corinne found herself asking.

The woman held her hand to her forehead. "For my sins," she said, but she couldn't stop grinning. "What did you think of it?" she asked.

"Very good indeed," said Corinne, trying to rein in her enthusiasm. "I wasn't really expecting such... professionalism. How long have you been married?"

Bethan warmed to her subject rather fast. "Five months. It just seemed – well – he'd had a pretty unsettled couple of years and he needed to feel secure."

Secure? The guy had filled a club with people who were queuing up to talk to him. The last word that Corinne would have used to describe him was 'insecure'.

It must have shown on her face.

"Oh, yes," said Bethan, with the intimacy of someone who knows her ground. "I know he seems confident but he's taken quite a battering. Really – he's pretty naïve and unworldly. He needs lookin' after."

Corinne glanced towards the bar where Tom bobbed and boomed in the midst of an adoring crowd. "Really?" was all she said. "And you trust him, obviously," she added, realising too late what an odd thing that was to say.

Bethan's smile vanished. She looked confused and suddenly thin and drawn about the eyes. "Of course I trust him. With my life. We're a family now. I have a nine year old daughter. He's completely committed."

He bloody well should be, thought Corinne, despairing. Actually, nothing was behind this woman's eyes but Tom, Tom, Tom, was it? But did that make him so very out of the ordinary? She looked round and caught sight of the pianist leaning against the wall, half-pint in hand. Like everyone at the bar, he was watching Tom, but with a detachment bordering on irritation. For a second, Corinne saw him as the butler charged with keeping the coffin nearby for the first hint of daybreak. Even as her throat tightened, she turned and offered Bethan her broadest smile. "He's wonderful. I'm really pleased for you. I'm off out for a fag," she said, though she rarely smoked and had no cigarettes. "See you later."

At the very least, she thought, heading towards the door,

a woman in Bethan's position should be mildly suspicious about Corinne's presence. A lone strange female in a town this small, coming to watch the performance of a man notorious for his infidelity? Yet when she turned to look, she saw Bethan still gazing at her husband, spellbound.

The cold air slapped at Corinne's face, sobering her. She joined a small crowd of smokers who were commenting that the cloud had dispersed and they were in for a cold night ahead. Someone offered her a cigarette but she'd only just lit it when the man himself arrived. No one shrieked or crowded round Tom, but still, Corinne immediately felt herself to be a member of some privileged backstage culture, some inner circle.

Tom didn't speak to her but the others were finishing their fags and almost immediately began to drift back, keen to get a drink before the second half. Within moments only the two of them remained. What should she say? 'You were really good?' 'Did you throw Gina Fulbright out of a hot air balloon?' Instead, she said, "I've met your wife. She's lovely, isn't she?" which to her own ears, sounded immensely stupid.

She held her breath, expecting him to make some predictable comment about his ball-and-chain. Instead, he stepped back and bent his head down until their eyes met. He smiled, softly. "Absolutely adorable," he said.

Certain he meant her, Corinne looked shyly away. If they'd chanced into a lift together, snogged and arrived unintended at a door that opened directly onto a bedroom, she could not have felt more exposed. She spent too long planning her answer. "It's good – er, good you feel like that," but her voice quaked and she felt subterfuge sucking her deeper.

His response was to sigh, but that only felt like a breathing space in which together they could acknowledge how sometimes (now, particularly) it was a pity that he had a wife at all. "I'm trying to give up smoking," he said, and Corinne heard, *I'm trying to stay faithful* while simultaneously feeling the pressure his wife put him under. "It makes my teeth hurt," he added and she felt her own teeth tingle against the cold.

She stamped her foot, putting the hard ground between them, alarmed by the speed at which his presence subsumed her. Even her stamping felt to be all about Tom. It *was* all about Tom. *Christ.* Was she this easy? This vulnerable? Thank God she'd stopped drinking. And now he was looking at her, all concern. "I've run out," she said, remembering they were discussing smoking but it sounded as if she'd run out of things to say that weren't directly about this sudden connection between them.

"It's not easy, is it?" he offered. "Here. Have mine. Keep it," and he gave her his pouch of Golden Virginia. Instantly, she felt guilty. *Why* was she hearing these things? Poor man, just being friendly, and here was she reading profound intimacy where none existed. She'd become obsessed from all the scary Crowley nonsense and now could see nothing else. Beside, she had to admit, she was blown away by the guy. Was that so surprising? Such talent. Such a generous, open-hearted gesture. A thing freely given. When she took the tobacco he asked her where she'd come from.

"Manchester," she said. That blind impulse again,

holding her tight. Keeping distance between them. But even as she nodded in thanks to the lie she felt mean. Like a child, she felt sure he'd know she was lying. *It doesn't matter.* Relieved, Corinne turned to go in. Only then did she feel his hand placed very, very lightly on her shoulder. "Manchester," he said. "It's very good of you to come all this way just to see me."

She turned back, smiling at him. "You were fantastic," she said, the need to hide her admiration gone now the encounter was nearly over. "Really. You were great."

She watched, wondering what would happen, but he just stayed with her words, like a child she'd handed an oversized lollipop. Happy. Open. Trusting.

It seemed they might stand there all night but the pianist appeared on the doorstep and flicked his head sharply towards the venue. With one nod to her and a lingering look of invitation, Tom was gone.

Corinne stared up at the sky, the whole of her body beating, lit by stars that saw everything and seemed to have placed her here, with foreknowledge, on purpose. *Well, probably beam me back up, Scotty,* she muttered to herself. But the feeling stayed – warm and sweet as treacle on a stove, her core full and wanting for nothing. She found herself reluctant to go back in for the second half – stupefied and at the same time, wide-awake. Very much as if, she realised, with a shudder, she had just shot her arm full of heroin and subdued the craving that was her constant companion.

She stood until her nose began to hurt. It had to be freezing of course, yet she was aware of it burning like a hot coal. She stayed, watching the layers of her own confusion as the tip began to lose all feeling. Had the great man made a pass at her? Maybe she'd made a play for him? Was there something rare and unusual between them? Nice girls surely didn't flirt with strange men and tell them how great they were? But then – he hadn't seemed like a *man* – not merely a fully-fledged, slightly threatening penis on legs. He seemed like – like... Heart pumping with alarm, she revisited their little scene in her mind's eye, saw his head framed against the sky as he bent solicitously down to speak to her. So tall. So big and strong. He seemed like the father every little girl ever wished she'd had. Gentle. Accepting. The centre of everyone's attention but available only to her. Was *that* what it was all about?

Maybe Freud was right after all. Flinching away from the implications, Corinne exhaled a dragon-sized cloud of vapour. Sleeping with daddy? That was quite a pull, but hardly the fault of Tom Hanson. Perhaps he *was* just naïve about women? The pleasure he'd taken in her flattery worried her now. Maybe insecure *was* a good description, hence his need for all that attention, she thought, even more baffled by her u-turn. Who was the victim here and who the prey? She heard the tinkle of the piano keys fade almost as soon as they began and turned just in time to see the front door closing. Surprised at the force of her thudding heart, she rushed back and slipped inside the hall to stand against the wall, convinced of only one thing. If he'd taken her number, she'd definitely be waiting for her phone to ring.

She had to tilt her head out of the way so the main lights could be switched off, but this time, as she saw with a shock, one of the spots lit the table she'd been sitting at. Her scarf still graced one of the chairs but both were empty. For one horrible moment she thought this was something to do with her, but as the piano continued to tinkle the other spot lit the stage and onto it strode Tom, dressed in jeans and a red football shirt with the words *Aberystwyth Town* blazing across the front and a snarl on his face. He spoke with a thick Welsh accent.

"Yeah, yeah, yeah, yeah, yeah," he said, projecting irritation toward the empty table. And out from the dark corner at the back came his wife with a huge red bandana round her head and her sleeves rolled up.

"Lissen to me!" she implored.

"Well, you said it already, I think. I certainly heard it already. So yoo're a bit pissed offf," shouted Tom. "So whatt?"

The audience tittered.

"Why are you always humiliatin' me, Dai?" pleaded Bethan, opening her eyes unnaturally wide. "You used to tell me how much you loved me." She put one hand on a hip and wagged her finger at him. "Now, I'm only going to give you one more chance. Do you love me or don't choo?"

Tom took several seconds shaking his head and raising his eyebrows, giving the audience an opportunity to boo and clap. Briefly, he divided them into the yeses and the noes before humming and hahrring. Then he stopped, paused and said, loudly, "No." The pianist crashed out a chord.

Quick as a flash, Bethan shouted, "Stop prevarrrriccatin'. I need a straight answer."

Tom looked to the ceiling and then over at Bethan as though she was the single most stupid woman to have walked the earth. "Lissenn," he said. "There's somethin' about you I just don' understand at all... "

The pianist honky-tonked out his introduction, grinned and away the two of them went. As Tom smiled the most winning smile Corinne had seen yet, she could hardly believe the lyrics that came out of his two-bit mouth:

> *"How could you believe me when I said I loved you*
> *When you know I've been a liar all my life?"*

By the time she inhaled again, Bethan had become some Judy to Tom's Punch. Picking up the rhythm, the crowd began to clap along. Plink, plink, plinkety, plink. One, two, three, four. Corinne scanned the audience. They were nodding and grinning with delight. Some of them mouthed the words. Most jigged in their seats. Her heart bashed against her ribcage: whack, whack, whack, whack.

Both onstage now, Tom and Bethan met at the back and strode together up the middle to the front where Bethan scowled and shook her finger again and Tom put his hands in his pockets before singing:

> *"I've had this reputation, since I was a youth,*
> *You must have been insane to think I'd tell you the truth.*
> *How could you believe me when I said we'd marry*
> *When you'd know I'd rather hang than have a wife?"*

Struggling to absorb what she was hearing, Corinne turned her attention to Bethan and felt the urge to slap her for colluding with the enemy. How could she be so... ? But she caught herself. This was a man who'd managed to destabilize Corinne with a five minute chat. Bethan seemed blind to anything more sinister than a bit of a laugh. 'Up for it' was she? Anything to avoid an accusation of spoiling everyone's fun.

So in the bright and apparent benevolence of Tom's comedy turn, Corinne watched Bethan play the stooge while Tom hit her again and again:

> *"...must be a loony...*
> *You're really naïve, to ever believe... "*

And her bewildered response:

> *"But you said you'd always love me... be faithful.*
> *What about the time you went to Aberystwyth?... "*

Oh what a fool the woman was! How loveable the boy-Tom! On and on it went, Tom's untroubled, revelling-in-it reply, over and over, more damaging than a lead cosh:

> *"But baby, let us not forget that I'm a heel...*
> *How could you believe me when I said I love you*
> *When you know I've been a liar. A double-crossing liar*
> *All my two-timing, double crossing li... i... i... fe."*

By now the audience were up on their feet, stamping and whistling to what had to be Tom's signature song. Like fucking *Deutschland Deutschland*, they sang along, never dreaming it could all end with the death of millions.

Or a string of used women too ashamed to fight back.

How did he live with himself? thought Corinne, as Tom in his red shirt scissored across the stage in a flash of hands and feet and teeth. Did he think he was being ironic? Did the local community see him as Fred Astaire accompanied by Irving Berlin?

Amidst all the shouting and whistling and stamping, no one noticed Corinne slipping from the room or clattering down the steps. She ran down the road, Tom's million watt grin burning on the back of her eye, the contempt in his cheer-filled voice ringing in her ears – *How could you fall, for that old lie?*

Crowley? Tom didn't need Crowley or any kind of satanic power. Just *that old lie*, a modicum of confidence and ordinary, run-of-the-mill misogyny would do. One seductive, blaming bastard to set you up and half the female population would do *themselves* in after that.

She stopped by a lamppost, breathing heavily, reining herself back, hearing the confusion that had so recently possessed her – *Make me? Did he make me? I'm blaming him now, but I shouldn't have believed what he said* – seeing how she bounced from shame to blame to shame ad infinitum, like two mirrors able only to reflect each other. She might be able to walk away now, but once upon a time, not so long ago she could so easily have been one of those women. Meanwhile, the originating two-faced, two-timing deceitful shit triumphed in applause. If even she, who had arrived specifically to observe the guy, had felt undermined and outmanoeuvred, what of adoring spellbound Bethan? What of Anita, or his other wives? Should they all have seen it coming?

Corinne walked on, hand on her chest, breathing lightly. Given the circumstances, how could a clever woman draw any conclusion but that she must really be stupid? How were they to know they had a daddy-shaped hole that left Tom with a target the width of The Grand Canyon? The man was like a pusher preying on junkies. She saw now how this final song could act as an escape clause he could refer to later when he needed to get out – *but I tried to tell you.* Using that, he could make women feel stupid all over again.

A puddle she'd skirted on the way to see Tom had iced over, all reflections lost to frost. Tom's honeyed words sounded by her ear. *It's very good of you to come all that way just to see me.* A bit of simple flattery. Easy come, easy go. Who needed Crowley when you already had two thousand years of women in need behind you, preparing the road ahead. A louder voice whispered in her other ear: *Who fucking cares if he's a Crowleyite or not – run away!*

She flushed right up to the crown of her head. The guy was so predictable that any benign, intelligent woman wouldn't believe it of him. You simply couldn't see the fucking join.

Outside number fifty-six she stopped and turned her phone back on. 9.20pm and a text message from Beatrice:

```
Roaming in Rome. Ralph elusive.
Back of a taxi, still looking for him.
```

Corinne smiled sadly. Perhaps Rome really would let Beatrice mourn as she needed to. She sent back a message of love and support. After that, the thought of Mrs. Bowen-

Jones's full English breakfast complete with doilies made her long for a kebab in front of her electric fire. Could she get a train? Now? The place seemed so settled for the night that the mass of traffic pouring around London could've been a dream.

The Bowen-Joneses weren't expecting her yet. They had the TV up loud. She crept upstairs, grabbed her bag, left £40 on the bed and caught what turned out to be the first of two trains to Crewe still to leave that night, and the last one back to London.

Chapter Twenty Two

Beatrice's accommodation for the weekend was a private bedroom in an apartment block around the corner from the *stazione* – a bit of a walk to the Trevi Fountain, but far enough away from the fancy shops to feel like a real place. She'd found it through an agency on the internet and arrived in darkness, relieved to have walked there without being mugged.

When she woke on Saturday morning it was to the sound of a small dog barking. She looked out of her fourth floor window onto a stone-flagged yard strung with washing that the sun never reached and studded with peeling wooden shutters, some open, some closed.

As expected, the apartment was empty, vacated for the day by her hostess, a young thin woman who had left a key in a copper bowl for her by the door. "To carm ant go as you pleass," she had so charmingly said the previous night, with no concern for her belongings or her own safety. After the grey months in England, the blue handkerchief of sky visible from the window gleamed, and Beatrice quickly showered and dressed. *For you*, she said to Ralph, shaking the thin cotton frock as if the creases might come out. She heard him then laughing at her, and allowed it; pictured him, last May, behind the ironing board, the blue sprigged material spread out in front of him as if smoothing it ready for this day.

Closing the apartment door behind her she entered a dark landing which led onto to an even darker, very narrow staircase. Just as she began to fear she might fall, it turned back on itself and she stepped into an immense bougainvillea-filled courtyard. In the centre a fountain jerked water six inches into the air and ahead, in the front wall, a great arced wooden gate, two storeys high, prevented her escape. This surely wasn't where she'd come in? Beatrice looked again and saw the small latched door set into the right arc that led onto the pavement. Beyond, in the empty side street, she turned left and saw the Colosseum towering like a gasworks above the buildings at the end.

Ridiculous, she thought. *And wonderful*, added Ralph. *Coffee?*

All that bright November day, Beatrice felt Ralph beside her. When she turned the corner of a street thick with shoppers to find herself staring at the Trevi fountain; when gazing in disbelief at the size of the feet of Constantine's statue, her feelings were intensified because of what Ralph would've said, because of what he *had* said in response to her on their honeymoon, and because beauty affirmed the love they had for each other and they loved each other unreservedly.

That Ralph was dead made little difference. Everything that had been so important to them felt vividly alive and present, here in the very objects she'd come to see.

On and on she went, grinning at satyrs, unable to leave Ralph in the Capitoline museum where she'd intended, because Romulus and Remus being suckled by the wolf seemed so... well... content. As she walked through the galleries, winking at a bust of Marcus Aurelius, she tried to remind herself that this was precisely why she'd come. To slip off for coffee in the calm, leaving Ralph for good. But

Ralph had caught up with her. *I don't know why I was so taken with them,* he said. *I'd rather be with you.*

On the bus to the Vatican her fellow passengers walked straight past the empty seat beside her. *So not dead then*, she thought, confused by the very idea as she stood, tired now, in the queue that snaked around St.Peter's square. *Dead?* Ralph joked, *What is dead?*

After an hour of waiting, her feet hurt. Even imagining Ralph's jokes about how the security staff at the Basilica looked like the mafia failed to amuse her. She felt him hanging back. Eventually, at the great wooden entrance, she heard the rustle of his pipe being removed from his pocket and imagined him sitting down on the portico where visitors were strictly forbidden. *I think I'll give it a miss.* He grinned at her, she turned towards the dimness and stepped onto the mosaic floor.

The Basilica smelled musty. Hushed whispers echoed in the vaulting spaces and the dark corners muttered. Beatrice sensed something rotten and foul lying beneath the building itself. Even the spiky frames of gold adorning everything looked dirty. If the church was a people, alive and filled with the holy spirit, rather than merely a building, then this place, with its dim paintings of popes and saints, was forsaken. Quickly – remembering now – she turned to her right.

There, in an alcove, light seemed to radiate from the stillness of the crowd that had gathered. People stood like statues themselves as they waited in silence for a view unobstructed by the shoulder or head of another. More quickly than she had expected, those in front of her moved away, as if what they had seen had opened their hearts way beyond their usual self-concern.

When Beatrice, who had half-shut her eyes, finally opened them to take in the complete statue of Michelangelo's Pietà, she stopped breathing. Even from behind the smeary bullet-proof glass put up to protect it since her last visit, the statue winded her. Never was death more pitiful than in the arms of life. Never was Jesus more completely just a mortal man than in that heavy head, slack on Mary's arm. Never was grief more spliced with love than in the rueful twist of Mary's mouth and the smooth surrender of her brow. Beatrice could feel that emaciated torso as if it weighed heavy on her own lap, against her own arm. Son. Lover. Protector. All of them gone.

Had she not – even now – thought first of the others around her, Beatrice would have fallen to her knees. She steadied herself by looking at the faces of those beside her, all filled with pity. So *much* pity, yet she knew that the softest washcloth, the lightest kisses, the finest linen would never be enough to raise the dead.

To turn away felt wrong. Like a desertion, though who was deserting whom, Beatrice couldn't have said. The needs of those patiently waiting behind her intervened. And of course, Ralph. The thought struck her like a lump-hammer in the chest. She had turned away from him after how long? She had kissed his cold face. His eyebrows had tickled her nose. And then she'd left, not because she'd spent a decent interval there, but because there had been nothing else to do. Nothing at all.

Quickening her pace, she stuffed a twenty euro note in the box on her way out. Perhaps they could use the money to get that smeary screen cleaned. A man in dark glasses ushered her through a side entrance. The queue had gone and the vast empty square blew her already chilly arms and legs cold. Where was Ralph? Someone had roped off the low portico. Starlings gathered, chattering in the dusky trees.

She longed to take the weight off her feet and get away from the Vatican. Without its palaces and pomp, the place felt like Southend. All plastic and postcards. She bought one of the Pietà before heading down a narrowing lane and through an arch to find herself outside the high walls of the city, beside a main road. Out here, the night seemed to have fully arrived, though it was only half past five. Would her hostess be home? She felt unwilling to leave behind her day and fearful of rejoining a world bereft of Ralph.

In a flush of extravagance, Beatrice decided to seek out the church that they had visited especially to see one of Bernini's sculptures. Once there, Ralph had sat for an hour or so. Perhaps that would be the place to say goodbye? The thought took root, and before she knew it Beatrice had convinced herself that he'd be there, waiting for her. *Got fed up*, he'd say. *Knew you'd find me.* All Beatrice knew was that the place was miles away, but the possibility of leaving the bustle behind calmed her. She refused to think about the taxi fare.

"Bernini?" she said to the driver of a shark-like Mercedes. "Er... Ecstasy St. Teresa? Er... Repubblica? Something to do with the Republic Piazza?" She grimaced helplessly.

Pronouncing each word clearly, the taxi driver provided punctuation by slapping the dashboard four times. "Santa Maria Della Vittoria. Si, si," he added before climbing out and offering her a seat in the back.

"But it's open? Now?"

He shrugged. "Of course, Signora. This is a church." He placed his hands together in a gesture of prayer.

From the car window, Beatrice watched Rome heave and spark around her. As they cruised up the slip road of a motorway she saw another below, neon-bright, jammed with hooting traffic. Behind each broad highway, tall buildings, close-packed, dwarfed ever-narrowing streets. A rosary jiggled from the driver's mirror as the air-conditioned car coursed away from the fever and heat and across the suburbs. Yes, this was Rome: the rushing, the rising above, the style and the squalor. She wished Corinne could see it and sent her a text:

Roaming in Rome. Ralph elusive.
Back of a taxi, looking for him.

Was this how her time was now dated? Before and after Ralph? Like the loss of Tom for Gina, was Ralph's death to become her high water mark, where everything afterwards sloped into insignificance? Gina had finally sent that letter because she'd been too broken to do anything else. Halfway across Europe, searching for the dead, Beatrice understood completely.

Burrowing into her bag for a pen, she pulled out first a tissue, then the postcard – a shine in the strobe of the motorway lights as blank as a single slab of marble. As the light passed, the picture resolved into two figures. Two figures in perfect relation. And in the moment before everything became again car, postcard, tissue, she saw that the two figures were essential to each other; that each created the other. She dug, frantically, for the pen, wrote on the back while she remembered: *Gina – For love*. Below that she added, *This is what happens when you try to fly*. Beatrice scribbled as if her own love depended on it. As if failing to make this clear would mean Ralph would never know. *And to prove it*, she wrote, adding a full stop just as the car smoothed to a halt at a traffic light.

Off they drove again down an avenue of villas standing unlit and empty behind high metal gates. Eventually, the car turned right past several shops and right again down a street where a huddle of old buildings overhung the pavement. The driver stopped by a cafe on the corner of a cobbled square and gesticulated at a church on the far side.

Beatrice took her purse from her bag.

"I wait for you here." He pointed to the gingham-curtained window of the squat cafe. The owner already stood at the door, hailing his friend. Concerned about the bill, Beatrice told him she had no idea how long she'd be.

"No matter. Is Saturday. I wait. No esstra charge," he said, waving her purse away, so obviously keen for his early evening sit-down that Beatrice set off across the square unconcerned.

By the time she made it up the stone steps and into the slim aisle, a fine mist had settled on her hair and her cardigan smelled of damp wool. Lit by many low flickering candles and lamps, the inside of the building glowed with more warmth than these flames could provide and the sense of many people quietly praying as she walked towards the altar was unabated by the rows of entirely empty pews to either side.

When she reached the front, a young priest came to receive her. "Welcome," he said. "Welcome," as if nothing could give him more pleasure than to be here to greet her this dark, damp evening. When she told him she had come to see the statue of St. Teresa, he led her left at the altar, to an unlit chapel. "Please," he said. "You know of our saint?"

When Beatrice hesitated he gestured towards a wooden chair and sat down beside her. Raising her head to look up, she could make out only the dull glow of marble above, lit occasionally by the reflection of a flame on an arm or head, but the priest smiled so kindly between his shiny, raven hair and his buttoned-up cassock, that she gave him her full attention.

"For her, prayer was the opposite of solitude. A chanze to be with someone who love her wholly and completely. Ans she spend a lifetime in prayer – but for her, this was being with someone who knows no hatred, no criticism. Who see only ourr gooodness."

Just like Ralph, thought Beatrice. A lifetime with Ralph – well, for her, anyway. She smiled, remembering his rage when he'd dyed his own vests pink by mistake.

"To spend enough time in prayer will, in the finish take away everrything that distract or confuse. Then all her own conscience pffft... " The priest waved his hands in the air as if sorting through one's own part in things was as simple as unpacking an overfull suitcase, but Beatrice already knew what the presence of love and forgiveness could do. How repentance so often followed. Now she found herself wondering how much more powerful that would be if you sought it every day, every hour, over a lifetime with God?

"And then?" she asked, politely.

"Many tears," said the priest, very matter of fact. "Tears before... well, you will see." He stood, a shadowy angel next to her, and gave a nod that seemed more of a bow. Then he walked away. Beatrice heard his feet tapping against the ornate floor, leaving her in the dark, presumably with Teresa and the God with whom Teresa had gone all the way.

But Beatrice had been pursuing not God or Teresa, but Ralph. Trying to get back to him. Trying to get him back for her. Up to now he'd always been there when she didn't know what to do. And now she didn't know what to do. Or where to go. Or what to think, or even why she'd come.

She heard switches being flicked. The sound seemed to come from both inside and outside her head and she stood, stepping back, to see the thing properly.

Much of the statue, set high on its plinth between two door-sized portraits was a cascade of shine and shade, reminding Beatrice of sheets in disarray. But the face of the saint rose not from bedclothes but from her nun's wimple, and at an angle not usually associated with humility. Eyes just closed, mouth part open, her hand loose but her shoulder pushed forward, foot dangling – this was not a woman leaning back but a woman attempting to greet, to match, to give. And Beatrice could feel the pressure that bore back down. This was a woman crushed by ecstasy, in the bliss of an orgasm. And judging by the smug expression on the face of the cherub with the spear in his hand, an orgasm that was much appreciated. And if that wasn't Eros, disguised as some law-abiding angel, Beatrice would eat her cardigan.

And she was almost hungry enough to eat her cardigan. The vision made her as ravenous as St. Teresa seemed replete. This body was as far from the pious and ascetic as the Pietà had been. Alive and tingling or dead and gone, truth shone from them both. No wonder Ralph had come here. Come here? Had he come here? Did it matter? She remembered now what it was to have hope and longing and hunger. To have youth and health and a future. To be twenty-five with a home and a job and a husband she loved.

Then, quite suddenly, she found herself kneeling, felt the spotlight, heavy and hot on the back of her head, penetrating her too, like warm rain soaking into earth. When she saw her tears spotting the hard floor, they seemed rinsed from her, all the sharp angles and pains in her body flowing away.

Standing eventually, she saw the light had penetrated not just her but everything. All that gold so much brighter in the chapel's reflection, and she, burnished on the inside, like the polished globes and the shining crosses. All of them, shimmering.

The priest thanked her for coming, smiled his compassion into her puffy eyes and tear-stained face and handed her an information leaflet. *For you to remember us.*

Beatrice offered him forty euros but he gestured towards a wooden box by the front door so she pushed the notes through the slit and left. She didn't look for Ralph, yet muttered a thank-you, as if leaving him behind.

Before her the dark square sparkled. Rain on cobbles. Rain and lamplight and the angle of her vision, ever-shifting.

She breathed in the air, damp enough for the back of her throat to catch, stepped out, missed her footing, went over on her right ankle and put out the other foot to steady herself. But she skidded on the edge. First her leg in the air, then her back, bump, bump bump. Then her head.

She saw everything explode. She knew that was it. That the big bang was still going on. And she wondered, in the most open-hearted and unknowing of ways, seeing no distinction between wet blood pouring and wet tears falling, whether she might find Ralph after all.

Chapter Twenty Three

According to Beatrice's passport, Ralph was next of kin. Once he was established deceased, her lanyard, still in her handbag, made Stoke Mandeville the first point of contact. Jeremy Frost had been called at home, late on Saturday evening. Someone was needed to fly out and formally identify her. He'd been returning on the plane, near the bottom of his second whisky when he'd looked at Beatrice's phone and opened her text message.

```
You're doing what you need to tho'. I'll be here
when you get back,
I know it's not the same but big hugs anyway.
```

Big hugs, from Corinne Brock? He'd known nothing of the intimacy between the two women and wished briefly that Beatrice had died a couple of weeks later, after she'd left his patch.

When he accessed the notes Dr. Samuels had kept on Gina and turned to the last entry: 'ready for discharge', he had a fleeting sense of work completed, even of a life run its course, but he dismissed it as self-protective nonsense. Beatrice, he knew, had suffered one of those random accidents, correlated with non-grip shoes, rain and stone steps. Although shocked, he put that aside, busying himself with members of staff; catching their first, naked response, and waiting a further five minutes until their slackened faces bounced back so he could leave them tearfully shaking their heads with colleagues.

Breaking the news to Corinne had been different. He managed to usher her into the tiny staffroom and close the door before she had time to notice how strange this was.

"Corinne," he said, taking a seat himself and waving her down. "I'm afraid I have some very, very sad news. I wanted to catch you before you heard it from someone else. It's about Dr. Samuels – Beatrice."

He watched her face swell, felt her battle to take control of herself. He'd never given a lot of thought to Corinne, but as he filled her in on the briefest of details he found himself impressed by the way she received the news.

"I know you were close," he added.

"Do you?" she responded eagerly, gladly. "Then please, Jeremy, let me make sure her patients – patient – gets taken care of in all this. Let me be the one to tell her. Please."

He recognised her urgency. Her need to face the matter from a professional viewpoint, at least while it sank in. Other than making a firm appointment in his diary to debrief her, he let Corinne get on with it. He found a postcard in Beatrice's bag too, of Michaelangelo's Pietà, addressed to no one, which since it mentioned Gina by name, he placed in her file.

*   *   *

Strange how sitting in Beatrice's chair felt all right. Not as if she was in the wrong place or had ideas above her station. Corinne wasn't even worried about not being up to the task of telling Gina what she had to tell. The idea that she could sidestep herself and make this a 'professional issue' seemed long gone. What could be better now than to meet Gina in shared bereavement? Who else loved Beatrice as much as they did?

Had.

Yellow light sliced through the windows to form squares on the walls. Buttery squares so thick they should be dripping. Outside, leaves, the last leaves, a hallelujah of leaves held down the light, sucked it in like a breath. Beatrice was behind all of it, blowing gold back out over everything, holding her warm and loose. She would. She would.

Corinne felt shot through with love as she'd once felt shot through with heroin. Beatrice seemed to have fulfilled her earthly mission and was now everywhere. Especially in this oozing, changing light that made it through that window at that time at precisely that angle.

Right on cue, perfectly on cue, came the knock.

Gina didn't move but stood outside the door, the rubber tips of her crutches squeaking slightly as they twisted on the lino.

Eyes heavy with a weight she couldn't push away, Corinne held open the door and saw Gina's face sharpen. "Hello," she said, stepping back. "Hello, Gina." Her lower lids filled with tears.

Gina saw a woman in half-silhouette and heard a low song of mourning in her voice as if from a well, all the darker for the thick sunshine around it. And this was her room. Hers and Dr. Samuels. Their special place.

So Gina's response was to feel herself to be Corinne's host, and for an odd few moments each tried to make the other comfortable, as though neither could quite figure out where authority lay. Corinne wouldn't sit until Gina did and Gina stood in the middle of the room not wanting to leave the spot where the sun was streaming warmth into her mending bones. She sensed that the future – the next five minutes of future – would take her somewhere from which she'd be unable ever to return. But she knew the fatal words were coming, even though in themselves, they meant very little.

"I think you should sit down."

"But the sun is shining so brightly," said Gina, tears running down her face. "I'd rather stand."

Hard luck? I'm sorry? I can't stop it? Corinne didn't know which of these words she spoke. Eventually she said, "Dr. Samuels would really want you to sit down." Her chest and shoulders shuddered and she pulled a chair to where Gina could surrender her crutch, lean on the back and manoeuvre herself into it. Then Corinne pulled Beatrice's chair next to Gina's in the yellow warmth and they sat side-by-side, looking at the empty space before them.

Eventually, Gina had to say, "She's dead then, is she?" but by that time, the words had become a full stop to a sentence that was already understood.

"Yes," said Corinne. "Fell down some stone steps coming out of a church in Rome. Hit her head."

"What was she doing in Rome?"

"Looking for her dead husband."

Gina's voice cracked into a high pizzicato stutter and Corinne heard relief. She responded by removing her phone from her bag. "This was her last text to me. Perhaps to anyone. Would you like to see it?"

Clearing away the tears, Gina squinted at the words: *Roaming in Rome. Ralph elusive. Back of a taxi, looking for him.* She smiled, and Corinne felt herself settle.

After a while Gina said, "I didn't know her very well, but all my hopes and all my beliefs about her were right. I thought they probably weren't. I thought she couldn't really be so... " She stared ahead.

"Compassionate?" offered Corinne.

Gina laughed again. "No," and she turned her head away, not meeting Corinne's eyes as she added, "Bonkers. She was bonkers."

Stunned by the obvious affection, the understanding, the intimacy the word so clearly communicated for Gina, Corinne shed a tear. Beatrice loved everyone so much that people didn't usually notice how truly unusual she was. But Corinne knew. What other psychotherapist described themselves as a 'very practised patient'? *I'm limbered up and super-bendy, that's all. Been everywhere. We're all crazy.* What other therapist acknowledged that?

Gina began to talk. "I mean, of course she was caring – I understand all that special attention stuff, but she wasn't putting it on. I saw her cry. I saw her put up with me being rude. I saw her put herself out for me."

"Go on," said Corinne, imagining the words *special attention stuff* flash above her head.

"Well," said Gina. "She just wasn't what I expected. Wasn't... straight. At all. She wasn't phased by anything. Nothing was out of bounds." *Nothing is forbidden. Everything allowed.* Tom's words still whispered and Gina heard, but let them be. "Everything was possible, but at the same time, muddle was muddle. That was how she saw things. She could – well – clearly she could travel across the world to look for something that didn't exist, but show her injustice and she'd pick it apart, show it up just by doing that. She'd destroy it by... by... just seeing it properly." So not, she realised, like Tom. At all.

"And now she's gone," said Corinne.

"Yes, that's really... difficult," said Gina, the word hopelessly inadequate. As she bent her head in appeal she caught the full impact of Corinne's waterlogged face staring ahead and knew she too, had no better phrase to describe what they shared.

Eventually Corinne responded, "It's s'posed to be difficult. S'posed to plug you into every unresolved death and loss you've ever faced. According to the books."

"Perhaps," said Gina, her attention on the shining squares that lit the wall – blank squares where so recently, squares of writing had been. "Perhaps the books are right, but the thing is... I s'pose... if it's not a stupid thing to say... Dr. Samuels resolved the – the deaths." Could death be resolved, Gina wondered? She heard her inaccuracy and realised she meant that Dr. Samuels had picked the deaths apart, too. With the greatest care, she'd laid out those bodies all over again.

"By dying?" Distracted by the thought that Gina really wasn't taking this in at all, Corinne couldn't help herself.

"Of course not," Gina responded. "But it's *clean*, isn't it?" she said, looking up, searching, Corinne saw, too late for a shared understanding, that Corinne wasn't reflecting back.

"Oh – no. I'm so sorry. It's not. Of course." Gina faltered. "She was your colleague. Maybe a close colleague. I can't talk to you about this."

So Corinne wiped her eyes and put her hands beneath the seat of her chair – Beatrice's chair. Scooting across the ground, she swivelled until she faced Gina. "I can put that to one side," she said, determined. "I want to hear, Gina. For Beatrice. I mean Dr. Samuels."

"Beatrice? Was that her name?"

"Yes." Corinne laced her hands together. "Look. If you can go on, please do. Don't be afraid of upsetting me. It's – it's important that you know how much I loved her too. I'm just really hoping that'll help you trust me enough to say what you need to?" Taking a deep breath, she reached into herself and found the truth. "I need to do this, too."

"OK," said Gina, shrugging her thin shoulders, just slightly.

"It's clean, you said."

"Well... she was the real thing. Even though she's gone... " a single sob caught in Gina's throat, "...she's... she'd given me something back. To do with being genuine. Just that. The fact that someone I loved. A person I believed I knew, was exactly what I thought they were, after... after... "

"Tom?" added Corinne, worried now about just how much she knew. Looking up at Gina's quizzical expression, she nodded. "I know a bit about Tom. Like you said, Beatrice was my professional colleague as well as my friend."

Gina sank back in her chair. "He was a crazy guy," she said, a look of amazement passing over her face as though he was in front of her all over again. "Lots of fields, in our relationship. Met in a field. Fucked in a field. Separated in a field. "

"Not forgetting the one the balloon was kept in? The balloon you stole, or he stole, or you stole together?"

"I stole." Slowing down, Gina put her head on one side and let her eyes half close. "After all this," she said, tapping her crutch, "thinking of him exhausts me. Mostly he made me feel like a small car in a low gear with its accelerator pedal down flat."

"Your engine racing?" said Corinne, remembering the star-filled skies of North Wales.

Gina sighed. "I've been thinking and I reckon I've always been stretching myself as far as I can go."

Corinne remembered her ballet class, felt the sweat trickling down her body, hamstrings pulling the backs of her thighs as she forced her head down onto her knee.

"Dr... Beatrice made me realise I'd always seen sex that way. Even before I knew what sex was." Gina giggled. "I fantasized about being tied to train tracks."

"But you'd be rescued?"

"Oh, yes. That was the point. I'd be pushed to the edge, then snatched from the jaws of disaster."

Tightening her fist, Corinne saw the vein outlined against her arm and felt her pulse thud for the needle. "Maybe it wasn't just sex you wanted to be that way, but everything?" They sat quietly until what was unsaid filled the room as densely as hot air had inflated that massive balloon.

"I jumped," said Gina, her voice louder. "I jumped. He said we should. And I felt him lift my trousers and tip me out." Clamping her fists to her mouth she managed, "but I know – I really know – because of Dr... Beatrice – that I made that up." Staring into Corinne's eyes, her voice cracked. "I don't think you have any idea how terrifying that is."

Corinne nodded, but the blood coursed through her body and she felt her hands shaking.

Gina began to blink, rapidly. "I couldn't stand that he didn't catch me. So in my mind I had to make it that he pushed me."

Several loud raps on the door had Corinne up on her feet, but Jeremy Frost had entered, crossed the room and dropped a file on the desk so quickly that he'd closed the door behind him before she'd even reached the handle. Too late she found herself standing, arms out and legs apart like a human shield, though for what, she couldn't really say. She couldn't say until she turned back to Gina. The woman was glowing white, then red, then white again, screaming, "How fucking dare he. How. HOW?"

Did she mean Jeremy or Tom? Lost for a response, Corinne found the tissues and tried to put one into Gina's hand but Gina pushed it away.

She returned to her chair, appalled. *I don't think you have any idea how terrifying that is?* Was that how she came across? If anyone knew what a trust, what love, what sex betrayed did to a woman – to a child... Yet Beatrice – professional, protective Beatrice – could destroy muddle, just by seeing it clearly? Could mend things, just by being herself?

Corinne glanced around the room for anything Gina

might throw and noticed the paperweight on Beatrice's desk, but the screams had turned to wails now, the eruptions slowing as rage turned to grief.

So she'd failed again. This time in the most basic task of keeping the therapeutic space uninterrupted. Even if Beatrice had managed to halt the interruption, she'd have found a way of using it to connect all the more deeply.

I couldn't stand that he didn't catch me. So in my mind I had to make it that he pushed me.

She'd have bridged the gap.

Corinne heard her own words then, echoing back from what seemed a lifetime ago. *Well it's just shame, Beatrice. It's a bloody plague where everything you say sounds stupid. Where you can't speak for hearing it scorned.* Easy enough to say, but to know? Yet Beatrice had made it possible for Gina to be bigger than the shame or the blame. Somehow she'd made it possible for Gina to feel a helplessness she hadn't believed it possible to live through. The room they sat in seemed suddenly a mile wide. Corinne heard a hissing in her ears. *Helpless not hopeless. Good enough not brilliant.* Was that the bridge? Was it that simple? Just some benign and trustworthy person, helping her bear the feelings, offering new words until they sank in?

Gina wept, silently. Broken, Corinne realised, but free to mend, her psyche no long irrevocably 'split'. At last the books made sense. But what if no one offered you those other words? If you had no one to hold and stroke away your despair? *Brilliant. Hopeless.* Narcissism or annihilation? She knew only too well which one she'd cling to.

She saw it then. That ashamed self. Looked straight at it.

But the little girl with the long dark hair wasn't looking back. She was looking away as if she didn't want to be there, the wing-mirrors of her mother's wood-veneer dressing table angled to reflect her likeness sideways on in a tunnel of endless reflection. *Blame to shame ad infinitum.* Avoiding. Always avoiding.

Determined, conscious, Corinne made that little girl look into the central mirror, to the figure behind it all – the complaining woman on the bed, mouth a loose snarl, a can of Superlager in her hand. Saw her raise her head. Heard her shout, *What's so bloody special about you, eh? Nothing's ever good enough.*

She felt a punch to her solar plexus and buckled in her centre. Stumbling, she saw Gina reach towards her and reached back to the outstretched hand. Kneeling now, and playing for time she stroked the fingers for a few minutes before pulling her chair next to Gina's and taking that hand back in her own.

Keeping her attention on soft skin touching, Corinne dared to look again but the image remained; the grey, supine form of a woman that looped and oozed between a weepy self-pity, a chin-up conceit and that spit of contempt she knew so well. Corinne didn't need to listen now. The words were always there. Always in her head: *DeadlossSelfishThoughtlessWorthless.* That face had colonised Corinne's point of view, leaving no alternative, but Corinne watched from Beatrice's chair now, no longer stared out of her wits. Now, she heard with just enough of Beatrice's love, just enough distance.

In her mind's eye, the bedroom gave way to a hospital bed, the horizontal mother no longer lit by Superlager. Only the whites of her eyes showed in the yellow sump of her face. Corinne could feel a different hand now, unresponsive to her own ever-hopeful squeeze. A hand that became colder and colder until the nurse had led her away.

Gina gave a tiny sigh. Crumpled and shrunken, she looked like an orphaned toddler who'd cried herself to sleep.

Corinne's own tears began to flow. Tears for Beatrice. Tears for her mother. Tears for herself. Outside, heavy cloud edged the sun. The room softened into dusky corners and bars of light and she felt Beatrice's presence beside her, lulling her, as warm as when she'd been flesh and blood.

So maybe Gina's not the only baby here?

Shaking her head, Corinne tried to shut the voice out. To face reality. Beatrice was dead and she of all people should accept that. Yet the sense of bodily warmth persisted, beating steady as a heart, right next to her ear. Despite herself, Corinne said silently, *You're back, then?*

Object relations, whispered Beatrice. *You've internalised the good object (me) – kept it inside you enough to refer to.*

Even though you're gone?

Especially when I'm gone. That's the point.

Gina shifted and settled, pulling her arm, which had rested on Corinne's, back into the crook of her own body. Corinne looked at the girl's smooth face. She saw Beatrice's smile and felt Gina jerk as if the last remnants of a nightmare had been shattered.

If you can just bear to go with the difficulties awhile, things tend to iron themselves out in the end. Like you said, 'It's grief that drives you mad. Shame's just easier than bloody grief.' Beatrice was whispering now and Corinne felt her attention drawn towards the desk where the file lay.

The postcard had been pushed inside the front cover. She glanced at the picture. At the body, broken beyond repair; at the woman stretched beyond endurance who yet held it close. Then she turned it over and read:

> *Gina... For Love – and to prove it.*
> *This is what happens when you try to fly.*

Corinne slid a thin sheaf of papers from the file. On the top lay a piece of A4 headed Projective identification from which a snake of ink ran down to the foot of the margin, ending at the word:

Borderline

Opposite it, in the bottom right corner was written:

Narcissist

and above them both, in the centre, Beatrice had written some notes before crossing them through and writing:

> *eeny, meeny miny mo,*
> *catch a wanker by his toe*
> *If he hollers squeeze it hard,*
> *next time be more on your guard or*
> *Love will tear you apart.*

Corinne felt the breath knocked from her. To love

someone so much? To keep loving so strongly that you couldn't imagine being apart from them? Even in the face of rejection? But just a glimpse of her hopeless, devoted self by her mother's hospital bed had been enough. Separation could be unbearable. For her. For Gina. Perhaps for everyone.

She fingered her blue laminate – CORINNE BROCK: WELLBEING COUNSELLOR – and shuddered at the photograph that smiled so confidently back. If she recoiled from her own vulnerability, how difficult was it to accept anyone else's? And how easy to problem-solve if you could stick a label on someone. *The Diagnostic and Statistical Manual of Mental Disorders* was rubbish. Dangerous. She'd campaign to have it banned.

She felt a soft breeze cross her face as though the fine hairs of her cheek were being stroked. *But you've been given a way of thinking about things that you never had. That can help you understand and help you use love more effectively – maybe that's something to keep? So much violence. Will it never end?*

Would it never end? Beatrice had moved onto her hair. Corinne sensed fingers running through the strands, slowing at tiny, unbrushed knots, smoothing over the bumps. The words soothed, no longer an imperative. More like a lullaby:

"As a child, the narcissistic individual is emotionally starved – (starved... starved) by a chronically cold mother. Her repeated failures of empathy create injuries (injuries... injuries) resulting in a chronically wounded adult self, self-persecution and self-hatred."

Poor baby. *Poor baby.* Poor baby. *Poor baby.*

"Are you OK?"

How long had Gina been watching? How long had she been so peaceful? "I'm... here," said Corinne. "You dropped off," she added, but Gina only nodded.

"I was resting. Thinking." After a few moments, she said, "You know, Tom sort of magnified, acknowledged and then forgave his own faults, all at the same time." And then, as though this were occurring to her as she spoke, she added, "So it felt like he forgave mine."

Corinne felt for herself what it was to be loved, soothed into acquiescence and then dumped with no one to catch her, and said, "So rejection by such a benevolent Tom would make it feel as though your faults could never be forgiven again." She paused, surprised by the sense she'd made. "You'd feel yourself to blame for everything." As she heard her own words unfurling, the spaces in between them echoed back through her as never before.

But Gina looked a different woman now, thinking in the quiet of a room that had witnessed so much. She gazed at Corinne. "I think Tom just simulated what understanding looks like. I think he did it so well that my need for him to understand made me believe that he did. But I forgot... I forgot that no one really knows anyone." She looked sad, adding with a tiny lilt of hope in her voice, "Do they?"

Corinne shook her head.

Gina sighed heavily. For the first time she looked as if she had no idea who Tom was at all. "One of the songs he sang – he was a performer – a good one... "

Corinne tried to look surprised.

"...was a question: What's it all about, Alfie? – and when

he sang it, he was so... pure. So genuinely confused. I'd have done absolutely anything for him."

With her arms drooping, hands on her lap as she leaned against the chairback, Gina's body looked so floppy that Corinne was put in mind of Beatrice's postcard. Another self-sacrifice, noble hopes sunk beneath a broken body.

Gina gave a rueful smile. "But really – it's a *what does it all mean?* song. A teenager's song, full of angst with all that, *the world's against us* stuff. It's a bit... simple, really."

Corinne smiled, thinly, because 'simple' – black and white – was precisely how people did see things, wasn't it, herself included? Pushing back those ideas felt like pushing the turning world back the way it had just come. Then she heard, very faintly, a voice of encouragement. *But you're doing it. You're doing it.* The words seemed to be coming from inside, from the urge to keep Gina going.

After a pause, Gina added, "No wonder he couldn't cope with carrying things on. In the end, he just gave everything up to passion."

"Don't forget the putdown. The *'you're nothing'* unless you go for the huge romantic gesture," added Corinne. *You're doing it, you're doing it.* The voice was louder now. But yes, she *was* doing it. She felt the same exhilaration as when she'd first learned to ride a bike – legs pumping, feet on the pedals, wind in her hair and her heart lifting.

"It sounds so bloody easy but it really isn't," said Gina.

"Well it doesn't look like Tom did you any favours," she said, concerned the moment the words were out of her mouth that she might sound critical, but Gina just said:

"I suppose there aren't any short cuts."

Corinne felt herself sailing along the pavement, heard the voice again, *Go on*, further away now. No one was running behind her holding the saddle, were they? And yet she was upright. Riding on her own. Look, no stabilizers.

"I did find love," said Gina. "I did. But now it's gone."

Corinne smiled. "I get it." She looked at the trace marks, almost completely gone from her own arm. "It's the buzz, Gina. *Without true love, we just exist.* But maybe that's not so bad." She thought of the women wrecked, that had gone before. "Tom's is not the only kind of true love."

"You know," said Gina wistfully, "his words blazed. They made everything brighter."

"Well Burt Bacharach's certainly did," said Corinne. But what use, in the end, was a buzz? Junkies rescued themselves from the torture they made of their own lives by jacking up. Dancers, like all performers, went for a roar of applause that for one vivid moment lit the darkness beyond the stage. She heard the cheers go up one more time, saw Tom's grin before she'd run from the hall. But weren't they all narcissists? Wasn't that how anyone managed at all? Wasn't what was going on here just her own performance?

Gina looked upset. Then very quietly she said, "God, I miss Beatrice," and relief washed through Corinne's newly emptied-head as she saw at last, that nothing mattered in therapy except the predictability and safety of the meetings. That, and a willingness to hear enough of Gina's suffering to make her feel able to bear the inevitable interruptions and losses in the world outside. Because the love Corinne could give her – the love they all could give one another – was only temporary. Conditional. Human.

So how would Gina do when brought up sharp against it? How strong *was* Gina's new found resilience, for Corinne knew without looking that this appointment was drawing to an end. Briefly the world reeled. Remembering there was no steadying hand behind her, she felt herself wobble, saw the kerb ahead glistening with gypsum. How would *she* do, with no Gina to give her focus? She'd lose her balance. She'd fall off. *You'll get back on.* She was weeping now, inside, as she watched Gina's tears running down her cheeks. How would either of them take it? This final goodbye? This confrontation with the real? *You're doing it*, said Beatrice, and Corinne felt a tiny splash of water fall on her hair. *Did you think I'd planned to go?*

Slowly, Corinne inclined her head, smiling a smile at Gina that she didn't feel. She looked at the clock on the wall.

But Gina seemed to understand, lifting her hand, palm up, towards it. Almost eleven.

"Yes," said Corinne.

The sun, which had turned from butter into gold, poured over the chairs and the desk, making the room a palace and turning both women bronze. Gina's crutches shone as Corinne lifted them upright and Gina pushed herself from the chair.

"I don't think Dr. Samuels will ever be gone for me," she said, hobbling to the door. The corridor beyond was as dim as the room had been bright. *Lucky you,* thought Corinne but she said, "Good luck. I really wish you well."

"Thank you," said Gina, and she reached out to touch her. "Thank you so very much for being the person who told me," and off she shuffled.

Corinne was still holding the door handle as the postwoman wandered up past the retreating Gina to Beatrice's office with a sheaf of envelopes. What now? The top one was handwritten. Corinne took them back to the desk and sat staring before absentmindedly opening it:

```
Dear Dr. Samuels,
Thank you for your recent correspondence. Just
to let you know that the Will has been drawn up
according to your instructions. Although this
document stands as legally valid, I would
appreciate a formally witnessed signing at the
first opportunity.
I look forward to hearing from you,
Yours sincerely,

pp. Polly Hatton (paralegal)
For Neat, Drew and Halmer.
```

She sighed, laid her head down on the desk and began quietly to weep.

Playlist

*If you've enjoyed this book, you might fancy listening to some
of the music it mentions:
https://tinyurl.com/tfamusic*

*If this book has been worth reading, please please go to
Amazon.co.uk and GoodReads.com and give it a star and/or
written review.*

About The Author

Gill Jackman has spent a lot of time at the Glastonbury Festival. She worked in Welfare through the mud/martial law years and saw a great deal of trench-foot. Even now, she can be found at the festival most years, in the Healing Field. She became a psychotherapist in 1997 and has just retired. *The Fantasist's Assistant* is her most recent novel. A serious descent into gaslighting and the struggle to transcend it, *The F.A.* is also a psychological thriller, full of dark and noirish romance. It couldn't be farther from chick-lit if it tried.

Printed in Great Britain
by Amazon